A WHOLE NEW CROWD

TIJAN

DEDICATION

This book was first written so long ago when I was just beginning. I posted it on Fictionpress and it was loved by so many. This was my first popular story and because of that, this is dedicated to all those readers who read it and sent me words of encouragement. This is also dedicated to those readers who kept messaging me and asked if I would publish it for them to own one day. I hope you enjoy the story again!

TABLE OF CONTENTS

PROLOGUE

Sitting on the patio steps, I heard the door open behind me, pulling me from my thoughts. I felt Carla's hot breath on my neck before my foster mother even said a word. She smelled of cigarettes and alcohol, but that was her perfume. She wore it daily. A fresh wave of her odor came down over me before she said, "You got everything?"

"Yeah." I wanted her gone. I didn't want to deal with whatever she would say when Jace pulled up in his truck. Her dislike for the Panthers, a gang that controlled Pedlam and another town, was well-known. I heard the growling sound from his engine, and it was too late. It wasn't loud, but it announced his impending arrival. There was no way she would go back inside and let me leave in peace.

She grunted. "Well damn. You got the leader himself giving you a ride over there. That's one good thing about this miracle adoption. It gets you away from the likes of him and his brother." Her toe pushed into my back, nudging me. "Since the brother is here, I'm assuming it didn't go over well with your boyfriend? That drug addict probably had a hissy fit; his girlfriend taking off, leaving him behind."

The truck slid to a stop, parked next to the curb, and Jace leaned forward so he could see me. He saw right away that she was bothering me, and his eyes narrowed. His door opened and he got out, rounding the truck to head up the sidewalk. I stood at the same time. I could've fought back, said some hurtful words to Carla, but she no longer mattered.

I was gone. She was the last foster family I'd be forced to live with. There'd been so many. I was moved around, from town to town, but for some reason, I kept being sent back to Pedlam. As Jace neared us, a wave of relief and bitterness crashed through me at the same time. He and Brian were the only ones I considered family. He stood there and slid his hands into his pockets; his eyes were trained on Carla.

I knew what he was doing; he was trying to intimidate her, and hearing her quiet gasp, I knew it was working. Either that or she wanted to fuck him. With Jace, it was probably both. He was the leader of the Panthers, but he was more than that. He owned different businesses in the community, and his nightclub, the Seven8, was the most exclusive one in town. Carla had asked me to get her in last weekend, and now the owner was right in front of her. I had no doubt she was considering the possibilities of getting something from him. He had money and power. She loved both.

I glanced over my shoulder. She wet her lips, and her eyes darkened with hunger. She was checking him out.

This was normal for Jace. He was gorgeous with broad shoulders, a trim waist, chiseled cheekbones, grey eyes, and dark blonde hair cut short in a crew-cut. His body was lean, but it was defined and sculpted into a lethal machine.

A faint grin hovered over his face. "You ready?"

I jerked my head in a nod. I couldn't get away fast enough.

He came up a step and grabbed the bags. Sliding his arm through the straps, he tossed my bags over his shoulder to land on his back. I only had one other bag. He eyed it, but I shook my head. I would carry it myself. He nodded and turned back to his truck. I started after him, but a hand came down on my shoulder, stopping me.

I held back.

Carla said, "Not so fast. You're not going to give me a hug goodbye?"

Jace had already made it to the truck. After the bags were inside, he paused, glancing back at us again.

I rolled my shoulder to get her hand off me. When it didn't budge, I'd had enough. Gritting my teeth, I jerked my arm up and knocked her hand away. Her eyes widened, and a second later, anger flooded her features. I moved down the steps, watching her warily as I made my way to the truck. I never knew what she would do when she was angry.

"You don't have to be such a bitch." She glared at me.

I nodded. I'd been quiet, putting up with her loathing long enough. I hadn't wanted to move again, which would happen if I would do things like talk back. The foster parents never wanted to deal with me, but this was the last one. I was going to a real home, with a real family, and I wouldn't have to worry about being kicked out or being taken away again.

I smirked at her. "You should repeat that to yourself when you look in a mirror every morning."

Her cheeks got red, and I knew she had an angry retort ready for me.

"Taryn," Jace murmured from inside the truck. I was at the truck now. The door opened behind me, and he added, stretched over the seat, "Come on. Get in."

"Gladly."

She was still on the patio, her hand clenched around the post. As I climbed inside and shut the door, I frowned. "Why isn't she doing anything? She usually yells by now or threatens to lock me in my room."

Jace leaned over to peer at her. "Because she can't." He shifted the truck into drive and pulled away from the curb. "She has no say over you anymore. Forget about her. You won't have to deal with her any longer, and you'll probably never see her again." He glanced sideways at me. "You nervous?"

He was right. She couldn't hurt me. None of them could. I really was done with getting new foster parents. Then his question registered, and my stomach clenched. "Yes."

"This is a good thing, Taryn."

Yeah. It was. "Then why are you driving me and not Brian?"

"Because my brother's an idiot."

Brian was my ex-boyfriend. Jace was not. Even though Jace was like a brother to me, it should've been Brian driving me. Starting a new future was a big deal. It was a once in a lifetime kind of thing, and he refused to be a part of it with me.

"He broke up with me last night."

Jace grimaced. "You and Brian break up every other week."

"I know, but…" This felt different. This felt final. *Maybe it should be,* said a voice inside my head, and I frowned. There was nothing more to be said. Jace had his own problems with Brian. Since their dad passed away, the two had a hate/strong-dislike type of relationship and couldn't stand to be in the same room as the other. The animosity was more on Brian's side. He had worshiped his brother, but then loathed him in high school. I never knew the real reason for the change and Jace wasn't one to communicate his feelings. I never knew how he really felt about Brian, but there were moments when I saw the wariness in him. If Brian came home, slamming the door behind him, Jace would sigh and leave. A fight was avoided.

"Taryn."

There was a dead serious tone in his voice. My stomach took a dive at the sound of it. I was going to hear something I didn't want to.

"You should leave us both behind."

I shook my head. "No."

"Yes." He kept driving, but his knuckles were white as he gripped the steering wheel. "I mean it. Brian's my brother, but he's an addict. He's probably always going to be an addict. He's violent, Taryn."

"Never with me."

"That doesn't matter. He gets into fights. At school. At home. With me. With guys who look at you too long. I love my brother, but I care about you too. It's better for you if you leave us behind. Don't visit."

"Stop." I wasn't perfect either.

"Don't come back. I mean it. When I leave you with them, I don't want to see you again." His voice gentled. "You know what I do. I'm not a good guy."

"You own businesses. You're in the Panthers."

"I sell drugs." His tone turned harsh. "I'm aware that it's fucked up, but that's what we are. We're fucked up. Me, Brian. Both of us. You can get away from us. You have to. This is the break that you need. You can have a better life. You know I'm right."

"Shut up! Brian's trying to get better, and I'm a thief. Are you forgetting that? I'm not perfect either." The tension inside me snapped. It imploded inside me, drenching my insides with shame, guilt, anger, pain, longing, and so many other emotions I couldn't name. They were becoming too much. I choked out, "You and Brian are the only people I have left." A tear slid down my cheek, and I grimaced. I hated crying. It was a waste. I never felt better afterwards.

"You can stop. You don't have to steal anymore. This family is a good family. Kevin's a doctor. Shelly's a stay-at-home mom, and you'll have a brother and sister. From what I've heard, they're both popular. The girl's in your grade. This is a new future for you—"

"Fuck you." I was seething. My hands curled in on themselves, my nails cutting through my own skin. "Shut up. Just...shut up."

"Brian's going to come crawling back to you. Don't take him back. Find a new guy at your school, someone who's not violent, someone who will go to college, someone whose future is not prison. We both know that's where Brian is going to end up."

"Stop it."

He did. The drive to Rawley continued in silence, and I couldn't stop the tears. They kept rolling down my face, falling onto the backpack I was hugging to my chest. I hated this. I did. A new future. A new family. Everything he said was true. I knew it was the right thing to do, keep going and never look back, but my god, it was killing me.

They had been family when I had no one. I never knew who my parents were. I had no intention of looking for them. They never mattered to me. Brian and Jace had been the ones that mattered. After getting off the Rawley exit, it wasn't long until he turned into a ritzy neighborhood. The houses were massive. The front lawns were perfectly groomed. White picket fences. All the shit that I used to make fun of. He turned down the last street, the truck slowed, and he pulled over.

I had never been to their house before, and I drank in the sight of it. It was huge with two large pillars in the front and a gated driveway. The gate was open and lights lit up the sides of the driveway, all the way to the house and attached three-car garage.

I rolled down my window. Nothing. There was no yelling. No one was slamming doors. No music with heavy bass was booming from the neighbors. It was too quiet.

I glanced at Jace. "I'm going to die of boredom."

He didn't reply. I didn't think he would.

The front door opened and the Parsons came out: the dad, the mom, a younger boy and a girl my age. They all filtered out to the patio, paused a moment, and then they slowly made their way towards us.

My nerves were stretched thin. My stomach was doing somersaults. "Do I have to take their name? Parson? I already hate that name."

"No, the social worker said you could keep yours. You're Taryn Matthews."

Damn straight. A flare of defiance shot through me, but I shook my head. I couldn't lie to myself. I was scared. Taryn Matthews was never scared, but my ass cheeks were quaking in my seat right now. "I can't do this."

"You can." Jace leaned over and pressed a kiss to my forehead. I closed my eyes, absorbing the touch. He whispered, "I love you, Taryn, but I hope that I never see you again."

CHAPTER ONE

Six months later

"Taryn."

I rolled my eyes at hearing my sister's voice. She could yell all she wanted. I knew what she was going to ask and I wasn't going to help her, so I kept going down the hallway. I had overheard her on the phone the night before. She wanted me to steal something. After taking Jace's words to heart, this was my new beginning, so that meant no more stealing. It was something I would've done in my old life.

"Taryn," Mandy shouted again. She was running now. The sound of her heels hitting the floor went from a normal clitter-clatter, to a constant staccato. I rolled my eyes. My sister was an idiot. No one should run when wearing high heels, at least those high heels—they arched halfway up her calves— but that was Mandy Parson. She wore high heels, clingy tank tops, miniskirts, and on some days, a cheerleading outfit.

She was one of *those* people.

I had been adopted into a family that was the opposite of everything I was—the God-blessed rich kids. Mandy was the epitome of the perfect daughter: blonde, petite, smart, and popular by all accounts.

"Taryn, stop!"

I ignored her and opened my locker. Hearing her stumble to a halt, panting behind me, my eyebrows went up. "Thought you were in shape. All those late night activities with Devon, right?"

"I'm not here to talk about Devon."

"I heard Devon hooked up with Stephanie Markswith at Brent's party."

She huffed. "Not gonna work, Taryn." I turned and saw the twitch in her eye. She knew I was trying to distract her. Her eyebrows were fixed, bunched together, and her mouth was pressed in a flat line, but then it all changed. Her eyebrows shot up, and she let out a dramatic sigh. "There's no chance he would hook up with her. No way."

"Not what I heard."

"She's not suicidal."

"She was drunk. I don't think she was thinking soberly." I shut my locker and moved away.

Mandy latched onto my side. "The girl's dead."

I saw Stephanie turn the corner up ahead. Talk about perfect timing. "Better tell *her* that."

Mandy didn't say goodbye; she veered off in her direction.

I stopped to watch this. I had to. Stephanie spread a rumor that I stole a biology exam my first week at Rawley. It wasn't true. She wanted revenge because her boyfriend had hit on me, but when I got called into the principal's office, my history was pulled up. Being known as a thief and being associated with Brian and Jace Lanser hadn't helped. I looked guilty and I got detention for two months with no chance to defend myself. They couldn't prove it was me, but it didn't matter. They didn't need to prove it.

When I heard Mandy yell, "Stephanie!" a grin came over me.
Revenge could be sweet.

Tray Evans dropped into the seat opposite mine at lunch. I looked up and tensed. Tray was gorgeous with sandy blonde hair, striking hazel eyes, and a jaw that girls melted over. While my sister was in the crowd at the top, he *was* the top.

"Your sis preaches about your skills."

"I don't do that anymore."

He narrowed his eyes.

I didn't want to tangle with Tray Evans. He was smarter than people gave him credit for. He watched people like I did, and he held an insurmountable power in school. I had dealt with guys like him from my other schools. I was toned and I knew guys liked my body. I had dark eyes, long brown hair, and a set of lips that caused a guy to groan. I wasn't boasting. This was fact. Guys found me sexy, which meant that I've dealt with my share of guys, all sorts from creepers to jocks. I knew how to deal with them, but Tray Evans was different. I had been aware of him since school started, but I relaxed when he didn't seem to care about me at all. That time was up.

Still holding his gaze, a shiver wound its way up my spine. He wasn't coming on to me, but it wouldn't have mattered if he had. The way he was looking at me was like he could read me from the inside out. His eyes pierced through me, through my walls, right into me. No one had looked at me like this, even Brian.

I didn't like it.

16

"Taryn!" Mandy landed in the seat next to mine. "Tray, hey!"

"Parson." He nodded at her, still looking at me.

"Is it true?" Mandy asked. "Is the party at your place?"

A faint grin teased at the corner of his mouth. Without looking away from me, he answered, "Thinking about it."

"Devon's excited. It should be epic."

I couldn't watch him any longer. He was winning our stare-off so I turned to Mandy. "Why are you here?" She didn't sit by me at lunch. I sat alone. That was my rule. After Stephanie's rumor and when I was found guilty, she told everyone that I stole her boyfriend. Not true. I kneed him in the balls, but that hadn't been added to the rumors. People had been welcoming until my new reputation had been spread around. Mandy was nice to me the whole time, but I knew it was causing a rift between her and her friends, so I made a decision. I went it alone.

"Come on, Taryn. We need your help."

"You guys are coming to double-team me?" I glanced around and noticed the attention we were getting. If Mandy was at my table, it was a big deal, but with Tray Evans there too, people's mouths were on the floor.

"Well...yeah."

Tray leaned forward, propping his muscled arms on the table, teasing me with a view of a tattoo peeking out from underneath his polo sleeve. "Mandy says that you're good at stealing stuff. She said you're good at breaking into places too."

"No." I paled. That was even worse.

"Taryn, come on, you're like a legend. Mom and Dad had to attend meetings about this stuff just to prepare the family for you."

The way she said it felt like a dagger stabbing me in the heart. "Sorry that *your* family had to learn how to thief-proof their home before their new defected adoptee moved in."

"I didn't mean it that way. I really didn't. Taryn—"

I wasn't listening. I left and ignored how everyone's heads turned to follow me as I went out the cafeteria door. Once in the hallway, I headed for the parking lot. I didn't think, I just went. It wasn't until I was in my car with the keys in the ignition that I stopped myself. What was I doing? I couldn't skip school. That was the old Taryn. I had to be the new Taryn. A wave of longing came over me. I missed Brian. He would've understood from the way I walked that I needed to get away, but he wasn't there anymore.

The passenger door opened and my heart stopped. Brian?—no— Tray. He smirked at me. "Going somewhere?"

"Get out."

He laughed, getting in. "All I did was sit down at your table and ask you a question. I'm wracking my brain, trying to figure out what I've done to piss you off, but I can't think of another time that we've even talked. Did I hit on you at some party and act like an asshole?" He grinned. "If so, I apologize right now. It was probably because you're hot and I was drunk."

He sounded all nice now, but it was an act. Every alarm was going off inside of me. He was not this innocent guy. As I stared at him, I found myself checking him out. He really was gorgeous, with eyelashes that girls would kill for and full plump lips. His shirt had moved higher and I saw the tattoo again.

I had a thing for tattoos, and the sight of his tribal one had me squirming. It'd been a while since I had been with Brian. Shit. Brian. Tray Evans was the rich and blessed version of my ex-boyfriend. The difference was that the Brian Lansers of the world never got away with anything. They got in trouble just because they existed. The Tray Evans of the world pulled the same shit and were worshiped.

Dangerous. He was just dangerous in every way.

"Like what you see."

I laughed softly. It hadn't been a question. "You got the package. We both know that, but I doubt you have the quality."

"You think so?"

"I've dealt with boys like you. You're all the same."

"Boys?" He flashed me a grin. "I'm all man. There's no part of me that's a boy anymore." He leaned forward so his face was close to mine. He came in slow and his breath teased my skin. Then he tilted his head to the side and his cheek grazed against mine.

I held firm. I had to. He was testing me, seeing if I would flinch or melt. I couldn't do that. I couldn't give him any reaction because if I did, he'd win. I would be the weaker one. Heat spread through my body and I gritted my teeth. My body was betraying me. No one had gotten that kind of reaction from me, not even Brian when we first kissed, and that knowledge made me hate this guy.

I smirked at him, he was so close to me. "Good for you."

His eyes were laughing and the hazel color darkened to an amber color.

"But I'm not interested."

A low chuckle slipped from him, and he moved back. "Listen, business only, okay?" He paused, an eyebrow lifted. "Next week is homecoming and we play the Panthers from Pedlam. They stole our game book last year, and we got screwed. We lost the game, and we lost going to the championships because of it. Some of my friends didn't get football scholarships."

"You want me to steal their game book?"

"Mandy says you used to do this stuff. I respect that you don't want to do it anymore, but we know that they've already been sniffing around campus. We caught a few of 'em Friday night. They were trying to take our state championship flag from two years ago."

"You don't even play football. Why do you care?"

"Because this is my school. Those guys are my friends, and I take care of what's mine."

I frowned. "I know people from Pedlam."

"You went to school there?"

"More than any others. I don't know if I want to help you screw with a school that I used to consider mine."

Tray sighed, rolling his eyes. "You're Mandy's sister. This is your school now, Taryn."

That was the first time I'd heard him say my name, and I hated hearing it from him. I hated him. A whole host of emotions were unlocked. Memories seared through me and Brian's voice, saying my name, was on repeat inside of my head.

I wanted it gone. I wanted him gone. "I'm not helping you."

Tray Evans was in my car, but memories of Brian were overwhelming me. I didn't want to remember him.

"What?"

"Get out." My voice was rougher than it needed to be. I couldn't help it.

"Fine." He got out and shut the door. As he walked away, I tried to calm the storm he had unknowingly unleashed.

I missed him. I missed both of them.

I let myself inside the mansion, dropping my keys in the bowl beside the coat-rack. The place was just massive. I already knew no one was home. My parents—it was hard to think of them as parents; I had to keep reminding myself not to call them Shelly and Kevin in my mind—were gone to a medical conference. It wasn't long until I learned that Kevin was rarely home. He was either on-call at the hospital or he was moonlighting at a different hospital. When he wasn't, he took Shelly with him for weekend conferences. When they both left, it was Mandy, Austin, and myself. A neighbor came over to check on us in the evenings. There'd been a few times when the neighbor slept over, but she always watched television in her room so we had the house to ourselves most of the time.

Grabbing a soda, I headed to the media room. It wasn't long until I heard voices coming from the kitchen, and I groaned. Mandy's friends' voices. The gods of the gods.

I muttered, "Kill me now."

"She's down here." Mandy bounced down the stairs and plopped next to me. Devon came in behind her and stood at the end of our couch, frowning at her. She beamed at me. "Hey!"

"Hey." I frowned.

"Tray said you said no. A big fat no actually."

I shook my head. I wasn't going to deal with this from her. "No, Mandy."

"Why not? This would be so easy for you."

"What's going on?" Jennica Kent asked, laughing as she sat on the couch opposite us. Tray and a few others came into the room. The only one missing was Amber Sethlers. She and Jennica were the two females at the top of the food chain.

I knew some about the others, Grant, Samuel, and I couldn't name the third guy. There were enough rumors swirling about every one of them. One hated the other. They had all slept with each other at some point. I never cared. They were rumors. I could barely keep track of the ones about me. This was the social circle at the top, and they were in my media room, well, Mandy's media room.

I wanted to run. I never mixed with Populars well.

"Leave her alone, Mandy. The girl said no."

I glanced at Tray in surprise. I didn't believe that he had backed down. "I'm not doing it. Wherever you want me to break into, I'm not doing it."

"We're not asking anymore."

"Okay." Mandy nodded. "We'll figure something else out then."

She bit her lip and glanced around the room to the others. The guys didn't care about the conversation. Devon had taken the remote and turned the channel to a basketball game. Jennica was watching Tray, who was staring at me. The longer he did, the redder her face got. I didn't look at him. I wasn't going to step back into that dark hole. He was like a vortex, a very hot and lethal vortex, but I couldn't stop myself from enjoying how upset she was becoming. Then she shot me a nasty look and I turned away, biting my lip. What was I doing? I needed to fit in, strip off my rebel ways, and assimilate into this pack.

I was screwed.

I glanced at Mandy. I should leave, but her hand went to my arm. Even though she hadn't said anything, I felt that she wanted me to stay. Oh hell. I knew she wanted me to be friends with her friends, but I couldn't. I belonged in the criminal crowd, not this one. This was a whole new crowd.

But…she was my sister and I was trying a new way. Going against my instincts, I tried to watch the game.

Mandy squeezed my arm.

CHAPTER TWO

As I headed to my car on Friday, I felt someone fall in line beside me. I knew who it was before I looked. Tray Evans. Since I hung out that evening with the group, he hadn't been around that much. He hadn't cared about pushing his agenda on me. In fact, he hadn't cared much about me at all. This was the first time since that day that he had even sought me out, but I had gotten used to his presence. There was a pull from him. If he was in a room, people knew it. They were aware of him and everyone migrated towards him. I couldn't deny that I didn't feel the same pull.

It was annoying.

I didn't have time to ask what he wanted. He grabbed my arm and pulled me from the sidewalk. We went into a group of trees, and with foliage surrounding us, we were cut off from everyone else. No one would know we were in there.

"Hey!" I pulled my arm from his hold.

He crowded me. "You lied."

"What?"

"I've been watching you, and I know you lied to me." He stood so close that I could feel the heat radiating off his body. "You said you don't want to steal anymore, but you lied. You get an adrenalin rush every time you take something. You're addicted to it. I've seen it in your eyes over the week. You miss it, and you were lying to me when you said you wouldn't do it anymore." He moved even closer. "You want to do it. I can tell."

He was right, but I pushed him back. "So what? I won't live that life anymore."

"I'm not asking you to."

"Right."

"I'm asking you to do one thing. One thing, Taryn."

He said my name. It was the second time this week and it had the same effect on my body. I gritted my teeth. I was starting to hate the power he already had over me. "What is it? What's going to screw Pedlam so much?"

He smirked, then hid it when he saw my anger. "We need to get in their school. They've got all this new security, some serious stuff, and we need you to get us inside. That's it. We just want to get in and do some damage. It won't be anything that will get us in trouble or you sent to juvie again." He softened his tone. "I promise."

And I was pure and innocent.

I snorted in disbelief. "I'm not stupid and there's a difference between helping you break in somewhere and lifting something for you. There's a big difference."

He flashed me a smile. Oh, whoa. I was suddenly burning up, and, judging from the look in his eyes, he noticed my reaction because the amber was back in his eyes.

"I know you're not stupid." He moved closer to wrap a hand around my neck. He bent forward slightly, his mouth just to the side of mine. He was almost kissing me. Without thinking, I closed my eyes and leaned

25

into him, bringing our bodies in contact. His other hand slid from my arm and down my back, ending just on the small of my back. He applied enough pressure, tipping my hips against his.

This was how Brian held me.

At that thought, I softened. My arm slipped around his shoulder, curving around his neck, and I moved my head towards his. Our lips touched, just slightly. There was no pressure. Just a small graze. I hadn't been kissed like in months. My body wanted it. There was a promise of safety and security. That old feeling I would get from Brian was there.

Brian...

I missed this, even if it wasn't real, even if it wasn't with the right guy. I could feel it again, for a small moment. I could slip away from the newness of my world, the fear from being out of my comfort zone and away from my real family. I was tempted. I was so tempted. Neither of us moved, we were at a standstill. Both of us were breathing deeply now and I slipped a finger inside the waistband of his pants and pulled. Tray's mouth opened over mine. His kiss was rough, taking command.

Opening my mouth, I dipped my head back and granted him better access. As his tongue swept inside, I moved mine against his, and my hands took hold of his shirt. Then I slid my foot around his leg and he grasped it, raising it, pulling my body almost on top of his.

Shit. This was too much, too quick. I pulled away and frowned. It hadn't been the warm comfort I felt with Brian. I glanced at Tray, seeing that he was just as affected as I was, and I shook my head clear. Tray was not Brian. He was a different type of danger than Brian, and with that thought, I shut it down. I wasn't going there.

"Just think about it." He had gone hoarse.

I didn't trust myself to speak so I just nodded.

"Fine."

I expected him to go. I expected him to pretend like I didn't exist, like he'd done over the week, but he didn't. He lingered and watched my lips.

Oh good god. My heart began beating faster. I hadn't signed up for this. Before this week, he had never said a word to me. Before this school and before my new family, he would've been in a different league than I was.

Guys wanted me. I knew this. I used it as a weapon at times. Guys were dumb. Girls were jealous and while they were experiencing those emotions, I used it, getting what I needed while they were distracted by their internal feelings.

But this guy, I licked my lips without thinking, this guy was different. I felt unbalanced with him. I didn't have the upper hand, and in those moments, I retreated. That's what I needed to do now. I started to go, but he hauled me back. My hand went to his chest and I stopped him. "Don't."

He ignored me. His hand slid inside my pocket and he pulled my ringing phone out. A new surge of heat rushed to my face as I realized I'd been so distracted by him, that I had missed that. Swearing in my head, I took it from him and pulled away, turning my back to him. "Yeah?"

I didn't check who was calling. I should've.

"Babe."

It was Brian. Memories of being with him, of being held in his arms, of being sheltered by him assaulted me. I shook my head. "You can't call me."

"Taryn," he said so softly, "come on."

I shook my head. "You can't. We talked about this."

He paused on the other end. I heard his pain. I felt it too, but he was my past, and he had become a bad part of my past. I glanced at Tray. Here was a different guy, one from the 'right side' of the tracks. He was asking me to go back there. Hearing Brian's voice was torture, but I was glad. The decision to keep clean was reaffirmed and I remembered what I could lose, or worse yet, I shuddered, what I could go back to.

"You can't call me." My throat swelled. "I'm sorry, Brian." Then I hung up.

"That was your ex?"

I didn't respond. No one needed to know my business.

"Look, I get it. I do."

He didn't, but I remained silent. My back was still turned to him.

"I wouldn't be asking if it wasn't important. Your sister said you could get into any building. That's what her parents had been warned about, that you're one of the best. I don't know that world. I don't. I know my school. I know my friends, and I know that I have to take care of us. Getting into Pedlam will help."

"It's a stupid rivalry."

"It's not. They fucked us up last time. A lot of guys lost scholarships. I know it sounds stupid, but it's important to us. It's important to them."

It was a stupid rivalry. I couldn't shake that thought. One prank couldn't ruin their lives, but it could ruin mine. I turned around. "I'm not doing it. Figure out another way."

Tray had a party that weekend. Mandy had invited me, but a house full of drunk people? It was not tempting. I went for a ride instead. The parents weren't home, Austin was sleeping at a friend's for the entire week and weekend, and Mandy had plans to sleep at Devon's. I didn't want to spend so much time alone in that massive house. The emptiness was too much at times, so I headed towards Pedlam. Tray mentioned they had new security, and I wanted to check it out. Rawley and Pedlam were two towns in the middle of nowhere. A large river ran between them, but there was no significance to either town. We were surrounded by fields and forest, set smack in the middle of the United States. So it was perplexing why Pedlam would want new security. As I pulled into the parking lot across from it, I wondered why they would post cameras at every corner, including the light posts in the parking lot, and why would they have armed guards? There were two going into the building.

As I watched, nothing stood out. There had been renovations done over the summer, but the new security didn't make any sense, especially when Pedlam was smaller than, and not as wealthy as, Rawley. That had been another reason why I hadn't been so ecstatic when I heard where I'd be living. Rich people were targets for me. I would steal from them, not rub shoulders with them, but it was what it was. On that thought, I headed back. As I pulled out onto the road, a truck was heading my way. It slowed and turned down a gravel road. As I passed it, I saw there were three men in the bed of the truck. They looked rough. No distinct facial features stood out. They were nondescript, but they looked hard. As the car disappeared around a bend in the road, I pulled over and studied where they had gone. The road led out to a field. I'd been down that road before. There was nothing there, a field, trees, and the river. Then I shrugged. They were too far ahead, and I didn't want to follow them. I drove home. When I got closer to Mandy's home, I stopped at the diner first. I knew it was the school's hangout, but since Tray was having his party, I figured it would be empty.

So color me shocked when I saw Tray, Samuel, and Grant in a corner booth. Before I could duck out, not sure if I wanted to stay or go home, Grant waved. "Hey, Mandy's sister!"

Ignoring the heat from Tray's scrutiny, I headed their way. "Yes, that's my name. Mandy's sister. It's a bitch to write that out all the time. The teachers are always confused. Mandy or Mandy's sister. They never know which one is me."

He laughed and popped a fry into his mouth.

Samuel frowned at him, but said to me, "We thought we'd see you at the party."

"It's not my scene," I lied. Parties were my scene, just not their parties. "Thought you guys would be at the party, since—you know—Tray, you're hosting it."

He grinned and leaned back. "Those parties can run themselves."

"Hmm." I wasn't sure what to talk about. These were Mandy's friends. I was Mandy's sister and that was extent of our relationship. They didn't seem interested in explaining why they weren't at the party, and I wasn't interested in having a conversation with them, so I headed to the counter and paid for a diet soda. After I filled the cup and headed back, I saw they were gone. I shrugged. Good riddance. But when I went to the parking lot, I wasn't that lucky.

Tray was leaning against my car. His arms were crossed over his chest, making his upper arms stand out under his shirt. That damn tribal tattoo peeked out of his shirt again, asking for me to lift his sleeve up so I could examine the whole thing. I groaned in my head. Brian had tattoos too, but none of them beckoned to me like his. I didn't like that. When I stopped in front of him, my eyebrow arched up.

I didn't say anything. It was on him to talk.

He didn't say anything.

Fiddling with my straw, I let my mind wander. If this was a game, I was going to win. I've spent time on stake-outs, doing surveillance for targets with Brian. For some of those, we had to remain still and silent for hours. This was a win-win for me. If I could piss Tray off as I beat him at his own game, score one for me.

He narrowed his eyes.

I smiled at him and thought back to Pedlam High School. There had been eight cameras. "You're annoying."

I pondered those cameras, wondering if there were more, but I focused on him again. "I've been told that."

He laughed briefly and shook his head. "Mandy went back to your house. She said you were gone."

"Oh?"

"Yeah. Where'd you go?"

"Why do you care?" I frowned. "I don't like the idea of my sister keeping tabs on me and reporting to you."

31

"Relax." He grinned. "She told Devon. I was right there so I heard. There's no tabs and there's no reporting going on, but I am curious where you went."

"Why? I'm none of your business."

"No." He shook his head. "But you are damned intriguing. Where do you spend your time?" His tone softened, and he grew pensive.

I reacted to his change. Heat started to build inside me, and there was a small flutter in my chest. Then I rolled my eyes. For fuck's sakes. What was I doing? Developing a schoolgirl crush? I shook my head. This was the last guy I wanted that to happen with.

I fixed him with a chilly stare. "Aren't you the busy bee with an inquiring mind."

He laughed. The sound of it rushed over me and I sucked in my breath. Oh boy. I was in trouble. A corner of his mouth curved up, and he murmured, "For some reason, I am becoming a busy bee with you. You're not like normal girls, you know."

"I do know." I flashed him a smile. "I'm smarter."

Another laugh from him. It slid over me like a spray of water on a hot day. It was refreshing.

I scowled. It was a headache.

He tilted his head to the side. "You may be right."

My eyes snapped to his. "Was that a compliment?"

He flashed me a grin. "What have I done to earn this horrible reputation with you? I'm being honest."

The truth from him came loud and clear. He was being genuine, and dammit, I felt myself softening towards him. His eyes were warm and inviting. His tone didn't reflect anything other than his honesty, and my interest was piqued.

I shrugged and forced myself to look away. "You haven't done anything except ask me to risk losing everything. Other than that," I smiled, "nope, you're right. It's unwarranted."

His eyes darkened and dropped to my lips. "I asked the first time because Mandy made it sound like you would want to do it. I asked the second time because I was testing a theory."

"Really?"

He nodded, his gaze never leaving my lips. "Yeah. A theory."

My chest tightened. His words were weaving a spell over me, one that I enjoyed and hated at the same time. I found myself asking, "What theory was that?"

"That it's a rush to you."

"What's a rush?"

"Stealing." His eyes lifted, pinning me in place. "Taking what isn't yours. You love it. You get off on it, don't you?"

I shook my head. "It's not that."

"It's not?" He reached for me, and I closed my eyes, feeling his hand take hold of my jeans. One of his fingers slid through a loop on my waistband, but he didn't do anything. He kept it there, as if anchoring me in place. I couldn't run. I didn't want to run, and I frowned as I realized that. He asked, "So what is it? What did I get wrong?"

Tipping my head back, I held his eyes. "It's not the taking something that isn't mine."

He grinned. "Somehow I don't believe you."

"It's the power knowing that I can. I can take it if I want to and no one can stop me." A shiver wound its way up my spine, but it was the good kind. It was the delicious kind. Remembering that power was overwhelming, beckoning me to remember what it felt like to yield it again. At the tips of my fingers, I could decide what was mine and what wasn't. It was intoxicating. "It's a rush."

His thumb fell from the loop. It was pressed against my stomach, warm against my skin. The heat inside me was building again. Then he began moving his thumb, rubbing it back and forth, and I closed my eyes. My breathing deepened. One touch and I felt scorched by this guy. Then I stopped thinking. His hand curved in, and he pressed his palm to my stomach now. I was pulled closer to him. His chest was inches from mine. As my pulse quickened, I lifted a hand to push him away. I needed space, but it didn't happen. Instead, my hand curved into his shirt and his other hand found my hip. He pulled me even closer. Our hips were touching now, a light graze against each other as we both stood there.

I wanted his touch. I wanted it in more ways than I had ever wanted Brian. My eyes opened and I realized what I was doing. I stepped away from him, breathing raggedly, but so was he.

"Shit." His eyes raked over me.

I turned. I didn't want him to see the evidence of his power over me. "Go to your party."

CHAPTER THREE

Mandy came in my room Saturday evening to inform me who hooked up with whom, who broke up with whom, who fought, and who barfed. It was an amazing party. She invited me out with them that night. I declined and continued folding my clothes. When she kept quiet, I knew—the rumors had already circulated—someone must've seen Tray and me outside the diner.

She didn't push it. Thank you for small favors. Instead I had to listen to her theory that Devon was cheating on her for the next thirty minutes.

"Are you serious? Devon? We're talking about Devon?"

"Yeah." She swung her legs around and sat up, still on my bed. "He was weird last night. I don't know. Maybe he really did hook up with Stephanie."

I paused, frowned, and then finished folding my shirt. "Are you going to talk to him tonight? About your hunch?"

"About Stephanie? No, but I am going to ask him if he's cheating on me."

"The sooner you talk to him, the sooner you'll know what's really going on and be back to being lovebirds again." The idea of Mandy and Devon not together was funny to me. It wasn't real. Those two were so lovey-dovey they made me gag the first time I saw it. The idea of Devon cheating was ridiculous. Then I glanced at her and saw the determined set of her shoulders. "Whoa. You're serious."

She stood and started to pace. "He's really off and it's getting to me, you know? He's been like this for a while, but last night it creeped me out."

"What'd he do?"

"He didn't do anything, just would put his phone away as soon as I came back." She hesitated. "Other stuff's happened too. I don't like it. I can't not say anything. No way. He's been like this for seven months. I can't ignore it anymore."

"Yeah." I knew how she felt. Brian had cheated once. I almost killed him afterwards.

She nodded, her jaw hardening. "Yeah."

"So where are you guys going tonight? Who's all going?"

"The gang and some others." That meant the top circle and the crowd beneath them. Stephanie. Ugh. "We're going to a party at Rickets' House."

Another ugh. Rickets' House was a big white mansion near Pedlam. Parties were thrown there because the house was abandoned, situated deep in the woods. Kids could scatter easily if the cops showed up, and it was notorious for being a mating ground. Brian wouldn't be there; he hated that place, but there'd definitely be others there from Pedlam.

"I'm in." I wasn't doing the job, but I wanted to know why Pedlam had so much security. It was nagging at me, and I knew I could get some answers there.

Devon and Jennica arrived a few minutes ago and planned on riding with us. It had been awkward. She gave my outfit a second glance. I couldn't dress like the new me. Boring, all covered up, and saint-like. I hadn't dressed like that at Pedlam, and I needed my old intimidation factor at full force to get the answers I wanted. So I dressed how I used to. I wore a leather miniskirt and a lacy black tank top that hugged my curves with a diamond necklace that was looped twice around my neck, resting above my belly-button. Even Mandy had been taken aback, and she'd seen the old me a few times.

She got over my wardrobe when she grew distracted by Devon's behavior. He'd been standoffish the entire evening. He arrived, gave her a chaste kiss on the cheek, and that had been it. After we traipsed into the car, he'd been silent, just focused on driving. Jennica sat in the back with me, chatting to Mandy, who was glancing at Devon every few seconds, trying to appear nonchalant. I was staring out the window tuning the conversation out.

Until I heard Jennica say, "...he was with Adrian last night. Seriously. Tray pisses me off sometimes."

I looked over and caught the heated look Mandy shot Jennica. She flushed when she saw that I had caught her, and I grinned. "What happened?"

Jennica turned to me. "I was telling Mandy that sometimes I'm embarrassed by Tray, especially when he screws girls like Adrian Casners. She's white trash."

"That's probably why he screwed her."

Jennica and Mandy were both watching me. Even Devon glanced in the rear-view mirror.

"What?" I asked.

"Nothing." Mandy looked away.

Jennica turned to face me. "We heard an interesting tidbit last night, about you and Tray." She was almost gloating. "Care to elaborate?"

I frowned. I had missed something, then how she said 'white trash' came back to me. There'd been an extra emphasis on those words. "Are you insinuating that I'm white trash? Because if you were, you worked too hard for the joke." I flashed her a grin and asked, "How long till we get there?"

I turned back to the window and ignored whatever her reaction was. A moment later, Devon turned into a driveway. "We're meeting up with Tray and the rest of the gang at his place first."

Tray's place was gorgeous. It was a mansion, bigger than Mandy's, and had four massive pillars right before the front door with a large porch extending off to the side. The living room could be seen through three large windows and inside there was a flat screen TV highlighting one entire wall. White leather couches aligned the sides of the room. The pool could be seen through the glass patio doors, shimmering on the other side of the mansion.

Walking inside, I saw a spiral staircase off to the right. There was an open doorway before the steps, leading into an expansive kitchen with an island in the middle, steel appliances, and granite countertops; even the kitchen looked like a masterpiece.

Most of the 'cool' crowd was lounging there, drinking, chatting, or in the process of making their drinks for the ride. Grant and Samuel were at a table talking with some girls I didn't recognize. Amber was sitting on the island, dangling her feet, talking with a guy that I thought was Brent…Garrett? Basketball team…I think. I didn't care.

Tray was nowhere to be found.

Mandy nudged me. "Tray just got here. He's getting dressed and then we're heading out."

"I don't get why we're all meeting here? Why don't we just go to the party?"

"Because Tray and Grant are the only ones who know where Rickets' House is and there's probably Pedlam students there. It's not like we all want to show up there alone."

"What? Strength in numbers? Can't handle a few Pedlamites?"

"You could?"

"I went to Pedlam, a few times."

"A few times?" a girl asked. I didn't recognize her, but she was already annoying me. She could've been the poster-girl for Hooters.

"Yeah. What about it?"

"She didn't mean anything, Matthews." Tray walked up behind me, wrapping an arm around my waist, pulling me into his side. To everyone else, he said, "Let's head out." He pulled me with him. "You can ride with me."

I glared at him and ignored the sudden attention he brought to us. Then I saw Mandy was watching Devon while Jennica paired off with Grant. It was a perfect time for those two to talk. "Fine."

Two other guys were behind us as we walked to Tray's SUV. Ignoring the heat from Tray's hand as it rested on my stomach, I brushed him off and rounded the SUV to climb into the passenger seat. The other two got in the back.

Tray introduced us inside, "Helms, Mitch, this is Matthews. Matthews, the guys."

"My name's Taryn, not Matthews." I recalled that they were both on the basketball team. They fit the description, tall and lanky in preppy clothes. It wasn't long before the three were discussing some recent game. All three ignored me, but I was fine with that. I wouldn't have to worry about talking with Tray the entire time. It wasn't long until he was pulling into a long driveway that started at the bottom of a hill and wound its way up. The house was at the top and the lights were already blinding through the trees as we started up. Cars were parked on both sides of the driveway, but we inched past them.

"Dude, where are we going to park?"

"Forget that. Look at all these people. We're going to get trashed tonight."

Tray kept quiet, glancing at me for a split second.

I grinned when I caught sight of an old friend's car. He would think it's a riot, me showing up with the crème de la crème from Rawley's royalty. No doubt he'd double over in laughter when he saw our entrance.

"Something funny?"

I looked at him. I hadn't been paying him any attention. I'd been working hard at that, but now, looking at him, my body grew way too aware of him. Feeling a sensation in my stomach, like a tickle, I couldn't

40

deny that he looked good. He looked more than good. He wore a soft blue shirt that molded to his trim form without being too tight. His arms and that damn tattoo kept drawing my attention. I was itching to explore it better, but I didn't. My hands curled into my lap. Tray grinned. A smug expression teased at the corner of his lips for a second before it vanished. Then his gaze lifted to mine, and I was burned by it. He wanted me. I could see it. When I flinched and started to look away, his hand touched my leg. I couldn't look away.

A soft curse slipped from me. A bunch of emotions threatened to unleash inside me, but I clamped them down. This wasn't the place to deal with this, not when I'd be seeing other Pedlamites.

When the car paused in front of the house, the other two jumped out. I saw my chance to get away, but he said, "Walk up with me." Anyone else would've taken it as a command, but I heard the questioning lilt to his voice. So I sat back and waited as he moved the SUV forward. The rest of our crew did the same thing; each car paused for the passengers to hop out and the cars followed the others, parking side by side at the bottom of the hill.

Tray didn't move to draw me against his side as we walked up. I was grateful, but at the same time, I was mad at myself—a part of me had hoped he would. I couldn't stop thinking about his hand on my back, and even now, a small tingle went through me at the idea of him touching me. We walked side by side, not looking at each other, but our arms brushed against each other's. Every part of my body was awake and anticipating the next touch or graze. He was pulling me in, just by being beside me.

41

By the time we neared the door, everyone had already gone inside. There were others drinking and lounging on the patio. I glanced around, recognizing a few of them from Pedlam.

"Holy shit!"

I glanced over and went cold. Veronica Teedz teetered on her high heels, beer sloshing over her cup. Her eyes were transfixed on my face as she drew closer. "Taryn? I can't believe it's you. It is you or am I that drunk?"

Veronica Teedz had never acknowledged my presence before. "You're that drunk." I moved past her, but caught the small grin that flashed over Tray's face.

People were everywhere inside. Each room was packed tight. A few tables were set up in the corners where people were playing cards. The main floor had a dance floor and music pounded throughout the house. The second, third, and fourth floors were the bedrooms. Hookups and smaller parties congregated there.

Tray grabbed my hand and pulled me towards the kitchen area. He paid for our cups, and after they were filled with beer, he pulled me to his side and murmured in my ear, "You know that girl out there?"

I tilted my head back, my lips brushed against his ear, and I rested a hand on his chest. He was warm and felt like cement under my touch. Even with that slight touch, I wanted to close my eyes and melt into him. Instead, I forced myself to say, "Yeah, not a friend." I gestured behind us. "I'm going to look around." I was asking him if that was all right? A part of me flared up. He wasn't mine. I wasn't his. Why was I acting like this?

He nodded and turned into the crowd, leaving me alone. There was no argument from him. As he went, people looked up, feeling his presence, watching him. These people didn't know him, but they reacted to him on an instinctual level. They moved for him, clearing a path so he could go by. Girls from Pedlam continued watching, even after he disappeared from eyesight. I couldn't blame them. I was struggling with the same need to stare at him. Pushing through the room, I worked my way through the crowd. A few recognized me and gave their hellos. It felt nice, to know that I hadn't been forgotten, but as I searched the house, there wasn't anyone I wanted to see. I couldn't find my friend so I headed in the direction Tray had gone and found him in a back room. Everyone from Rawley had taken root in there. Tray was against a far wall. He was swamped on both sides by people. Even if they didn't know him, they were pulled in by him. Tray had that power. He had a presence that told the world he didn't give a damn about anyone or anything. It made him all the more appealing.

Then I saw my friend, Grayley. He was sitting in the middle of a couch. His hair was longer, touching the tops of his shoulders, and his shirt swallowed him, hanging loose over his baggy pants. With almost delicate features, Grayley was given the nickname of Pretty Boy growing up. When he got a few tattoos and a scar down the side of his neck, that nickname went away. To everyone, he was just Grayley now. He fit in with anyone. It was one of his gifts. He was a likeable guy. He had become friends with me and Brian years ago, but he was also good friends with the crème de la crème of the Pedlam circle. If anyone would know why Pedlam had such high security, it would be him.

I started for him, and Tray noticed my intent. He straightened from the wall and frowned. I threw him an uneasy look. I wasn't doing the job for him, but I was still curious. If he came over, he'd start getting thoughts I didn't want him to have.

Grayley glanced up and he began to grin, but then a guy I didn't know stepped in between us. After an obnoxious wolf whistle, his gaze raked me up and down, and he sneered at me. "My, my, my. I know who you are."

"That's nice—"

"I thought so." He winked at me.

"But I don't know you—"

His hand grabbed my hip, and he tried to pull me close. "That's okay. We can fix that."

Removing his hand, I finished, "And I don't care to know you."

"Then we have a problem." He stepped back and looked me up and down in an exaggerated motion. "You have got one of the nicest bodies I've seen in a long while. In fact." He tried to draw me to him again. Tray narrowed his eyes. He remained against the wall, and I didn't know if I was relieved or disappointed. I stopped thinking about Tray and stiffened as the guy's hand slipped under my shirt. This bastard was going down. My hand lifted, ready to grab his thumb and twist his arm so he would be forced backwards, but I heard from behind me, "Goddamn, Clint. Let go of her." He was thrown from me and shoved against a wall. The people standing around us scattered, and someone began punching him, hitting him in the face and stomach.

It was Brian. His back was tense, his shoulders tight, and he kept raising his fist to deliver another blow.

For a moment, I couldn't move. It was Brian...that knowledge seeped in slowly. It had been so long since I had seen him. Then Grayley was in front of me. He yelled at me, "Matthews, do something."

Shit.

I lunged for them.

"Brian," Grayley bit out as he moved closer to the fight, trying to wedge himself between them. But Brian and the other guy were inches taller than Grayley and heavily muscled. I knew Brian's body. He didn't lift weights, but he didn't have to. He did construction during the summer, so his body was toned. Grayley was gangly and not athletic at all. He'd be snapped in two.

Tray straightened, hearing the exchange, but he didn't seem interested in pulling Brian off the guy, though it didn't matter. Brian was punched, and it wasn't long before a full scuffle was going on in the room. I grabbed Grayley and tugged him back. He cursed. "They fought over another girl this week too. This ain't good. Brian's going to get arrested again."

Hearing that, a pang went through me. Another girl? Then the rest registered with me, and I knew he was right. Brian was always arrested before the others; the cops hated him because of Jace, but Brian was beyond listening. The guy had delivered a few hits and then Brian turned his body. He shoved the guy down and delivered hit after hit. No one moved to stop him, and I shot Tray a look. He sighed and then nodded. As he did, his friends waded in and grabbed Brian off of the guy. When the other guy jumped up, ready to lunge for Brian, he was grabbed as well.

Tray gestured to the door. "Take 'em out."

They were ushered from the room. As the rest filed behind them, no one complained about the early exit. Tray held back and crossed over to me. Ignoring Grayley's presence beside me, he asked, "That was your ex?"

My throat had grown thick with emotion. I nodded. I didn't want to deal with the questions at that moment. Tray seemed to understand. "Let's go." He grasped my hand and led the way, weaving through the crowd. We were out the door when Veronica stopped us again. She was even more unsteady on her high heels this time, if that was possible. "I called him. You know, Taryn, Brian's been miserable. We all know it's because of you. He wanted to know if you showed up."

"You called him?"

"Yeah. I did. He loves you. It was the two of you. You guys were so…you guys are perfect together."

"Yeah, except that we're not."

No one knew why we couldn't be together, or no one cared to understand. Even now, Brian was still fighting against the guys holding him. He wanted to hurt the other guy, who had stopped resisting. He was wary now, his eyebrows bunched forward in concern. Brian yelled at him, "You ass punk. You touch her again and I'll cut you."

I sucked in a breath. Brian meant it.

Tray stood beside me, but I couldn't look at him. I didn't want to see any condemnation he might have for Brian. Forcing the tears back, I started down the stairs. "Brian." He paused and turned to me. I said, "Stop it."

"Taryn."

"Stop." He grimaced, hearing the pleading in my voice. "Please, just stop." I wasn't referencing just this night. Memories of our past came back to me. The nights I would crawl into his bed, how he took care of me. I felt them as if I were reliving them. His fighting. How he wanted to be a part of Jace's lifestyle, how he wouldn't listen to me when I begged him to stay away. Brian wasn't Jace. Jace was smart and dangerous. Jace would survive no matter what, but Brian wouldn't. He would get caught. He would go to jail, and I would lose him.

Flashbacks of our fights came to me. The hurt was there, every time he didn't listen to me and went to buy more drugs. I couldn't deal with it.

"Taryn," he started.

The fight had left him, but I shook my head and went past him. I felt Tray beside me.

"Taryn," Brian called after me.

I couldn't. I just couldn't face him. Any conversation with him always ended the same way. He would promise to change. He never did, and I would pick up the pieces. I couldn't do that tonight, not this time.

I kept going, hugging myself. Tray never touched me. The sight of it would've enraged Brian again. I was relieved, but a part of me wanted it too. I shook my head. I couldn't deal with Brian's jealousy, not tonight anyway.

"TARYN!"

I turned and disappeared from his sight. Tray's SUV blocked his view. When I got inside, he asked, "You okay?"

"No."

He didn't start the engine. Instead, he sat there and waited a few minutes. Then he asked, "What do you want to do?"

47

"Leave."

He did as I asked. As we drove past the house, Brian was gone. I didn't want to know where he had gone, but Grayley was still there. I told Tray to stop and rolled my window down. "Gray."

Grayley approached the car. "Holy fuck, Tar." He groaned, shaking his head. "Holy hell for fuck's sake."

"I didn't know that was going to happen. I didn't know someone would call him."

Grayley was eyeing Tray, but he murmured, "Yeah, well, for what it's worth, he's been off the rails since you left him. Everyone's on edge at school. That guy was one out of ten that he's fought *just* this month."

I shook my head. "I couldn't handle being with him anymore."

"We know. *He* knows. I think that's why he's like a loose cannon more than normal lately. He can't blame you for leaving. No one can."

Those words should've made me feel better. They didn't. "Will you watch him for me? Call me if anything bad happens to him?"

He nodded. "Yeah, sure. Another day in the life of a Lanser, huh?"

A sad laugh came from me. "Yeah."

"Okay." He leaned around me and said to Tray, "Take her home. Knowing Taryn, she's ready to crash."

"Thanks, Grayley."

He nodded. A rueful smile graced his features and his eyes grew solemn. "Miss you around town, though."

"Miss you too."

He laughed and stepped back, then gestured to the road. "Get out of here, Matthews. I'll call if I need to."

"Okay." I nodded. As Tray pulled forward, I kept looking at Grayley until he was out of sight. Then I rolled the window up and huddled against it, pressing my forehead against the glass.

CHAPTER FOUR

It wasn't long until Tray's phone went off. "Yeah," he answered. A moment later, "Nah. Have fun. Grant knows the way back."

His phone rang again, then again. He had the same conversation.

I glanced over. "A lot of people want you to go back to the party."

He glanced sideways at me and then my phone rang, interrupting anything he might've said. I reached for my phone, but Tray caught my hand. "What?" It kept ringing.

"You know who that will be."

Brian.

A weight dropped onto my shoulders and I nodded. I knew. This was part of breaking up. When he saw I was going to answer anyway, he let go and I held it to my ear. "Brian?"

He demanded, "Where are you?"

"I got a ride home."

"I saw you, remember? Where are you? Why are you with that punk Evans and why was Clint hitting on you tonight?" He paused. I couldn't answer before he added, "Were you teasing him? Shit. Are you teasing both of them?"

I frowned. This wasn't Brian, or this wasn't my Brian. He was hotheaded and a loose cannon, but he had never turned his rage against me before. I looked at Tray and saw that he had heard. Judging from the chill radiating off him and the set of his jaw, he wasn't happy.

"Brian, you need to calm down."

"The fucker was all over you. He was two inches from—"

"I was handling him."

Tray pulled the car over and watched me. A knot had formed in my gut and the longer he remained silent, just listening, the more it grew. I didn't know how this was going to turn out, but I closed my eyes and concentrated on one thing. Brian needed to calm down.

"You were handling him? You're the one who's delusional, Tar. He needs to know that you're still my property. He fucks with me if he even goes near you."

"Brian." I wasn't his property. He knew that. "Are you trying to piss me off now?"

He stopped, then let out a harsh laugh. "Are you kidding me? Are you fucking kidding me?"

"Brian, stop."

"No, you stop. You left, Taryn. You walked away from me, but you're still mine—"

I ended the call. Grayley was right. Brian needed to be reined in, but I couldn't do it. That wasn't my place. I didn't know why I asked Grayley to keep tabs on him. I couldn't do anything about him anymore, but someone could and I knew only one person that Brian might listen to. His brother.

"We need to go somewhere."

"Where?"

"You're not going to like it."

51

He frowned, then started the car. "Just tell me where."

It was thirty minutes later when he shook his head, eyeing the nightclub. "Am I going to get killed in there?"

I laughed. I couldn't help it. The Seven8 was home to Jace Lanser, Brian's older brother. Brian and Jace had a love/hate relationship, but Jace had something that Brian didn't: discipline. Brian was smart. But Jace was smarter and ruthless.

"Come on. You'll be fine." I climbed out of the SUV. Going to his side, I added, "Just don't say anything."

Tray didn't look appeased, but he followed me.

When we neared the door, the bouncer scanned Tray up and down. "He going to be a problem?"

"No trouble. Is Jace in?"

"Hmm. He's in. He's with Cammy."

I grinned. "Those two back on again?"

"Don't care. She's either here or she's not."

"Right." I rolled my eyes. When he kept glaring at Tray, I sighed. "You going to let us in or do I need to get in my way?"

His glare turned my way. One night he refused to let me inside, so I went through the roof. The bouncers still hadn't lived that down.

"He's in the back. Take the small hallway."

Tray followed me as we circled around the front entrance, the pounding music already blaring in our ears. Catching Casey's attention, the front bartender nodded in greeting as we slipped behind him and trailed into the hallway that led its way around the club to the back offices. At the closed office door, I knocked and waited. A second later, it opened as Cammy slipped out. She slid the strap from her halter-top up her shoulder. When she saw it was me, she stumbled. "Taryn, I didn't know—"

"Let her in, Cammy," came from inside.

Flushing, she rolled her eyes and slipped around us.

The sight of a shirtless Jace with his pants unbuttoned, hanging low on his lean hips, welcomed us as we went inside. Raking a hand through his tousled hair, he grinned at me, his abdominal muscles highlighted against the neon lighting inside. Brian was solid, but Jace was in a whole different league. He had a lean build, dirty blonde hair, and piercing eyes. His eyes skimmed over me and settled on Tray. He stood there, studying him and as he did, as he breathed in and out, every muscle in his body rippling from that slight movement.

"Heya, Terry." He flashed me a grin as he buttoned his jeans. He crossed over to us and gave me a hug.

Jace was the only one who could get away with calling me that name. Brian tried once and he got a swift kick in the balls. He'd never done it again, although he sneered every time Jace said it, which made him say it every time he could.

As his arms wrapped around me, a nostalgic feeling came over me. He and Brian had been my family. Each of them protected me for years. When he started to move away, I grasped onto the back of his arms and held him tighter. I just needed a moment longer.

He stayed there, wrapping his arms even tighter, tucking his chin into the crook of my neck and shoulder. I felt his lips brush against my skin as he murmured, "Missed you too."

I nodded. I couldn't talk. For some reason I was thankful Tray hadn't heard him. I stepped back, brushed the tear that had escaped, turning away so he couldn't see that either. I felt both of them watching me and swallowed the emotion. When I looked back up, I was all business. There was a reason we had come, but I couldn't help myself from asking, "You and Cammy back on?"

"For the night." He gestured to Tray. "Who's he?"

"Not important." I cleared my throat. I wanted to tell him about Brian and get out of there, before even more emotions came over me.

"Wait—" he murmured. A light of recognition sparked in his eyes. He snapped his fingers. "Evans."

Tray looked at me and waited.

I laughed. "I didn't mean it literally. You can talk. I guess he knows you."

He winked at me before turning to Jace. "Yeah. I'm Evans."

Jace regarded him with caution, but he shook his head. "You're with Taryn?"

Tray looked at me. A jolt went through me at what Jace was insinuating. I shook my head. "No, no. Um..." I bit my lip, my cheeks warming, as both of them waited for my answer. "No. He's friends with my sister."

"The sister from your new family?"

I nodded. "Yeah. Her." I grinned. "She's popular, Jace. Can you believe that? I got one of *those* families."

"Yeah." He looked at me with fondness. "I can, Terry. You deserve it. You know I always thought that."

"Yeah." Other memories started to come to me, but I pushed them away. "Listen, we're here because of Brian."

54

"Aw. The real reason you came." He shook his head. "What's my brother done now?"

"He's…" I hesitated. If Jace went after Brian, it could get nasty, but there was no one else who could reel him in. "He's a little nuts, to be truthful. I'm scared of what he's going to do. He saw me at Rickets' Hou—"

"Wait." Jace was startled. "You went to Rickets' House?"

I nodded. "Yeah." I glanced at Tray. "A bunch of people from our school did. Why?"

"Don't go there anymore."

"But—" This didn't make sense. He had never cared before. It had been Brian who had been worried about me. "Why?"

"Just don't, Taryn."

He said my name. My eyes widened. I knew Jace could be serious and sometimes deadly, but he usually kept his lighthearted side for me. He was serious now. He was very serious. He said again, "I mean it, Taryn. Don't go there. Changes are happening and it's not safe."

"What do you mean?"

He shook his head. "It's not for you to worry about."

"But—"

"Taryn." He silenced me, moving towards me. "I mean it. I don't want you there. I don't even want Brian there."

"You don't?"

Jace gestured to Tray. "Drive her back." As Tray took my arm, Jace said to me, "I'll keep Brian away from you. I promise. Go back to Rawley." He took both my shoulders in his hands and leaned forward to press a kiss to my forehead. "Go back to that new family. You're better off." He squeezed my shoulders. "Make something of yourself, Taryn. A chance like this don't come along often. Grab it while you can."

As we left, I couldn't get Jace's words out of my head. A shiver went down my back, and as we left Pedlam behind us, I couldn't shake the uneasy feeling.

His phone kept ringing as we drove back to Rawley.

"Why aren't you answering?"

He kept his eyes on the road. "Because they're drunk."

As it began ringing again, I saw the name Adrian Do Not Answer flashing across his screen. Tray knew what I was going to do. A small grin lifted the corner of his mouth, but he kept driving. He was going to let me do whatever I wanted. At that idea, my own wicked grin formed on my face, and I hit the answer button. "Hello?"

For thirty seconds, there was silence before she said, "Who is this?"

"Tray can't talk right now. He's too busy with me." Tray turned to me and my cheeks warmed, but I didn't look at him. I moaned into the phone then. "He's soo good, ooh my gawwd."

Silence again. I waited. When the silence stretched, I let out another groan and then she screeched. "Who are you?"

I laughed. "The girl that took your place." Ending the call, I handed it back to him. "I hope that was alright?"

He took it, pressed a button, and dropped it into the console between us. "I think you took care of a problem for me. I should be thanking you."

I laughed; the idea of Tray owing me sent a host of sensations through me. Then my phone rang and all that went away. "Are you kidding me?" Expecting Brian, the small burst of anger fizzled to concern. "It's Mandy."

She rushed out, "Devon and I broke up. I was right. He's been sleeping with Jennica. Jennica of all people! I caught 'em in one of the bedrooms." She stopped as a sob came out. "I hate that bitch!"

"Mandy, I'm so sorry."

"I hate her, I hate her so damn much. What am I going to do? It's going to be all over school!"

"Fuck school. You don't let her get away with this."

"I know, but what can I do? I'll get caught whatever I do and then I'll get suspended. I can't do that. Mom and Dad would be furious with me. I might lose my scholarship to Brown next year."

Here it was. This was when I stepped forward and offered my criminal skills. Fuck my family. Fuck my future. My sister was hurting. I might not have been willing to throw it all down the drain for Tray, but this was different. My old protectiveness came out. Mandy was family. Enough said.

"Mandy."

Tray frowned, hearing the sudden seriousness in my tone. He glanced at me. I didn't know exactly what I was going to do, but I was going to do something, and it wasn't going to be legal. I wanted to give her some form of comfort, but if she knew, she'd want in and she could get in trouble with me.

"What?" She paused in between her sobs and a hiccup. "Taryn?"

"Nothing." I forced those words down. "Where are you?"

She hiccupped again. "I'm coming back. I made one of the guys drive me back. Taryn," she started crying again, "I couldn't stay there. They didn't even stop. She saw me and kept going. I couldn't stay there. I would've—"

I jerked forward in my seat. She couldn't do anything. It was better if I got in trouble, not her. Mandy was good. Mandy was normal. She had a future. Mine was still in question. I shook my head. "You didn't do anything, did you?"

"No," her voice dropped to a whisper, "but I wanted to. I wanted to hurt them, Taryn. What am I going to do? Oh my god." She dissolved back into tears. "I hate Devon. I absolutely hate Devon. I'm going to...I'm going to key his car; that's what I'm going to do."

The car slowed as we turned into Tray's driveway. I said to her, "Just come to Tray's. I'm here. I'll wait for you."

"Thank you, Taryn, just thank you." Her voice was hoarse now.

"It'll be okay. I promise."

"O...o...kay." She hiccupped again.

After we ended the call, I glanced at Tray. His lack of surprise set me on edge. My teeth gritted together. "You knew." It wasn't a question. It was an accusation.

Compared to the mob that had been in his house earlier, his mansion was eerily vacant. I followed him inside as he went to the kitchen and opened the refrigerator. He had ignored my statement, but when he handed me a beer, his eyes caught mine. I couldn't place what was going on in his head; he was wearing a mask. It was one that I had witnessed on him since I arrived in Rawley. It was the same mask he gave everyone, his friends, his teachers, and now it was directed at me. Tray

Evans wasn't normal. I had forgotten during our recent interactions, but I remembered now.

I stepped back and ignored the beer he handed to me.

He dropped his arm with a sigh and shrugged, leaning back against a counter. "Would you care if I said it was bro code?"

I snorted.

He laughed softly. He sighed again and shook his head. "I'm not a narc, Taryn. I know a lot of shit and don't say a word. That's not me."

"Mandy's your friend."

"So's Devon."

"You don't care that your friend is getting hurt?"

"She wasn't getting hurt. She wouldn't until she found out." He straightened from the counter and advanced towards me. He walked with purpose, stalking his prey, and I bit down on my lip. I should've moved. I couldn't. The mask fell and someone dangerous was looking back at me. My heart leapt into my chest. There was more to him. I felt it. My body responded to it and responded to him because of it. I didn't know what it was. My mind wasn't thinking, but I couldn't move away. As he stopped in front of me, just an inch separating us, he looked down to my lips. He said, "I'm no narc."

I hated that word. I really did. I hated narcs, and I hated myself because I understood him. I had to ask, "If the situation was reversed? If someone was cheating on you and your friends knew?"

He merely smirked and set the beer in front of me. Keeping both arms on either side of me, he trapped me in place. Nudging the barstool I sat on with his knee, he twirled me around until I was facing him.

My throat swelled up. "How long has it been going on?"

He had started to move even closer. His hand lifted from the counter, and I closed my eyes, not knowing where he was going to touch me. My body was burning up. I felt alive from the anticipation of his touch, but as I asked that, I felt a cold chill instead. He stepped away. "I'm not answering that either."

"What?"

He shook his head, the same mask falling back into place. "It's not my business. It's not my job to do clean up." His nostrils flared as disgust filled his tone. "It's not yours either. Stop making it your job."

"She's my sister."

"And that's her relationship."

I didn't care. She had taken me in, treated me like family. It was my job whether he agreed or not. "She said seven months before. He's been acting off for that long. Has it been that long?" I wanted to grab hold of him. I wanted to feel him against me. No. I frowned as I corrected myself. I wanted to be in his arms again. They had been like a shelter to me. My frown deepened. I had never felt that with Brian...

"I'm not telling you." His cold tone pulled me from my thoughts. I felt as though he slapped me across the face with his harshness.

"How long?"

"Stop pushing this. Nothing good will come out of it."

"I'll do it."

He paused, eyeing me with caution. "Do what?"

"I'll get you into the school." No! A voice cried from the back of my mind, but I wanted to do something right. Mandy would want to know. She would be coming here, and her insides would be killing her. Giving her all the information I could was one way to help her, whether she would realize it or not. She needed to know because I had needed to know myself. "Tell me what you know and I'll get you into that school."

"Fuck you."

I needed a new tactic, so I pulled him closer and slid a leg around his, twining it around his waist, bringing him into full contact against me. I slid one hand up his chest to curl around his neck. He wrapped both arms around me, one tilted my neck back and the other was on my butt, grinding me against him. Our mouths were slightly apart.

"I want to know how long." My lips grazed his as I spoke.

"And my response is still fuck you."

His hand left my neck to grasp my other leg and twine it around his waist, both legs now wrapped around him. I fell against the counter slightly as he arched me against him. I gasped as heat seared through my body. He slid his hand to the front of my pants and moved underneath my shirt. I panted silently as his fingers caressed, moving upwards to softly flick against one of my breasts.

"I'm going to get you off." His eyes darkened at my words. "But you're going to tell me what I want first."

"And my response will be the same, I want to fuck you." His intent glittered in those amber eyes as he slammed his mouth against mine. It wasn't exactly rough, but it was fire.

I tilted my head back and opened my mouth, feeling his tongue sweep inside where it met with mine. As I felt him lift me from the barstool and plant me higher on the counter, I heard a soft moan and realized it had come from me. One of his hands was keeping my leg firmly wrapped around him as the other was exploring underneath my shirt, moving to the other breast. I slid one of my hands underneath his shirt and explored him in return, the other wrapped firmly around his taut shoulders.

And then he ripped himself away from me.

"What…?" I murmured, dazed.

Tray ran a hand through his hair. "Fuck."

A flash of headlights filled the room, illuminating him a moment. It cast a shadow over him. He looked so gorgeous in that moment. Then the door slammed shut and I hurried out of there. When the front door opened, Mandy was there. I grabbed her arm and pulled her with me. "We're getting out of here."

CHAPTER FIVE

Mandy cried the entire ride back to our house. After she showered, she curled up on my bed and cried herself to sleep. I wasn't sure what to do, so I slept on the couch in my room. I figured Mandy didn't want to be alone. The next morning, she cried again—through breakfast, lunch, and dinner. She didn't once ask about getting revenge. After she went to bed early that night, around eight, I dressed in some black work-out clothes and slipped outside to my car.

I needed to do something to help take the heat off her tomorrow.

Driving to school, I parked on the road by the football field. It was far enough away from the normal parking lots that no one would look at it suspiciously and, if need be, I could run through the football stadium and evade anyone in the trees that outlined the perimeter if I got caught.

When I got to the school, I circled around to the janitor's office and hooked a leg onto the fire escape. Darting up, I pulled myself onto the roof and crossed to one of the heating fans. Seeing it had been turned off, I unscrewed the shaft, lifting it clear off. Then I went to work on the fan—wedging a rock between the blades, just in case it turned on—I slipped my hands through the blades and found the bolts. After they had been unscrewed, I lifted the fan up and then slipped through. My feet touched the ceiling, and I ran my hands around the flooring until I found the hatch that led to the venting shafts. I lowered myself down and then began crawling, counting until I thought I was over the main office. My estimation had been correct—I was in the main office.

The P.A. system was located in the principal's office. I turned it off and changed the alarm settings. When I was done, school tomorrow wouldn't be filled with their daily announcements or warning bells. Rap music would be playing instead, and when they tried to shut it off, a bunch of firewalls and requests for passwords would pop up. I wasn't dumb. They'd get it shut off, but it would take most of the morning and by then, most people wouldn't be paying attention to the love scandal of Devon and Jennica. Mandy would be free and clear to be miserable all alone amidst the chaos.

As I climbed back up through the shafts and headed back to my car, I made a mental note to bring earplugs. My hair would have to be done to cover them, though. It wasn't revenge against Devon, but it would happen. I would wait until an opportunity presented itself. Then Mandy would have her justice.

They canceled school. They couldn't get around my passwords, which surprised me. Pedlam blasted through my walls within an hour. The house was empty when I got there, but that wasn't surprising. Shelly and Kevin had left a message the night before to tell us they wouldn't be home till the following week, but the neighbor would be checking in daily. When I played it for Austin the next morning, he let out a whoop of joy and said he was headed back to his friend's house. Mandy burst back into tears.

It was hours later when I heard people downstairs. As I left my bedroom, I heard Mandy giggling. "We can get so much done now that we have the whole day off. I heard it was Mark Jenkins and his gang."

"I heard it was Tyler Guerros."

I paused on the stairs.

"Whatever. We all know who was behind it. He might not have done it, but I bet he knows who did. Tray Evans."

My frown grew. Another stranger.

"Ooh, did you see him today? Tray Evans is seriously hot."

Then it clicked. The entire cheerleading squad was in our living room. That meant that I was out of there. I turned around, but Mandy spotted me. "Taryn!"

I plastered a fake smile on my face, but it dropped as soon as I saw hers. There were no traces of the sobbing mess I had forced fed this morning. She looked ready to take the world by storm. "What's going on?"

"We're going to have practice here since school and all," she paused, "and I'm going to have our student council meeting this afternoon too."

Okay. Message received. I started back up the stairs.

She stopped me. "Are you staying or..." She frowned. "What are you going to do today?"

"I thought that was code for me to stay in my room?"

"Oh." Her eyes got big. "Um...well, Devon is coming because, you know, he's on student council. So..."

One of the girls snorted. "And because he's your boyfriend." She fixed me with a hard stare. "Or are you not allowed to have your boyfriend around with this…sister…in the house? Is there some weird rule about that or something?"

Mandy hadn't told them. Her head dropped down and I knew what she wanted now. "I'll stick around."

Her petite shoulders moved in a relieved sigh and her head lifted back up. I saw the thanks from her, though she didn't say it.

"What time is your student council meeting?"

"At 2:30."

Nodding, I murmured, "I'll be back down later." I wouldn't go far.

After doing homework, I put my earbuds in, laid in bed, and listened to music. I needed something to silence the shrieks, giggles, and 'no ways' from downstairs. It was much later when I sat back up and realized that I had fallen asleep. I sat up and listened. The annoying chatter was gone, but I still heard voices downstairs. When I got down there, Mandy was in the kitchen alone. She was pressed against the sink, her face glued to the window.

"He's here?"

She jumped around. Blood drained from her face and her hand jumped to her chest. "You scared the crap out of me."

"Sorry." I grinned.

She shook her head, shooting me a rueful look. "You enjoy scaring people, don't you?"

"Kind of." I laughed then grew serious. "Is he here?"

She nodded. The slight humor fled from her, and she turned back to the window. "He's out there with Tray and the guys."

"They aren't saying anything?"

"He hasn't said anything. He's acting like everything is fine."

"Is *she* here?"

"No," she hissed, turning back to me. "I don't know what I would've done if she had showed up. I want to scratch her eyeballs out and pull her hair and then fling her body in front of a moving car." She shuddered. "I'd like to do all of that without going to jail."

I grunted. Sometimes jail was worth it, but I kept quiet. That wasn't good advice. My phone was buzzing in my pocket. Mandy started to say more, but I tuned her out. When I pulled it out, Grayley's name was on the screen. I held a finger up to her and headed outside. After shutting the door, I said, "Gray?"

"Brian's on his way to your place."

"What?" My heart stopped.

"He had a huge fight with Jace. The cops were called, but Brian split. He said something about sorting it out with you. He's headed your way." He paused. "Are you safe there?"

I got over my fear and frowned, gripping the phone tighter. "Brian would never hurt me."

"He's nuts, Taryn. Make sure you're safe. If he won't hurt you, I wouldn't put it past him to hurt someone else."

The same heavy weight that I always felt with Brian settled back on my shoulders. Moving to the street, I turned as if expecting him to come around the corner already. I had no idea what to do. Brian was coming here. This was off-limits. When we broke up, when I explained my new adoption, he had agreed not to come to Rawley and now he was breaking that last truce. I nodded to myself, gripping the phone so damn tight. It was pressed against my ear, and I was surprised Grayley couldn't hear my heart beat through the phone. It was pounding in my eardrums.

"I'll be fine," I murmured, not believing myself.

"Call Jace. I think he sent some of his guys after him to make sure, but call him anyways."

"Okay." A different terror spread through me.

I didn't see his car. Great. Just great.

"Okay." I sighed. "Thanks for giving me the heads-up."

He hesitated on the other end, but said, "Good luck. Do you want me to come? I can hop in my car real quick."

"No." I shook my head, even though he couldn't see. "I'll handle it. I'm not alone." Glancing over my shoulder, I saw more than ten cars parked outside of the house. These weren't the people I wanted Brian around. They wouldn't understand he had a heart or how he wanted to be like his father so much, or how he was so envious of Jace who had known their father before he died. They wouldn't see past his anger to the hurt that was the real fire sparking everything.

They would only judge him.

A hollow ache formed in me as I dialed Jace's number.

"Hey, Terry." He was somber.

"I heard." It's all I had to say. We both knew this side of Brian. "He's coming here?"

"Yeah. He was getting fired up again and didn't take it too well when I told him to stay away from you."

I closed my eyes. It had been what I wanted, but it had been the wrong person saying that to him. This was on me. "I thought you were the right person to talk to him about this. I didn't think he would listen to anyone else."

"He wouldn't, except our dad, but he's gone so what do you do?" A static sound came over the phone and he said, "Look." He had pulled away from the phone, but came back to it, speaking clearly again. "I couldn't come after him or I would've. The cops are here. You know they're looking for any excuse with me."

"I know. He's coming to me. I'll handle him."

"Terry," I heard the same hesitation from him as well, "Brian's never hurt you, but he's not handling your break-up well. Are you with people?"

"I am." They would only see the angry and ugly Brian. "I might have to call the cops, Jace, or someone else will. Mandy has people here. You know these people; they don't understand."

"I know. Listen, I sent a few men. Just stall Brian until they get there. They'll handle him. Brian wants into my organization. Remind him of that. If he acts up, if he gets pinched, he can't get in."

A different terror formed alongside that ache. Brian wanted in? That meant... I whispered, "Jace, no."

"No, I know. I'm not letting him. He's a hothead, but he's a good kid. Don't worry, but if you have to use something to get him to calm down, use it. If he gets pinched, you don't know what the cops will say to him. They'll turn him against me and if that happens..."

He didn't finish the sentence and I didn't want him to. I didn't want to hear about that other world. I was trying to leave it. "I'll take care of him. I gotta go." Jace said something more, but I hung up and stuffed my phone into my pocket. Hurrying through the house, I went to my room and took out my locked box. I hadn't unlocked it for months, but this was a moment I had to. Pulling a long-sleeve shirt on, I took out my Taser from the box and put the box back in its hidden spot. As I went back outside to wait, I slipped the Taser inside my sleeve. I used a strap to secure it, but it was within reach if I needed it.

Then I sat on the curb and waited.

My heart was pounding.

I didn't have to wait long. I heard Brian's car screech around the corner and slam to a stop right in front of mine.

Part of me wanted to hop in and tell him to go to a park. We could hash it out there, but Jace's guys were coming to the house and wouldn't know where we went. So I braced myself when Brian slammed his door shut and strode to me.

Oh yeah. He was in a rage.

"You bitch!" he snarled, crossing the street.

I stood up, but held firm. I would stand my ground. "Brian."

"You told Jace to handle me? Jace!" His snarl deepened to a scowl, but I saw the hurt behind it. "Are you sleeping with him? First Evans and now him? My brother?" His top lip curved higher. He said, "You whor—"

I kneed him in the balls. "No one talks to me like that."

He doubled over, but twisted so he could see me. "You're a bitch."

My sympathy was gone. "And you're crazy."

He flinched. The storm came back over his face and he tried to straighten. He had more to say, but then he groaned and bent back over.

"We're over, Brian."

His head twisted away.

I moved closer and lowered my voice, "I loved you. I did. I probably always will, but you want to go in a different direction than me." I gestured to Mandy's—no—to my house. "I want this. I want college. I want a good job. I don't want to have to work four jobs to make ends meet or worse, to end up in prison. This is my way out. Let me have it."

He shook his head. He still wouldn't look at me.

I waited. We were still alone, but it was only a matter of time before we were seen. "Brian, please."

He stood now, swallowing his pain down. "You love me, baby, you just want this future so desperately. I know you."

"And I know you."

"You do, but I know you better than you know yourself, and you won't last. This life..." He looked past my shoulders and the sneer appeared again. "You won't get the adrenalin fix you need. I gave you that. Your old life gave you that."

I started shaking my head. I already knew he was wrong.

He kept going, "No one knows you. Not like me, baby." He stiffened and an ugly laugh came from him. "Look at them."

A new horror filled me, but I knew who he meant. Turning, I saw them standing there. Mandy was on the lawn. A hand was pressed to her mouth and her eyes were wide with fear. Her friends spread out behind her and the guys. I flinched when I saw them. Tray was leading them down the driveway. They were heading towards us. I held a hand out, stopping them.

He stopped, but he was waiting for my say-so. I shook my head. It wasn't time.

Brian laughed and raised his voice, "You guys think you know her? Huh? Evans? I've heard about you and your daddy. You're all the same."

71

My heart was breaking. Brian moved as if going to them, but I lifted a hand to his chest. His heart was racing under my touch. He acted as if he didn't know I was touching him. He lifted his arm and pointed over my shoulder. "You're weak. You're targets. That's all the good you are. You have no idea who you're messing with. No idea!"

"Brian," I whispered.

"She's mine. She's one of us." He spread his arms out wide and raised his voice even louder. "We persevere. We're the strong. We take on any circumstances and we still thrive. We're going to keep thriving. Hell, we're going to conquer. She's got that rush in her and she won't be satisfied with you. None of you. You just wait and see." He looked down at me, his eyebrows lifted, as if seeing me for the first time. He fell back a step. Sweat was running down his face. He whispered to me, "I'll wait for you, Taryn. I love you. You're mine. No one else can take your place."

Tears were rolling down my face. I ignored them.

He pressed his forehead to mine. His hands came up and cupped the sides of my face. "I'll always love you. I will. Don't forget me. Don't give up on me. Please, Taryn. Please."

I couldn't do anything as waves of sadness crushed down on me. As he kept going, I felt an ache, big enough for an ocean to fill, opening inside of me. Then he pressed a kiss to my forehead. So had Jace. I had taken comfort from that one, but this one, I suppressed a shiver. Brian was my past. If I hadn't been sure before, I knew now. I held my tongue and bit down on my lip. He wouldn't accept it now.

Then I heard car doors slam.

I had stalled long enough.

Brian glanced back and a strangled laugh ripped from him. His hands fell from me and he shook his head, backing away from me. "My big brother, Jace." He faced Jace's men, three large men that were coming our way, and lifted both his middle fingers in the air to them. "My fucking big brother, Jace. Mr. High And Mighty, so fucking powerful he's got these monkeys to run around and chase down his little brother." He stopped and then shouted at them, "We're good. You don't need to come and protect little *Terry*. You can report back to big brother that the cops don't need to be called."

"Go with them, Brian."

"No." A growl came from him.

"Go." I didn't look, but I lied, "They have their phones out. They're calling the cops now, Brian. Jace said..." I hesitated.

He turned around. "Jace said what?"

I couldn't. I shook my head and said instead, "The cops are already coming. Go, Brian. You're not sober enough to drive. Give your keys to one of those guys."

"Taryn?"

My jaw hardened and I turned away. "Go, Brian. Get out of here. I mean it."

"Taryn, come on—"

It was killing me. Seeing him like this, remembering when he would carry me and comfort me, and knowing what everyone thought of him now felt like a knife had been sliced through me. It had slowly been pushed in and the person took their time, pulling it up through my whole body, causing irreversible damage on the way.

73

"GO!" I snapped and let loose the strap. The Taser dropped into my hand and I raised it. "I mean it, Brian. Get out of here."

He looked at the Taser, but he didn't move. He didn't react. He only stared at it and then me. A hurt little boy looked back at me, but I turned away. One of Jace's men came forward. He saw the Taser as I kept it hidden from the crowd behind us. "We'll take him back."

I turned it off and slipped it back into place. As he took Brian with him, a rush of relief soared through me when he went with him without a fight. I turned away and walked to my new home.

Tray came to the street to meet me. I stopped just in front of him and closed my eyes. The storm inside of me was raging on and on. I jumped when I heard their car doors shut. I listened as they pulled away.

Tray asked in a soft voice, "What do you need?"

I couldn't handle anyone else. "I need to get out of here."

"Done."

We went to his car. I never looked at anyone, but as soon as he pulled away, I felt some of the weight lift from my shoulders again.

CHAPTER SIX

I didn't care where we went. He asked once if I wanted something to eat. I nodded and he pulled into a drive-in type of diner. The waitress came out. When she asked what we wanted, I felt Tray glancing at me. He ordered for me and I was relieved. I didn't know this guy, but he knew me. If I hadn't been emotionally drained, I would've been scared by that. I wasn't. I found it comforting instead.

When the food came out, a small table was hooked onto his door, and he handed my water to me. The food was left alone.

"Thank you."

He nodded, but didn't do anything. He didn't eat. He didn't drink his own water. Nothing.

I frowned. "Where are we?"

He shrugged. "Some other town. I figured you wanted to be long gone from Rawley and Pedlam."

"Thank you." Again. I started to smile. That was somewhat funny to me, that I kept thanking him, but it fell flat. The humor was forced in me. "He's not that bad."

"Save it."

"What?"

"Save it." His head was resting against his seat and he never lifted it forward, but rotated it to meet my gaze.

There was no judgment. He didn't care. I frowned. "Most people would say I'm an idiot to care about him."

He shrugged. "Who cares? You broke up. It's obvious the guy's having a hard time letting go."

I glanced at my lap. No one had really seen through Brian like I had, except his brother.

Tray added, "Yeah, he's a little unhinged, but I can be too. So can you. So can a lot of people. Now, if the guy was going to be violent towards you, that's a whole other story, but if you're asking without asking if I give a damn about your ex? No. I don't give two shits about him." The same blank expression looked back at me. "Do you really care that I don't care?"

"No." I was honest. "It's refreshing. Most people would give me a lecture to stay away from him."

He gave me a half-grin. "That's a waste of energy. You're already trying to stay away from him."

I nodded. "He's not a bad guy. He's just—"

He cut me off, "No excuses to me. I don't care, remember?"

"Yeah." A relieved grin escaped me. "I care about him still, and I don't want to hear someone else that I care about judge him. He's not below anyone. He just shows his feelings more than others."

Tray snorted. "That's the kicker, though, isn't it? There's a lot of people who hide their true shit better than others and because of that, they think they're better. It's a load of bullshit to me."

I frowned. "I had no idea you thought like this."

He shrugged, but lifted up a burger and began to unwrap it. "Yeah, well, to me you were just another hot chick with an attitude. Guess we're all due for some surprises, aren't we?"

I eyed him, as I let his words filter in. There was more to him than what he showed everyone else. Then I realized that he knew me better than my new family, than even Mandy. "Don't tell anyone about Jace."

He was inspecting his burger, but glanced back up.

"Please. They were both family to me."

"I'm not saying a word. I get it. You don't want to hear bad shit about your family." He flashed me another half-grin and a dimple appeared this time. I sucked in my breath as the power of that one dimple, of that smile from him, and his honesty struck deep inside of me. I swallowed. This guy was dangerous to me. I'd been through the emotional wringer from Brian and twenty minutes later a few words, a few smiles, and he was almost forgotten. Tray was front and center.

I forced myself to turn away as a tingle of fear slid inside of me. Tray could have devastating effects on me if I allowed it. I shook my head. I couldn't allow it.

I finished my water and handed him the cup. "We should go back."

He tossed it in the garbage, along with the rest of the food; none of it had been eaten. He eyed me for a moment.

I didn't look away. Something happened. He knew it. My behavior had changed, and he was trying to figure it out. I couldn't look away, but I wanted to. My body was starting to burn up. I wanted to go to him. I wanted to wrap my arms around him, and I wanted to feel the pressure of his lips on mine. I wanted to taste him and even thinking that, the desire went up a notch. I tried to hold back from squirming under the weight of his gaze, but it wasn't without its consequences. I was suddenly starving and dying of thirst.

He won.

I ripped my eyes away from him and focused outside the window. My chest lifted and a ragged breath left me.

He didn't say anything. It was like before. We left, but the air was charged, unlike when we first arrived. The emotion had been thick in me from Brian. This time it was because of him. I grasped onto my seatbelt and made myself consider what we'd be walking into at the house.

I couldn't have prepared myself.

Before we opened the door, I heard my sister. "You're a fucking tramp, you bitch!"

Tray reached around me for the door. He murmured, close enough so it teased my skin, "You up for this?"

My body reacted to his closeness. I leaned into him, resting against his chest as he continued to hold the door. He didn't move. He didn't open the door, and I remained there. I drew strength from him in that moment. Then I nodded. I was ready.

Tray pulled open the door and I stepped inside first.

They were in the living room. "Oh please," Jennica huffed. "What do you expect from me? An apology? You're never around and when you are it's all cheerleading this, student council that, not to mention yearbook crap and your perfect little family with your perfect little GPA and your precious scholarship to Brown. No, you're a great girlfriend. You're a perfect girlfriend, except you don't give a shit where your man is or how he feels."

There was shocked silence after that. Devon was watching Mandy. Jennica was being held back by Amber, whose brother was next to her. Samuel and another guy were lounging on the couches looking amused.

"I can't believe you just said that." Mandy leapt towards her. Devon moved to intercept her, but stranger guy beat him to it, leaping from the couch. Grabbing her shoulders, he held her back as Mandy tried to get around him. "Get off me, Dylan!"

"Mandy, stop."

Jennica took a step back. Devon was in the middle, arms half raised between them, looking uncertain about which girl to go towards.

Amber turned to us and sneered. "Where have you two been?"

Tray smirked at her. "I was hungry."

"You were hungry?"

"Yeah." Tray settled against the wall and lifted an eyebrow, daring her to push it further.

She didn't. Her chin went down and Mandy let out another scream, trying to claw her way through Dylan's arms.

"Mandy, go to your room."

She swung to me, startled. "Taryn—"

I shook my head. "Go."

She glanced around, her eyebrows bunched forward and she was biting her lip. Then she jerked her head in a nod. "Fine." She shoved Dylan aside and swept out of the room. I didn't wait for her to go up the stairs. I turned on my heel and got in Jennica's face. I had already dealt with too much crap that day to care about this minion. She saw the storm in my eyes and readied herself. Her little chin raised, her eyes grew haughty, and her skinny shoulders lifted.

"You're pathetic. You screwed your best friend's boyfriend. Congratulations. You got into a guy's pants. Wonderful achievement for you. Revel in it. It'll last a week. He's going to drop you." I glanced at him, saw he was already uncertain, and rolled my eyes. "She's already dropped you and you're now known as the friend who sleeps with her friend's boyfriends. Congratulations on your new reputation. The only people who will want to be your friend will be people like you. You'll never get the good friends, the ones who are actual friends." I never looked away. I never faltered. The longer I talked, the more she withered beneath me. I was finished. "I've kept quiet, but I'm done. Mess with Mandy again and you will be messing with me." I stepped closer. "That's not a threat. It's a fact. Ball's in your court if you decide to take me on and with that said, get out of my house."

"And who are—" she sputtered, taking another step back.

"I'm her sister. Enough said."

Everyone was silent. Jennica had grown pale, shrinking away.

I said, "I'm waiting."

Devon cursed, grabbed her arm, and hauled her behind him. The door slammed shut behind them. It wasn't long before the rest followed them. Amber and Grant were next. Samuel, Dylan, and Tray remained for a moment.

There was more silence. Then Dylan threw his head back and a deep laugh came out. "Oh, I like you. I really like you." He thumped Tray on his chest and chuckled. "She's a cold-hearted bitch."

I took it as a compliment, then heard him head upstairs and knock on Mandy's door. I asked Tray, "Who is that?"

"My cousin. He's not from around here." Samuel stood up and flashed me a grin. "Evans, I could go for a burger."

Tray nodded, but said, "I'll be out in a minute."

As he left, leaving the two of us alone, I shivered from different anticipation now. One smoldering look from him and every cell in my body stood straight up, jumping alive. I didn't think I would get used to this from him. Ever.

Then he nodded. "Congratulations."

"On what?"

"You earned their respect."

I snorted. "I don't care."

"I know." A smile teased at the corners of his lips. "They saw that too and because of that, they fear you now."

As he left, he walked past me and the backside of his hand brushed against mine, making me moan softly. My head went down. I couldn't hold back my own smile.

He paused.

I waited...

Then he kept going, but I heard him pause and turn back. I never looked up. If I had, I would've gone to him. I wanted him. Amidst all the drama, that truth flooded me and overwhelmed me. I wanted Tray Evans like I had never wanted Brian before. I was beginning to lose the battle if I cared about that or not.

Mandy knocked on my door that night and told me that I had a visitor. I swung my feet from the bed and sat up. Tray? No. She wouldn't have called him a visitor. It wasn't Brian. She would've been scared. "Who is it?"

She shrugged. "I don't know, but he's hot. Like really, really hot."

I caught the shadows under her eyes, the ones that weren't from the dark hallway. "You okay?"

She didn't answer. "Dylan's staying over." Then she walked into her room and shut the door.

I frowned at her bedroom door a moment and saw the light turn off. When had that happened? Then I shook my head. Maybe it was best if I didn't ask. When I got downstairs, I stopped on the last step.

It was Jace.

He was dressed in dark clothing. I grinned. "If you're going for dark and deadly, mission accomplished."

He laughed softly. His blue eyes scanning over me. "You're unscathed, I see. The men said Brian wasn't too kind to you."

"He wasn't happy that I involved you."

"My brother should've been smarter. He's blinded by his hurt. You two are done. He won't accept it. Who else would you go to?" Jace folded his arms over his chest, then glanced upwards. "So that was the sister?"

He had driven me to their house, but he hadn't met them. "Yeah."

"She's sad."

I wasn't surprised by his quick deduction. Jace hadn't risen to be the leader of the Panthers at the young age of twenty-two by luck. He was sharp, he was quick, and he was lethal. Mix all that together with his looks and he was a charismatic walking weapon. I had witnessed it most of my life. People followed Jace. They wanted to listen to him and do as he said. He learned of his affect when he'd been in high school and used it to his advantage. The school expelled him because he had led too many protests and riots in their classrooms. Being restless, angry, and too smart for his own good, I hadn't been surprised when he showed up at the house wearing the Panther colors one day. Their dad went nuts, but soon he grew fearful of Jace while Brian began to worship him.

Then their dad died and all that changed. Brian began to hate him too, even while he continued to idolize him. I stopped trying to figure out how that worked long ago. All I understood was to stay away from Jace. For a few years, we barely talked except in passing when I would go to Brian's room and he'd come home early in the morning. A few of those times, he had blood on him.

I was relieved when the blood started to disappear altogether, but then I learned he still had blood on his hands. It was the invisible sort instead. Remembering those years and how I had been fearful of him, made me chuckle softly.

"What?"

"Nothing." I didn't want to remember when they changed. "Brian's okay, right? That's why you came here?"

He sighed. The air suddenly dropped to a serious feeling. "I didn't come about my brother."

"Why then?"

"Evans."

"Tray?"

He nodded. "Stay away from him, Taryn."

No Terry. He always said Terry. I frowned. "What does that mean?"

"He's not what he seems. That's what that means."

He started to leave. I grabbed his arm and held him tight. His bicep shifted under my touch and he waited for me. An urgency filled me. "Why? Tell me what that means." He wasn't going to. "Please."

I saw the surrender. He murmured, softly, "He knows people in my world, Taryn."

As the full implication of those words hit me, I let him go and stepped back. I shook my head. "No." But I couldn't disregard his words. I remembered Tray's own words hours earlier.

There's a lot of people who hide their true shit better than others.

But that didn't mean anything. "You're going to have to do better than that, Lanser."

His eyes went flat as I said his last name. Then he smirked. The sight of it was deadly. "I don't care who's in your pants, Terry." A stab of pain went through me. He used to use that word as a term of endearment, in times when he had been soft and gentle with me. He was using it as a shield now. The cold stranger in front of me now added, "I can't give you facts. If I did, you'd be dead and I would have to do it. This is a warning for your own good. Stay away from Evans. Everyone will be safer if you do."

I shook my head and closed my eyes. "Stop, Jace." This wasn't my brother. He was the Panther's leader now. "Stop."

"You heard me." Then he disappeared. The door closed a moment later. When I returned to my room, I curled underneath my blanket and flicked a tear away. I wouldn't cry.

CHAPTER SEVEN

Mandy acted like nothing had happened. I was eating breakfast when she came down. She didn't say a word to me and headed out. I grunted. Maybe I should take that way of living? Pretend nothing happened? It felt good and I nodded to myself. That sounded good to me. It was how I was going to handle the day, act as if nothing happened yesterday. When I got to school, no one said a word to me. I didn't see Tray or Samuel. Mandy ignored me and was talking with a group of girls I didn't recognize. Moving around them and the guys beside them, I headed to my locker and grabbed my books. Then I headed to class.

I took my usual seat in the back, then realized my table mate wanted to talk. She kept ducking her head down, glancing up, and would duck her head into a book again. When she repeated the process three times, I looked over at her.

She gave me a tentative smile.

Oh hell. "I'm Taryn."

A squeal escaped her mouth as she extended her hand. "Molly Keeley. I'm your—"

"Classmate. I know that."

"Yeah, and I'm in your health and gym class."

Wait. "I'm in health?"

"You skip for study hall."

"I thought I had study hall."

"You should probably tell your teacher that."

"Oh." I sat back. "Thanks."

"No problem. We're playing volleyball next week in gym too. That should be fun."

"You play volleyball?"

"Only with my family. I can't wear contacts so I have to wear those goggle things in class." Her cheeks flushed again. "It's embarrassing. They look like microscopes, but my mom won't let me get new ones. They're not 'cost-effective.'" She ducked her head again. "That's what my mom says."

"Keep your glasses." The teacher stood up, and I leaned down in my chair. "You won't give a shit in two years. They'll help you find your soul mate in college anyway."

She laughed, her voice squeaky. "You're not like the rumors say."

"That I'm a stone cold bitch."

"Yeah and that you screwed Tray Evans."

"Where?"

She listed them off with her fingers. "In the school parking lot, in the parking lot at the diner, at one of his parties, at Rickets' House, and in his car."

"I've been busy."

She giggled and then squeaked before turning away. Her face got red. I looked over and saw Tray staring back. He had knelt beside me.

"What?" I gestured to the teacher. "He's going to start class."

"We have two days."

"For what?" I wasn't an idiot. I knew. I was just playing.

He wasn't amused. "Will you please help?"

"I told you I would, but you didn't spill the details. I had to hold my sister when she sobbed and asked questions. I couldn't answer any of them." He had helped me yesterday. Then Jace told me to stay away from him. I was getting whiplash from being pulled in so many directions. I sighed. "Let me think about it."

He hadn't gotten the answer he wanted. His lips pressed together, but he stood. "Saw Jace Lanser leaving town last night. Stopped at the diner for a burger."

"Yeah. So?"

He backed off, taking his own seat across the room, but it didn't matter. The entire class was listening. "Nothing. The guy's a loser."

"Keep talking and maybe I won't help after all." Jace was family. No one talked bad about my family.

Mandy hushed me. "Taryn, don't talk to him like that."

I ignored her. Everyone was waiting. No one spoke back to Tray Motherfucking Evans, but I just did. He didn't shoot back and I could feel the confusion from everyone. My classmate leaned over and whispered, "You are officially my idol. No girl who's slept with him has gotten away with talking to him like that, and he sought *you* out."

She was so excited about the last fact. I sighed. This would be the number one rumor going through school for the rest of the day. I caught sight of Mandy's warning glare and rolled my eyes. Another day that I had saved her from the gossip mill. When she waved her finger in the air, I flipped her my middle finger. No one was going to tell me how to think, speak, or feel. If she kept trying, she'd learn like everyone else did

87

that they could kiss my ass. When she gasped again, I was tempted to make it a double deuce and flip my other middle finger too.

"Okay, class," the teacher started, and I ignored my sister for the rest of the class and the rest of the day. I ignored everyone else while I was at it, not that it was a sacrifice. As the day went on, Jennica pulled her friends to the side. All of them gave me varying looks of hatred. Mandy ignored me with her sudden new group of friends and all the other girls took cues from the reigning crowd.

I was a social leper. The only person who didn't understand it was my table mate. When I went to another class, she saw me in the hallway and waved. Two other girls were with her. One gasped and the other grabbed her hand, pulling it down.

The next day was the same. Mandy still adopted the same philosophy to act like nothing happened in her world. She barely talked to me at home and that same guy slept over. I wanted to ask what the deal was with him, but since she wouldn't even say hello to me, I assumed it would've been a lost cause to ask. The only thing different about the day was that Samuel and Tray were missing. People noticed. Towards the end of the day, I started thinking people had forgotten about me, but nope. Jennica and her friends stopped talking the second I entered the hallway. Their hatred was still going strong.

I shrugged. It was peaceful to me, but I couldn't help myself. As I passed by, Jennica stared at me the whole time. I pretended to scratch my ear with my middle finger again. I was fully aware how immature it was, but I enjoyed it and she had heeded my warning. No one talked about Mandy and Devon. No one seemed to notice that they weren't standing next to each other, holding hands, cuddling, or talking even. My sisterly duty had been fulfilled. At the end of that day, as I headed to my car and saw Tray leaning against it, I wondered if my friend duty needed to be fulfilled also.

Then I paused and asked him, "Are we friends?"

His arms were crossed over his chest and in that moment, I was reminded about his 'god-like' status around the school. Square jaw, his striking hazel eyes directed on me, and those perfect lips curled up in a small smirk. He really was gorgeous.

He smirked. "Only if you want us to be, Matthews."

He had pissed me off. He had comforted me in a way no one knew how to do, and he knew how to read me. No one knew how to read me like he did.

My nostrils flared. "I think we are friends."

He flashed me a grin. "Does that mean you're going to help me?"

"I think it means that I have to." I snorted. "I'm sentimental like that. I tend to help friends and family whether they want it or not." My eyes narrowed. "But is that all you want?"

The loaded question held between us. His eyes darkened back to that amber color, and I knew he was thinking the same thing I was. My chest tightened and my pulse started racing. I had a strong feeling we were going to be more than friends. When that happened, I'd deal with it. I was starting not to be able to control myself when it came to Tray Motherfucking Evans.

His eyes fell to my lips and stayed there. "I think," he flashed me another heart melting grin, "that the whole ball is in your court."

"Shit." I shook my head. "The innuendos I could make with that one word. You couldn't have used a different word?"

"Sorry." He wasn't. He was laughing.

"Ball. You used the word ball." I rolled my eyes, but couldn't hold back the grin. "A set of balls. A pair of balls. A bowling ball and a pin. Ball. Just one? I think it could get lonely. I think you should add onto it. Maybe say the whole donkey's pair is in your court."

He barked out a laugh. "That makes no sense."

I shrugged. I was trying to slow my hormones so I joked some more. Tray stopped listening and grabbed my hand. I stopped talking. He pulled me in front of him and I stood there, feeling all girly. I had never felt like this with Brian. None of it made sense to me. He rested his arms on my shoulders, his head bent so we were eye level, and I stood in front of him. He didn't wrap those arms around me. He didn't pull me against his chest. My hands lifted and held onto his biceps, and I stared back at him.

Then he smirked again. "Thank you for helping me."

Yep. A tingly sensation had started in my gut, but it kicked up a notch now. I wanted to curse my hormones and since I couldn't say a smart-ass comment, I nodded.

This was my moment. This was my element. Standing on top of the roof of my old school with the black night as my backdrop and the wind rushing behind me, I closed my eyes for a moment to savor the feeling. It was like nothing I'd ever experienced. I didn't know what it was, or how I could describe it, but even the hairs on my fingers were vibrating. I felt alive.

I got the blueprints for the new school from Grayley. He hadn't been happy about getting them or handing them over. He hadn't been his usual carefree easygoing way so I pressed him. "What's wrong? Tell me or I'll find some computer nerd to hack your email."

His eyes got big, but then he scowled. "You would, wouldn't you?"

"Spill it, Gray."

When he told me that his dad had returned to town, my senses went haywire. Grayley's father wasn't a good guy. He got out of prison for transporting drugs over the border six months ago. Gray hadn't been worried. His dad chose to remain in the south, but I could see the concern and knowing the reason behind it, I asked, "You want me to talk to Jace?"

His head whipped up. "What? No. Why would you offer to do that?"

I shrugged, tucking the blueprints into my bag. "Because you're a friend and Jace is family."

"No. Don't do that." He frowned. "Aren't you supposed to be leaving us behind? I mean, I heard that you had been told to stay away from Rawley." He pointed to the blueprints in my bag. "Why do you need those? They renovated, but trust me, not much is different."

I shrugged. He didn't need to know any of that, but I asked, "I noticed they upped the security. Why? I meant to ask you that at Rickets', but you know how that night went down."

He sighed. "You're not getting into trouble, are you? I have a hard time imagining that Brian or his brother would be happy about that."

"Leave Jace to me." I wanted to ask about Brian, but I wasn't sure if I could handle hearing it so I bit my tongue. "I'll be fine." I lifted my arm and bounced the bag up and down. "I'm a cat burglar. We always land on our feet."

He groaned. "You are *so* not funny. It's painful."

I had laughed. He had laughed, but the unease lingered. It was in the bottom of my gut, and I sensed it was with him too. Gray never questioned me when I asked for odd favors in the past. This has been the first time and knowing his father was back in town, that unease was mounting. Something else was going on in town.

Coming back to the present, I watched the guards change their positions. If my calculations were correct, they would change again in two hours for breaks. I didn't want to be weaving through them when they would be moving around so I had to go now. Questions about Gray and his father were pushed to the back burner. Tray was waiting for me to deliver an entrance to the school and that was what I was going to do. So, with that thought, I grabbed my rope and began rappelling down the side of the building.

The window to an art room was always left open, so I snuck in that way. Then I used the vent shafts to crawl all the way to the security guards' room. According to the blueprints, the camera room was their headquarters. I still couldn't believe the school had a freaking camera system, but it was the obstacle for me to tackle. Figuring out why would be for later, after Tray and his friends did what they needed.

There was one guard sitting at the controls. I waited until the pizzas arrived. Tray promised to pay for them, put the drugs in them, and have Samuel deliver them wearing his old pizza delivery uniform. When the guard caught Samuel on the camera, he pushed his chair back and stood.

"What the hell?" He was on the radio as he left the room. "Did you guys order pizza?"

I didn't wait to hear their answer. I dropped to the ground and hurried to the cameras. I didn't have long. Switching off the recording, I looped it so it would continue to play the earlier feed. By the time they caught it, I hoped the drugs would be ingested or Tray would be done with whatever they had planned. As soon as I hit the button and the screens filled again, I heard voices from the hallway and darted back into the bathroom. I was back up in the vent and screwing it into place when I heard someone say, "They delivered it by accident?"

"Yeah. That's what the guy said."

"We're not supposed to eat anything we didn't order."

"Who cares? The kid said it's already been paid for and he can't find the right address." His voice was muffled as he continued, "He said when they called, they could tell them it was already delivered."

"Yeah." Someone sighed in surrender. "Might as well."

"Grab your slices and get back to your positions. Boss hired us for a reason."

"Yeah. Yeah. Okay, heading out."

Mission accomplished. Instead of leaving through the art room, I waited until the guards headed back to their spots and began to move. Cameras were taken care of so I dropped to the hallway and headed to the gymnasium. Tray said that's where they wanted to get inside first. When I propped open the back door, I turned my small flashlight on twice.

Dressed in dark clothing, they came running from behind their cover, moving fast. As they filed past me, Tray stopped and grinned. His face was covered in camouflage and there went that same tightness in my chest. It was becoming annoying.

He asked, "Guards can't see us?"

I shook my head. "Nope. You came in the right vantage point. It's the blind spot from what I mapped out."

"And they should be sleeping soon?"

I nodded. "Give them ten minutes. I can't guarantee they all ate the pizza right away, but I heard two of them eating."

He nodded, then frowned at me.

"What?"

"Not many would think or have the guts to drug a pizza."

I shrugged. "The two people I call family, before Mandy's family, are criminals. This is who I am."

"Tray," one of his friends whispered from inside the gym, "come on."

His gaze dropped back to my lips, and he murmured, "Never thought I'd be hot for a criminal chick."

Oh shit.

He flashed me a grin. "See you tomorrow. It's homecoming. After the game and dance, Dylan's having a party."

"Who's Dylan again?"

His grin stretched wider. "Samuel's cousin. His parents have a house here."

"I don't do dances." Brian would've laughed if he knew I went to a football game in the past, but I wanted to go. Then I blinked in shock. Another shit. I even wanted to go to his party. As I headed out, I couldn't believe it.

I was becoming normal, but I needed to go see a certain gang leader first.

CHAPTER EIGHT

I stood across the alley from the Seven8. I did not want to go into that building, but I wanted to see Jace. I missed him and Brian every day, but new things had come to light. His warning about Tray. Grayley's dad was in town, and because I cared about him, I promised myself to ask. His dad wasn't good and if he was in town, Gray would be hurt. It always happened. I tried to calm my nerves. Jace had something to do with it. I knew it. Jace was behind everything, and so he was the one I had to approach for my favor.

The building was pumping in music, sweat, and drugs. I could hear the shouts from the crowd from where I stood. There wasn't usually a waiting line, but there was one tonight, trailing around the corner.

I crossed the road. There was no issue at the door, and I was waved in. When I started to head down the hallway, I saw Krein, Jace's second in command, walking towards me. He grabbed my arm. "Taryn."

I frowned and pulled away, but he didn't let go. "Krein," I warned.

He pulled me close and yelled into my ear, "He's not back there." Then he let me go and nodded towards the dance floor. "Follow me."

We moved through the crowd, and he pointed to a corner. Jace was standing in a corner with two girls pressed against him while he was nodding to another guy speaking into his ear.

Krein leaned close again. "Stay here." Then he muscled his way over to them. A guard let them through, one that I hadn't known was there, and the other guy moved back so Krein could talk to Jace. A second later he was pointing at me. When Jace spotted me, I saw the slight widening around his eyes. The rest of the world would see the same poker face, but they weren't privy to the storm that was brewing in his eyes. Great. His jaw tightened and I got ready. He was pissed.

Jace broke away from the group he had been standing with, leaving the two girls disappointed until Krein went over to them. One girl glared at me, as Jace grabbed my wrist, pulling me behind him. He wasn't nice and gentle like his second in command had been. He didn't wait for his guards. He shoved through the crowd and kept his cement hold on me. When a drunk stumbled in front of us, Jace lifted me in the air and placed me in front of him. He didn't pause. He swept the guy out of the way, then ushered me forward and kept his arms on both sides of me until we were at the other end.

Then two guards materialized out of nowhere. They took point and led the way down a back hallway.

"Jace," I started.

"Don't." He didn't let go of my arm, but I was transferred to his side. He held onto me as we went to his office. As we neared the office, a girl left the room and ran in the opposite direction.

"Get her. I don't want her going that way."

The guard nodded and went in pursuit. When we were at the door, the guard passed us, holding onto the girl's arm in the same manner that Jace was holding onto my arm.

"Hey!" she protested, trying to twist her arm free. "Let me go."

97

She was ignored and then Jace had me in the office and the door was shut.

I prepared myself. He was working. I had known that the second I saw he wasn't happy to see me. That meant I had about two minutes until he would kick me out. He'd done it countless times to Brian over the years. Jace never liked us showing up on his territory, and this was the second time I had broken that rule.

Jace kept the room dark and my eyes strained to adjust themselves. He didn't say anything. He brushed past me and disappeared inside his bathroom. Emerging a second later, he pulled off his shirt and grabbed another one that had been laying on the chair. Pulling it over his head, I diverted my eyes when I saw his stomach muscles ripple from the movement.

Here I went. "Jace," I started.

"What are you doing here?" His tone was all-business. There was no family warmth, and I shivered, missing it.

"I came for a friend." My heart was pounding in my ears. "My friend, Gray—"

"You're here about his dad."

"Yeah."

"You want to know if he's working for me?"

"Yeah." I willed myself to look up and hold his gaze. Even in the darkness, his eyes could pierce their way through me. "Is he?"

"Why should I tell you?"

I flinched. He was so harsh. "Because I'm family."

"You're not, Taryn. Not anymore."

Another slap across my face; his coldness hurt. "Why are you being like this?"

A hollow laugh came from him. "Don't fool yourself, Taryn. I'm not you. Brian's not you either. You're out. Why do you keep coming back?" He strode towards me and I was unsure what he'd do. "I told you to stay away the last time you were here."

"Yeah." I rolled my shoulders back, ready for whatever was about to happen. "Then your brother showed up in my town—"

"Your town."

I heard the mocking from him. "Yes," I clipped out. "My town. You've made that abundantly clear. My town. My life. My future. You want the lines drawn and you want me on the other side, don't you?" I sneered. "Screw you. I came back for one thing. Gray. Is his dad working for you or not?"

There was silence for a beat. Then a soft laugh came from him and the cold from it sent chills through my body. This was the gang leader Jace. This was the mastermind behind the Panthers who kept them from being touched by the police. Cunning. Ruthless.

He said, "Leave, Taryn. You were given an out and if you don't take it, it might not be there anymore."

I snapped to attention. "Is that a threat?"

"Yes." There was no hesitation from him. "Stay out or I will fix things so there's no longer an out for you to go."

"Jace." My family member was gone. He had been gentle with me, but that was gone as well. "I'm here for a friend. How can you be mad at me for that?"

"Because this isn't your life. He's not your friend. Stay out, Taryn. I mean it."

I shook my head, pushing past the lump in my throat. "Stop. Please."

"Get out."

"I take care of my friends and family." He started coming for me, and my voice rose. I didn't have much longer. "It's the same quality in me that loved Brian." He took my arm and we were going towards the door. "Please, Jace. Please." He didn't have the cement hold like earlier, but his hand would still leave bruises.

He wasn't being gentle anymore.

I shook my head, clearing that thought as he opened the door. "Please, Jace. I know his dad must be working for you. Cut him loose. Send him away. Gray always gets hurt." He was taking me out into the hallway. I slammed a hand against the door to stop us and lowered my voice, "He abuses him."

Jace stopped.

"He hurts him. Please get rid of him. I don't want my friend hurt. That's all. That's the only reason I'm here."

A guard straightened from the wall. He'd been waiting. "Boss?"

Jace held my arm out and the guard took it.

"Jace." I strained against the hold. "Please."

The small light in the hallway cast his face in shadows. He was unmoving, a cold stranger. He said, "Go home. This is no longer your home. These people here are no longer your concern. Get out and stay out. This is my last warning."

I frowned. My heart leapt into my chest. It was pounding with fear. What did that mean? "Jace—"

"STOP!" He gestured to the guard. "Get her out. If you see her again, shoot her in the goddamn leg. I don't want to deal with her again." He stepped close to me. His eyes were primal as he stared into mine. "Do you hear that? I don't want to deal with you again. I gave the order, Taryn. They will follow it. Come back again and you'll lose a leg. Keep coming, I'll have them shoot every fucking limb. It's your decision. Get lost."

Then he disappeared inside, locking the door behind him.

I stood there, staring at the door for a while longer until the guard led me out. I didn't pay attention until we were in the cold and the door was shut in my face. I couldn't believe what had just happened.

Jace threw me out. He meant it.

I drove home that night and went straight to bed. Tray called, but I didn't call him back. My heart was breaking. I didn't even notice if Mandy was mean to me or not the next morning. I remembered a faint good morning from her. I didn't care. Then I got to school and I almost got back into my car as I looked up.

It was homecoming. Fuck me. I already had a headache and when I got inside, another headache came at me. Mandy darted over. She grabbed my hand. "Did you hear?"

"Uh—" I guess she had been nice that morning. I still didn't care.

"Pedlam's coming here to play. Their football field got tilled last night. Can you believe it?"

"What did you just say?"

"Their football field was tilled. Can you believe that? I heard that their gymnasium got tarred, too. Seriously. Who's crazy enough to do that shit?"

Yeah. Who was crazy enough? My body went numb. "Excuse me." I went right back out to the parking lot and spotted Tray in the back corner, getting out of his SUV.

I went over to him and opened his door again. He glanced up. "Hey." I pushed him inside and got in beside him. I didn't wait for him to say anything. I started right away, "You tilled their football field? You tarred their gymnasium?"

"Yeah." He was looking at me like I'd gone crazy.

"Are you stupid?"

"What are you so pissed at? You knew we were going in there to do some damage."

"Not this. Not damage that'll launch an investigation." A different fear from last night settled in my chest. It dug deep, and I knew it wouldn't to be leaving any time soon. "I didn't know you were going to do damage like that. I thought you were going to deflate their basketballs or something? Not tar their gym."

"Why are you so bent about this?"

"Because I have a record." How could he not have thought about that? "Because I could go back to juvie. I don't want to go there. I hate it and…" I stopped. I could lose my family. I lost one last night. I couldn't lose my other one. It was me, only me. I was back to that way of thinking, but shit, who was I kidding? I never allowed myself to really let them in. I didn't know my parents. They took off the same week I moved in. I knew Mandy, but she only talked to me half of the time, and Austin spent most of his time at his friend's.

There was no family.

I'd be arrested. Somehow they would connect me with the vandalism last night, and I would be removed from their home. Jace kicked me out. He meant it. I didn't have him and Brian. I shook my head. Brian wanted to be a Panther. I couldn't do that life.

It was just me. Again.

"Get over yourself."

"Excuse me?"

He snorted and rolled his eyes. "I don't even know what you're thinking, but I can tell you're overreacting to this." He cursed. "If anyone takes the blame, it'll be me. You were in the dark. The other guys didn't even pay attention to you. I told them I had a guy on the inside. That was enough for them, and trust me, no one will talk. You cut all the footage. The stupid security guards will get canned. That's the extent of it. We didn't hurt anybody. I highly doubt Pedlam will launch an investigation. With that security, I don't think they'll want the cops poking their noses around there."

My eyes shot to his and I tried to absorb his calm. "How do you know?"

"My dad was a cop. I'm not dumb. Schools don't keep security like that unless there's something worth a lot of money or illegal on the premises. They won't want cops getting curious. You have nothing to worry about."

His dad was a cop? I had to laugh. "You would've been my enemy if I was still in Pedlam." Holy hell. "How did I not know your dad was a cop?"

His tone cooled. "Because he's not around anymore."

"What?"

"He moved south. It's just me. My mom killed herself before all that happened." He bit out a hard laugh. "Hell, that's probably why he went down the path he did."

His mom killed herself. I froze at hearing that. Fuck. I didn't know what to say about her. He said, "It's for the best. Don't feel sorry for me because of her. She was in so much pain that she couldn't endure it. She did what she had to do."

My god. He sounded hard and unforgiving. He was like me, but no. He wasn't like me. He had friends. He had a school that followed him. I met his friends. They would do anything for him.

"I'm sorry about your mom."

He chuckled. "Don't feel sorry for me. My mom's in a better place and my dad is a piece of shit."

"How can you afford that huge house?"

"My mom was rich." Then he scowled. "My dad left me money, but I don't touch it."

"Oh." I frowned.

"It's not something I talk about." He grimaced. "Sorry, I just...don't like to think about it. I'd go crazy if I did."

I nodded. I could relate. "At least you know who your parents were."

"Yeah?"

He was watching me and the air switched again. Gone was the fear and a camaraderie took its place. I wasn't sure how I felt about that, but I couldn't fight it. "I never knew mine."

"You grew up in the foster system?"

I nodded. Even Mandy hadn't dared to ask me that question. My throat grew thick. "I never talk about it."

"Not even to that ex-boyfriend?"

"Not even him." Brian never wanted to talk about our parents or our families. He wanted to talk about sports, how he was going to be the toughest guy in school, or what Jace was doing. Realizing that I had confessed more to Tray in a few weeks than I had to Brian in a few years sent shock waves through me.

"It's his loss." Tray's voice grew light. He pretended to punch me in the arm. "Come on, Matthews. Let's go and reap the rewards from being awesome. That prank was one that will go down in history. Everyone knows I did it, but no one can prove it. That's the best thing about this life."

"What I would give to have your easy life."

I had crawled out of the vehicle, but I paused when Tray stopped behind me. I turned back. His eyes were narrowed, but he wasn't looking at me. I had a sense he wasn't even present with me anymore. His mind had wandered off. After a few minutes, he muttered, "Things aren't always what they seem, Taryn." Then he brushed past me and headed inside.

I didn't talk to Tray for the rest of the day. Well, he didn't talk to me. I hated to admit it, but it bothered me. It bothered me a lot.

CHAPTER NINE

I would've known where the party was from a mile away if Mandy hadn't left directions. Okay. Not really, but the music was blaring so freaking loud, I finally chose to turn my own radio off. I parked at the end of the lane and walked closer. When I got to the lawn, I recognized a group of Pedlam students. What the hell? They were supposed to wallow in their own parties. In Pedlam. Not here. I hadn't gone to the game, but Mandy told me my old town lost. That couldn't mean anything good was going to happen with them here.

I hugged myself, suddenly chilled, and wished I'd kept my sweatshirt on, but to no avail. I was dressed in a sheer sweater, a black tank top underneath, and a pair of jeans.

"Yo," a guy hollered and followed that with a whistle. "Hey, it's Lanser's bitch."

I gritted my teeth. Real original, asshole. I kept going. Since most the people outside were from Pedlam, I figured my allies were inside. I doubted Brian was in attendance.

"Hey." The guy tried to grab my elbow.

I wrenched my arm out of his grasp. "Let me go."

"Whoa. Calm, bitch."

I didn't know what I would do or say.

"Whatever." I darted past him.

"Hey!" He tried to follow me, but I got lost in the crowd. When I headed to the back patio, I saw Mandy on that cousin's lap, his hand under her skirt. My eyes narrowed. The fact that this had gotten past everyone's attention mystified me, but reinforced my theory that people were dumb. She tipped her head back and laughed. I groaned. She was drunk. That wasn't a normal Mandy laugh.

At the same table was Tray and also…I stopped walking when I saw my lab partner? A double what the hell?

Dylan spotted me first. "Hey, you made it."

"Taryn!" Mandy screeched. She stumbled over and threw her arms around me. "I love you so much, do you know that? You came. I'm so happy. I didn't think you would."

I hugged and patted her on the back. "I know. Football games and dances are not my thing."

"They will be. If you're my sister, they have to be, but you came. So yay!"

"Yeah."

"You're the best sister I've ever had."

I didn't know what to say to that so I patted her on the back. Again.

Dylan rescued me when he laughed. "Leave her alone. You're suffocating her, Mandy."

Mandy giggled and pulled away. She crawled back into his lap. "I know," she murmured, curling her arms around his neck again. "I really do love her so much."

Tray kicked a free chair out for me.

"Thanks." I dropped into it, still giving my sister a confused look.

Tray frowned, studying me. "You okay?"

"Yeah," I said quickly. Looking over at Molly, I asked her, "How'd you end up at this table?" Then I cursed when I realized how that sounded. I groaned, wiping a hand over my face. "I'm sorry. I just meant," gesturing to the odd couple and Tray, "these aren't your normal peeps. That's it. No judgment."

Tray grinned. "Nice save."

Dylan lifted his hand to Molly. "She said she was your only friend."

Mandy burst out laughing.

Tray chuckled. "I think she got you back already with that one."

"My only friend?" I echoed. "She's not my only friend." Yeah she was. I glanced sideways at Tray. He was watching me intently. A secret grin appeared and I knew it was just for me.

Crap. It felt as if my body exploded. I readjusted myself and tried to get comfortable, but it was useless. This damn attraction I'd had for him wasn't going away. I knew that now, and had begun to get used to it, but with a little look like that from him, knowing it was meant only for me, a girl could only handle so much.

I let out a soft sigh.

His laugh softened so it was only for my ears.

There went that tingling sensation again. Another explosion. I'd have to do something about it. This was killing me.

Dylan grinned at me. "Your friend is pretty cool."

I nodded. I hadn't known we were friends, but okay. I'd take it. Molly started giggling, and that was when I figured she was drunk as well. I skimmed an eye over the table and cursed my stupidity. It was covered in wine bottles.

Tray leaned closer and asked, "You want a drink?"

A WHOLE NEW CROWD

"Yeah. Maybe one."

"Be right back."

As he left, I commented to Dylan, "You're one of the few around here who doesn't seem drunk."

He smiled, his thumb rubbing against Mandy's thigh. "Yeah. It's turned out to be a good party."

"A lot of crashers."

"Yeah, but what can you do?"

"Having Pedlam and Rawley together, that means there's going to be some fights."

"I know." He shrugged. "We've got our crew. We can handle ourselves." He threw a frown in Tray's direction. "Besides, I doubt Evans would stand for that. If he thought there was a problem, he'd have me kick them out."

"Taryn."

Turning around, I saw Grayley standing just behind the patio gate.

"Hey." I waved him to the table. "Have a seat."

Mandy and Molly stopped laughing. Dylan sat up straight. He'd been warm and friendly a second ago. He was cold now. "Pedlam student."

"My friend." I leaned forward and kicked Tray's seat out for him. "Sit down, Gray."

He did.

Once he was seated, I asked, "Heard we spanked you guys."

He snorted, running a hand through his hair. "Please. As long as we can drink, we're happy." Then he grew serious, lowered his voice, and leaned closer to me. "Can we talk? Somewhere private?"

I knew what he was going to ask. "I'm sorry."

"Okay. Another time then?"

"No." I shook my head. "I went to Jace and he wouldn't tell me anything. He kicked me out."

His eyes widened. "He kicked you out? For real?"

I nodded. Remembering it brought some of the old emotions back up. "I'm trying not to think about it, to be honest."

"Man." He sat back, dazed. "Whoa. I'm sorry, Taryn."

I jerked a shoulder up. "It's no big deal." It was. We both knew it was, and he patted my hand, sighing softly.

He added, "I'm still sorry."

"Yeah."

He glanced from me to the table. Mandy and Molly were both staring while Dylan was watching the house. I knew who he was waiting for, but Tray wouldn't kick him out. They had met already, somewhat, at Rickets' House, and Tray knew I had gotten the blueprints from a friend. Gray sighed and leaned close again. "You want me to go?"

Did I?

I shrugged. I should've been clearer about a decision, but I didn't care in that moment. Gray was a friend, maybe the only one from Pedlam that I could still talk with. He knew me better than the people at the table, but Tray chose that moment to return with two cups in hand. He gave Grayley a brief nod in greeting as he placed the drinks on the table and pulled a chair to sit between us.

I said, "We can talk later."

"Yeah." An uneasy laugh came from him. "When it's not enemy territory, right?" He clapped a hand on Tray's shoulder. "That was an awesome prank, by the way. The guys are planning their revenge already."

Tray nodded. "Good. I wouldn't want it any other way."

Grayley laughed. "I'll let the guys know—" He stopped. "Or maybe I'll keep quiet since I got a friend on your side." Nodding to the others at the table, he tapped me on the shoulder as his farewell before he headed away.

Mandy asked, "Who was that?"

"A friend."

"Like me," Molly piped up, then her cheeks got red, and she ducked her head again.

"He seems like a good guy," Tray spoke up for him.

I could sense an interrogation from Mandy coming, but it was halted at those words. No one went against Tray Evans, certainly not my adopted sister. Knowing what he did and that he had done it for me, I turned to him. "Thank you. He means a lot to me."

"I know."

"Yeah."

Then Mandy shrieked in laughter and I sighed.

"Come on," Tray murmured in my ear. He took my hand and stood up.

I didn't care where he was taking me. He tended to know when I needed to get away so I went, with another wave of gratitude going through me, but paused when Molly jerked her head back up.

Tray pulled me into his side and leaned around me. He handed Dylan a twenty. "Can you call a cab for Taryn's friend? For when she wants to go home?"

"Sure thing."

I ignored the knowing look from the cousin and the confused expression from my sister. Molly was grinning from ear to ear. This would be spread over the school as well. Maybe I should've been happy. My goal for a while had been to distract the gossip mill from Devon and Mandy's break-up, but at this point, I didn't think it mattered.

We left. When he headed out, I asked, "Where are we going?"

He didn't answer. He took my hand, glanced over his shoulder, and flashed me a smile. Oh fuck. It was one of those smiles. It was earth-shattering, heart-melting, and a fireworks type of look. A lot of promises were attached to that look, and I swore my panties were soaked through. Yes. I definitely needed to deal with this. My body was starting to develop a mind of its own, and it was starting not to listen to me.

He squeezed my hand and slid both of them into his pocket. It was snug and too close to where I really wanted to put it. My body was ready to erupt. I couldn't remember the last time I'd been like this with a guy. A part of me loved it. The other part was in one giant pretzel-like knot.

His SUV was blocked by other cars. I climbed inside while Tray took his phone out and called someone. A little while later, three guys came out with keys and moved the cars. Then Tray climbed in beside me and backed out onto the road.

We drove in silence, just like before until he pulled up to his place and cut the engine.

Once we were inside, he went to the refrigerator, and I sat at the table. No lights were turned on. I was starting to realize Tray enjoyed living in the dark, but the light from the refrigerator flooded the room as he grabbed two beers. He came over to the table, sat across from me and slid a can to me. The room had gone back to the darkness again, and I shivered. It was like a blanket had been thrown over us. I'd been raw since my visit with Jace, and this was what I needed.

One night. I already made up my mind. One night and Tray Evans would be out of my system. We could be friends after that. Maybe? I wasn't sure.

He leaned back in his chair and opened his can. The sound was jarring in the silence between us, and I jumped, then gritted my teeth. Of course he was going to open his beer. I should've been expecting that, but I was so overwhelmed with so many emotions. They were swirling all inside of me. Lust. Desire. Fear. Pain. Those four were the main ingredients that made me, mixed with fury. A counselor told me when I was younger that I had an unhealthy amount of anger inside of me. She'd been kind. It was fury, and it made me who I was. It was my foundation, but I didn't count it. It was just there. Always would be.

"You have some messed up relationships."

My eyes jumped to his, and my heart leapt in my chest. "What?"

He was watching me. The darkness didn't matter. He could see through me anyway. He put his beer on the table and leaned back again. "You. Your ex. Jace Lanser. What is it with you and those guys?"

"They're my family."

He didn't comment.

"They *were* my family."

"Was there something going on with you and Lanser?"

"Brian."

"Jace."

Oh. "I was with Brian."

"That's not what I asked."

"Why are you asking that?"

"Because I was in the room with you two. It seemed like more than some nice family thing you think you had going on." He leaned forward, his tone turned hard.

"It's none of your business, if there was." I sighed and shook my head. "I was with Brian. There was nothing going on with Jace, and besides, my relationships with both of them are done. I was given explicit instructions to stay the hell away."

Tray started laughing. "I didn't think you were like most girls."

"Really?" My chest tightened from tension. What the hell did that mean?

"Most girls are dumb. Guys are assholes, but girls tend to romanticize that shit."

"Aren't you an asshole?"

"Yeah." He never looked away. He never wavered. The truth was right there for me to see. "I am and every single girl thinks she's the exception, that I'm going to change for her, but it never works. No girl will control me. The more I make that known, the more chicks I have coming onto me. You," he lifted his beer to me again, "I thought you were different. I thought you knew what an asshole was and that an asshole will stay an asshole."

"I'm an asshole," I said quietly, and it was the truth. "I'm the one they want to change."

"But you won't be changed?"

I shook my head. "Brian tried to make me dependent on him. He wanted one of those weak girls." Shit, this hurt to admit. "He'll be better off without me. He can be with someone who needs him more, who makes him feel—"

"Powerful?"

He understood. That knowledge settled deep in me, and I nodded. "Yeah."

He was still watching me, seeing inside of me. "And Lanser?"

I wasn't confused anymore. I knew who he meant. "Jace was family because I was with Brian. That was all. He was tied to his brother and his dad because of blood, but if he could live without them, he would." That meant without me too. I had never accepted that truth, but I had known it. It'd been there, one of those truths I ignored. "He leads the Panthers, and he's involved with that world. He wants me out."

"Are you out?"

He wasn't asking for my benefit. The need for him had been there between us from the beginning, and it had grown until I couldn't handle it. I knew why he was asking, but instead of answering his question, I said, "This is uncomfortable."

The air shifted once more. It was the first time this thing between us was being addressed.

His nostrils flared and his eyes darkened. He couldn't hide his feelings for me either. Then he smirked. "I know."

I was relieved first and then the floodgates opened. All the desire and sexual tension that had been banked down was let loose. I almost stood from my chair for him, but grasped onto the table to keep myself still. I blinked back tears from the sudden desire. It was powerful and almost blinding.

My voice had grown raw. "I'm tired of dancing around this."

"So stop."

"It's you too."

He leaned forward, his hands slid closer to me on the table, and I stared at them. I wanted to feel them run over me. I wanted to feel his arms around me. Fuck. I wanted him, all of him.

The need for him was growing stronger and stronger. I was starting not to care about staying in my chair. "I won't change," I rasped out.

"Neither will I."

We were both assholes. That had been established.

The ache was throbbing in me. My chest was moving up and down. I was damn near panting for him. A part of my brain was yelling at me to remain calm. I couldn't give in. When I did, nothing good could happened. This guy, this self-proclaimed asshole, would hurt me. The writing was on the wall, and if I went to him, I knew what I was signing up for.

I didn't care.

I cared to taste him. I cared to have him inside of me. My hands started to push up from the chair. I felt my body following, and a part of my brain went away. A primal need had taken over. He stood too and walked towards me. I stopped, waiting for him to round the table, and then he was in front of me. I couldn't look up. His chest was rising in in sync with mine. I lifted my hand to his chest and felt his heart racing.

"Taryn." His voice was a sensual whisper to me, like a caress.

I looked up.

His eyes were a dark amber and he moved another step closer. The table was pressed behind me. I couldn't move, and he leaned down to me, his lips coming towards me. I licked mine, waiting for his, and then his hand shocked me. He touched my hip and lifted me so I was on the table.

I gasped, but he swept down. His lips were on mine and the fire took over me. I became alive in that moment.

I pushed away. "I have to say this now or I might not follow through with it later."

His hand curved into the back of my head and he leaned forward.

I held firm, turning away. "I mean it."

"That's fine," he soothed me and brought me back. His lips rested on mine. He didn't apply pressure and my god, I wanted him too. No. I pulled away again, but he caught me. He didn't let me go far. "What is it, Taryn?"

Even the way he said my name. It was almost impossible to think clearly.

"Taryn."

"Right." He was like a drug. "I won't have sex with you."

He chuckled, pressing a kiss to the side of my mouth.

Oh fuck. "I mean it." I tried to sound firm.

"Stay the night anyway."

I couldn't. I'd be straddling him in the middle of the night. "No."

"Please." He kissed the other side of my mouth, and I closed my eyes. It was such a soft graze, but I trembled. He was adding fuel to the fire with each touch, each tease. I was blind with lust. It was like a blanket that had folded over me, and I was beginning to not give a damn about what would happen when the blanket completely swallowed me.

His hand spread out over my thigh and his thumb dipped down, rubbing the seam of my jeans. It was so close to where I wanted it and I squirmed. Just an inch further and he would be right there. My legs spread, just a tiny bit, and I felt him grin against my lips. He knew what spell he was weaving over me. Then he said the magic words, "I won't let you, if that's what you're worried about."

My heart leapt up and was held suspended.

He brushed his lips across mine again. It was tantalizing and he said again, "I promise. Stay the night. We won't have sex."

I tried to joke. "Some good old fashioned humping?" The corner of my lip curved up in a grin, but brushed against his from the movement. We both paused at the caress. A whimper left me. I wanted him so damn much.

"Just stay."

I found myself nodding without realizing that I had given in. The night was going to be torture, but I wanted to be in his arms. I wanted to sleep in them and that was the real reason I said yes. Then I stopped thinking. I didn't want to question where that need came from and I opened my lips.

It was all he needed. He took command.

CHAPTER TEN

I woke when Tray got up and padded into the bathroom. The shower was turned on and I groaned. Images of us flooded me. On the table. In his bed. He had carried me up the stairs. Oh god. I was beginning to want him all over again. Then my phone beeped and I lifted it. Four calls from Mandy, one from home. Holy shit. I bolted upright. That meant Austin had called me.

Something was wrong.

Calling Mandy, I braced myself when I heard her panicked voice. "Oh my god. Where have you been? Where'd you go last night?"

"I'm at Tray's." Bomb dropped.

She didn't care. "Get your ass home. Mom and Dad are showing up in an hour."

"Fuck."

Mandy hung up.

Just then the shower cut off and Tray came back to the room. A towel was around his lean hips. I jerked away. I would be reaching for that towel in two seconds if I let myself go where my body was screaming to go and had been screaming the entire night. I shifted and tried to force that need to feel him inside me away. True to his word, Tray stopped us every time we got close. I had yelled at him a few times, but he chuckled, ducked my fists, and started to kiss me again. I would end up clinging to him seconds later.

"What?" He reached for his pants.

"My parents are heading home." Fuck my life. A night filled with torture, pent-up sexual tension, and now the parents. When had this become my life?

"Alright." He grabbed the rest of his clothes and dressed in front of me. Then he grinned. "You planning on teleporting? Is that how you do your cat burglar/thievery stuff? It would explain a lot."

"Shut up."

He laughed. "We gotta get over to Dylan's to pick up your car."

I'd forgotten about my car. I was still reeling, thinking of the illegal acts I committed since my adoptive parents had been out of town. If they knew what I had been doing, they'd give me back or never let me leave the house again.

Tray sat beside me and nudged me with his leg. "Is this about last night?"

I shook my head. "I'm not used to having parents."

He laughed and then rolled over so he was above me. He braced himself up with his arms on either side of me. "If it's any consolation, Mandy's parents don't give a shit."

I laughed. "Yeah, right. Thanks for trying."

"No, they don't. For real." He dipped down and pressed a kiss to my lips. Dear god. My hand found his cheek. As he pulled away, I tugged him back down. Each nibble from him was a morsel to my starving hormones. Then I heard what he said and pulled away. "Wait. What do you mean?"

He pressed another kiss, this one chaste, before sitting up. "I thought it was a joke when I heard they adopted a girl. They're never home. Mandy's dad is a doctor, but he hardly practices. Then I saw you." He looked at me wolfishly and made a show of scanning me up and down. "I got a different idea. Maybe Kevin wanted to adopt you for a different reason."

I hit him. "Are you kidding me?"

"No." He laughed, pretending to rub at his arm. "I'm not, not about Mandy's parents. They're not real nurturing parents. Mandy's fucked in the head because of them."

"What do you mean by that?"

He gazed at me in disbelief. "She's high-strung."

Yeah? I lifted an eyebrow.

"She's got some perfect complex. That's all from her parents."

"I don't believe you."

"You don't have to. Go home and watch how fake they are."

I couldn't argue that. They were fake. They acted like they were perfect with no problems, no worries, and there was some truth in what he was saying. Still. I shook my head. "Why did they adopt me?"

"Exactly. When do you turn eighteen?"

Two months. I frowned. "They must care about me. Why would they bring a teenager into the house if they didn't?" I glanced at the bed, remembering what we had done. Parents cared about that, right? My fosters hadn't. They cared if I broke curfew, but that had been it.

"Come on." He softened and tapped my hand. "I'll stop and get us some breakfast on the way to Dylan's."

121

"No." I stood and grabbed my clothes, dressing in record time. "Let's just get my car. I should be at the house when they show up."

I bent down for my shoes and Tray groaned from behind me. "We could shower first. You should be clean. You want to shower?"

"We don't have time."

He chuckled. "I'll drive fast."

I started for the door. "You're going to have to drive fast anyway. I don't have long anymore. You know," I winked at him as we went outside, "with all the talking just now."

He laughed, and followed behind me to his SUV. After getting to Dylan's house, he pulled next to my car. I got out, but Tray called after me.

"Yeah?" I turned back.

"Call me tonight. If you want to, I don't know, come over and watch a movie or something."

"Thought we were both assholes."

He shrugged. "Assholes can watch movies too."

"Okay." I laughed. "I'll call you later." Then I stopped thinking and took off for home. When I got there, I was relieved—the parents weren't home yet. Hurrying, I swept inside and up to my room where I grabbed my robe before heading into the bathroom. I could hear Mandy in her room on the phone.

After my shower, I went downstairs, and caught Austin poking around in the fridge, his lanky form wearing basketball shorts and a Rawley jersey.

"Hey, kid," I spoke up, reaching around him, grabbing a yogurt.

He raked his eyes over my form. "Showering doesn't hide your recent lay."

"Excuse me?" I muttered, startled. The kid was in eighth grade.

"Mom and Dad are going to know."

"Hey." I shot a leg out and blocked his exit from the kitchen. "What the hell's your problem?"

"Nothing. I'm just telling you—you look like you got laid last night, and showering isn't going to hide it."

I tipped my head to the side. "You get laid last night?"

He snorted. "I'm fourteen. Mom and Dad would skin me alive."

Would they? I still played with him, seeing how uncomfortable he was. "So what's her name?"

Austin scowled at me, shoved my leg off the counter, and walked out of the room with a plate of pizza. I heard him mutter as he went, "I don't have a girlfriend." A second later the television was turned on at full volume.

"When did you leave last night?" Mandy asked, coming down the stairs.

"When you and Dylan decided to start a make-out session at the table."

"Everyone saw you and Tray leave together. Seriously. Jennica and Devon showed up with Grant at the party. Jen still has it for Tray and I guess they showed up just when you guys were taking off. I loved it!" she chatted happily, grabbing a Pop-Tart.

"Except it has nothing to do with you, Jennica, or Devon." I jumped on top of the counter, swinging my legs, watching Mandy rush back and forth in the kitchen. "What are you doing?"

"Trying to make some food for when Mom and Dad get home. They should be here any minute."

"So, you and Dylan," I started. I figured this was the perfect time. She couldn't scream or run off. "What's going on with that?"

She shrugged and, if possible, started to busy herself even more. "I don't know. Nothing. He's Samuel's cousin, and he's hardly ever here in Rawley."

"Where are his parents?"

"They live in Europe. He usually lives with his sister. He goes to a private school and is on break for the month. He's going back in a couple weeks."

"And Devon? What do you think Devon thinks about Dylan?"

She stopped and fixed me with a dark look. "Why do you care?"

"I don't." I told her the truth. "I'm trying to figure out the dynamics because no one seems surprised that you and Dylan are all touchy-feely."

"Oh." She shrugged. "Dylan makes out with whatever girl is single when he comes. If I get back with Devon, Dylan will be macking on a different girl next time. He doesn't care."

We heard car doors shut at that moment and Mandy froze, staring out the window for a moment. She muttered, "Yeah, well, a lot of things are messed up." Then the door to the kitchen opened, and she fixed a bright smile on her face. "Welcome back, Mom!"

Shelly came in first. Like Mandy, she was petite with blonde hair, and today she wore Capri pants and a white, light-weight sweater with a floral tank top underneath. She was a soccer mom. She had called herself that the first time I met her with a bright smile and a cute pixie-like face.

She hugged Mandy, letting go of the luggage behind her. The two of them looked so much alike, they could've been twins.

I did not fit in with them.

That feeling doubled as Shelly ran a loving hand down Mandy's hair, smoothing it out, hugging her tight one last time before letting go. "Oh, honey. I've missed you so much."

Mandy pulled back, then burst into tears. "Devon and I broke up."

"Oh my god. Oh no." Shelly glanced at me, graced me with a kind smile. "Taryn. It's so good to see you too." She held a hand out for me to squeeze and as I did, she turned back to Mandy. "What happened, darling?"

The story was then unfolded. They turned to go upstairs as one unit. Shelly reached for her luggage and Mandy took the other carry-on that was on the floor beside it. I heard Mandy say as they went up the stairs, "He cheated on me, Mom."

"Oh no." When they were at the top, "With who?"

"Jennica."

"Her? I never liked her, you know." Then they were in the master bedroom and the door shut. I couldn't hear anymore.

"Taryn."

I'd been gazing towards the stairs, but turned at Kevin's voice. He was in the doorway. While Shelly was petite and cute, Kevin was tall and handsome. He was six feet, had broad shoulders, and a trim waist, and greying specks in his hair that gave him a refined appearance. When I took in his threads, I shouldn't have been surprised, but I always was. Shelly dressed rich, so did he. His khaki golf pants and vest over his short-sleeve shirt were custom tailored. Even his shoes screamed they were expensive.

"Kevin." I didn't go to him. Mandy's dad had always made me nervous. He never did anything. He'd always been polite and kind to me, but he wasn't a loving man. I had never witnessed a hug between him and Shelly, or Mandy either as I thought about it.

"Dad!" Austin came barreling up from the basement. He threw himself at Kevin and a genuine laugh came from my adopted father as he hugged him back.

I had to correct myself. Kevin was loving with Austin. He hugged him tight again. "Oh, man." Pulling back, he ruffled his hair. "Two weeks I've been gone and you shot up a good three inches. You're getting as tall as me."

The fourteen-year-old grinned from ear to ear, but he ducked away from his dad's hand, then smoothed his hair back down. "Whatever, Dad. You're back, right? You're staying a while this time?"

"You know it."

"I gotta show you my score on the game downstairs."

"What were your stats for the basketball game last weekend?"

Austin stiffened, then shrugged. "They were okay."

"Austin."

"I missed my top by two points."

Kevin shook his head, but still smiled at him. "It's my fault. You and I need to throw the basketball around some more. We'll do that tonight."

Austin lit up. His eyes flooded with warmth and his smile stretched even wider. "That'd be great. Can I show you my score on the game now?"

"Sure." Kevin laughed and draped an arm around Austin's shoulders. The two went downstairs and continued talking about some game.

My phone buzzed and I pulled it out. It was a text message from Tray: **Afternoon party at my place if you and Mandy want to head over?**

I replied: **You couldn't have picked a better time. I'm on my way**.

He never asked about Mandy, and I never explained that she was busy with her family. As I headed out, I wasn't even sure if they would notice I was gone. Then I frowned as Tray's words came back to me. *They're not real nurturing parents. I thought it was a joke when I heard they adopted a girl. They're never home.*

His words were still with me when I pulled up to his house, but I shook them off. I'd tackle that later.

The guys were downstairs with a football game on the screen. Beer bottles were everywhere and a pizza box was opened on the coffee table. Grant saw me first. "Hey, Taryn."

Everyone else looked over and I waved, now feeling out of place. "Hi. I heard this was a party?"

Tray stood up and grinned. "Hey." He took my hand and pulled me upstairs as he said, "It will be. People are starting to come over now. Leading me into the kitchen, he opened the fridge. "Want something to drink?"

"You're always trying to get me drunk." I meant it as a joke, but it came out as an accusation. I folded my arms over my chest. What was wrong with me?

"Trying to be a good host."

I looked away.

"Hey." He turned my face back to his. "What's wrong?"

I thought it was a joke when I heard they adopted a girl. I shook my head. "Nothing."

He trapped me against the counter and leaned in close. "Is this where you're an asshole and lie to me? I thought we had more time before the asshole side of us came out."

He was teasing. I knew he was and I sighed. *Get over it, Taryn. No one gives a shit. Remember that and you'll be fine.* With that reminder, I shoved down all the insecurities and awkward feelings. I smiled back. "I would love a beer."

He gave me a quick kiss and pulled away. "Good. You can have fun tonight and maybe we could do another all-nighter. Last night was torture, but I loved it."

"You want me to get drunk at a party where I don't trust anyone?"

He frowned. "They're my friends."

"They're assholes."

He lifted a shoulder. "You're right. Okay. Get drunk and I'll watch over you."

"Promise?"

"I may be an asshole, but I'm an asshole you can trust." He smirked as he reached behind him and then placed a cold bottle in my hand. "I promise." He took my other hand and led me back downstairs.

Maybe it wasn't a great decision, but I gave in. The fight was always in me to survive and for once, I didn't want to fight. I wanted to be watched over. If he volunteered for that position, so be it. Brian never watched over me. I watched over him, and Jace had rarely been around.

When he sat on the couch, I curled up next to him and enjoyed my place among his group of friends. As the afternoon passed by, I heard and saw the respect they had for Tray. They listened when he spoke. Everyone turned to him and no one ignored him. They genuinely liked him.

People had never genuinely liked Brian or Jace. Jace was feared. He was respected, but I didn't know if anyone in his life liked him. It was the opposite for Brian. He was tolerated. He was a hothead. No one knew when he would explode, and so he earned a reputation as being unpredictable. He was met with caution wherever he went.

It was an alien feeling, watching this different world unfold before me.

I liked it.

CHAPTER ELEVEN

"Fuck."

"You shit."

"Asshole."

One of the guys playing grinned and flipped his last card on the table. He shot his arms up in victory. "Pres-i-dente!"

We were playing Assholes and Presidents. I was neutral, which pissed me off, and this other fucker, Aaron, slammed his last card on the deck and shouted, "Vice-President! Vice-President. Oh yeah! Oh yeah!"

I spotted my turn and slipped in my last pair of sixes. "Neutral." Then got flicked off by another player and laughed.

I'd been recruited into the game when Samuel grabbed me and pulled me to the empty chair beside him. The last two hours had gone by quickly. The place was overflowing with people now. Tray was outside manning a keg that Dylan brought over while Mandy showed up with friends that I still didn't know. They were at the pool. When she started glancing at Devon, who was manning the keg with Tray, I saw the hope in her eyes and knew where it was going. Mandy was like so many girls, crying about a guy hours earlier and then trying to get his attention. Jennica was there as well, but she kept inside with the other girls from their group.

I didn't want to be there when their love triangle hit the fan. It was inevitable, but Tray said to have fun so I was going to try.

"Take that!" Samuel hollered as he threw his last card on the pile, bringing me back to the present.

A guy rolled his eyes. "You're neutral, dumb-ass."

Samuel shrugged. "Just wait. I'll be Prez pretty soon and then you'll be my beer bitch." Downing the rest of his drink, he turned to me. "How about it, Taryn? Another shot?"

"Right and give you the chance to drug my drink?" I stood, but winked at him. "I'm not a complete idiot. I'll get my own drink."

"I said a shot. Not a drink. There's a big difference." Samuel followed behind me as I started through the crowd.

I just laughed and went around a large group, half-stumbling to the keg. Samuel caught my arm and righted me a few times on the way. I turned to tell him thanks and saw that he wasn't looking at me. He'd been watching Tray, who could see us through the crowd. Samuel chuckled beside me. "I told him I'd watch over you. The guy needs to relax and delegate sometimes." Then he winked back at me. When we drew closer, he hollered over my shoulder "I need two shots."

I winced and elbowed him. "Back up. I need to be able to hear, you know."

Samuel grinned and ignored me as he reached for the two shots. One was pushed into my hand and I frowned. Was I—never mind—I'd tossed it down my throat and grinned at Tray. "That was good. What was it?"

He lifted an eyebrow. "Does it matter?" Then poured another one.

"Sweet." Samuel took his and gestured to him. "I love this man." He was talking to me, but grinned widely at Tray. "I love you, man."

Tray chuckled. "Good to know because you need to go downstairs and grab a few more bottles for me."

"On it." He turned to go, but bounced back. Brian was there with a glower on his face, glaring down at him.

"Brian." I started for him, but Tray pulled me back. It didn't matter. My first instinct was to go to him. Always. Even now, Brian was furious, but I saw the little boy in him. He was hurting. It would never matter how violent he might be. That's all I would see.

He transferred that look of hate to me. His nostrils flared. "I was told to stay away from you." He laughed, cursing at the same time. "You told me that. Jace told me. Gray told me. That's all anyone says now: leave Taryn alone."

"Shut up."

I was pulled back and Tray stood in front of me. A different feeling hit the air. It grew serious and oppressive. People sensed it and turned to see the reason. Within seconds, a small circle had formed around them.

"Evans."

"Lanser." Tray wasn't affected by Brian's growl. "This is my house."

"That's my woman."

Tray lifted his head, raising his chin a centimeter higher. "She's not, actually."

Brian stiffened. His jaw clenched, and he swung his accusing eyes my way. I gulped when they hit me. I felt punched in the throat by them and looked away. By that movement, I had submitted my guilt to him. Then I realized what I had done and I got pissed. I jerked my head back and snarled at him. Brian saw it and frowned. I moved forward. Tray reached a hand to me, but I bypassed him. No guy was going to put me in the back.

I shoved between them and poked at Brian's chest, pushing him back a step. "It's none of your goddamn business."

"You're his woman?"

"I'm not anybody's woman. I'm mine." I was ready to tear some shit up. "You came here. This is Tray's house. I bet you heard there was a party and couldn't help yourself. Am I right?"

Guilt flared over his face.

I'd been right. I nodded. "This is on you. You knew where you were coming. You know I'm moving on. You won't let it go so this whole thing, how shitty you're feeling right now, this is all on you. I won't feel guilty because I'm trying for a better life. I won't, Brian."

He wasn't fighting back. The more I spoke, his shoulders dropped. The anger was leaving him and for some reason, I was disappointed. I frowned, not understanding that at all. I wanted him to fight back, but why? Then Tray was there again. His hand touched my wrist, and he pulled me back again. It was a gentle touch and a slight movement. I was lost in my own head. Why did I want Brian to fight with me? That made no sense.

Dylan shoved through the crowd at that moment. He took in the sight of Brian, Tray, and myself, then sighed. "Um...we have a problem."

"What?"

He looked right at me. "Mandy wouldn't listen to me. She insisted on going upstairs to use the bathroom. She might find Devon and Jennica."

My stomach dropped.

He added, "They're having sex."

"Oh my god."

Samuel laughed and thumped Brian on the shoulder. "You got trumped, dude. Crazy scorned chick always wins out against the angry/hurting ex-boyfriend." He glanced at me. "You know your sister's going to go nuts. In fact, we should be hearing her screech in about three, two," his finger lifted in the air as he said, "one."

A scream came from inside the house, followed by, "GET OFF EACH OTHER!"

I groaned. "Oh no."

A second scream came next and I started forward. Brian caught my hand. I stopped to look at him, but before he said anything, I shook my head. "Stop."

"Taryn?"

"Go, Brian. This is the last time. Just go."

"YOU WHORE!"

I glanced up at the house, towards the second floor. Tray said from behind me, "Go, Taryn. We'll handle this."

I didn't wait another second. Half the crowd was still watching us and the other half had started inside to watch that fight. I shoved through them, but I heard Tray as I did, "Get him out. Lanser, don't come back here again."

I had seen the hurt in Brian's gaze; he wasn't going to fight them. As I headed up the stairs, I pushed thoughts of Brian to the back of my mind. I didn't want to analyze my own life. It was easier to deal with someone else's love life.

When I got upstairs, I couldn't believe where I found Mandy. A small sitting room was on the second floor. No door. It was room that opened to the hallway, and sitting on the couch was Devon and Jennica. His pants were pulled up, but were unbuttoned and the zipper was still down. Both were staring at Mandy with messed hair and a glazed look in their eyes.

They didn't care. I saw it plain as day. Shaking my head, I wasn't going to intercept whatever Mandy was going to dish out. Morons. They deserved whatever was coming their way.

Mandy shrieked, "I can't believe I ever thought you were my friend!"

"Oh please. Get over this. You already know about us." Jennica snorted and rolled her eyes. "All you give a damn about is your perfect life. Devon called me four times a week when y'all were together. He was begging me for it. You were so frigid and now it's every day, Mandy."

Devon hung his head and folded his arms on his lap.

I stepped forward and kicked the bottom of the couch. He glanced up, and I gestured to his pants. "The least you could do is zip it up."

His face flushed in embarrassment, and he fastened his pants.

Mandy's eyes were wild. She seemed focused only on Jennica. "You're so second class. You're a second class friend. You're not even his girlfriend. You're second class in everything, even in school. I'm first. You're second."

Jennica's eyes flashed in anger, and she shot to her feet. Her pants slipped down, showing a white lacy thong, but she didn't care. "I'm not second. Not with him." She swung her hand back and pointed at Devon.

He shifted down on the couch, but she didn't care. Neither of the girls did. Jennica added, "You've had him forever, but he's been mine. He was always really mine, Mandy, not yours. How does that make you feel?"

"Horrible," Mandy yelled back in her face. "It makes me feel horrible. I loved him. I loved him with everything I had, and I still do."

"Mandy." Devon started to stand.

I pushed him down.

She kept going, her voice hoarse, "He's been with me since seventh grade. I thought he was my best friend. I thought you were both my best friends. My life fell apart a week ago because of you two. So when you ask how that makes me feel, I'm going to answer you. It hurts like hell. You hurt me, Jen. You were supposed to be my friend and you weren't. I'm not ashamed of what you did to me."

My heart swelled with pride.

She said, "I'll never be ashamed of being hurt by two people I loved. I was the hurt one and maybe I'm a fool. I thought maybe…" she trailed off, lingering on Devon for a moment. Yearning mixed with sadness flared in her eyes, but her jaw hardened. She turned back to her friend. "I'm hurt by what you did and no matter how you try to spin it, I'm not the bad guy. You were supposed to be my friend and you weren't. That's the truth."

There was silence as she finished. Jennica looked away, her eyes cast down. Mandy might've gotten through to her. But when she looked back up, her jaw had hardened, and her mouth was strained. I sighed and stepped forward. "Stop." Jennica's top lip curved in a snarl. She was going to start on me instead, but I shook my head. "She won just now.

You know it so accept it and walk away. Give her time, stay away from this guy," I pointed to Devon, "and apologize when you finally accept how low of a friend you are. She'll take you back because she's a good friend. She's a better friend to you than you deserve."

The snarl left, her anger faded, and a look of defeat came over her. By the time I was done, a tear had formed, and she flicked it away.

The crowd had started to lessen. This wasn't the chick fight they had been hoping for. It was just an emotional scene where a girl lost two people she still cared about.

It was then that I realized why I was disappointed with Brian downstairs. He was doing what I kept telling him to do and the less he fought, the more he was letting me go. It was the hardest thing to deal with, actually letting go. As Mandy began crying and Jennica couldn't stop her own, my own tears appeared. They weren't falling, but I felt them.

Dylan came forward and took Mandy. He told me, "I'll bring her home later."

I nodded.

After they left, Jennica started to say, "It's not—"

"Shut up." My words were harsh, but my tone was thick with emotion. I shook my head. "Look at what happened just now. You lost a friend." I nodded at Devon. "He won't stay with you and you know it. He's going to try and get her back and where will that leave you?"

The blood drained from her face.

I finished, "Alone."

"I have friends."

"Who are friends like you. Do you really want those people as friends?"

Tray came through the crowd at that moment. He scanned over everyone and touched my arm. "Taryn, let's go."

"Tray." Jennica turned to him. Her eyes were big and pleading.

He shook his head. "Don't, Jen."

"Tray?" Devon had stood, frowning.

Tray didn't answer. He took my arm and led me away from them. As we left, this was the final nail in their coffin; their leader didn't want to associate with them. He took me back through the house and around the pool. A small house was on the other side and we went inside.

I glanced around. It was a small oasis from the crowd outside.

"Come on." He took my hand and led me to a room on the second floor. A king-sized bed was in the middle with a couch beside it. A large television was in the corner.

I shook my head. "How rich are you?"

I expected a laugh, maybe an offhand comment, but there was none. He jerked his head towards the main house as he pulled me to sit with him on the couch. "What do you think will happen with those three?"

"Nothing." I hated to admit it, but I was a realist. "Devon will go back to Mandy. Jennica will act like nothing happened and they'll be friends again."

"Really? It seemed intense when I got there. I saw Mandy leave. She didn't look ready to forgive and forget."

"I want to think things will change, but I don't believe it. They'll be fake with each other. They may actually think they're friends again, but they won't be. The real friendship is gone. It'll be replaced with a fake friendship and even when she goes back to Devon; she'll never really trust him."

He narrowed his eyes, studying me.

I laughed. "You're not disagreeing with me."

He shrugged. "Mandy caught Jennica and Devon kissing in eighth grade. It was the end of the world. They had a big fight like just now, but those two got back together the next week and Jennica and Mandy were best friends within two days. I was just impressed that you called it."

"So you agree with me."

"Mandy wants to believe her friendship is real with Jennica, but it isn't. It never was. There aren't a lot of real friends out there."

"Are there real relationships?" My chest grew tight.

He didn't answer right away and the tension grew with each second that passed until he did. "Yeah. I think so, to people who don't lie to themselves. Then yes."

I wasn't sure how to take that. Fear, hope, happiness, and caution all swirled inside of me as I sat there. For the first time in a long time, I was speechless, and I had no idea why. When his hand slid to my cheek and tipped my mouth to his, I stopped thinking about it. As he pressed me down, I enjoyed his touch. It was healing, in a roundabout way, and I really didn't want to try and explain that to myself. I just enjoyed it.

CHAPTER TWELVE

The next week was strained. Mandy kept with her new group of friends while Jennica held firm with Amber and the guys. The only one who seemed affected was Devon. He kept to himself. I saw him a few times with Samuel and Grant at school. Tray was with them sometimes. He was with me at other times. He had begun to hang out at my locker, drawing more attention to me than I wanted. A few girls tried to start fights with me, but I knew it was because of him. They were jealous. When I walked away, leaving Tray in their presence, I knew they were confused. Watching Mandy and how she pretended that nothing was the matter affected me. I didn't understand it, and I didn't like it. It left a sour taste in my mouth so I tried to keep to myself.

"Taryn." Shelly knocked on my door and stuck her head inside. I took my earbuds out, but didn't get up from my bed. She smiled. "Honey, Kevin and I are going out. Mandy said to let you know some of your friends are coming over for the night."

I nodded. "Okay. Thanks for letting me know." I had no intention of hanging out with them.

She frowned. "Are things okay with you and Mandy? You two have seemed off this last week."

Had things been okay? Mandy rarely talked to me anymore. She kept with her new friends and I remained alone. I shook my head. "Things are fine. Her break-up with Devon is still hurting her, I think."

"I'm sure that's it. You're right." She waved again. "Okay. We're off. I'll bring some ice cream home tonight."

When she left and shut the door, I let out a sigh. An hour later, there was another knock on my door. Instead of waiting for me, it opened and Tray slipped inside.

My heart paused and a rush of sensations overwhelmed me. He'd been doing this to me for a while, but the feelings had doubled the night of his party, when we talked about real relationships.

I didn't say anything. Neither did he, and I moved over so he could crawl onto my bed. When he turned so he was facing me, we stared at each other for a moment. As his gaze fell to my lips, he murmured, "You've been avoiding me all week."

I could lie. I didn't. "You scare me."

He lifted a hand, and his fingers caressed my cheek. As he lifted a strand of my hair and tucked it behind my ear, a knot loosened inside me. A different feeling was spreading through me, overtaking me, and it wasn't just lust anymore. That terrified me even more.

"I do?" His hand skimmed back down, pausing at the corner of my lips, and my pulse kicked up a notch. He was going to kiss me, then he pulled back. His hand fell to my chin, softly, and down my neck. He let it slide down my arm, the entire gesture a caress before he tucked his hand around my waist. His thumb slipped inside my shorts and he rubbed back and forth. An ache grew. I wanted to feel him there. I wanted to feel him inside of me.

Fuck it.

I closed my eyes, leaned forward, and found his lips with mine. The feel of them, the slight graze, was like a promise, and I sighed, melting against him. He traced my lips with his tongue, then swept inside. It had been like this the other night. One touch, one taste, and my body was writhing with the need for more. It built, wanting more and more of him until I was panting at the slightest feel of him now. Twisting my leg around his, I pulled him even closer. He rose above me, bracing himself, twisting one of my legs around his, pulling him tighter against me.

Then my phone rang.

I groaned.

"Leave it." Then he began trailing kisses down the side of my face. As he went to my neck, I arched my back and neck for him. I wanted to feel his hands on my breasts. I wanted to remember the feel of him cupping them, caressing them with his hands.

The phone kept ringing.

I reached for it, but didn't recognize the number. I tossed it to the floor, and Tray switched our positions. I straddled him and wrapped my arms around his neck, pressing against him, savoring the feel of his strength underneath me. He was like a drug. The more I got from him, the more I needed.

His hands found my arms and he lifted me up. His eyes were dark amber again, and his voice was thick with lust. "If we don't stop, I won't be stopping for the rest of the night."

I tried to remind myself that everyone was downstairs, even Austin. This was a bad idea, but I went back to suckling his neck.

Tray groaned. I felt the fight in him as he tensed. His hand fell to my thigh and curved into me, holding me, anchoring me to him. His other hand grabbed the hair at the back of my neck, and lifted my head for his. Our lips met again and the feeling of being drowned came over me once more.

I couldn't get enough of him.

Then his hold switched on me and I was lifted in the air. He sat up, scooted against my headboard, and pulled me back onto his lap. My legs were on either side of him and we were sitting eye level. My hand lifted to his hair and raked through it. I grabbed a fistful and leaned forward. His hands held firm on me, still on my hip and the back of my neck. It was a possessive hold, but so was mine. My kisses grew more demanding. He answered with a deep groan, tilting my head for better access, pulling my hips forward. I went with him, grinding against him, feeling him between my legs. He was where I wanted him, but it wasn't enough. I wanted him in there. No clothes. No protection. Him and me.

At that thought, my hand trailed down his stomach to his jeans, but he caught it with his and interlaced our fingers together.

Dammit. I strained against him, rubbing my chest against his, and a low growl emanated from him. "Taryn," he whispered against my lips.

He was going to tell me to stop. Maybe I should, but I didn't. My lips opened over his once more, then I lifted to kiss his cheeks, his eyelids, his forehead, and then his throat. Bending down, I lifted his shirt over his head and moved further down his chest. I swept my tongue over each dip and between each muscle. He quivered under my touch. He was so strong, so powerful, but I had the control. With a sweep of my hand down his chest, he trembled.

143

He wanted me. I wanted him. My hands went back to his jeans. This time, he didn't stop me. I wrapped my hand around him. His forehead fell to rest on my shoulder as I started stroking, back and forth. I felt him unbutton my jeans, and in seconds, his hand slipped inside, his fingers dipping inside me. I paused, gasping as he found my core, thrusting in and sliding back out.

My phone began ringing again.

Make it stop. I willed it to stop. I didn't want to pull out of this haze, but it kept ringing. Tray paused. Then it went to voicemail and I started to relax again. He swept his lips against my shoulder, lingering there and a moment later my phone began going again.

God, no.

I began whimpering as his fingers went back inside me. I wanted him to go further, harder, but he pulled them out when my phone kept ringing.

"I'm going to kill whoever is on the other end." I fell back, but he caught me so I wouldn't fall all the way back, and then pulled me to rest against him. His head bent forward and his lips went back to my neck, nibbling there, such a teasing caress, and I sighed as my own began tasting his chest. I wanted to explore him again and a part of me was tempted to throw my phone, then come back and not let the world interrupt us again. I didn't. Instead, I leaned over to the floor. Tray trapped my waist, holding me on him so I wouldn't fall, and I grabbed my phone.

It was the same unknown number. I frowned, but tucked the phone away. Whoever it was would be dealt with later.

144

Tray skimmed a hand up my arm, sending new shivers through me as he did. He murmured, "You never said why you're scared of me."

A helpless laugh came from me. "You mean beside this? What we just did?"

His hand curled around the back of my neck, and he moved me so I was looking up at him. Our eyes caught and held. He was somber. "This scares you?"

"What you can do to me scares me." I was being honest. It was freeing. Then I frowned. I had never been this open with Brian.

"You mean this?" His hand dipped down and went between my legs again. He paused, his fingers right where I wanted them and he smiled. "Or this?" His other hand rested between my breasts. My pulse was racing, and my heart seemed to leap to meet his touch.

He felt it and his smile grew tender.

I swallowed. "Both. You're real." Real relationships. That's what we had talked about. "That makes me want to shit my pants."

His fingers teased me and slid back inside. Then he grew serious again. "This shouldn't scare you."

"Spoken from someone who knows his family, who's had the same friends probably most his life, who never had to move from home to home."

He frowned, but said, "Spoken like someone whose father is a disgrace to me."

I sat upright. "You've never said much about your family."

"Neither have you."

"My family was Jace and Brian. I'm trying to move on from them."

He touched my bottom lip, drawing my attention back to him. "What are you thinking?"

I hesitated, then said, "About letting you in."

His eyes were so serious, but the corner of his mouth lifted in a slight grin. "I thought we were assholes, and we were going to remain assholes together?"

"Sometimes assholes lie." I felt like I couldn't breathe. "And they aren't assholes to the ones they let in."

His chest moved up and down beneath me. His hands rested on my hips, and I remained there. What the hell were we going to do? No. What the hell was I going to do?

"Yo!" A hard knock came to my door.

Tray cursed and ran a hand through his hair. "Great timing." I grinned at the sarcasm, but couldn't deny the relief that went through me. He tucked me against his chest and raised his voice, "What do you want, Dylan?"

"We're going out to eat. You two want to come?"

Tray glanced at me. "You want to?"

I shook my head. "I've never been one for crowds."

He laughed. "Who couldn't like this new crowd?" Then he lifted me off him and placed me on the bed. The entire movement was gentle, so gentle that an unnerving emotion began to spread in me. I didn't want to name it. It was too uncomfortable for me. He rose from the bed and pressed a kiss to my forehead, tucking some of my hair back at the same time. He whispered against them, "For what's it worth, you affect me the same way, Matthews."

My throat was thick as he left. Then I heard them go downstairs and drive away. "Fuck."

Austin left to eat with them, and I didn't want to sit alone with my emotions so I went swimming; fortunately our school's pool had late hours. As I dove into the depths, I ducked my head down and swam.

I hadn't thought about swimming in a long time, but when everyone left I needed to do something. I couldn't steal anymore. I was good at swimming. The water absorbed me, taking me away from the world, until it was only me. It was me, the water, and my thoughts.

Lining my feet against the wall, I held myself there and stared at the end. The water rippled, as if daring me to go faster and plunge through it, and I was itching to answer its challenge. I felt the excitement building inside, and shoved off from the end. My arms were already circling when I ducked my head down and kicked out.

I started out limber, going slow to get into a good pace, but I knew what would happen. I would use every muscle in my body. My lungs would strain, stretching to their fullest capacity, before I turned and took a relieving breath. I would suck air in, and my head would go back down. Each kick would match each stroke and I would take myself to the end only to duck down and repeat the process.

This was the warmup when it was fun and freeing, but soon, I would hit a wall of fatigue. That's when those muscles would protest. My lungs would scream for relief. Every cell in my body would want me to quit, but I wouldn't. I never did. An hour later, then another thirty minutes after that, I kept going. I didn't stop. I pushed through the pain until my mind screamed, 'enough.' It was then I went to the end of the lane and stopped. My fingers clutched the edge and I panted. I had reached the point where my brain stopped working. All thoughts had fled and the emotions had been cleared from me.

Swimming was pure.

I had missed it. I had needed it.

CHAPTER THIRTEEN

It was in our first class when I saw the reunion of Mandy with Amber. Since the Jennica debacle, Amber had sided with her, but my sister was whispering with Amber in the back of the classroom. My eyebrow went up and I grunted, then sat and turned my back to them. I had tried to help my sister out enough.

"Morning, class." The teacher shut the door and put her bag on the desk. She lifted up a novel, *Of Mice and Men*. "Who read the chapters? I want to know your thoughts."

I snuck a peek at Mandy and Amber. Talk about friendship and sacrifice. Then I smirked when Amber raised her hand. "Mrs. Tationa, Mandy and I were wondering if we could be excused. We'd like to finish up some posters before the pep rally this week."

"Oh, Amber, of course—"

I burst out, "Are you kidding me?!"

"Taryn," Mandy hissed.

The teacher looked startled. "You don't agree with my decisions in this classroom, Miss Matthews?"

I shot my sister a glare, but turned to Amber. "You're not even on the pep rally committee. Trust me, I know. I live with the president of the pep rally committee. Two, you're not a cheerleader, and three, if anyone should benefit from this discussion—it's you!"

A strangled gasp ripped from Mandy. "Shut. Up." She gritted her teeth.

"No," I ignored her. "I'm sick of you guys running around this school like it's your personal playground. All the teachers just let you guys get away with whatever you want. I'm so tired of it."

Someone snorted behind me. "Aren't you being hypocritical?"

A guy wearing a polo was glaring at me. I snapped, "What?"

"You're one of them." He leaned forward. "Have *you* ever been in trouble for anything?" I laughed at that and then heard him say, "Aren't you dating Tray Evans?"

My grin fell flat. "No."

Amber scoffed. "Then what were you doing Friday night in your bed?"

"We're not dating." We weren't, but I held tight to my desk so I wouldn't squirm all over.

"Whatever," Amber shot back. "You get on your high horse about us, but we haven't done half the shit that you have."

I went livid. My eyes narrowed. "Excuse me?"

"Like it was just 'by chance'," air quotes, "that the Monday after Mandy and Devon break up, our school gets canceled. That stuff's never happened here before, and I'm sure you had nothing to do with it." She rolled her eyes. "And we all know how Pedlam got broken into."

Mandy paled. "Amber, stop it."

My eyes narrowed to slits. "You've got balls, Amber."

She frowned, and I saw the confusion on her face.

I spelled it out. "If you spill one word, who do you think you'll be pissing off?"

It wouldn't be me. When she realized her mistake, her eyes got big. I grinned, but then she rolled her eyes. Her snootiness came back and her lip lifted in a half snarl/half pout. "Whatever." She looked around the room. "No one will tattle. I'll say it was you. You all hear that, everyone? It was Taryn Matthews who brought up the break-in."

"Girls." The teacher stepped between us and held her hands up. "Stop this or you'll be sent to the principal's office."

I ignored her. "Let's talk about you, Amber."

She stiffened, but leaned back in her chair. "Fine. Bring it. I doubt you can say anything that'll upset me."

"Did you apologize to Mandy?"

She frowned.

I smiled and looked at Mandy. "Mandy, did she apologize to you?"

My sister's face was as white as a ghost. "For what?"

"Since your good friend here brought it up, everyone will now be talking about your break-up with Devon, if they weren't already." I smiled at Amber, who flinched from what I said. "Let's go with that. Mandy, you were the one that was hurt by it, but Amber remained by Jennica's side during the whole thing. This is the first time I've seen you guys talk to each other since that night even. So," I drew out, "did you apologize to my sister for abandoning her?"

The anger flared bright in the depths of Amber's eyes. She pressed her lips together in a flat line and swallowed a knot, before throwing a sideways look at Mandy.

I shook my head. "That had been a hunch, but damn. It's nice to know that I was right."

Mandy's head went down, and her hands folded in her lap. She didn't fight for herself. Amber was never a blip on my radar, but I knew if she was friends with Jennica and supported Jennica, she wasn't a good person. Seeing my sister take this from her made my stomach roll over on itself.

An ugly laugh ripped from me. Mandy looked up. Amber seemed to hold still. All eyes were on me again. "This is a joke. *You're* a joke."

"Taryn."

I ignored the teacher again. I said, "People like you will hurt people. You'll go through life with this entitled attitude. You'll walk over people, step on them, do whatever it is that will hurt others, and you won't care. You might say you're sorry if you're called on it, but you won't be sorry. You'll keep going and keep hurting people. I've seen people like you all my life." I felt sick. "It's people like you who get to the top and you don't look down. You don't look at the trail of bodies left behind you." I turned to Mandy now. Her eyes enlarged and she bit her lip, but she didn't turn away. A small modicum of respect came back for her with that. She was going to face whatever I had to say. I frowned. I wasn't going to mince my words because of it. "You're one of those people who take it. You let people like her win because you don't say a word. She should've been your friend during that time. She wasn't. She chose the girl who hurt you, who," I snorted, "I'm sure will be your friend by the end of the week. What you accept is what you'll always be given. Stop accepting their crumbs."

Amber glanced around. She'd been smirking, but it faded when she saw others had the same anger as me.

"I hurt people." She looked back at me so I finished, "But I hurt people like you and your friends."

The room was silent and the air was heavy. One second.

Two.

Three.

No one had her back. She fled the room.

This would be a problem. I just called out one of the top people. Mandy started to get up. My mouth fell open. She was going to the door. No, no, no. She couldn't...

She reached for the handle, but paused and looked back. She didn't say a word and then left.

No one talked in the room after they left. Even the teacher was silent. Amber was at the top, and I called her out, disgracing my own sister in the moment. Fuck me. Great job, Taryn. Sighing, I frowned. I couldn't take it back, and it was how I felt. I slid down in my chair, knowing there would be repercussions. There were always consequences when people like Amber were humiliated. They didn't change. They just fought back.

Then I remembered—Tray ran this school. He was one of those at the top too. Oh hell.

I didn't have long before I started feeling some of the repercussions. Jennica glared at me when I left first period. Grant and Samuel glared too. They cast a glance at the girls to make sure they had noticed. When they were positive they'd been noticed, they dropped the glares and went back to their conversation.

When I walked up to my locker before my last class, a girl was writing 'whore' in permanent maker.

I grabbed the pen from her hand and threw it. "Fetch."

She started to retort, but I opened my locker, grabbed my book, and left before she got one word out.

I felt attention everywhere I went. People were watching me. I wasn't dumb. I knew they were going to wait and see what happened, but when I got to my last class, I stopped in the doorway and wanted to groan. I always thought I had study hall during this period, so I decided to go to health instead. I was surprised when I saw who else was in this class. Tray.

He was at a table by himself, lounging back in his chair. As I stared at him, unsure what to do, conversations hushed around the room, and he looked up. His eyes were narrowed when they landed on me. I groaned on the inside. The anger was there, but it was banked.

The teacher saw me too. "Miss Matthews, you've finally decided to grace us with your presence. I see someone took it upon themselves to let you know that we are, in fact, not study hall and that you are, in fact, supposed to be here."

"Yeah."

"Good. Good. Take a seat. I see an empty one by Mr. Helms."

I glanced at Helms and saw a look of disgust pass over him. He stood. "I'll sit with Tray."

He was gathering his books when Tray stopped him. "She can sit with me."

Oh joy.

Helms froze. He looked at Tray, read something on his face, and sat back down.

I met Tray's eyes again. Yeah...no. "I can sit on the floor."

"Oh no." Tray kicked out the empty chair beside him. "Sit with me. Really."

As soon as I sat down, the class started, but I couldn't pay attention to the teacher. I doubted anyone was. His entire body was rigid. I stole a few glances his way, but was met with a cold, even stare back. I could feel the tension in his body. Jace's warning to stay away from Tray came to me again. Shit. I should always listen to Jace. He never lied to me.

I heard the teacher ask for two volunteers to go to the counselor's office. I had barely registered his words when Tray spoke up, "We'll go."

I never got time to decide if I wanted to go. He grabbed my arm and hauled me out. We were in the hallway before the teacher could say thanks.

I wrenched my arm away. "Ouch."

That's when I was met with the full force of Tray's fury because he grabbed my arm again and yanked me into the empty gymnasium.

"This isn't the way to the counselor's office."

"Do you really want to go to the counselor's office?" Tray snapped, hauling me into the equipment closet. The heavy door slammed shut behind him.

He had a point there, but taking in his tight jaw and set shoulders, I said, "I would today."

He ignored me and rolled his eyes. "What the fuck do you think you're doing?!"

"Excuse me?"

"You know what. The entire fucking school is going off about you and Amber. You said that we hurt people, that we don't give a shit about them."

I crossed my arms over my chest. This could get technical. "She doesn't."

"You lumped her in a group at the top. I'm the top. Anything you said about her, you said about me too."

That was the problem. I sighed. "Okay, listen. I can see the confusion."

"Stop messing around, Taryn. You called out my group of friends, and they're pissed."

I snorted. "Yeah, I'm sure. The guys didn't look that pissed. I was calling out the girls, and you know it. Everyone knows it."

He stepped close, curbed a hand around my neck and leaned close. He didn't touch me otherwise, but I felt the heat from him. Even though I was in trouble, I wanted to touch him. I wanted to lift my hands and press them to his chest. I wanted to feel him tremble under their touch and then I wanted him to close the distance, put his mouth on mine, and press me against the wall.

"Taryn!"

I jerked back to the present. "What? Yes. I didn't mean you. I'm sorry."

He groaned, raking a hand through his hair. "What the hell am I supposed to do? Everyone's looking at me to reprimand you."

Not really. I gave him a tentative smile. "You know, you could just make it clear that this is a girl thing. Amber would have to fight her own battle and you're in the clear." I nodded. "That could happen. We'd be covered and I can handle her."

He cursed and shot back, "When did you decide to be the school's personal savior and call out everyone at the top? The girl thing won't fly and you know it. You're pissed because your sister is letting Amber and Jennica walk all over her. You're trying to fix her problem, like you've always done. You set the alarms to save Mandy from gossip, and now you're covering your own ass by going after all of us."

"I didn't mean you."

"Tough shit. I'm at the top. You said 'people like you.' That means me, my crowd, my people."

"I'm not going after you. This has nothing to do with you."

"Yes, it does," he retorted fiercely. "This is my school; you're messing with my friends."

"No—"

"Mine," he bit out.

"Look," I spoke a little calmer, "I'm tired of how Amber gets away with everything at this school."

"So am I," he stated.

"I know, but," I faltered, "this isn't about you. About you and me."

"Oh no. You're goddamn right about that one. This has no bearing on you and me."

I stopped at his words. There was a possessive note in his voice and heat rushed through me. The ache to feel him against me started again, but I cleared my throat. My voice was hoarse when I spoke, "Look, I was just pissed. Amber and Mandy wanted to get out of class for some pep rally posters. I'm tired of how they can do whatever the hell they want.

So I said something and then Amber brought my shit up. About the alarms last Monday, about how Pedlam got broken into." My hands lifted to his shirt and I grasped onto his collar. He remained standing so close to me, his gaze bearing into me. Oh god. It was such an intimate look. My chest swelled and I ignored how my pulse picked up speed. I added, "She called you out too when she brought up the Pedlam thing."

Tray sighed, raking a hand through his hair.

My lips were dry. God, he was freaking gorgeous. And those lips…his shoulders…

Tray gave me an exasperated look. "You got pissed and went after her. My friends aren't saints. I'm not a saint." His look switched to a pointed one. "Neither are you. You've got serious history with the biggest drug-runner in Pedlam. You used to date a guy that's violent." My eyes got big, but before I could argue, he said, "Maybe not towards you, but he's known to be violent with others. Both Lansers aren't good people."

I sighed, turning away to rest my head against the wall. I didn't know what to say. I'd opened a can of worms, but—hell—I wasn't one to sit back and let stuff slide by. Not if I was pissed enough and could stop it. Or, to be more accurate, if I wanted to stop it. Tray was right, I let a lot of stuff by because I didn't care about it, but this time, I cared. So I opened my mouth.

"How did you know about Jace?"

Tray snorted, rolling his eyes. "I know more than you think about that world."

He knows people that I know. I remembered Jace's warning. A shiver went through me, but I folded my arms across my chest and leaned back

158

against the wall. Tray was becoming my only ally here. I didn't want to lose him. "He's not a drug lord."

"No, he's a drug dealer. That's a lot more prestigious."

I rolled my eyes, hearing his sarcasm. "Jace is—"

"Jace is someone you should stay away from. He might care about you, but he's not going to change. One day he's going to end up in prison or dead."

That was enough. "And how do you know so much?" The guy was insufferable.

"I know. Trust me."

"But how?"

"My dad," he remarked. "He used to be the chief of police here, and my older brother's with the DEA. I know both sides, trust me. My family is messed up, but I know where to step and where not to step." Tray sat on a roll of wrestling mats against the wall. Bracing his elbows on his knees, he said further, "That's how I know Lanser."

"Jace said you knew people he knew." This was important, whatever Tray was going to tell me might not be brought up again. I had this one shot. We were in a back room, tucked away from the world. Right now, it was only him and me. "What did he mean by that?"

Pain flashed in the depths of his eyes. The sight of it surprised me. There was more than pain, though. There was anger and grief too. He was haunted.

Then he said, "My dad was a dirty cop."

"Oh."

He laughed, and the sound sent chills down my spine. "Jace is a dealer for Sal Galverson, a drug lord from South America. They tried to recruit my dad to help with the distribution in Rawley."

"Did he?"

He nodded. "Yeah, for the longest time. Bad stuff happened. My brother got involved. He came back home. We thought he was home to recuperate from an injury, but he was really undercover. My dad was so dumb. My brother told us he had been shot, and his leg was broken, so my dad didn't think he could follow him."

"What happened?"

"My brother was faking. He got a ton of evidence on my dad. Some of it was turned over, but Galverson's lawyer found a loophole. My dad was the only one that would've gone to prison."

"Would've gone? He's not?"

"No, he's in South America with Galverson. He still helps him because of his contacts with the cops here. My dad kept the other evidence. If anything happens to me, it goes to DEA. I guess it's the stuff about their current suppliers. Galverson's not scared about prison. He doesn't want his distribution and suppliers messed with so everyone's at a standstill." He grimaced. "My dad is with him as an act of good faith; it's not just to hide from the government."

I blinked, not believing what I just heard. "Does anyone else know about this?"

He shook his head. "No. I never said a word to my friends and all the stuff that went down was swept under the rug. A lot of the Rawley cops are dirty. My brother went back to the DEA. I haven't talked to him since it all happened."

"When?"

"Last year."

I sighed and moved to sit in front of him. Tray pulled me back against his chest and wrapped his arms around me. I laid my head on his chest. "I'm so sorry, Tray. I had no idea."

"It's not a normal thing people go through or tell anyone about." He tipped my head up and peered down at me. His eyes were fierce. "I'm only telling you because I know Jace Lanser. He showed up at our house when they thought my dad was going to flip on them. I know what he's capable of."

So did I. A wave of sadness crashed down on me. "Jace has never said he was a good guy. I know he's dangerous."

"You'll stay away from him?"

I nodded. I felt that he was asking more with that question. It wasn't only about Jace and me; it was about Tray and me. He was claiming me again with this request. Jace had been family, but I couldn't go back to there. He didn't even want me back there anyway. I whispered, "I'll stay away from him."

He chuckled. "They're expecting me to put you in your place." One of his hands began caressing my leg.

I was confused, then remembered Amber and Mandy. "I can't back down to Amber. I won't. I hate girls like her."

"I know, but it's going to make things a lot more tense with the group."

"Why? It's not like I'm exactly friends with you guys." I turned to face him, and his hands moved to my waist. "I just don't like how Amber and Jennica treat people."

He nodded, his thumb coming to my bottom lip. He rested it there, then pulled it down. My eyes held his. I was melting, just looking at him, feeling him against me. Tray grinned, running his hands up my arms and back down to my waist. He pulled me closer to him and leaned forward, nuzzling my neck.

I wrapped my arms around his neck. The conversation was officially over.

Tray kissed his way up my neck, along my chin, and found my lips.

I lifted my legs and turned to straddle him. He slid a hand down my back, slipping it inside my jeans, then up my back, moving to softly caress my breast, underneath my bra.

"—this place is usually—whoa."

The door opened. Tray clipped out, "Out." The door slammed shut and then I started laughing, hiding my face in his neck. We were always getting interrupted.

"Sorry, guys," Samuel said through the door.

"Get lost." Tray nuzzled my neck again.

"Yep. On it." His voice sounded farther away and another door shut a moment later.

I didn't want it to end so I found his lips again, and we started kissing as if nothing had happened. When the bell rang, I pulled away and stood. My knees were unsteady. Tray held onto my elbow for a little bit.

"I'm good."

"This isn't just for you." He flashed me a grin, breathing heavy.

I chuckled, feeling relieved that he was affected just as much as I was. A moment later we left the equipment closet, and once we were in the hallway, I started in the opposite direction. Tray's locker was in the senior hallway. My locker was in a separate hallway, but he stopped me.

I glanced back. "What?"

He flashed me a grin, his eyes were still a darkened amber color. "Come on," he said, pulling me behind him as he walked us back through the hallways. "We're going to my house for the rest of the day." He pulled out his keys when we approached his SUV.

Nothing else sounded better.

CHAPTER FOURTEEN

We spent the afternoon and evening at his house. His phone was turned off because people didn't stop calling him. My phone never went off so I never thought to check it. When I was thinking about heading home, I looked at it. I regretted it.

Tray looked over. The movie had ended, but neither of us had gotten up from the couch. He asked, "What is it?"

I showed him my phone. "Mandy called and she never calls much. She called three times."

"So call her back," he suggested, "and then once she starts in, hang up."

"Oh and it's so easy," I mocked him.

Tray laughed and wrapped his arms around me. He scooted down and pulled me on top. As I straddled him, I called her back. Tray started tickling me under my shirt and I laughed as I tried to twist away from him.

"Taryn!" Mandy yelled into the phone.

I frowned. There was loud music in the background. "Where are you?"

"Oh my God, Taryn. We did something really stupid," she scrambled.

Hearing the panic from her, I froze. Everything stopped. The laughing stopped. My hand fell from Tray's tickling ones. I sat completely still. "What did you do?"

Tray stopped, hearing my tone.

"Amber went off about you and Tray. How you're just screwing him and that's why you get away with everything you do...and so," she paused for some air, "Amber remembered your ex and she wanted to get even with you..."

A knot of dread forming in my stomach.

"She knew that his brother owns the Seven8 in Pedlam so we..." She stopped.

I groaned. "Please tell me you didn't go there. Please, Mandy. That place is dangerous."

Her voice got so small. "We did."

My heart stopped. "The Seven8 is dangerous, Mandy. People go there in masses for safety reasons. Girls don't go there unless they're connected. You are not connected."

"Yeah, well...we kinda figured that out for ourselves."

Fuck, fuck, fuck. "This is bad. You need to leave. I don't care if you're alone or where you are. Leave that place. Now."

An unspoken decision was made between Tray and I. He had undone my pants earlier, and fastened them now. I didn't ask. He understood. My shirt was straightened, and he sat up. He reached around me and fastened my bra. Then he pressed a kiss to my cheek and whispered, "Let's go get them."

I nodded. Mandy talked as I followed him up the stairs and waited as he got whatever he needed. She said, "No, I can't. *We* can't. We're in trouble."

"What kind of trouble?"

"We finally got in and these guys started hitting on Amber and Jennica."

My hand clenched around the phone. Jennica? For real? *No, Taryn. Be calm.* The rage in me would have to wait. Get my sister to safety and then murder her. That was the new plan.

She kept going, "When Samuel tried to step in, they beat him up, Taryn. He can barely walk and he's bleeding everywhere and they won't let us leave."

"Grab one of the bouncers. *Make* them help you."

"We can't. This place is packed and these guys have us in a back corner. We have to go past them to get out and they won't let us." She lowered her voice and I could barely hear it. "I'm so scared, Taryn. I don't know what to do."

Tray touched my arm and gestured to the door. He was ready. I nodded to him and followed behind him. I said to Mandy, "Are all of you guys in the corner? Is there anyone who isn't?"

"Yeah, Grant. He's not in the corner with us. He went to the bathroom, but we haven't seen him since we got here. Amber thinks he got beat up too," she cried out. I could hear a hitch in her voice.

"I'm coming, Mandy." Tray turned onto the highway, but he didn't go towards the school. I put a hand over the phone. "Where are you going?"

"You're not going to the Seven8 alone."

166

"Jace owns that club. I'll be fine." I pressed my lips together. Tray didn't need to be told about Jace's last threat, that if I went back, his guards would shoot me in a limb. I'd have to tackle that when we got there.

"I don't care if God owns that club. You're not going in there alone."

"Taryn!" Mandy yelled from my phone.

I raised it back up. "Hold on. We're coming. Don't do anything."

Pedlam was an hour drive. Tray made it in forty minutes. When he parked, he was out the door and crossing the street by the time I unbuckled my seat belt. I darted after him. "Hey! Wait up."

He stopped down the street, and we both studied the line. He frowned. "Why is one of the most dangerous clubs in town the most popular? Are all people idiots?"

I nodded. "Yes." Then one of the guards saw me and I ducked behind him. "Um..." Crap. The guard lifted his radio and talked into it. This could be a problem.

Tray frowned at me. "What are you doing?"

"I might have forgotten to tell you something."

"Might?"

The guard was coming towards us, reaching for his gun. I froze. Then another guard joined him.

I appeared on the other side of Tray and held up my arms. "Please don't shoot me! Please don't. Jace would be mad. I promise. He didn't mean what he said before."

Tray whipped back around. "What?!"

The guards were so close now. I could hear the one saying, "Got it, Boss."

Oh god. I closed my eyes tight. The other guard had been raising his gun. The bullet was going to hit me. I tried to prepare myself.

Then I heard, "Girl, you shouldn't be here."

I opened one eye. The gun was put away. "Oh my god." I patted myself down. "I didn't pee myself, did I?"

Tray was glaring at me.

The guard shook his head. "You're lucky Jace had a change of heart. He took the order down the next day and said to notify him the second you showed up again." He grunted, taking my arm. "He said you were trouble no matter if you had your limbs or not."

The other guard poked Tray in the back, gesturing for him to follow us.

Tray shot me a dark look. "You and I need to learn how to talk a lot more."

I laughed. "Yeah. Just as soon as we rescue my sister and your shitty friends, it's on the agenda." I ignored Tray's growl and asked the guard, "Is Jace here?"

"He's in a meeting."

We were taken through a back hallway and waited. After ten minutes passed, I sighed. "How long do we have to do this? My sister is here. That's why I'm here. Just let us go and get them, then we'll leave. I don't need to see Jace."

The guard didn't care. I looked to the second one. Neither did he.

"Come on."

They still ignored me, then the radio beeped and a voice said, "Almost there. Hold tight."

The guard lifted it and pressed his button. "Got it. Out."

I didn't recognize the voice, but the door opened from down the hallway and Krein stepped out. His hair was messed up and he wasn't wearing a shirt. He gave me a crooked grin when he came closer. "Hey there, Taryn. How's it going?"

I gestured to his pants. "I'm thankful your pants are on."

"Yeah." He laughed, but his hand dropped to double check they were fastened. Then his grin spread. "So what brings you back? I heard big brother Jace wasn't too nice to you when you were here last."

I rolled my eyes. "My sister is here with a bunch of her friends. One of the guys got beaten up and some other guys won't let them leave."

"Oh." He frowned, scratching his head. "That's not good. What's your sister look like?"

I held up my phone and showed him a picture. He nodded. "Got it." He gestured to the guards. "Show her to the back room. I'll get some other guys and get her friends."

"My sister," I corrected.

He wasn't listening. One of the other guards asked, "What back room?"

Krein started off, but shouted over his shoulder, "The big back room. The main one. Keep 'em entertained. Taryn talks big, but her attention span is like a fly. She'll be buzzing around and getting into shit if you don't distract her."

"Hey!" I shouted at him, but it didn't matter. Krein disappeared around a door and my arm was taken in a hold again. The guard led us further down the hallway until we were shown in to a big room. It was empty. A few tables were set up in one corner, but no one was in there. The floors were made of cement. The lights barely worked and it looked like the floors had recently been hosed down. Puddles of water were spread out all over.

I didn't want to ask what that room was for. As soon as we were inside, I pulled my arm from the guard.

He protested.

I pointed to the table. "I'm going to sit. I'm not going anywhere."

He frowned, but kept quiet. Tray followed me and I was relieved when the two guards remained by the door.

It wasn't long before the door opened again and Krein led the group in. He walked towards me and spread his arms wide. "I deliver, Taryn. I always deliver. You can remember that for the future."

I sighed in relief when I saw Mandy run around him and head towards me. Catching her in my arms, I hugged her tight. Her arms wrapped around me. I cupped the back of her head, holding her close. "Taryn, thank you so much."

Four guards walked around us, carrying Samuel. He was laid out on the table and Amber went to him, crying, as she held his hand. The others sat around him. I was going to ask Krein if they could help with Samuel's wounds, but a first aid kit was brought over and two of the guards started treating him before I could ask. Krein stopped beside us. "So this one's your sister?"

Mandy stepped away, brushing away her tears, burrowing under my arm closer to me.

I nodded. "She is." She stiffened next to me, and if she could get any closer to me, she would've. She was terrified of him. I was about to ask if Samuel needed an ambulance when the door on the opposite end opened.

Everyone stopped. The guards froze. Krein's light-hearted attitude fled, and I turned to see who had entered.

Jace. He was dressed in black cargo pants and a black shirt that clung to him. A gun was holstered on his side and he held a radio in one hand. He looked at the group with one glance and scowled. "Get 'em out, Krein. No parties. Not tonight."

"Jace," he started.

He wasn't listening. He started towards the door Krein and the group had come through. "I mean it. I want them out. Now."

Krein called after him, "Even Matthews?"

Jace was reaching for the door, but stopped and swung those piercing eyes my way. He didn't say anything for a moment. Then Tray stepped up beside me. "We'll get out of here as soon as we get our friend."

Jace narrowed his eyes and started for us. "Evans."

Tray gave him a tight nod in return. His gaze met mine for a second. I felt his warning in them again, but he turned and went to Samuel. The group helped him to his feet and then towards the exit door.

"My friends were here," I told Jace. "That's the only reason I'm back. I'll leave as soon as we have them all."

Krein asked, "I thought this was all of them?"

"We have one more."

"My brother," Amber spoke up. "Can I go with you?"

Krein waited for Jace's approval.

He nodded. "Take her with you, find her brother, and then get *all* of them out of here." He was staring right at me as he stressed the word all. I clamped my mouth shut, feeling a burst of anger. I wanted to say something. I didn't, but I wanted so damn much to tear into him.

Amber headed after Krein, but she turned around and her eyes raked Jace up and down. When she finished her perusal, she ducked through the door. The noises from the club filled the room for a moment. It faded when the door shut once more. I looked around. Mandy had gone with the group out the exit door. The guards went with Krein. It was only Jace and myself.

He didn't waste time. "Did you really only come because of your friends?"

I flushed and narrowed my eyes at him. "Are you calling me a liar? It was my sister, Jace. You know how I am with family loyalty."

Unlike him. That was the unspoken message. He received it, and his glare lessened. Then he asked, his voice softer, "Are your friends okay?"

"I don't really care about any of them except my sister." I paused. "And Tray."

"Evans."

It wasn't a question from him, but I nodded. "Yes. He's my friend."

"I told you to stay away from him—"

"The second you threatened to have me shot is when your advice was no longer wanted." I wanted to hurt him like he had hurt me. "Tray's never hurt me like you have."

He laughed, shaking his head. "I see your verbal skills are still intact. You haven't gotten too soft over there in white picket fence land."

"Fuck you."

The words were out of my mouth before I could hold them in.

He barked out another laugh. "I have a lot I can say on that one, but I'll keep it to myself." His radio sounded and Krein's voice came over, "We got him in the back." Jace lifted it and spoke into it, "I'm sending

172

Taryn back to you." Then he pointed to the exit door. "Your friends are out there waiting for you. Go away, Taryn."

I flinched. It didn't hurt any less than the first time. A lump formed in my throat, but I refused to accept it was there. Screw him. I swept past him. "I hope Brian continues to hate you. I hope he hates you so much that he doesn't want anything to do with you and leaves town, just like I did." I got to the door and started to push it open.

"So do I." His words stopped me.

Then I shoved through the door. The pain mixed with fury and I stopped just outside the door, bent over, and took gaping breaths. Then I brushed away the tears and headed to the back parking lot. Everyone was waiting for me, everyone that mattered now.

CHAPTER FIFTEEN

Samuel was taken to the hospital. Mandy cried into Devon's arms, and Jennica rolled her eyes. Grant was fine. He'd been in the bathroom the entire time. No one asked what he was doing in there, but Amber remained by his side. Tray gave me a ride to the school and I went home in my own car that evening.

That was a week ago. Shelly and Kevin decided it was family weekend so Mandy wasn't allowed to have friends over. They looked at me, ready to say the same warning, but it died in their throats. I snorted. I saw it on their faces. The same thought had flashed in both of their minds: Taryn doesn't have friends. That was fine with me, though. After seeing Jace again, I was fine with some hibernating. When we went to school the next week, things remained quiet. A few others remembered my stand-off with Amber and were confused when the fighting hadn't continued. I had to laugh at that. Her plan to get revenge backfired.

It was the next Friday when Mandy told me her and Devon were back together. I wasn't surprised. She was an idiot, and I realized my sister would continue to do idiotic things. Did she enjoy hurting herself, because that's what this would do to her. He was going to cheat again. She would be hurt. She would forgive him, forgive Jennica again, and the cycle would continue.

I was done. I washed my hands of my sister. When she told me about a party that night, I had no intention of going. I went home instead. Austin was downstairs and I could hear other voices, including a few girls.

"Hey, honey," Shelly said as she bustled around the kitchen.

I hopped onto a stool. "What are you doing?"

"Austin brought a bunch of his friends home. He never acts like it, but it means a lot to him if I prepare food for them." She put a grocery bag on the counter and threw me a grin. "Gotta do it, all those kids like to eat, you know."

I grinned. "He got a girlfriend down there?"

Shelly laughed. "That's my thinking too. Maybe we should 'investigate' later, hmmm?"

As she took out a pan from the oven, she washed her hands and then pulled out pizza dough. "You're making homemade pizza?" I had never had homemade pizza. That was what normal people did with their normal parents. This was my family now.

"It's Austin's favorite. Mandy's too before she decided her life was a diet. They have the same tastes in a lot of ways. Pizza, lasagna, but now Mandy loves salads. Poor thing." Her eyes lit up. "So, Taryn, you and I haven't had a lot of alone time. You're not going out tonight? I know from Mandy that there's always a party going on."

I looked away. "Yeah, there is."

"No party for you?"

I shrugged and turned back. She was staring at me, a slight glimmer of concern there, but she gave me another soft smile. There was pity instead. I hated seeing that. "You know, I could have friends."

175

The pity disappeared and she straightened from the counter.

I added, "Just because I grew up in the foster system doesn't mean I'm less than anyone else."

"Taryn, I didn't mean—"

"I'm here tonight because I want to be, not because I don't have friends or I wasn't invited to the party. I could go to any party I want. You might think to ask yourself why your adopted daughter is staying home and your real daughter isn't?" As soon as I said those words, I cursed in my head. There was a fine line and I didn't want to narc on Mandy.

Her hands fell away from the pizza dough. "What are you talking about?"

"Nothing. Never mind." I had to get out of there. Shoving off the stool, I went upstairs and grabbed my swim suit. I was heading back downstairs when the doorbell rang and Shelly came back with a stack of delivered pizzas. She saw me on the stairs and laughed. "Teenagers don't want to wait for homemade pizza." She put them on the counter and yelled down the stairs, "Austin! The pizza's done, guys. Come and get it."

I had enough time to step out of the way when Austin and five pubescent boys and three girls rushed upstairs, zeroing in on the pizza in record time. The girls were slower, looking at the pizza with caution. I knew how they were feeling. They wanted it, they were salivating for it, but being skinny meant not eating, *especially* in front of boys, who were inhaling the food without chewing.

"Hey, your sis is hot, man!" one guy said as he stuffed an entire slice in his mouth. He nudged Austin. "You never told us that."

The girls stared at me.

"Shut up, dick," Austin retorted, wiping his mouth.

"Austin," Shelly reprimanded. She tried to look stern. She failed. The adoration she had for her son was evident.

"Whatever." Austin rolled his eyes. "Mom, where's the soda?"

"Oh. I'll go and grab them. I left them in the car."

He leaned back to wait.

Uh, no. I spoke up, "Why don't Austin and all his friends go and get them?" One of his friends stood next to me and his hand was too close to my ass. As I said that, I shifted away from him. He looked up, saw he'd been caught, and his head went back down. He shuffled away, but I saw the smirk on his face. He was another little punk.

"Oh, come on!" Austin cried out.

"Go," I ordered. They went, but Austin flicked me off—it was becoming his favorite gesture—just as they slipped out the door. I didn't even waste my time wondering if Shelly saw that. She wouldn't reprimand him anyway so I turned to the girls. "Grab your pieces and head downstairs. I'll hold them off for a while."

They didn't wait a second longer. They grabbed their pizza and ran downstairs.

"Well," Shelly gave me an appraising look, "I didn't even think of that."

"I'm a girl and I remember what it was like when I was that age."

Pretty soon, the guys bounded back inside, each with a twenty-four pack in their arms. Unloading them on the counter, they grabbed another piece of pizza, but I tapped one of the boxes. "These can go in the pantry, where the soda *always* goes." I gave Austin a pointed look. The kid was testing the boundaries right now; he knew where they went. Shelly was letting him get away with it.

Grumbling, Austin showed them where to go—half of the guys knew where they went anyway—and when they came back, I saw his hand slowly raising, his finger was inching upwards…

"If that finger touches the air, you're computer's going to come down with a virus and all your porn's going to be gone."

The finger stayed in place, and the hand was lowered back to his side, but he still glared at me. The rest of the little dudes inched away from me. The one who tried to touch my ass suddenly looked like the pizza had gone down the wrong tube.

"Whatever." Austin shrugged, grabbed the rest of the pizza, some soda, and headed back downstairs.

Shelly was fighting back a grin and burst out laughing the second they were around the corner. "Oh, dear. I shouldn't be laughing, but I've never seen Austin handled like that. I've never been able to get him to do anything."

I gestured to the door. "I'm going swimming. I'll be back later tonight."

"Oh. You swim?" When I didn't stop to answer, she yelled after me, "Okay. Have fun!"

The water felt great. No one else was there and I took longer than normal. I lost track of my lap count after the first hour and when I finished an hour later, I saw a guy sitting at a table in the corner. Pulling myself out, I went to grab a towel, and said to him, "That's not creepy."

He was in an area that wasn't lit so I couldn't make out who he was, but I saw his teeth when he smiled. He stood and came over. As he drew closer, I noticed he was wearing a Rawley High School staff shirt with a whistle around his neck. He was in his mid-forties, trim, with specks of grey mixed in his black hair. He nodded to the pool. "You're a good swimmer. Is that the fastest you can do?"

"No. That was fun tonight."

"Can you go faster then?"

"I can go a lot faster."

He nodded, narrowing his eyes at me. Then he said, "I'm the coach. Our season is starting up soon. Can you try-out?"

"I'm not into team sports."

"Yeah, but swimming doesn't have to be all-team. You do your own thing and I see the fight in you. My gut is telling me you want to try-out because you want to see if you're the best."

"I doubt I'm the best. I just started swimming again."

"Yeah, I'm still going with my gut. You've got an itch in your eye. You're a fighter. Swimming for fun, alone, on a Friday night won't satisfy you for long. We've got try-outs Monday. I'll pitch you against my best swimmers. You can tell me then if you're interested or not."

He nodded again, going to an office door in the corner. Before he shut it behind him, he said again, "Try-outs are on Monday. Here. 4:00. I'll see you then."

I wasn't going to do it. I already knew I wouldn't, but I couldn't shake his words. He had a gut feeling. I was a fighter. I wouldn't be satisfied with swimming alone. Maybe... No.

I stopped thinking about it. When I got home, the house was dark. The lights were still on in the basement, but I went upstairs. It wasn't long until I heard Shelly take Austin's friends home. When they returned, she told him in the hallway, "Go to bed, honey. I'll give you a ride to Patrick's tomorrow." Then she knocked on my door. "Taryn?"

"Yeah?" I was at my desk and I closed my computer when she opened the door.

She smiled, skimming over me. She leaned her head against the door. "How was swimming?"

"It was good." I tried to suppress the small surge in me when I saw her warmth. My throat swelled up. "The swim coach was there." Why did I tell her that?

"Really? Coach Hayes?"

I nodded.

She gave me another tender smile. "He's a good man. He's a good coach too. Did he talk to you?"

No other foster parent had been interested in my swimming. The fact that she was even asking questions sparked a longing in me that I hadn't known was there. My voice was hoarse when I said, "Yeah. He invited me to try-outs."

"Oh good. That's great, Taryn. Are you going to try-out?"

"No." I shrugged. "I don't know."

"I think you should. I think sports are always a good idea. I know you aren't that fond of Mandy's friends, and if you're on the swim team, you might meet other girls like you. Who knows. Maybe they like swimming for the same reason you do."

"Yeah. Maybe." My chest was so tight. She seemed so interested. I was having a hard time remembering why I'd been angry at her before.

"Okay, honey." She came in, smoothed back my hair from my forehead, and pressed a kiss there. "Have a good night. When Mandy gets in, let her know that I have to take Austin to Patrick's early in the morning. They have a tournament this weekend."

"I will." My throat was still so full. I could barely get my words out. She left and I closed my eyes. A tear slid free. I let it go. I never had an adult care before. My chest tightened and then I wiped another tear away. I tried to ignore the fear I was feeling. They adopted me. They must love me. This wasn't a charade. I kept telling myself that when I got ready for bed and laid there, staring at the ceiling. It wasn't a charade. They really did love me.

My phone buzzed and distracted me. "Hello?" I didn't want to analyze why I was glad for the distraction.

"Hey, where are you?" It was Mandy.

"At home."

"Mom and Dad home?"

"Yeah. Everyone's in bed. I don't know where your dad is and your mom said to tell you that she's taking Austin somewhere early tomorrow morning."

"Thank God." She breathed in relief. "Listen, if Mom and Dad ask, tell them I came home late and left early."

"Are you at Devon's?"

There was a moment of silence on the other end for a moment. "Are you going to be mad if I say yes?"

"No," I muttered. "You already know how I feel."

"Yes, I do," she said, "but this is my decision."

"I know, I know. I'm just looking out for you, you know. We're sisters and all," I mumbled. All this family stuff was new to me.

"Okay," she trailed off for a moment. "I thought you'd be at Tray's."

"No." Since we went to the Seven8, things had cooled between Tray and me. I wasn't sure why, but I hadn't been ready to tackle that either. We were at a standstill. I hadn't seen him around other girls and I had kept to myself too. "He wasn't with you tonight?" Then I heard a muffling sound on her end. "Is that Devon?"

"Yeah. Amber and Erin are here too. We just ordered some food."

"Who's Erin?"

"A friend of mine. She's on the student council with me," Mandy replied, her voice half-turned from the phone. "If Mom asks, tell her what I said. I came home late and left early. Tell her I went running. She's all about exercising."

"Alright, I'll pass along your lie to Shelly." I paused a beat, frowning to myself. "Watch Devon. Make sure he doesn't cheat on you with Amber or that Erin girl tonight."

"Taryn!"

I hung up, rolled over, and stopped thinking about everything.

The next morning Shelly woke me up, a frazzled expression was on her face. "Taryn, I have a huge favor to ask of you."

I scrambled upright. "Mandy went running this morning. She came home late and left early."

"Oh, okay," Shelly mumbled. "Can you give Austin a ride to Patrick's? He's packed and ready to go. Kevin called. He's waiting for me at the airport. He needs me to go to a workshop with him. I won't have time to take Austin."

Oh. Relief flooded me. I nodded and got out of bed. "I'll get dressed and take him."

"Thank you so much, Taryn. The neighbor will stop in every now and then to check on you guys too." She pressed a kiss to my forehead. "I don't know what we would do without you."

I frowned, but she was gone in an instant. I found Austin outside, waiting on the curb with a sullen look on his face. He was dressed in athletic clothes and his bag was beside him, a basketball in his hands.

"Hey, punk. Need a ride?"

He glowered at me for a moment and then stood up, following me to my car. As I pulled out onto the road, I asked, "So, another workshop, huh?"

"This one's in Switzerland." He slumped down in his seat. "They're going to be gone for three weeks. It's a month-long conference, that's what Mom said."

"And your dad?"

"He's an asshole," Austin mumbled, looking out his window.

I dropped him off at his friend's house. When I started to get out and go inside, he pointed to the mini-van in the driveway. "They're waiting for me."

I stayed in my car. "Okay. Have fun. Call me when you're back."

He nodded, his shoulders were slumped over, but when he got to the mini-van, the cockiness came back over him. When I pulled away, I mused to myself. No middle finger again. We were making progress.

CHAPTER SIXTEEN

I was sitting on the front step when Tray pulled up to the house. As he strolled over, he turned to survey the street. Then he twisted back and arched an eyebrow. "Are you people watching or waiting for winter?"

I laughed. As he sat next to me, I scooted over. His legs pressed against mine. I didn't scoot over that far. "I like to people watch. Austin's at a tournament. The folks are gone and Mandy's with Devon. What else should I do?"

His voice dropped to a soft whisper. "Hang out with me?"

My heart slowed. Even with those four words, I was affected by him. Excitement and warmth began to build in me and a small shiver ran through me. It was a good shiver. I hugged my legs to my chest and rested my cheek against the top of my knees. Turning to him, I flashed him a smile. "After this week of friendliness?"

He laughed softly. "It was you too."

It was. We had both been circling around each other. I let out a sigh. "It's that time, isn't it?"

"What is?"

"You and me."

He frowned, but his eyes darkened to an amber color. "You and me?"

I nodded. "We were going to be assholes, right?"

He laughed, raking a hand through his hair. "We aren't being assholes anymore?"

I shook my head, but I couldn't wipe the grin off my face. "Maybe we could try. We can be true to our asshole insides."

"You're such a bitch," he teased.

I teased back, "And you're such a dick."

He nodded. "You'll never change, will you?"

"I'm all about being selfish. It's only what I want. Everything's about me."

He tried to keep a straight face but failed. A grin slipped out. "We'll never have a future like that."

"I know." A laugh was moving up my throat. I kept my lips pressed tight and tried to swallow it. When the other corner of his mouth curved up, my laughter almost boiled over. I sputtered, keeping it in. "You're such an asshole."

He ran a hand over his face. The smile was forced away and a blank expression looked back at me. His eyes sparked in amusement. "Don't try to change me."

I barked out a laugh, but silenced it. "Don't try to change me."

"Still an asshole. I stand by that."

"I do too." My head lifted up and down in a nod.

"Good." He snorted from a choked laugh, but widened his eyes and put the blank wall in place. "So we're on the same page again?"

"I think so."

He put his arm around my shoulders and pulled me against him. His tone softened. "If we're still going to do the asshole thing, are you up for Crystal Bay?"

"What's that?" His hand dangled off the side of my shoulder and I reached up, lacing our fingers together. I leaned into him. In that moment, I didn't feel so alone.

Squeezing my hand back, he answered, "It's a cliff over the river. There's a cave and a waterfall there. A lot of us like to go and jump from the top. It's pretty nice, actually." He hesitated. "A bunch of us are going."

Of course. I should've known. "Mandy?"

He nodded. "She'll be there."

When he grew guarded, I asked, "Were you with them last night?"

"I stopped by. They were having a movie night. I just went to see if you were there."

There it was. That same shiver wrapped all the way around me. I was beginning to forget what it felt like to not have this feeling around him. I was too far gone. At this point, I only hoped that I wouldn't be crushed at the end of it. Whenever that would happen. My throat swelled.

"You'll still come?"

I nodded. "Yeah."

"Good." He squeezed my hand once more. "But I have to warn you, there's a lot of others coming too."

"Oh god."

He laughed.

"Not the student council, yearbook committee, and cheerleaders?"

"Don't forget the basketball team and football team."

"Why not invite the entire school?"

His chest was shaking from repressed laughter. "It pretty much is." Then he hugged me. Both of his arms folded over me and I was moved so I was sitting on his lap.

I turned so I was facing him. My legs wrapped around his waist and my arms wound around his neck. Closing my eyes, my head tucked into the crook of his neck and shoulder. This wasn't a sexual hug. This was one of comfort and security. No matter our joking conversation before, I was realizing that he was mine. I didn't know the definition or terms of how he was mine, but he was.

He hugged me back and we sat there for a while longer. I didn't want to leave, but when we did, it was later, much later. Tray asked me to pack a bag, just in case we went somewhere else after the bay. When we got there, I was glad I had. He hadn't been lying. There were twenty cars parked on the road. I glanced at him when he parked. "Something tells me this might be an all-day event."

He nodded, getting out of the car. As I did, he said over the top of the car, "They talked about grilling at my house tonight."

I should've known. They didn't party last night so, of course, they would tonight. I shook my head as we started down a trail to the beach. "Is there a requirement that there has to be one party every weekend?"

Tray laughed, leading the way. "At least one. Most want two, though."

I shook my head, but then we got to the bottom and I saw the cliff part. I stopped, speechless for a moment. Crystal Bay was a cliff that jutted out into the river. Large boulders and rocks sat around the opening of it and waves crashed onto them. I had known the river was big, but I hadn't realized how big until I saw the power of those waves. They slammed onto the rocks before retreating back into the water, only to come back with renewed strength.

Tray started up the rocks. He glanced back and lifted his hand. I shook my head. "I'm a cat burglar, remember?"

He flashed me a grin. "That's right. I forgot your illegal ways." When we headed around the mouth of the cave, voices from inside drifted out. They echoed off the cliff walls, growing louder as we got closer. The light grew dim, but it was still manageable. A moment later, the light exploded and filled up the entire interior of the cave. A waterfall fell into the middle of the cave into a pool of water. As we rounded the last curve of the cave and stepped into the clearing, someone yelled out, "Hell yeah!" before they dove down from the top and into the pool at the bottom. The splash sent shrieks from the girls sitting around the edge of the bank.

It was a party inside a cave. I drew next to Tray and asked, "I'm surprised there's no deejay."

He laughed. "Dylan tried to lower down speakers one summer and ended up ruining his entire stereo system." He gestured around the cave. Almost everyone was in their bathing suit. After the guy who had jumped pulled himself out of the water, he went over and shook his hair out over a group of girls. They shrieked, but I could tell by the looks on their faces that they enjoyed it.

"Taryn!" Mandy waved from the opposite corner. Since Jennica and Amber weren't with her, I told Tray, "I'm going to head over and say hi."

"Okay. I'm going up top." As he headed for the side of the cave where people were climbing up, his hand brushed mine. He flashed me a grin over his shoulder.

I sighed. He had slipped under my skin. He was inside and the more time I spent with him, the deeper he burrowed into me.

"Taryn!" Mandy called again.

I ignored her. I couldn't take my eyes from Tray. He stripped his shirt off and dropped it on the ground. As he did, the muscles in his back rippled from the movement. He was gorgeous. Every inch of him was perfection. Then he started up the makeshift ladder. There were steps carved into the wall. He climbed up them, grabbed hold of the rope that was attached from the top, and hoisted himself up, his feet going to the rocks that stuck out from the wall. The last few feet looked like they were the hardest. He pulled his body up and stuck his hand in the air. He was grabbed from on top and hauled up the rest of the way.

"Taryn!" Mandy waved at me again. "Hey! You made it."

"Yeah." I grinned at her. She was drenched in a white bikini, but she was smiling. She looked happy. "I'm here." I was going to keep my mouth shut about Devon. It was her life and her suffering that she was signing up for.

When she latched onto my arm, I smelled alcohol. "That's so awesome. I wasn't sure if you would come, but I'm happy you did. You have no idea. I love you, Taryn. I really do. You're like my sister now."

"Okay." I untangled her hand from my arm and pushed her back a little. "You've been drinking."

Her cheeks were red, and she started giggling. When she couldn't stop, she clamped a hand over her mouth.

189

"You've been drinking a lot."

Mandy doubled over, still laughing, and reached for her drink. As she took a sip and kept drinking, one of the other girls spoke up, "Want a drink? There's some coolers they lowered down from the hole." She pointed to a corner. "Dylan brought a pony-keg, but it's on top. Half the guys are up there."

I saw mostly girls were in the cave. The guys were jumping from the top and climbing back up. As I watched another one make his way up the side of the wall, I asked, "No girls can climb up?"

Mandy was still laughing, curled up in a ball now. Her friend saw my frown and laughed nervously. She said, "A lot of girls are scared, plus you have to pull yourself up using the rope. That'd be really embarrassing if they couldn't get up, you know." She shrugged. "We mostly just come through the base like you did and hang out."

My frown deepened. "That's bullshit. Someone could bring a ladder so the girls could have fun too."

"This is fun." She shrugged. "Enough for me."

It wasn't. I muttered, "Not to me."

"What?" Her eyes widened. "Are you going to try it?"

I nodded. Damn straight I was going to try. This was what I did. If there was a wall, safe, lock, or any barrier put in front of me. I would tear it down. Standing up, I noticed people had grown quiet as I approached the wall. Someone whispered behind me, "No girl's made it all the way up there, have they?"

Another whispered back, "No and shut up. I want to watch this."

Ignoring them, I gritted my teeth and started up. My feet covered the first steps easily. I held onto the rope as Tray had, pulling myself up as the spaces between the rocks grew wider and wider. I was almost there. I could feel the breeze from up top and could hear the boys laughing up there. They didn't know I was coming up. They pulled Tray up, but they'd been watching for him. They were so loud, they wouldn't be able to hear me if I called out. Then I glanced down. Every single person below me was watching. Mandy was pale. Her hands were pressed to her open mouth. Amber and Jennica moved out from a corner. Both were waiting for me to fall and they crossed their arms over their shoulders. Smug smirks appeared on their faces.

I grew harder in my resolve. I'd go it alone. With that thought, I gripped harder on the rope and wrapped it around my arms and shoulders so if I slipped, my fall would be slowed enough I could stop myself. The rope burn would hurt, but I was going to tackle this one way or another. Wrapping the rope around my leg, I looped it so my foot fit into a small pocket and then I began to climb. When I broke into buildings, it was rarely a full-out climb like this, but I had done it on a few occasions.

I kept going. All of my muscles were stretched tight and they began pulsating as I held my weight, then climbed up one handful at a time. As I neared the top, the guys still didn't know I was there. My head had almost cleared the surface. I heard someone shout from below, "Help her!"

I glanced down, surprised. It was Mandy's friend. She stood to her feet and walked to the edge of her bank. Giving me a thumbs-up sign, she cupped her hands around her mouth and yelled again, "HELP HER!"

"Yeah!" More girls clambered to their feet and stood with her. They all started hollering. "Help her! You helped the others."

Mandy's hands fell from her mouth, but it still hung open. She was gazing around the group. Amber and Jennica shared a dark look, their mouths in flat lines. I grinned at them. That made this even more satisfying, and with that last burst of adrenalin, I used it for momentum and clambered up. My head broke the surface.

All the guys were sitting in a group around the keg. Their backs were to me. I rolled my eyes, but grasped the rope at the top and pulled myself the rest of the way. When I was at the top, the bottom broke out in cheering and clapping. The guys heard that and turned. A few jumped when they saw me. "Holy shit."

Tray moved around the group. His eyebrows shot up, and he began shaking his head. He came over to me. "Why am I surprised? I shouldn't be." He helped me up and patted me on the back. "Want a drink?"

I shook my head. Ignoring the stunned looks from the guys, I turned and headed towards the opening of the waterfall. "I'm jumping. I came up here to have fun and that's what I'm going to do."

He nodded, moving back. His eyes were full of approval as they roamed over me. I climbed up in my clothes, but took them off now so I was standing in my bathing suit. It wasn't meant to be a show, but with all eyes on me, it was one. Even now, as I stood there, a few girls had went over to the wall. They were assessing if they could do it too. Then I lifted my arms up and jumped. As I soared down into the water, a sense of liberation went through me. I was alive. I did what I wanted. It was a freeing moment. Then I pulled myself up from the pool of water and went right back. My body was aching from the swim last night and the climb, but I was going again. Then again. Then again. I would go until I was done having fun.

I started back up when Mandy's friend came over. "You're going again?"

"Yeah. You could too, you know."

Regret flashed over her face and she shook her head. "I can't. I can't pull myself up at the top." She lifted her arms. "These aren't strong enough."

I shook my head. "Start up after me. I'll haul you up the rest of the way if I have to. They do it for the guys. They can do it for us too." Fierce determination came over me, then I heard a mocking tone.

"When did you become all about women's lib?" Amber folded her arms again over her chest. Mandy's friend melted away, so did a lot of the girls, and Jennica took their place, coming to stand beside her friend.

Mandy frowned. She started forward, but stopped. Fear flashed in her eyes. Jennica and Amber saw her too. We all waited to see if she would speak up. She didn't. Her head went down and she sat back with her group.

That pissed me off. When I saw the smug looks in Amber and Jennica double, I gave them a polite 'fuck off' smile and asked, "Care to give it a try? Women's lib or not, it's a rush to jump from the top."

The smug smirks disappeared. They shared another look, but this was one of matching hesitation. Then I smirked this time. "Yeah. That's what I thought." With that last parting shot, I started to climb again. When I got to the top, Tray was there. He reached down from the rope, but I shook my head. I had a point to prove. "No, I have to do this alone again."

He saw Jennica and Amber and nodded. "Okay."

He was there when I finished and drew me against his chest. Hugging me to him, he dropped a kiss to my lips. We were in plain view of everyone, on top and down below. I didn't want to think about who would be pissed or who would be surprised. I answered his kiss, deepening it, and knew in some way this was giving Jennica and Amber the middle finger. When I pulled back from him, Tray caught me. His hand cupped the back of my neck and his forehead rested on mine.

The climb and diving back down had my blood pumping. The adrenalin was addicting, but it didn't compare to this. His thumb rubbed back and forth over my neck in a soothing motion, giving me goose bumps. Whatever unspoken agreement we had before, the joking banter we shared earlier in the afternoon, was done.

Tray was claiming me in front of everyone.

CHAPTER SEVENTEEN

It was later, when it was growing dark and everyone was packing, that one of Mandy's friends came over and stood next to me. She didn't say anything, just gave me a smile and ducked her head down. I wasn't used to shy girls, and she hadn't been shy earlier so I asked, "What's up?"

"Um..." She paused and flashed me another grin. "Everyone's going to Rickets' House. I mean, we're going to Tray Evan's house first, and I'm sure you're riding with him since you know, the kissing." She gestured to the top of the cliff. A look of awe appeared in her eyes. "But...um...I was wondering if you're going tonight to Rickets' House? You do your own thing, but some of the girls are going to your house to get ready with Mandy..."

I made sure no reaction appeared on my face, but my insides were going, 'what the fuck?' "What are you asking me?"

"Um..." She gulped. "Are you going out with the group tonight?"

"Oh." I shrugged. "I don't know. I guess."

"Good."

"HALEY!"

She looked around and then motioned to her group of friends waiting at the front of the cave. "I guess I'll see you at Rickets' House. I'd say Tray Evan's house, but people probably won't get out of their cars. If you don't have a ride, you can ride with my friends and me. We'll make room, but I'm sure you're probably going with…" She trailed off as her eyes widened, looking past my shoulder. When I felt an arm come around my waist, I realized why she was so nervous. Tray pulled me snug against his side, and she lowered her head. "I'll see you later, Taryn."

She darted off and I glanced to him. "What was that?"

He grinned. "You changed the status."

"What?"

"You changed the status." He gestured around. There were more groups lingering behind. Most of them were watching us. I expected jealousy or condescension, but there was none. There was a different look in their eyes, guys and girls. They weren't in awe; they were something else. I couldn't put my finger on it.

"I don't get this. What's going on?"

"I know it's dumb, but no girl's climbed up there. You did it more than once and you got other girls to do it." He shrugged, a look of pride in his eyes. "They're surprised, Taryn." Then he laughed softly. "And they're wondering why the hell they hadn't done it themselves."

"Oh." They were surprised. As I looked over, a few of the girls gave me smiles before they followed everyone else. A couple of the guys gave me quick nods. I'd seen that look before. It happened when guys learned that I knew Jace or I was able to steal something no one thought could be taken. It was respect, but seeing it from the girls now made me pause. Girls hated me. That had been the rule, but it was changing now. A lump formed in my throat and I swallowed around it. Jeezus, where did that come from?

"You okay?"

I nodded. "Yeah. Just…surprised too."

He grinned down at me, a fond look appearing in the depths of his eyes. "Something tells me you shouldn't be. It's you, Taryn. You're badass."

I snorted and elbowed him in the stomach. "Right. Is that you trying to get in my pants?"

He laughed softly as he caught my elbow and held it in his hand. He thumb started to rub over it in a soft caressing motion. "No, just me stating a fact. You're not normal, Taryn Matthews. You're different. You're someone who sees the right path when no one else does and follows it." The corner of his lip curved up in a slight smirk. "You show them the way. You're not normal. Thank god." He let the last sentence out in an exhaled breath.

I had no idea what to say. The shock at seeing their reactions doubled after hearing his words. Tray meant it. If I'd been in Pedlam and the school's golden-prick said something like that, I would've laughed in his face, delivered a retort, and sauntered away without a backward glance. He wasn't that guy. He was more.

Then he let go of my elbow. "I'll wait for you at the car. I need to talk to the guys quick."

I tried to say 'okay', but he was gone before I could get a word out. As he weaved through the crowd and left from the cave, I was left with a storm raging inside of me. I pressed a hand to my stomach, trying to calm myself. My god. It was him. He was wreaking havoc on me, filling me with emotions that were too scary for me to handle. Hope. Warmth. Other things, other emotions that I didn't know how to process. He made me feel safe. That, right there, set me on edge. I couldn't be safe. I couldn't allow myself to pretend it was real. Every time, as soon as my guard dropped, something bad happened. Tray Evans was nothing special. The second I let myself feel more than I should, something bad would happen. It always did. I couldn't let that happen. Drawing in strength, determined not to let him get too close, I began to follow the line of people out of the cave.

I was standing behind a group of guys. They were tall with bags over their shoulder so I was hidden. As we kept going, a pair of voices trailed back to me.

"Can she be any worse?"

"I know. Honestly. I was trying not to gag."

The first one muttered, "You know she didn't sleep last night. She was at Devon's all night."

The second one groaned. "Trust me. I know more than the rest. He's a sex addict. He's got to be."

"My god. And she was so fucking hyper today."

"You know she was creaming her pants when Tray kissed Taryn up there." Another groan. "I don't know what she expects. She's treated her sister like crap—"

"Please," the first one interrupted. "She is not her sister. They adopted her and from what I heard, they were forced to adopt her."

A sick laugh trailed back to me. "You're right. I forgot that rumor. Whatever. That's a ridiculous rumor, but god, I'd love for that to be true."

"Yeah. I know. Did you see Mandy hanging all over Tristan's group today? If she wants to pretend to be Queen Bee in that group, she can try. Tristan's going to kiss her ass to try and get close to Matthews. You know she's been wet for Tray since seventh grade."

"I know. What was Mandy on today?"

A snort. "Must be nice to have a rich daddy with a prescription pad."

"I know, right? I wish I could pop a pill every time I feel like taking a nap."

"Ugh. You know that bitch hasn't slept a full night in months. She takes those pills from her daddy, and she sleeps for maybe two hours. Must be nice."

"I know, right."

"I'm having a hard time trying to be nice to her. Please tell me I can't sleep with Devon tonight. Please tell me that's not the right thing and we need to be nice because of her and her wacko sister. Please tell me to do the nice thing. Amber, help me out, because I really want to cause havoc in their lives."

Amber chuckled. "You do whatever you want. What kind of friend would I be if I held you back?"

"Oh god. This could get ugly tonight."

The two laughed and moved further away. I wasn't able to hear them anymore. I felt like someone had punched me in the face. They were forced to adopt me? Mandy was a pill popper? I frowned, feeling the blood drain from my face. That couldn't be... There was no way.... Then I closed my eyes. I couldn't process this. Mandy. Tray. Even Austin. Those were all good things that had happened. An old ache took root in my stomach and I felt a hole open there. It was vortex, sucking all the good emotions into it, leaving me feeling hollow.

"You're Matthews, right?"

"Huh?" I lifted my head and blinked. I realized that I had stopped and was now the last in the cave.

A guy from school was frowning at me. He was waiting at the mouth and he waved for me. "Come on. You're the last. Most everyone's taken off already."

"Oh. Okay." I hurried forward, but I was too dazed to focus on walking over the rocks. I wasn't paying attention and a moment later, I was out of the cave and on the road again.

"See you." The guy gestured farther down the road before he hopped in a car that was waiting for him. The door was opened and as soon as he was inside, it took off. His friends yelled out, "Hell yeah! Party at Rickets' tonight." Their sounds faded and I turned to see Tray waiting for me.

He was standing by his car, his arms folded over his chest. His head was tucked down and he could've been asleep from how casual his posture was. He wasn't watching me, but I knew he was alert and aware of my approach. When I stood in front of him, he lifted his head. His eyes were guarded.

For a moment, we stared at each other.

The air was thick. There were so many emotions inside me, all of them were swirling around to form a vacuum. He terrified me. He always would, but as I continued to hold his gaze and as his wall began to slide away, I saw the same fear in him. Then an emotion flickered in me, so deep that I was surprised to feel it at all. Hope. It swept through me, a small flicker that grew to a full flame and it mingled right alongside the empty void that had been placed there from overhearing Jennica and Amber's conversation. Tray must've seen the pain in me. His wall fell away completely and he lifted an arm, beckoning to me.

I went to him.

He wrapped his arm around me, sheltering me, and even though he had no idea what was wrong, he pressed a kiss to my forehead. Brushing some of my hair aside in a loving gesture, he comforted me.

I didn't like depending on people, but I would for a moment. I'd allow myself this pause in my normal living to be weak.

Tray held me for a while longer. He didn't ask what was wrong. He knew me well enough to know I would tell him when I was ready. After standing there, hugging him back, allowing myself to be comforted, I swallowed and pushed the storm down inside me. He felt it and stiffened. His arm fell away the same time that I moved back from him.

We continued to look at each other, then he nodded. As he went to the driver's door, I went to the passenger door and we both got in. He drove me home. We still didn't talk. The farther we got from Crystal Bay and the closer we got to town, I slid down in my seat and watched the scenery go by. I had conversations ahead of me. I knew all of them were going to be painful, but I needed to find out the truth.

If my adopted family had been forced to adopt me, then why? By who? I needed to find that answer and I needed to find out about Mandy. I loved her already. It wasn't until then, at hearing my relationship with her might be a farce, that I realized it.

When Tray pulled up to my house, I saw the other cars. The curtains were pulled back so I was able to see into the kitchen. It was full of Mandy's friends. Assuming these were from 'Tristan's' group, from what I overheard, I prepared myself for weirdness and ass-kissing.

"You okay?"

I glanced over. The concern in Tray's eyes was evident. I nodded. "I just heard some things that I have to deal with."

"You need help?"

I shook my head. "No. This is on me." A shriek of laughter came from the house and I looked over again. They were all giggling, moving around the kitchen with drinks in hand. A girl was filling their glasses with more wine.

"Okay. Everyone's heading to my house tonight to go to Rickets'. Are you coming?"

"Yeah." Then a plan began to formulate. "Can you pick me up? Everyone's meeting at your house, right?"

He frowned but nodded. "Sure. When everyone takes off, I'll just let them know I'm going to swing by and pick you up first."

"Okay."

"You didn't want to get a ride to my house with your sister?" He leaned down so he could get a better view of my house. "Although, they look too drunk to drive anyway."

There was one girl who looked sober. She was thin with white-blonde hair, and she stood out among the group. She'd been the one pouring wine into the glasses. I was willing to bet she was Tristan. It was obvious she was the leader. She stood with confidence. Her shoulders were straight. Her chin was lifted, and it looked like she was watching over her minions. I hadn't paid attention to Mandy's friends earlier, but despite the distance between the house and car, I could tell she was pretty. She had a heart-shaped face, small petite looks, and higher-set cheekbones. I was starting to suspect she was a rival to Jennica and Amber in the looks department. All three girls were beautiful.

As I continued to study Tristan, I said to Tray, "No, they have a sober driver." I looked to him. "I need Mandy out of the house. I have to look for something when no one else is around. The timing is too good for me to pass up."

He nodded. "Okay. I'll send the group ahead without me and I'll wait outside until you're ready."

"Okay. Thank you."

"I hope everything's okay?"

I gave him a fleeting smile. "So do I." I got out of the car and headed in. I had been exposed to a hornet's nest and I was going to step right on it.

CHAPTER EIGHTEEN

I understood the drug life. It wasn't because I took drugs. It was because I had taken care of someone that did. Brian. Standing in front of Mandy's room, all those memories flooded back. I had taken him to rehab twice. Jace took him the last time, and he had kept clean so far—so far. He might've relapsed, but I had no idea. A small knot formed in my throat as I realized that truth. Brian wasn't my concern any longer. Mandy was.

When I left Tray's car and went into the house earlier, I played nice. I stood around. I joined in with the fake banter, fake smiles, and fake politeness. The truth was that I wanted to tear upstairs and demand to know if it was true. I held back and when the girls started to leave, I shook my head. No, I didn't need a ride. Yes, Tray was picking me up. Yes, it was wonderful. Yes, we were together. I had frowned as I said that, but he did kiss me in front of everyone. I knew it meant something, even though there'd been no actual conversation between us.

That could wait. Finding out Mandy's secret was my priority now, and with that thought, I reached forward and opened her door. It swung open, showing her pink picture frames, her desk, her pink laptop, and her queen size bed with its beige bedspread. She had her own bathroom attached to her bedroom. That was where I headed first. Pushing past the nagging feeling that I was violating her trust, my jaw firmed. My hands clenched.

I began searching.

As I did, the storm of emotion inside of me calmed. The anxiety, the fear, the tension, the need to demand answers—all of that silenced, and as I opened her bathroom cabinets, my hands didn't shake. I moved with purpose. Each drawer was looked through. Underneath the drawers were explored. On top of her mirrors, then every corner in the room was felt for any loose tiles or framing. I felt inside her Kleenex boxes, on the inside of empty toilet paper rolls. I lifted her garbage, then took the bag out to make sure nothing was hidden beneath it. I ran my fingers over every dip and turn of the toilet, feeling the screws to make sure they weren't loosened.

Nothing.

The closet was next. Thick hangers were examined to make sure nothing was taped to the opposite side of it. I lifted the closet dowel itself and ran a hand over the end, no opening had been carved into it to hide drugs. Each shoe box. All of it. Every pocket, every inch inside of her clothes, under the soles of her shoes, there was no space unexplored by me.

I felt the door frames and doors themselves, making sure no room was carved out. The knobs were tested to make sure they weren't loose. I found nothing so I turned to the bedroom.

Brian hid his drugs in a small box under a patch of carpet. I wondered if Mandy would do the same, so I looked at the corners of the room, making sure there was no slack in the carpet. There was none. She couldn't lift any corner of it. The bed was next. Each blanket and sheet was lifted, then investigated. The pillow case and pillow were too. Then I checked the mattress, still nothing, so I flipped it over. Nothing was taped to the underside of it. I moved that aside and rested it against the wall, then turned and studied the bed frame. Nothing.

After I put it all back and remade her bed, I went to the desk. Nothing. Her dresser was last and I found nothing there.

I sat in the middle of her room. It was all back in place. Each picture frame was adjusted exactly how she left it. She would have no idea how deep her room had been searched by me. Maybe it wasn't true. Maybe Jennica and Amber were being spiteful and jealous, but even as I thought that, I shook my head. "No, it can't be." They weren't lying to each other. They were telling the truth. I had heard it in their voices. They didn't think anyone could overhear them. The guys that were between us didn't care and they knew that. That meant it was true. Mandy had a stash. I knew it.

My phone buzzed in my pocket then, and I looked at it. It was a text from Tray: **Outside. Take your time.**

I sent a reply to Tray, telling him I'd be out in five minutes. As it sent, I stood. I needed to grab my things, but when I turned for the door, a shadow behind her curtain caught my eye. They were light-colored, thin enough to let some light through, but as I went closer, I saw it. A small box was pushed in the corner. The words 'PRIVATE' were on top in pink, glittery letters. A lock was attached to it, but I used a bobby pin I found in the bathroom and popped it open within seconds. Lifting the lid, there were three rows of prescription pills. As I looked through them, I read the labels. Ritalin, Vicodin, Xanax.

A heaviness settled over me. It had been hovering over my head as I searched the room, but it now rested on my shoulders. Studying the bottle, I notice that Dr. Parson prescribed each bottle to her. Whether he was aware of it or not, her own father was her drug dealer. I had no idea how to handle this. If it had been Brian, I would've packed up his bag and taken him straight there. The idea of waiting and talking it out with Shelly and Kevin wasn't an option. It wouldn't get done. Whatever was going on with this family, I couldn't keep lying to myself. I wanted a family. I wanted something better, and they had given it to me, but this was wrong. They were never home.

I packed a bag for Mandy. I put enough clothes and toiletries in it to last a week, then I tucked it in my room. Mandy was going to rehab tomorrow, whether she wanted to go or not. Brian had denied his problem. He had accused me of having the problem. He yelled. He pounded the walls. He broke chairs. Then he broke and started to plead. There were tears every time, but I made him go in every single time. He had to. So did Mandy. Whether this family wanted me or not, I loved her. I would do what I needed to take care of my sister, even if it meant protecting her against herself.

As I got into the car, I didn't say anything.

He was studying me. Then he asked, "Are you okay?"

I shook my head. "I will be." And I would.

Rickets' House was busy like it always was. Cars filled the parking lot and were lined up on one side of the driveway. Groups of people were walking to the party as we passed. One guy signaled at Tray and said, "The lot's full, but you can try, man."

Tray nodded and lifted a hand in thanks, but he still turned into the driveway and through the parking lot. A car was pulling out, so he pulled in, but instead of getting out right away, he looked over at me. I knew what he was going to ask, so I said first, "Mandy has a drug problem." Then I waited. A moment of silence lingered between us. I sighed. "Did you know?"

"I heard rumors. I didn't know for sure." He paused, then murmured softly, "I'm sorry."

I jerked my head in a nod. Whatever. My sister had a problem. "Yeah, well, she's going to get help. I'm going to make her get help."

"I have no doubt." He reached over and squeezed my hand. "I'll help you in any way I can."

"Good." Relief flared through me. "I might need to stay at your place."

"Sure, but why?"

"I'm taking her to rehab tomorrow."

"When are Shelly and Kevin getting home?"

"Does it matter?"

He frowned. "No, I guess not, but what about Austin?"

"I'll bring him with me." I lifted a shoulder and let it fall in a helpless motion. "I don't know what else to do. They took me in, but there's something off with this whole situation. I'm taking Mandy to rehab tomorrow. I'm making that decision without their consent. I don't feel quite right staying in their house."

"You don't think they would approve?"

"I have no idea." That was the truth and the admission hurt. "I have no idea what they would do. But this is what I have to do."

"Okay." He squeezed my hand again. "Austin will flip when he sees the gaming system and you can stay as long as you want."

"Thank you."

"What you're doing is the right thing to do. You're a good person."

Shit. That sent a host of emotions through me and I grinned at him. "Now I just want to jump you."

He gave me a half-grin. "I've still not gotten those pants off. I'd be game."

I laughed, but I had no witty comeback. I didn't think he expected one. With another soft squeeze of my hand, we got out of the car and headed up the hill to the house. As we drew closer, people looked over. I stiffened, remembering the last time we were there, but then realized people were watching Tray. Then I had to laugh at myself. I forgot who I was walking in with. It was Tray Fucking Evans, and he was holding my hand.

When we went inside the house, Tray went for the keg and I spotted Mandy. She was sitting on Devon's lap. Her arms were curled around his neck, and she was pressed against him. Even as I started for them, his hand slid up her thigh, lifting her skirt. A smug smirk was on his face as he nuzzled Mandy's neck. The sight of them made my stomach churn, but I wasn't surprised.

Stopping next to them, I waited until Devon became aware of my presence. He lifted his head from her neck and grinned at me. "Hey, Taryn."

"Taryn!" Mandy squealed, throwing herself off his lap. Her arms were in the air, and she grabbed me. She was jumping in place as she hugged me. "I'm so glad you got here." With her face pressed against my neck, her voice came out muffled. Leaning back, I saw her eyes were dilated and she had a dream-like smile on her face. "I'm so happy for you and Tray. That's so awesome."

I frowned and glanced at Devon. "How much has she had to drink?"

"Nothing." He lifted his shoulders in a shrug. "Whatever she had at the house. Some of the guys went to get shots, but we haven't made it to the kitchen yet."

"I didn't think you drank that much at the house," I said to her.

She started laughing. When she couldn't stop, she covered her mouth with her hand. The laughter kept coming and she bent over, her shoulders shaking. "I'm sorry," she gasped. Her head flew back up and her cheeks were bright red. "I didn't. The girls drank all of Dad's wine, but I didn't have any." She looked to Devon. "Why can't I stop laughing?"

A faint grin was on his face. It was clouded in concern, but faded to pure amusement. Tugging on her hand, he drew her back onto his lap and wrapped his arms around her again. His head bent back into her neck and he said something, which sent a renewed wave of laughter from her, and she shook her head. "Devon!" she shrieked.

She was on something. "Hey." I tugged on her arm. "Where are your friends?"

Her laughter faded and the glazed look in her eye lessened. She tried to focus, chewing on her lip. "Um...Jen and Amber?"

"No, the ones you were with at the house earlier."

"Oh. No idea." She sent me a blinding smile and turned back to Devon.

I raised my eyebrows. "Some Tristan chick? Where is she?"

He frowned a little, starting to pick up the serious tone in my voice. "They're outside on the patio. Is everything okay?"

Mandy was still giggling, sucking on his neck. I glanced down at her, frowning, and said, "No, it's not." I headed for the patio. As I did, I heard Mandy say, "Taryn? What's wrong?" But I kept going. When I got to the patio, it didn't take me long to find Tristan and her group. They were in the corner. The girls were sitting on the laps of guys. As I approached, Tristan looked up. When she saw me, a bright smile beamed back at me, and she waved. "Taryn! Over here."

I had to laugh. Two days ago, this girl would've laughed behind my back and called me a whore. Even if she wasn't friends with Jennica and Amber, she was close to their ranks. I could see it. Her group of friends were all beautiful, catty, and snobby. I didn't know how I had missed them in the school hierarchy, but I shouldn't have been surprised. I didn't give a shit about ninety-eight percent of the people at school. When I saw Stephanie Markswith perched at the end of one of the couches, I shouldn't have been surprised. She sat in a timid manner. Her shoulders were hunched over, and her arms were crossed over her chest. She was on the outskirts of the group with no lap to sit on. I could tell she was the lowest one on the totem pole with this group. I smirked at her. Without anything spoken, I knew this was the group she was trying to get 'in' with. They were the next rung on the social ladder for her. She looked up and saw me then glared.

It seemed ages ago when she spread the first rumors about me. Things were much different now. She couldn't touch me.

I grinned. "Still not over your boyfriend wanting me instead of you, huh?"

"Taryn!" Tristan beamed up at me.

Stephanie looked ready to strangle me, but she ducked her head and never said a word.

As soon as I was within arm's reach, Tristan took my arm and pulled me closer. "Is Tray with you?"

"Yeah, he went to get drinks."

"Wonderful." The beam kicked up a notch.

I frowned. I was tempted to let her know that ass-kissing worked better when it wasn't obvious, but I held my tongue. Instead I asked, "My sister is wasted in there. How much did she drink at the house?"

"Oh." She seemed taken aback by that question, but shrugged it off. "I don't think she had any. I gave her a glass, but I don't think she drank it. The others drank enough for both of us, I guess." Her eyes switched so they were more focused. She had a goal. "Does Tray know how to find you? We can make room for both of you here." She scanned their corner. There was no room. The entire couch was packed tight. She lingered on Stephanie. Her lips pressed together, and my smirk came back. She was thinking about asking Stephanie to leave, for Tray and me. I loved it. Stephanie realized the same thing because an instant frown appeared and she sat upright, watching Tristan back. A look of disbelief was on her face and her mouth fell open an inch.

Tristan must've rethought it. She turned back to me. "We'll make room somehow."

I waved, dismissing her. "Don't worry about it. I got what I needed to know. Thanks."

When I turned to leave, she called after me, "Wait."

I glanced back.

Her mouth was hanging open this time. "Uh, I thought you guys could hang out with us?" She closed it and another fake smile plastered on her face. "I mean, I know you're not friends with Jennica and Amber. I get that. Trust me, I do. We could talk and plan their demise." She laughed a little. "I'm just kidding. They're friends with Mandy. I'd never do anything to hurt her—"

I almost rolled my eyes as she said that last statement. That meant she had considered doing something to them. I was all for that, but she kept going, "—I'm so happy her and Devon worked things out. Aren't you? I think it's great. Those two are going to get married. I'm calling it now."

Gritting my teeth, visions of Mandy's future flashed in my head. He'd cheat on her. She'd catch him, cry about it, threaten divorce, and would go back to him. The cycle would be on repeat for the rest of her life. "God, I hope not."

"What?"

I paused and realized I had said that out loud. Tristan was frowning at me, and from the corner of my eye I could see that Stephanie was grinning like a mad fool. What was she smiling about? But, instead of dealing with Stephanie, I said to Tristan, "I said, 'God, I hope not.'"

Tristan's eyes got big. "You don't like Devon?"

"I don't like the idea of Devon and Mandy. He's a cheater. He always will be."

"Oh."

I could tell she had no idea what to say, but it didn't matter. I didn't like her. I already knew we would not be friends, whether she knew it now or later didn't matter to me. I started to turn back for the house, but stopped again. The crowd had shifted, and I got a glimpse of the backyard for a second. Wait… I moved forward. Tristan said something, but I didn't care what she was saying. I kept going. As I got closer to the edge of the patio, the crowd moved again. I saw him again, and my stomach dropped.

It was Brian.

CHAPTER NINETEEN

He was sitting on a picnic table. His feet were resting on the seat and he was focused on a girl that was standing between his knees. Wearing a black shirt, he was almost camouflaged against the night's darkness. His black hair blended in, but then he smiled. My heart started to ache. I remember when he used to smile at me like that.

Without thinking, I started for him, but someone grabbed my arm and pulled me back. "Don't."

Tensing, I rounded with a snarl, but it fell away. "Gray?"

A tense look was on his face. His hand dropped. "I'm sorry. I saw you talking to your friend, and I was worried you'd see Brian. Don't go over there, Taryn. Let it go."

"Why?"

His lips pressed together. "Just take my word for it. Don't go over there. He's in a better place since he got kicked out of Evans' party. If you go over there now, it'll set him back. Please."

It killed me. I loved Brian. I still did, but hearing Gray plead on his behalf, he was right. If I went over there, I would've hurt him. I opened my mouth, ready to agree when I stopped. A guy approached Brian, and they exchanged something. I got a glimpse of money folded into a big wad and then the guy left. Brian returned his focus to the girl in front of him once again. He ran his hands up and down her back, settling on her hips, tugging her even closer so she had to kneel on the seat. As they started kissing, I turned to Gray.

His eyes were stricken and held mine.

I gestured to Brian. "That was a Rawley guy."

Gray's shoulders dropped, his head went down, and he cursed.

As he shoved his hands in his pockets, I continued, "Brian hates Rawley students. Why would he give a shit about that guy?"

Brian gave him something. The guy paid for it. My mind was racing as I connected the dots. When it all clicked, I groaned. "Please tell me you're not going to say what I think you are."

"Taryn."

I shook my head. "Tell me that Brian isn't working for Jace, that he's not selling drugs, and that kid wasn't a paying customer just now." My heart was pounding and my chest tightened. "Please goddamn tell me that I have this all wrong, because if you don't, I am going to flip out."

Jace never wanted him involved, I repeated over and over in my mind as betrayal formed in my gut. He promised never to involve Brian, but now he was. A defeated look came over Gray. Shaking my head, I started for Brian.

"Taryn, no."

I shook off his hand. "No, Gray. I have to confront him now." With each step, the anger and hurt bloomed brighter in me, but there was another emotion. This was going to be goodbye, but this time it was for real. I had tried telling him goodbye so many other times, but as I got closer, I realized that I never accepted those because I knew Brian would still fight to be with me. He wouldn't anymore. He had moved on with his life, and I saw that now.

"Don't." Tray got in my way, holding two drinks in his hand. Judging from how he glanced at Gray and then to Brian, I assumed he figured everything out.

"You knew, didn't you?"

His shoulders were tight and his mouth was pressed in a flat line. "Yeah, I did."

"How?" Goddamn. I wanted to yell. I wanted to throw something. Eyeing the drinks in his hands, I was tempted to overturn them on him. I didn't, though. I let him see the anger in me instead.

His eyes narrowed. His jaw clenched. "He was expelled from Pedlam. Then I heard he got back in. Seeing what went down just now, I'm assuming he's the new drug connection in their school."

"How do you know this?"

"I hear a lot, Taryn."

There was more. I could see it in him, but he was holding back. I closed my eyes and cursed, rubbing my forehead. A pounding headache was forming. "I am going over there. I am going to have my say to Brian and then I'm walking away. I'm done after this, but you and I are going to have a conversation later."

"I have no doubt." He never looked away.

I felt like I had been smacked in the chest again. My heart stopped, just for a second. Tray wasn't holding back from me. A weird form of excitement began to fill me, but I shook my head. I didn't have time for these lovey-dovey feelings. Brian was watching us now.

His head was up. His eyes were alert, but he was wary.

I knew, right then and there, that Brian had never been my equal. I didn't know how to explain it, and I didn't know if I wanted to, but it never would've worked with us. We weren't meant to be. Sadness took root in me. Leaving the one who was my equal, I headed towards my past. A lump formed in my throat. I'd have my say and I wouldn't look back any longer.

The girl was glaring at me when I got to them. I glanced back over my shoulder. Tray remained behind me. A guarded expression was on his face, but I was thankful he stayed back. I said to Brian, "Tell her to take a hike."

She gasped, and her face scrunched up in anger. "Excuse me—"

He patted her hip twice. "Get lost, Dee."

"What?" She twisted back to him, and her mouth had dropped open. "Are you serious?"

He nodded to me. "I have *business* to attend to," he said, stressing the word business.

She shut up. "Oh. Okay then." When she stood up, she glared at me again. "Watch your hands, honey." As she walked away, she ran right into me.

I hid a grin. I had been ready for her move. As her shoulder collided with mine, I had locked my body up so I was unmovable. She bounced back off of me and gasped again. Muttering, "Fat-ass," she melted into the crowd.

I laughed. My body was solid with muscle, and no one could call me overweight. I wasn't skinny, but I was slender, and I knew guys loved my curves. Then I stopped thinking about her and locked eyes with Brian.

It was time.

"You're working for Jace?"

"No." His jaw clenched. "I'm working for Galverson."

"Same thing. Jace is your boss."

"Jace's boss is my boss."

I snorted. I couldn't believe we were having this argument. "That makes no sense."

He shrugged. The irritation vanished and a sullen look came over him. "Does it even matter? Jace doesn't want me there, but I am. So what? What do you care, anyway?"

"I care," I said softly. "I care a lot."

He flinched. "Yeah, well..." He turned his head away. He clasped his hands together, still leaning forward on his knees, his jaw clenching. "What do you want, Taryn? You're going your way. I'm going mine."

That was the crux of it. A sadness like I hadn't experienced in a long time came down on me. It settled over me like a heavy blanket, wanting to pull me down to the ground. "Yeah. Looks like."

"It is." Anger flared in the depths of his eyes. After a moment, it was banked, and he forced himself to calm down. "I'm doing my thing. That's what you wanted. I don't know why you're over here. I'm not your business anymore. Just like he," he nodded towards where Tray was standing, "isn't mine. Let it go, Taryn."

"Jace never wanted this for you. I don't understand—"

"You don't have to. Let it go." His eyes were cold, bearing down at me.

"I still care."

"It doesn't matter. We're through. We were your family, but you got a new one."

I grimaced. "I wouldn't say they're a family."

219

"Whatever. A new crowd. It's a new life. This is what you wanted. When I wouldn't walk away, you argued for this. I'm giving it to you now."

"Yeah, but," I gestured to his hand, "I know what you gave that guy. You're dealing for Jace."

"I'm not—"

"For Jace's boss. Same thing."

"Stop."

I had stepped close to him and his hands came down on mine. I glanced down and was surprised to find my hands were under his, resting on his knees. I blinked and stepped back. When had I reached for him? Then Brian's soft murmur distracted me as he said, "I'll be fine. Nothing will happen to me. This," he dangled a packet with white powder inside from his hands, "will give me that security. I don't need to be a Panther or Jace Lanser's little brother to make a name for myself. I'll be fine, Taryn. I will. I have it all covered."

He didn't. He *so* didn't, and my heart hurt even more because of it. I shook my head. "You're so stubborn. You always think you know what you're doing."

He sat upright, straightening his back, and a cold wall fell over his face. "I'm taking care of my own back. That's what you're doing, right? You got handed a brand spanking new family. Do us all a favor and pretend you don't know us anymore."

A harsh laugh rippled up from my throat. It was out before I realized I was even laughing. When it registered, I couldn't stop it. A small note of hysteria mingled along with it. I couldn't stop that either.

Brian frowned. He looked ready to say something. Concern filtered in, but then he masked that too. "Just go, Taryn."

I jerked my head in a nod. My neck muscles were tight and I felt like I was breaking tendons as I nodded, but I tightened my jaw and forced my head up and down. I would be fine. Fuck him. He was going down the wrong path. Not me. He would be the one who got screwed in the end... I couldn't stop it. I couldn't protect him anymore. That had been my job for so long. I turned, but I couldn't stop myself from murmuring, "I wasn't given a family. They were forced to take me in." I began walking away. I didn't stop, even as I got to Tray, I kept going.

That was my last exchange with Brian. I knew it and it had gone horribly wrong. I didn't stay at the party. When Tray offered to drive me back, I shook my head and asked for his keys. He wouldn't let me drive alone so we compromised. He drove me home, but we didn't talk the whole way. When he dropped me off, I didn't ask if he was going back. I didn't want to know, not at that moment. I wanted to sit and be alone. Brian was really gone from my life. I didn't know how I knew for certain, but I did. After pulling Mandy's suitcases down to the kitchen, I sat and waited for her. This was something I could do, someone that I could still protect.

I waited until the morning. It was after six when she was dropped off. When she came inside, she looked haggard. She had bags under her eyes. Her dress was plastered against her. The smell of cold sweat clung to her, and her lips were swollen while her eyes were dilated. When she tossed her keys on the counter, she took one step, saw me, and stopped. Her eyebrows bunched together and she lifted a hand, scratching at her head and messing with her hair before she asked, "Taryn? You're up?"

"I made coffee." I pointed to the coffee pot.

"Oh." She glanced over and frowned. "Okay. That's a weird thing to say. Um," she kept frowning, then shrugged, "I'm going to bed."

She started for the stairs, then saw the suitcases and stepped back. "Uh, Taryn? What's with the luggage? You going somewhere?" She seemed to reassess me. "I heard you had words with your ex. Did something really bad happen between you? You think you're in danger or something?"

No, not me. "I'm not going to beat around the bush. I suck at that stuff." I watched her. I wanted her to see me and see how serious I was. When she did, she kept frowning, but a small amount of fear filled her eyes. "I found your stash."

I let that hang in the air between us.

When she realized what I meant, her eyes went wide and her shoulders stiffened. Her mouth fell open. "You had no right. You searched my room? Who do you think you are—"

"You are eighteen."

She stopped, confused by what I said.

I stood from the table. "You have a problem." She opened her mouth. I knew there was an argument on the tip of her tongue, but I held a hand up. I kept going as she fell silent again. "I know you're going to try and justify it. You're going to tell me that your dad knows and he doesn't care. Or you'll tell me how it's perfectly fine; you just use them when you need extra energy. I don't care."

I felt dead inside. Mandy saw it and the façade fled away. She wasn't going to deny it, but I saw the storm beginning to brew inside her.

I added, "Those are your bags."

"Excuse me?" she asked, her voice low and deadly.

I stepped closer and lowered mine to the same pitch. "Those are your bags. They're packed because I'm taking you to a rehab facility. Unlike your parents, I give a shit. You're lying to yourself every time you take a pill and you know it. You're so full of lies, I don't think you know what's right anymore. It's right to leave a boyfriend when he cheats on you. It's right to be angry when he cheated on you with your friend. It's right to demand better friends, better relationships, better parents who give a damn. Those are the right things to do." Jeezus. I stopped and forced myself to calm down. Anger was coursing through me, setting me on edge. I wanted to rip into someone and bleed them dry. I realized that I was saying those words to myself as well, to the little girl in me. The one who wanted to be loved, who wanted a mother like all the other girls had in their lives, who wanted a regular home and didn't have to be locked inside her room since she was a flight risk.

I had been lying to myself too.

Closing my eyes, I turned away. I hung my head and forced myself to see the truth. I wanted that so much that I hadn't acknowledged the truth. Shelly and Kevin were never home. They were polite, but that was it. They didn't care. They didn't want me there. They weren't the family I thought I had been gifted. Gritting my teeth, knowing this was all a lie forced on me, I whipped my head back up.

Mandy fell back a step. The color drained from her face.

"I love you," I said, forcing my tone to soften. "Because of that, I'm taking you to a facility. None of your bullshit will work on me. I've gone this route too many times with Brian. I won't go through it again. Because you're not fighting as much, I know you're early in the process.

You can be helped, and you have to be helped. Mandy, you have to be." She was my family. "With this fucked-up situation, you became my sister. So I'm here and I'm fighting for you. Take the bags, Mandy." Please. I mentally prayed. She needed to go of her own choice. I couldn't force her to go so I pleaded. "I'll drive you and I'll help you."

"Taryn?"

Her voice cracked and a tear fell down her cheek. I saw the shame. It flared over her face and then she hung her head.

That was when I knew she wasn't going to fight it. I stood there, shocked. Brian always fought. He denied. He yelled. He threw things. Then he would cry and he would plead and he would beg me not to leave him. Mandy did none of this. She went straight to crying, and she crumbled on a chair by the table.

CHAPTER TWENTY

I was still in shock at how easy it had been to convince Mandy to go to rehab. She didn't say much on the car ride there. She sat, slumped down, and cried most of the way. As we filled out the paperwork and sat in the lobby, she still didn't say much. The counselor came out for her assessment and she followed him into the office without a backward look to me. After that, she was admitted. As they led her through a back hallway, I could still see where they were searching her bags. That was when she looked up and I saw a frightened little girl staring back at me.

The counselor spoke her name, but Mandy looked haunted. I narrowed my eyes, wondering if she was more scared of herself than of going into rehab. Then he touched her arm and she looked away. The small window she had given me to see inside of her closed up. Taking her bag, she followed him and I couldn't see them anymore.

When I left, with a doctor's note to give to the high school administration, a ball of emotion was in the bottom of my stomach. It wouldn't move. How I drove home, I had no idea. I was on autopilot and I stayed like that for the rest of the day. Tray texted to see if things were fine. I told him to expect Austin and me that night. I waited for my little brother to get back from his tournament. When he did, I picked him up. When he saw my face through the car's window, he stopped walking. He was dressed in low-riding, baggy athletic pants and a large jersey with his earbuds in his ears. Someone yelled goodbye and he lifted his hand, but it was an absent-minded farewell. As he came closer and got inside, he didn't say anything for a moment. He tugged his earbuds down and then asked, "Where's Mandy?"

I studied him before I replied. He was fourteen. I could tell he was popular. He was athletic. His friends were good-looking and wealthy. He was jaded. He didn't have the innocence most others did at his age. Weighing all of those factors together, I knew Austin wasn't dumb. "I took Mandy to an in-house treatment facility."

His eyes narrowed. "What does that mean?"

I didn't hold back with my answer. "Your sister has a drug problem."

"How do you know?"

I hid a grin. He wasn't fighting me. I heard what he hadn't said. "My ex used to be a drug addict. I just know."

He jerked his head in a nod. "She's at some place getting help?"

"As long as she stays."

"What do you mean?"

"She signed herself in. She can sign herself out."

"She can do that?" He snorted and leaned back in his seat, plopping his head back against the headrest. "She'll be out by tonight."

"Maybe." I hoped not. "If she does, they'll call. You can still talk to her."

He rolled his eyes. "It won't matter. This shit's been going on forever."

"What do you mean?"

"Mom and Dad took her in last summer. It didn't do anything. She came out and was popping pills on the drive home. It was a joke."

I frowned. His words rocked me. They had known? "The bottles I saw were prescribed from your dad. Why would he continue to do that?"

"He doesn't. He cut her off a long time ago. I bet she just uses them to store the pills in there."

She got the pills somewhere else…that information seared through me. She had another drug dealer, and her family was forced to take me in. I didn't think those two items were random. In my life, I learned there weren't many coincidences. As I drove home, I knew that I would have to go see Jace. He didn't want me there, but I didn't care. I was going to find out some answers. When we headed inside, I told Austin to pack a bag.

"Why?"

"It doesn't seem right to stay here, not after I took Mandy in without your parents' permission."

He frowned. "Oh. Wait a minute, if they don't know, how are you paying for this?"

I had no idea, but I wasn't going to admit that to a fourteen-year-old. I shrugged. "I'll figure something out. Go pack a bag."

"What about nosy neighbor?" He gestured to the house next door. "I think Mom was going to have her stay with us a couple nights, you know, to 'check' on us." He laughed. "We could just leave a note. She doesn't care anyway."

"Oh." He was right. "The neighbor is the least of our problems. Go get your bag."

He started up the stairs, but paused again. "Where are we going?"

"We're staying at Tray's."

"At Tray Evans'?" He smiled widely, blinding me. He added, "That's awesome. We're staying till Mom and Dad get home?"

"Or if Mandy leaves rehab."

The smile fell right away. "Oh. Yeah." He darted to his room, and I heard him shoving things into a bag.

As I waited for him to finish, I pulled out my phone and dialed Tray's. When he answered, I asked, "Is it still okay if Austin and I stay at your place?"

"You already asked and yes." He paused. I could hear his hesitation before he asked, "Are you okay?"

"I will be." I was angry. I was more than angry, but my voice was tight and controlled as I gripped the phone. My hand clenched around it. "I have to run an errand tonight."

He didn't say anything at first. "Should I ask what the errand is?"

"No."

"Taryn, I don't like it."

I didn't care. "Tray, someone messed with my life. I have questions that I need answered, and I will get them." At any cost.

"Just be safe."

Hearing Austin's door slam and him barreling down the stairs, I said into the phone, "I gave you a second chance to back out. Too late. We're heading over right now."

"Sounds good."

"Okay." I moved to end the call when I heard him say, "Taryn?" I pressed the phone back to my ear. "Yeah?"

"Be careful."

My heart skipped a beat. Those two words were spoken with intensity and tenderness, but it was the raw emotion in them that had that alien feeling blossom again in my chest. It was another one of those moments when he spoke and his words went right into me. He could do that, more and more lately with just a look or a touch or a word.

That, in itself, was a whole other issue that I didn't want to tackle at that moment. Instead of feeling vulnerable and stripped open, I was going to take on a fight that I could handle. Jace Lanser.

I drove Austin to Tray's, dropped him off, and then left. Tray waved from the door, and Austin didn't seem to care if I went inside with him or not. He was happy. I still didn't know why, but I wasn't going to question it. Then I drove towards Pedlam.

I wasn't going to call Jace. I wasn't even going to walk across the alley and try to get through the guards. For this conversation, I wanted to surprise him and if he wasn't around, maybe that was even better. I could snoop around for my answers.

Jace had been kicked out of the house when he joined the Panthers. When their dad died, he moved back in to watch over Brian and me, since I was there so much, but I knew he still had his own house. Knowing that, I debated if I should head to his house first or gamble and try my luck with his office at the Seven8 first.

I decided to gamble.

Standing across the back alley, down the block from the nightclub, I saw it was another busy night for the establishment. The security guards were busy and as I was watching, two guys began fighting near the door.

This was my shot. Knowing I only had a couple seconds, I sprinted down the alley and then pressed against the wall of the opposite building. I could hear shouts from around the corner. A crowd formed and more guards rushed from the side alley, running around the corner. They ran right past me, and after the last one shoved open the door, I jerked forward. I slipped through the opened door and immediately stepped behind the door. Two more guards rushed out, passing by where I was hiding. When they were gone, I heard shouts from inside—more guards were heading my way. I heard a voice yell over a radio, "Three fights! Get it under control!"

From farther down the hallway, someone answered, "On it, boss. Six more were dispatched."

"We do not want the cops called."

"On it." Then static came over the radio and it grew in volume; they were getting closer. The hallways were lit up. The lights were bright. I had nowhere to hide. The door closed. I couldn't open it or they would be suspicious so I hurried to the light switch. When they were right around the corner, about to turn towards the door, I plunged the hallway into darkness.

I had a small window again, and I sprinted for them, keeping on my toes to be silent. As they stopped and cursed, I pressed against the wall, moving past the first one's elbow as he reached for his belt. A flashlight switched on and I melted backwards, keeping to the darkness.

Jace didn't like when we were in his territory, but I'd been in his office a few times. Going to the back exit doors, I knew they weren't alarmed like the others. His office was at the top corner. When I got there, the floor was in the dark. Good. That meant Jace wasn't there.

There were two doors on the whole floor. One was a large set of doors and the other was further down. It led to a small back room. I headed to the latter. Jace liked having his office next to the stairs that led to the roof. It was a better exit, if necessary.

The room was locked, but I pulled out two pins from my pocket and bent down to work on it. It didn't take me long to unlock the door. I knelt down and blew under the door. He could have another security measure, and I was wondering if he had sensors set up on the other side of the door. Nothing happened so I felt around the entire doorframe to see if any other secret paneling would spring open. He'd been known for having secondary alarms installed, but when nothing opened for me, I stood back and frowned. It couldn't be that easy. Still. I took a breath and opened the door. I'd have to risk it. When I stepped inside and nothing more happened, I let out that breath.

So far, so good. I eased further into the room. No secret alarms flared up or went off. I sat down at his computer and typed in his daughter's name. Not many people knew about his daughter; Jace didn't even know I knew about her. It worked. I began looking for anything that tied Jace to Kevin Parson. I knew he had something to do with my new adoption. I needed proof before I confronted him about it.

"How do you know that name?"

His sudden voice, low and deadly, set the hairs on the back of my neck upright. I froze, my fingers poised over the keyboard, my heart pounding, before I looked over. Jace was standing in the doorway. He was dressed all in black. A black t-shirt hugged his body, outlining his ripped torso. It wasn't tucked inside his black cargo pants, but hugged over top of the waistline. I saw the bulge in the front and knew he had

231

tucked a gun there. My mouth went dry. Did he have other guns? My heart sped up. I couldn't believe I was nervous about his guns. Six months ago, he'd been family.

"Jace," I started, cautious, as I stood from the desk.

A lethal storm had taken over his face. His jaw clenched as he stared back at me. "How, Taryn?"

I licked my lips and tried to keep myself calm. I needed to think rationally around him, especially when he was acting like a caged animal. Somehow I had stepped into the cage with him. He was ready to spring, and I had no idea what he would do.

"How, Taryn!?"

I jerked back, slamming into his desk from my movement. It cut into my arm, but I didn't feel it. I didn't dare look away from him. "You printed out an email from her mother. It fell from your pocket one day at the house."

His eyes went flat. "Tell me the truth. Now."

Shit. "There *was* an email you printed out. I just found it one night in your pants."

He took a step towards me. I could feel the danger radiating off him. It was coming off of him in waves. "What were you doing going through my pants?"

"I wasn't snooping on purpose—"

"Not like now."

I flushed. "I was looking for a condom. Brian ran out. We knew you would have one."

He cursed and moved the rest of the way into the room. Shutting the door behind him, he turned the lock and pressed a code into a compartment beside it. I chewed on my lip. I had completely missed that. As he pressed the right buttons, the red light turned green and then yellow. He had armed it. It would go off when I left, drawing the guards to the top floor. I stored that in the back of my mind, but then he looked back at me as he took his gun out.

"Jace." My heart was pressed against my chest. It felt like it was trying to break out of me.

"Stop." He shook his head and moved to the table. He put the gun down, then stripped his shirt off. As he turned, his muscles moved, and his skin glistened from sweat and dirt. He reached for a clean shirt that was laid on the table and pulled it over his head. It was another black one, hugging every inch of him. He glanced back over at me, his eyes were still dead, but the fear in me went down a notch. He moved away from the gun. Instead of coming towards me, he went to the far wall and leaned against it. His head went down.

I didn't dare say anything. I had to wait for him to start.

"I keep telling you to stay away and you keep coming back." His head lifted, his eyes pinning me back in place again. "Why, Taryn? No bullshit lies. Tell me why right now or I'll do something you won't like."

Anger spiked in me, but it mixed with fear. I read the threat in his eyes and knew it was true. He really would do something. A shiver went up my back. I didn't want to find out what it would be. "Did you set up my adoption?"

"Yes."

My eyes widened and my eyebrows shot up. A gutted laugh spilled out of me. "I hadn't expected that honesty."

He tilted his head to the side, narrowing his eyes. "Why? Because you're so honest with me?"

"What are you talking about?"

"You sent Brian on a mission when you should've come to me first."

"I did not. What are you talking about?"

"He came around asking a lot of questions last night. He wanted to know about your family. He went to anyone who would talk to him. Word got around." He stopped. Pure agony flashed in his eyes and my alarm shot up again. He wasn't saying something. I knew it. There was more to come and I started to shake my head.

"I never said anything to him."

"You told him about your family. Why did you say anything to him?" His voice was strangled and it stopped in a whisper. The anger left completely and I saw only pain in him. It hurt to see. It was deep and there was so much. I felt it in myself, just from seeing it, and I turned away. I didn't want to hear what he was saying.

I said, "Whatever Brian did was on him."

"It's on you."

I stopped, then gulped. What did that mean?

"He didn't come to me, Taryn. He doesn't want anything to do with me anymore. He went to others, and *they* went to others. I was told too late."

"What?" I shook my head. "What are you talking about?"

"He said your family was forced to take you in. He wanted to know the social worker that put your adoption together." His chest lifted and I heard the pain in his voice. His voice hitched on a sob. "That's a government worker. Do you know what happens when there's rumors a drug dealer wants to talk to a government worker?"

"No, no, no," I started whispering, starting to put the pieces together. *No, no, no.* I couldn't think anything else. There was no way.

"They didn't come to me. He didn't come to me. I was too late."

"No, no, no." I kept shaking my head.

"He's dead, Taryn."

No, no, no, no, no, no. I heard what he said, but I couldn't accept it. It couldn't be. I had talked to him twenty-four hours ago. He had been fine. "He's fine."

"He's not." Jace's eyes looked dead. "Trust me, he's very far from being alive."

"No…" I couldn't talk. Burning pain filled me. It washed all over me, branding me as each wave crashed over me. I couldn't think anymore. I could barely stand. "No…"

I heard Jace's voice from a distance now. "Kevin Parson owed me a favor. I cashed it in. I needed you out of here. Do you get that? I wanted you gone. I gave you something you wanted, a family. I handed you a better future on a silver platter and you refused to take it. What THE FUCK were you thinking? Just take it. That's all you had to do. Sit down and accept your new family." His voice rose as he kept going, "I don't give a shit if they don't like you. You shouldn't either. You have a home. You have a sister that I can tell you already love. You could've just accepted your new life, but you kept coming back. You kept asking fucking questions, questions that I knew you would ask even if you were here. My god, Taryn." His head fell back down. An anguished sob came from him. "Why couldn't you have just let it go?"

TIJAN

Brian wasn't dead. I wouldn't accept that. There was no way. "How do you know?"

"Because I know you."

"No." I shook my head. I was dizzy. The room was starting to spin. "I meant Brian. How do you know he's—" I couldn't say the word.

"I identified his body." He closed his eyes. His body wavered, and he had a cemented grip on the table in front of him. His shoulders were bunched together tightly. His voice came out raw. "It was an execution. They shot him in the middle of his forehead."

I couldn't talk anymore. I felt myself falling, and I reached out for the desk. I was going to crumble to the floor. As I found the chair and held onto it, trying to steady my knees, Jace said further, "Someone—a very bad guy—came to town. My boss. He's here, and I wanted you gone before he got here. I wanted you away and distracted by your happy life. I thought you would be. I really thought you would stay away, especially since that's what you always wanted. You wanted out of this life. Why didn't you just let it go? I didn't want you involved. I didn't want Galverson to know about you. Brian hated me, but you—I care about you. He would realize that. He could've used you to hurt me, but now…" He stopped. Then his voice grew rough. He was hardening himself back up, closing the wall. "It's too late. He knows all about you now, and he's curious why I tried to hide you."

His boss did this? His boss killed Brian? A hoarse cry ripped from my throat. I couldn't comprehend any of this.

Jace came towards me. There was nothing in his eyes anymore. He was looking at me like I was a stranger once again. He grabbed my arm. I flinched from his hold, but he held firm and dragged me to the door. As he opened it, I saw three security guards. They were waiting for me. He handed me to them and said in my ear, "Stay out of my life." The guard pulled me into the hallway, but Jace called my name again. I looked up and he added, "If you come back again, I will kill your sister."

I opened my mouth, but he interrupted me. "I will go to the rehab facility *myself* to do it." Then he shut the door in my face.

I had never told him about Mandy, but before I could let that sink in, Brian's face flashed in my mind and blinding pain overwhelmed me. I fell to the ground. I didn't know how I got home after that. I didn't care how I got home.

CHAPTER TWENTY-ONE

The next day, Tray told me one of Jace's men had driven me home, and he came out to carry me inside. I couldn't walk. I couldn't do anything. I just sat and stared straight ahead, like an empty vessel. He told me that Austin had been scared. When I heard that, a pang of regret went through me. Austin didn't deserve that. His sister was away. His parents were gone, and now I was acting like a walking corpse. No, that wasn't true. A walking corpse didn't feel. I was feeling too much; I couldn't handle it. I felt like someone thrust a large butcher knife into the middle of my chest, leaving a gaping hole. It was becoming infected, and I was rotting from the inside.

Tray asked if he should call Shelly and Kevin. I asked him why. He jerked his head in a nod, then climbed into bed behind me and wrapped his arms around me.

The week passed like that. I didn't go to school for the first half of the week. Tray took the counselor's note to excuse Mandy's absence, and he explained what happened with me. I was allowed three days to miss and when I went back Thursday, I shouldn't have been there. I went from class to class. No one talked to me. Everyone watched me. They had all heard about Brian's death; they just didn't know I had caused it. Tray helped me. He remained by my side. He had people take notes for me. When he couldn't be there, he had people carry my books for me.

He told me a few days later that Mandy had called. She wanted to know how I was doing. For some reason, I began laughing at that. She was in rehab, trying to comfort me. Brian had never cared when he was getting help. It had been all about him. She was in his old place, and she was reaching out because of him. Somehow, that was ironic to me, and I couldn't stop laughing. Austin was in the living room at the time. When he saw the tears rolling down my face and heard the hysterical note in my voice, he threw his video game controller and ran upstairs.

I couldn't blame him.

Tray frowned and said into the phone, "Maybe in a few days." He paused, listening to her on the other end and then replied, "Just keep getting better. That helps her."

I wiped a tear from my face, but couldn't stop laughing. I sighed. "I'm a mess."

He didn't respond. He slid an arm under my leg and the other behind my back, lifting me so I was on his lap, tugging my head so I was leaning into him. My shoulders were shaking as more laughter poured out of me. The laughter soon faded and then there were only tears. When the irony left me, it was replaced with a deeper sadness. The void inside me doubled.

Each night when Tray took me to bed, I laid there, closed my eyes, and willed myself to sleep. Sometimes it worked and sometimes it didn't, but when morning came, I got up. I showered. I dressed. I ate. I went to school. I went through the motions. My birthday came and went. I didn't remember until it was the day after. A sad laugh formed, but died before it slipped out. I was eighteen now. I didn't even need to be adopted anymore.

I never told anyone. I didn't want to deal with any more pity, from anyone.

It was the next week when I found out that Jace had held a small funeral for Brian. I hadn't been invited. I couldn't even process that, but I knew it would hurt me later. All I could process was that I wanted to make Jace pay, even more than he was now. This was his fault. No, it was mine too.

I closed my eyes and felt another wave of grief roll through me. It was both of our faults.

"How'd your friend die?"

Austin asked the question from across the table. It was Saturday morning and everyone had slept in, so we were having a late breakfast.

Tray looked to me, waiting to see if I would answer.

A lump was in my throat, hell—it was always there now. I spoke around it, "He was shot."

"Oh." He glanced down at his plate and moved his eggs around with his fork. Then his hands gripped the fork tighter and he looked back up. "Why?"

"What do you mean?"

"Why was he shot? Mandy said you had dated a psycho."

I frowned. "When did she say that?"

"Before." He lifted a shoulder and looked to Tray for a moment. "It was before you moved in. She heard Mom and Dad talking one night. She said that we were asked to take you in because the guy you were dating was dangerous. If that's true, why aren't you happy? I mean, isn't this a good thing he's dead?"

I couldn't form a sentence. The pieces started to fit together even more now. Jace told Shelly and Kevin about me. He used the excuse that Brian was dangerous. They had been lied to as well. A new wave of hatred spewed through me. It was like poison, affecting every pore inside of me, turning it so all I could think about was Jace. This was his fault. It wasn't mine. Brian's death was on him.

"Taryn?"

I didn't know who said that. The need to find Jace, the need to hurt him, was overwhelming.

"Austin, why don't you get ready? I'll call Eric's mom and have her pick you up."

A chair was shoved back. They were moving away, then I heard Austin's faint voice, "Yeah…is she going to be okay…" Then I couldn't hear anymore. They had both left the room.

I had loved Jace. He and Brian had been the only constants in my life. I would move away, then come back, and they would still be there. That cycle was repeated every time I was sent to another foster home. Somehow, I always ended up going back to Pedlam. I would sneak out to see Brian. He was my first love, but Jace was family too. Now they were both gone and I felt stripped open. I felt like I was bleeding everywhere and I couldn't stop.

A door shut in the distance, and I heard Tray coming back to me. He didn't say anything. I tensed up; I didn't know if I wanted to hear any more condolences. I gritted my teeth. With every, "I'm sorry," I wanted to hit someone. My hand curled in a ball. I was going to swing if I heard sympathy from him. Without saying a word, he knelt and scooped me up from the chair. He tossed me over his shoulder, and I waited to see where he would take me.

He carried me outside and into a gym. As he set me down, I looked around. A punching bag was in one corner with a boxing ring in the other. Against one wall was a sheet taped up with a silhouette of a person in the middle. Little holes were punched through it along with rips. As Tray went to grab a knife from the wall, I knew it was used as a throwing target for him. He came over and opened his palm. A knife was in his palm, the handle towards me.

"What is this?"

I knew how to climb, how to break locks, how to sneak into buildings, but I had never been taught how to throw a knife.

Tray kept his hand steady. He was looking right into my eyes, no hesitation, no judgment, nothing. I flashed back to the last night I had seen Brian, when Tray had looked at me in the same manner. He was there, right in front of me, and he wasn't going anywhere. I had felt as if I had been punched in the chest that night, and the feeling came back again. In one look, as he stood before me, I felt him under my skin. He forced the black hole to move aside and an alarming emotion bumped my heart into beating faster.

My mouth went dry. I was scared of Tray. He didn't treat me as anything except his equal. Brian had worshiped me. Jace had taken care of me, but Tray was different. The strength in him was more than I ever imagined. He lifted his hand again. "Take it, Taryn."

"Why?"

"Because I know you. You're a fighter and once you've mourned Brian enough, you're going to want to go after Lanser." He stepped closer. His hand was still lifted. The knife was beckoning to me, but I was distracted as Tray's body was so close. He had held me every night, but those were nights of comfort. This was different. He changed the dynamic between us. He lifted the tension between us and raised it another notch until I couldn't ignore how much I wanted him. I swallowed, needing more air. His voice dropped to a whisper, "You won't win against Jace Lanser. He's a deadly weapon in himself, but I can teach you how to defend yourself. I can teach you how to hurt whoever you're fighting."

"You want me to go after Jace?"

"No." His hand closed around the knife, and he pulled it away. "You'll lose, but if you're cornered and alone, I want you to have a fighting chance." His hand lifted again. The knife was uncovered once more. "Take it, Taryn. I'll teach you how to use it."

I did. As my hand closed around it, knowing that I would learn how to yield it, I felt powerful. No, I always felt powerful. It was just coming back to me. "How do you know this?"

"My dad taught me. It was one thing he did right by me before he left." He moved so he was behind me. One hand took my arm and the other splayed out on my hip. My heart was racing, but I tried to push all of that away and listen to him. He lifted my arm and moved my other hip back. He murmured into my ear, "If you're fighting someone, you won't have time to grab a weapon. If you're lucky, you will see them coming, but most times they'll get the drop on you."

I frowned. "That's not helpful."

He chuckled, his breath caressing over my ear and the side of my face. It warmed me and sent shivers through me at the same time. His hand tightened on my hip. "When you're fighting for your life and this is all you have, you don't hesitate." He jerked my hand out in a straight jab. At the same time, he pushed my hip forward so my whole body went with the motion. "If you fight someone bigger than you, don't hold back. Don't stab and keep half your body away. It won't do anything. You'll just graze the guy. If you go in, go all in and push all of your weight behind your knife."

Jace and Brian had been in fights, against each other and against others. The violent world wasn't new to me, but the idea that it was me and one other person in a back alley had my mind spinning. Jace never taught me these things. Neither had Brian

He stepped back from me and I missed his warmth, but he took my shoulders and turned me around. As he did, his hazel eyes had a grave look in them. He dropped his chin so he was staring right into my eyes. He said, "If you have the opportunity, go for the throat. If it's you or him and its life and death, you can't hesitate. If you can, jab the entire knife into the guy. Go in through the side, but if he's holding you at an angle and you can't get a good rush at him, slit his throat. Right in front." He ran his finger across the front of his throat. "Fighting with a knife is about being smart. If you're given a window, do it. Don't hesitate. Use your whole body. You might have a couple seconds, if even that. He's bigger than you. If he's going against you, he won't hesitate. You can't either. It's you or him, you fight with every last inch in you and when you don't think you can fight anymore, you search for more inside of you. You need to be a wild animal. Do not hold back. I mean it, Taryn. You can't hold back. Fear will paralyze you. It'll be hard enough to fight just through that, but you have to. Okay?"

He waited for me to nod. When I did, he lifted my hand, the one with the knife, and pressed the blade against his neck. He said, "Press it into me."

"No."

I tried to pull back, but Tray caught my hand. "You need to feel what it's like to have a knife to a throat. This is where they're vulnerable."

I nodded. His hand fell from mine and I kept the knife there. He stared at me, and I felt his trust in me, but his eyes were blazing. He was fighting for me. "I want to kill Jace."

"I know you do."

I had loved him. Now I hated him.

His hands framed both sides of my face. Bending over, he rested his forehead to mine and stared right into me. "I can't promise you will get the chance. He leads the Panthers. He works for Sal Galverson, and he's one of the best fighters I have ever heard about."

"I can hurt him in other ways." My mind was connecting the dots. He wanted me out of the way. He had connections to my adopted parents. I was his secret. "He didn't want Galverson to know about me. Why? That makes no sense."

Tray stepped away. "What are you talking about?"

"He said Brian hated him. He said Brian wasn't a threat, but I could've been. What did he mean by that?"

"In that world, there's no guarantee. People can turn on you in a flash."

"Yeah." I lifted my chin up. "I could get Galverson to turn on Jace."

"No, no. That's not a good idea."

"But what if—"

Tray caught my arms and pulled me back in front of him. "No, Taryn. That world is dangerous. I had my own brush with it, remember? I'll never see my dad again. You can't do anything. I'm teaching you this stuff on the off chance that you do find yourself in an alley against someone."

I snorted. "I'm a thief. I can usually find my way out of a situation."

"Yeah." He tapped my forehead. "You've always used this, but it's personal now. You're all heart now. You're not going into anything clear-headed, not until you really grieve Brian Lanser fully." His voice grew soft. "And I'll be honest, I don't think you ever will. When you love, you love hard. I know that about you. I also know you're not going to let him go because you blame yourself."

I reared back as if he had slapped me. "I blame Jace."

"Yeah, but you blame yourself too. I can feel it in you. You barely eat. You're a walking zombie. The girl who was so full of life and fight before is a shell now. You're empty, but I know everything will slam back and you'll go crazy. The need to hurt Jace will be too much and you'll do something that could hurt you," he pulled me close again, "really hurt you. That's why I'm showing you this."

"So what do you want me to do?" My hand wrapped around the knife. I felt the razor's edge against my skin, pressing into it. I was fighting myself. I wanted to hurt myself, but I wanted to hurt someone else more. With a concerted effort, I relaxed my hand. I let the knife slip down, and I caught the handle of it. Then I looked at it. It was a small weapon, but it could be so deadly at the same time.

"Nothing."

I flashed him a grin. "Brian died because of him."

He let out a sigh.

"There's a snowball's chance in hell that I won't do anything."

"Taryn."

I pointed the knife at him. "Jace wanted me gone. His boss is in town." I remembered another fact. "There was a ton of security at the Pedlam High School. I'm going to figure out why. Something's going on. I want to know what and then I'll figure out some way to turn Galverson against Jace. He's going to die, whether at my hands or not."

As I left the gym, my shoulders were straight. My walk was steady. There was a calm that settled over me. It replaced the turmoil inside me and I felt good. I had a mission. I owed Brian. I was going to make his death stand for something, even if I died trying. So be it.

I kept the knife.

CHAPTER TWENTY-TWO

Mandy remained in treatment. Austin worshiped Tray. I became less of a walking zombie. People began warming back up to me. A few even said hello to me, but then I got a note to go to the counselor's office in my last class on Friday. Tray and I had plans for more training; we had started to spar against each other in the boxing ring. As I stood up and headed for the door, the teacher called me back. "Take your books, Taryn."

I paused at the door. Everyone lifted their heads, looking from me to the teacher. He pointed to my table. "You won't be coming back today."

"Well, that's ominous."

The room started laughing, but the teacher frowned. "This isn't a laughing matter."

I frowned, glanced at Tray, retrieved my books, and left. After stowing my books in my locker, I headed to the office, and when I got there, I stopped outside the door. Shelly and Kevin were already there. I could see them through the window. Shelly wiped a tear from her eye, and Kevin was bent forward, resting his elbows on his knees, a fierce scowl on his face.

This was about Mandy. They had finally found out.

As I headed inside, I flashed them a smile. "So who told you? My bet's on the neighbor. She finally figure out we've been gone?"

Their heads snapped to me and varying levels of outrage stared back at me. Shelly was dressed in a yellow dress, clutching a string of pearls around her neck. At my question, she yanked on the necklace and broke it. When they fell to the floor, spreading all over, Kevin raked a hand through his hair. He cursed and knelt, tossing his tie back over his shoulder so it wouldn't get in the way. His suit coat had been discarded. It was folded over the third chair. As he reached under it, grabbing a fistful of pearls, I saw the sweat running down his back. I went to the chair in the far corner, my back to the door. Shelly was leaning down, and the counselor had joined Kevin in his search. When she crawled to me, I saw the pearls she was reaching for. As her hand stretched out, my foot came down on the pearls and she looked up, seeing the storm in my eyes. Her hand retracted. Kneeling upright on her knees, she stood and went back to her chair.

Kevin grabbed the last of the pearls and stuffed them in his pocket; he and Shelly returned to their seats. They rolled their shoulders back and lifted their chins.

They thought they knew what was going to happen. They thought wrong. I said, "Let me start."

Everyone looked at me. I caught the expression that came over Kevin's face. It was arrogant and superior.

He was my first target. "I took Mandy to a treatment center."

He said, "You had no right—"

I interrupted, "You had no right to take me in when you didn't want me."

He stopped, his eyebrows bunched forward, and he glanced at Shelly. She wore her own small frown, and her throat moved up and down as she swallowed. Then she asked, "What are you talking about, Taryn? Of course we wanted you."

"You didn't." I nodded at Kevin. "What'd you do?"

He grew still, sitting to his highest height on the chair. "What are you talking about?"

"You owed Jace Lanser a favor. He cashed it in." I gestured to myself. "Me."

His eyes widened.

"Oh, dear." Shelly paled.

The counselor shrunk down in her seat, her head jerking from me to them.

I asked again, "What'd you do? I'm assuming he covered for you with something. No one does anything for free." I saw the guilt flare up over his face. "It must've been a pretty bad mistake for Jace to call this favor in. I mean, taking a daughter in for life, that's a big-ass favor for you to agree to."

"Honey." Shelly reached for her husband.

He brushed her hand off and turned to the counselor. "Maybe we could have some privacy?"

Her eyebrows shot up. "Oh. Uh." She clipped her head in a nod. "Of course. I have some work I can do in the other office." She stood, pushed up from her chair, and paused in the middle of the room. She swept another look over them. Her lips pinched together and she said, "I will be referring you to Mr. Daniels, the other counselor, due to my own ethical obligations. Jace Lanser is a known drug dealer. Because of your association with him, I am uncomfortable continuing my work with your children so I will no longer counsel any of them."

Kevin rolled his eyes and waved at her. "Fine, fine. Just go."

Her eyes darkened. Then she left and the door shut a second later.

He was worked up. His cheeks were red and he was wringing his hands together in his lap. He was going to go on the offensive, but I beat him to it, "Don't try to deny it. Jace already told me the truth."

"Oh, honey." Shelly reached out to me. Her hand was trembling. It was so thin and frail. "I don't know where you get these ideas, but that isn't true. We wanted you. We did." She glanced to her husband for support.

There was none. His eyebrows were still furrowed together and his lips were pressed in a flat line.

"Kevin?"

He ignored her and said to me, "What did he say?"

She sucked in a dramatic breath.

"That you owed him a favor. What was it? Someone overdosed on your pills?"

He looked away. Bull's-eye.

"Oh my god." Shelly started rocking back and forth. She wrapped her arms around herself.

"The person died."

Holy shit. I hadn't expected him to confess.

He closed his eyes, cursed, and looked at the ground. His hand raked through his hair again. He grabbed a fistful of it and he remained like that as he took a moment. Inhaling, then exhaling, his voice dropped low, "I messed up. They sent a girl to me. She was on other meds, and she was asking for a different painkiller. I didn't read the file. I was sent an email. It was in code, but it said the patient's name and what I was

251

supposed to give her. I swear," he raised his haunted eyes to me, "I had no idea what would happen."

I sat there in shock.

A disgusted and wrangled sound came from him. "I've been holding onto that for so long." He looked at Shelly. "I'm so sorry, honey. I am."

Her hands were pressed to her mouth. It was hanging open and her eyebrows remained arched high. She shook her head in a tight motion and whimpered, then jerked to her feet. "No. No, you can't do this."

"Honey?"

"You can't—" She stopped, look at me, and another whimper slipped out. She pressed her hands even tighter to her mouth. "I am so sorry, Taryn. You're right. We never should've adopted you. Our family is not good enough for you. I am so sorry." She bit back her next words, glared at her husband, took her purse and left.

He started to go after her.

But I needed more. I didn't know what for, but I knew I needed him to tell me more. "Wait!"

He sat back down. "Taryn, I have to go after my wife. She's going to divorce me if I don't. I know how she gets when she's in these moods."

"But—" I needed more information. "What did Jace do?" I swallowed over a knot and pushed it down. I was so close to having the information I had been craving. "To make everything go away, what did he do?" I waited, but he kept looking at the door. He was going to go. I only had a few more minutes. "Please."

The indecision cleared away. He leaned back in his seat. "I don't know. I can't tell you much." He laughed. "I shouldn't be telling you anything, but I know he asked out of love. He told me how violent and

252

dangerous his little brother was. I'm glad we were able to get you away from him, if anything else."

My stomach dropped. The darkness was forming again in me. "Brian could be violent, but he wasn't to me."

"What?"

I shook my head. "Jace lied to you. He said something to make you feel better about taking me in. Brian never would've hurt me and in the end, if you hadn't adopted me..." Grief crashed down on me. "He might still be alive."

If I had turned the adoption down, Brian would still be alive. I wouldn't have left. He wouldn't have gone asking questions.

It wasn't only Jace's fault. I had to accept my part. I shook my head, my voice hoarse when I spoke next. "I shouldn't have believed it. The whole thing, this whole family thing, was too good to be true. I knew it in my gut. I should've listened to it more."

"Taryn," he started.

I heard the sympathy in his voice and shot my hand up. I glared at him. "Don't start. His death is on you too."

He frowned. "Death?"

"Brian. The guy that you were supposedly saving me from." I didn't only hate Jace. I hated Kevin too. "He's dead. He wanted to talk to the social worker who set up my adoption. Word got to his boss that one of his workers was trying to find a government employee. What do you think they did?"

"He's dead?" Blood drained from his face and beads of sweat formed on his forehead.

Finally. He was getting it. I gritted my teeth together. "You fucked with my life. Someone I care about is dead because of that. His death is on your shoulders too." I had to leave. I couldn't stay there any longer. The thought of being in the same room with him was suffocating me. Going to the desk, I turned one last time. "Austin and I have been staying at Tray Evans' house. He's enjoyed it. He likes Tray. And leave Mandy in treatment. She needs to get better, and she's trying. I know she's really trying. Don't mess up her life."

I swept out of there just as the last bell rang.

"Taryn!" Shelly was waiting for me outside the office. She lifted an arm, but the doors burst open and the hallway flooded with people.

I ducked my head and disappeared from her sight. Whatever they did from here on out, it had nothing to do with me. I was no longer a part of their family.

Austin moved back in with them, and I learned from his text messages that all things were good in their household. For some reason, that sickened me. Shelly had tried contacting me, but Tray became my guard dog. She showed up at the house a few times, and he would ask her to leave. She would call and send text messages, but I never answered. I should've. That would've been the adult thing to do, but I wasn't ready to listen to any justifications or promises filled with empty words.

A week later, I shut my locker and started for the parking lot, but stopped. Jennica stood by her locker. She was a beautiful girl with almond eyes, dark black hair, and an olive complexion, but at that moment her eyes were strained. Her lips were pressed tight and she had a heated look in her eyes.

I waited and lifted an eyebrow.

"Mandy dumped Devon last night."

My other eyebrow shot up, but I kept my shock hidden.

"I'm sure you're ecstatic about that."

I gestured to my face. "You can't see it, but I'm doing somersaults on the inside."

She grunted and flicked a strand of hair out of the way. "She dumped me too."

Now I really was doing somersaults on the inside. "Really?"

"And Amber." Jennica's lips pressed together again and she looked away. It was the last day of the week. The hallway was emptying. "She's done with us. She told us last night." She crossed her arms over her chest. Her chin went down and she fixed me with a stare. "So congratulations. You got what you wanted."

I sighed and shook my head. "Having my sister lose her friends is not what I wanted."

Jennica paused.

I continued, "I want my sister to have good friends, friends who are true to her, who care about her, who treat her right. That's what I wanted and if you're the friend who's going to change and do that, I'm all for it." I shook my head. "But I highly doubt you know how to be a true friend, so yes, I am glad that she ended her friendship with you. Would you want your sister to be friends with someone like you?"

She frowned, biting her lip.

I put my bag over my shoulder. Tray was waiting for me and I nodded to him. "I have to go."

"Wait."

I started past her, but stopped and turned.

She rolled her eyes. "Look, I know I'm a shitty friend, but I do care about Mandy. Just let her know that. Please?"

"I will."

"Taryn."

I glanced back again.

"Can you let me know how she's doing? I know I have no right, but..." Her head went back down and she looked away.

I nodded. "You care about her." I was beginning to see that.

She nodded. "Thanks." The corners of her mouth curved up in a small grin. She looked grateful.

"You do care about her, don't you?"

"Yeah, I do. I don't show it, but I do."

I shook my head. "Then why the hell do you treat her how you do?"

She frowned, then lifted a shoulder up. "I don't know. It's the cool thing to do."

"It's not." Disappointment flooded me. "Treating people like you do is the farthest thing from being cool. Stop lying to yourself. If you want a good friend, be a good friend. That's all there is to it."

She rolled her eyes and scoffed, "Yeah, right. What do I do when someone treats me how I treat people? Better to be the bitch on top than to be the bitch who gets kicked around. Come on, Taryn. You're lying to yourself if you think people are going to be the good friend that you think. Do you not know people? They're all assholes. They lie. They

256

think they're better than others. They manipulate. There's no good friends out there."

"Yeah." I clapped for her. I was drawing attention to us, but I ignored them. "People do shitty things. Welcome to the real world. It happens, but you keep doing what you want done to you and someday, it'll happen."

She looked away.

I shook my head. "Keep doing what you're doing. I'm sure you'll land a wealthy husband who will cheat on you your whole marriage…with the women you meet for lunch. That's where you're headed."

"Taryn," Tray said from close behind me. I felt his hand on my shoulder and turned, taking it in my hand, I held it.

I gripped it hard as I said to her, "I'll give you updates on Mandy, but to answer your initial question, yes. I'm happy. She's clearing out people who have treated her horribly. That's a good sign."

I left before she could say anything more. I didn't want to hear it because it didn't matter. Mandy was getting better. Somehow, that helped me. All the anger and darkness I felt for Jace shifted and hope blossomed inside of me. I didn't know if it would stay long, but it felt good having it back there. That meant some things were changing. Some things *could* change.

CHAPTER TWENTY-THREE

Mandy stayed in rehab for another thirty days, but she called the night before to let me know she was getting released. There was a ceremony and she invited me to come, but her parents would be there.

I wasn't ready to see them. So, instead, knowing they would be there and at Mandy's side, I went to the school's pool. I wasn't a thief anymore. I hadn't been in a long time so my trips to the pool were increasing. They had an Olympic sized one, unlike Tray's that was half its size, so once I dove in, I could really let my mind go.

When I finished my last lap, a light was on in the corner office, but as I got out of the pool and went to my bag, it switched off. The door opened and Coach Hayes nodded at me. He shut the door, tested the knob, and headed towards me. He was dressed in a navy blue mesh coat over khaki shorts. A Rawley Swim Team cap was pulled down low over his eyes. Stopping in front of me, he frowned at me. "You didn't come to try-outs."

I stiffened. "I was busy."

He nodded. "I get that. Everyone's busy."

I narrowed my eyes. "Then why do I feel like you're giving me a hard time?"

He grinned. "I'm not." He held his hands up, a clipboard in one. "I heard about your sister and something else, someone close to you died?"

"My ex-boyfriend."

"Yeah, that's it. Some of the teachers were confused. They weren't sure of the relation."

I frowned. "You guys talk about me in the teacher's lounge?"

"Yeah." He hiked up his pants. "Don't feel all special because of it. They talk about a lot of things, but you were a hot topic for a while."

I finished drying myself off, still frowning, before I dropped the towel and reached for my clothes. "I'm not sure if special is the word I would use."

"Come on. Everyone thought you were another foster kid."

I scowled. "What? Another kid riddled with problems?" I raised my chin up, tugging my shirt over my head at the same time. "Because I do, you know. I have enough baggage to fill up a jet."

He narrowed his eyes. "Why are you telling me that?"

I shrugged, bent over, and pulled up my shorts. "I figured you should know."

"You missed try-outs. There's no reason I need to know."

"And what if I asked for another chance?"

He shrugged, looking pensive. "That'd be interesting."

I chewed on my lip, studying him. He wasn't giving anything away, but I caught a spark in his eyes. I couldn't tell for sure, but my gut was telling me he was thinking about it. For some reason, I wanted a second chance more than anything at that moment.

I said, "It'd be good for me. I'd have a purpose, you know."

He laughed, took his hat off, ran a hand through his hair, and tugged the hat back on. He shook his head. "I'm not one of those coaches who look for projects to nurture. I don't care about the underdog kind of kid. I maybe should. I know if some other teachers heard that from me, they'd take up their self-righteous torches, but you don't strike me as a kid that cares about bullshit."

"If I wanted someone to bullshit me, I'd still be in the Parson household. They're awesome at pretending every pile of shit is dyed gold."

He barked out a laugh, then caught himself. "You're something else, Matthews. You think you deserve another shot?"

He was serious. I could tell he was no longer fooling around. He meant it. I nodded. "No, sir. I don't, but I'd appreciate a shot."

"You don't think you deserve it?"

"I don't deserve anything, but like I said. I'd appreciate a shot."

He grunted. "You're like a breath of fresh air. I don't think I could stand another self-entitled student."

Did that mean what I thought it meant...

He nodded. "You got your spot, Matthews."

He started for the door, his car keys in hand. As he was almost there, I called out, "So I can try-out?"

"No." He turned, using his back to open the door, grinning at me. "You're on the team. I've been watching your speeds the last hour and I already know you'll smoke my best swimmers." He paused with the door on his back. He had one foot still in the pool area and the other out the door. The grin faded and he grew somber. "I wasn't bullshitting you before when I said you have talent. I don't know why you haven't been swimming this whole time, but this could be a future for you, Matthews. If you work at it, that is."

He had been watching me and I was on the team, just like that. I stood there, my insides all wrapped up around each other, stunned by how quick I'd been given this shot. *Brian would've been proud.* That was the first thought in my head. Then I remembered he was gone and my jaw tightened. My hands turned into fists. Just like that, in such a short span of time, I felt on top of the world and then my chest was tight. The anger was pounding through me again.

When I left the pool, I heard my name called out, "Taryn!"

Shelly had been waiting for me. She got out of her car, raised her hand, and waved. "Taryn! Hold on." Then she ran to me.

I rolled my eyes.

"Hey, honey."

Reaching for the car, I tossed my bag inside and turned around. "You look ridiculous."

She frowned and pressed a hand to her chest. She was wearing a light scarf and it was billowing in the wind. Her hand settled it down, but she tugged at her sweater, closing it around her, and then smoothed out her skirt. With a string of pearls around her neck, her diamond earrings, and a pair of three inch heels, she looked ready for either a socialite dinner or church.

The corners of her mouth dipped down, but she lifted her chin again. It was like she had reaffirmed herself about something. She nodded and her shoulders dropped down to a ready position. "I can understand if you're upset with me."

"What are you doing here?" I didn't want to hear anything she said. It would all sound pretty, but it would all be a lie. "Mandy called. She said you're supposed to be at her graduation ceremony."

She swallowed with an audible gulp. "That's why I'm here. Kevin and Austin went. I came to see you."

"Why?"

"Because they're with one daughter. I'd like to be with the other one. And," she gave me a timid smile, "I'd like to ask if you'd come to the house? We're having a small get-together for Mandy. All her friends are invited. Everyone wants to celebrate how wonderful she's done."

I smirked. Of course. "You're an idiot. You believed Kevin's lie about adopting me and now this? Mandy dumped her friends. Wanna know why? Because they're assholes. I hope you didn't invite Devon, Jennica, and Amber? Mandy's done with them and I'm proud of her for doing that."

She blinked rapidly, as if shocked, then she forced a smile on her face. "Of course. I invited her friend Tristan and anyone Austin told me that was 'cool.'" Her cheeks pinked and she laughed softly. "He told me to trust him with the invites so I did. If he invited anyone you don't think should come, we can still toss them out. No one will impede on my daughter's well-being."

I was watching her. I cursed. "You mean it."

She blinked, and her eyebrows bunched forward. "Of course, I do. Why wouldn't I?"

"Kevin lied to you. You were brainwashed to adopt me. Are you not getting that?"

She shook her head. "No, Taryn. I wasn't brainwashed and I wasn't manipulated. I wouldn't have taken you in if I hadn't wanted to." She stepped close. Her hands lifted and she took hold of my shoulders. Leaning forward, her voice lowered to a hoarse whisper, "The moment I saw your picture, I fell in love with you. Then I read your file and I fell even more in love." Her fingers curled into me, holding on tight. "I am not happy with my husband. There are things we have to work out, but I am happy about you. I am so thankful that you're a part of our family." A tear slid down her cheek. She ignored it, giving me another shaky smile. "I'm not as blind as you think. I can see that Austin's hurting. When we picked him up, he didn't want to come home. He's your fiercest defender in the house. He asks us every day when you're coming home. And Mandy..." She closed her eyes. When they opened, there were fresh tears there. "I'm ashamed that I haven't reached her like you have. I'm ashamed that so much was going on in my house and I never did anything about it."

The tears. The heartfelt proclamation. I bit back a smart ass retort and fought from rolling my eyes. Then I couldn't help it. It slipped out. "For real?"

"What?"

Her hands uncurled from my arms and she moved back a step. Searching my face, she saw the disbelief on my face.

I shook my head. "Who do you think I am? You really thought I would fall for that act?" I couldn't forget the history. She left me with Austin. She took off whenever her husband called for her. Her daughter was a drug addict. "You shouldn't be ashamed by what your husband has done. You should be furious. You should leave him."

"Taryn," she started.

"No." I moved further away from her. "You're one of the worst kinds of people. You're the kind that sees something horrible has happened and you sweep it under the rug. You want it to go away so your life isn't interrupted."

Tears were rolling down her face, but it was like she didn't feel them. She stared back at me. Her eyes were unblinking. There was a glazed look in them.

"Look at me. I'm the one who survived not having a family and I'm schooling you how to fix yours." I snorted, feeling an empty void open in me again. "I can't undo how I feel about Mandy and Austin. I already love them, but I'm thankful now that no relationship was built between you and me, or Kevin and me. So thank you for being shitty adoptive parents. You did me a favor."

I sat in my car after that and waited. Shelly stood there, pale as a zombie, for a few more minutes before her phone rang. As she answered it, I heard her words muffled through the window, "I'm coming, honey. No…" Then she turned and went to her own vehicle.

I sat there, even after she drove off. I couldn't bring myself to leave.

I hit the punching bag. *They lied to me.* It barely moved so I hit it again. *They didn't care that they lied.* I gritted my teeth. My fist tightened and I rolled my shoulder back, lifted my wrist again, and bent forward into the stance. One foot was in front, the other behind, and I was on my toes. I was ready to switch them, jab back and forth, and bounce back as the bag should've been swinging to me.

Nothing.

With a deep growl, I hit it as hard as I could. It moved an inch.

"You're using your arm."

"Duh." I didn't look as Tray came into the room. He left the lights off, so the only light on was the small lamp positioned over the punching bag. Sweat rolled down my back and I'd lost my shirt long ago. Standing in my black sports bra and a pair of boy shorts, I felt fine. I was heated, but not overheated with the air conditioner in the room.

He circled around me. I glanced down, saw he had kicked his shoes off as well. After another moment of studying me, he took his shirt off too. He tossed it to the corner, then tilted his head to the side, and his hazel eyes narrowed at me. A slight smirk lifted the corners of his lips. As he stood there, his muscles clenched. His chest lifted and he breathed in, his stomach muscles clenched in and then out. There was hardly an ounce of fat on him.

We'd been sharing a bed for two months now, but as I drank him in, it was as if I was seeing him for the first time. Hunger and lust slammed into me. My mouth opened and I swallowed.

His smirk widened and he gestured to my arm. "Use your shoulder. Hit with your body, not your arm. Your strength comes from your core. The hand is the weapon."

"I want to bone you right now." I frowned.

"You're working out. Your adrenalin is pumping." His hand gestured from his chest to his stomach. "I can't blame you. I'm a prime specimen."

I snorted. "You don't need to work on that confidence. Your arrogance just sucked all the oxygen out of the room to inflate your ego."

He laughed, but switched his body and punched the bag. It swung away and his hand lifted. It caught it as it swung back. "The shoulder. I leaned back and threw my body forward. You don't have to be obvious about it. Twist your body. Let your feet help guide you." He stopped and paused for a moment. "We've been sparring for the last month and a half. You know this."

A single droplet of sweat rolled down the side of his face. It moved to his chin, settled on the cleft of his chin before it fell to his chest. I watched as it went all the way to his chest, making a smooth trail in its wake, all the way down, over his abdominals until it hit the waistband of his shorts. A heat that had been in me since I started, the fury from Shelly and Kevin, had been boiling, but now the flame lit up as if gasoline had been poured on it. I was burning up from the inside out and the need to take Tray and shove him against the wall was climbing. I wanted to push him to his knees, shove his pants down, and position myself over him. I could imagine the feel of him inside me, and my legs clenched. The ache was throbbing.

I started for him, wanting to feel him going in and out of me.

Tray's smirk turned cautious, but he didn't move. I stopped an inch from him. I could feel his body heat and moved my head to the side. I wasn't trying to be seductive. I was trying to hold myself back. As his eyes held my mine, he saw what I wanted. His responded and darkened in lust, but he didn't move. I wanted him to touch me. I wanted to feel the graze of his hand up my arm, over my shoulder. He would circle my throat, cup the back of my neck, and pull me the last inch to him. I would feel all of him against me. All his strength and power. I craved it.

Then I murmured, with a slight frown, "You've been holding back."

"What?"

"Why do you hold back? You've been treating me like I'm fragile."

A slight chuckle. "I'm not holding back and you're not fragile. You were mourning. There's a difference."

For two months we've held each other at night. He would pull me against his chest, wrap his arm around me, and caress my arm until I fell asleep. He had fed me. He reminded me to shower at times, even told to dress for school a few days. I'd been a mess, then I'd been angry and demanding as he taught me how to fight. And now, I wanted what he'd withheld from me. I wanted him. I wanted all of him.

"I've only slept with one other guy."

"I know."

"People have always called me a slut. They assumed I was experienced, but I've only been with Brian. He's the first guy I let in."

"Hey." His finger went under my chin and he tipped my head up. "You're feeling a lot of different emotions right now. You were sad for a while. You were angry. You wanted to hurt someone." He gave me a half-grin. "You might always feel that, but now you've moved past some of those emotions. Wanting to have sex is normal. You're alive. You want to live. I understand, but I'm not making one damn move on you until I know it's pure. Until I know that afterwards, you're going to want me again and again and again. That you're not going to curl in a ball with self-loathing or guilt because you're alive and he's not." As he said those words, his finger tightened under my chin and I was pulled slowly to him. He looked straight down into me. I felt as if he was seeing my soul. I was bare to him. All the lust, pain, fury, everything was stripped clean until he just saw me, whoever I was.

A lump formed in my throat and I swallowed over it, shoving it down. I didn't want to feel that. It was awkwardness, it was self-consciousness, and it was pain. I was tired of feeling this emptiness.

He lowered his head, his lips just above mine. If he moved a fraction of an inch down or I pressed up, they would touch. I could feel the brush of him.

Another touch. That was what I wanted. I didn't want just sex with him. Realizing that, feeling the hunger for more, I pulled back. My heart stopped and fear crashed into my chest. I'd felt this before, the last time I saw Brian, a few times before that. Tray was my equal. He was the all. He wouldn't play games. He wouldn't hold back. He was real. Brian had... I turned away from Tray as I realized the truth.

It wasn't the same. I felt more with Tray than I did with Brian.

"Taryn?"

I shook my head and cleared my thoughts. Moving back to the punching bag, I hit it. It barely moved again.

"Taryn?"

I couldn't talk so I swung again, then again. I didn't care if the bag didn't move. I was moving. I was doing what I needed. I wanted all the shit from inside me out of me. As I kept going, punch after punch, I imagined a huge dump truck coming in and scooping out all the crappiness from me. With a guttural cry, I switched my feet, switched my fighting stance, and swung with my left arm. Then I kept going.

Tray came to stand on the other side of the bag. He held it, hugging it, as I kept pounding. I didn't care if my hands bled or if my knuckles bruised. My head went down and I kept hitting. I went until my arms wouldn't lift and my body was exhausted. Even then, after an hour, I wanted to keep going. Too many emotions were still swirling inside me. They were slithering around like snakes and I couldn't get them out. I didn't know how anymore.

CHAPTER TWENTY-FOUR

"I thought Mandy dumped her friends." I paused, then added, "Your friends."

Tray chuckled. "She did, but I guess the girls went to visit her last night. Plus, Dylan's in town again. This get-together is at his parent's vacation house. I think he wants to try his hand with your sister since she dumped Devon."

I frowned. "Why am I jealous that you know more about my sister and her friends than I do? I'm the girl. Isn't that what we do? We get the gossip."

He laughed again, turning onto a different street that headed out of town. "I think the girls would give you the info if they weren't scared of you, and Mandy's only been home a day. I only know because Dylan called to explain it all last night when he invited us."

"She should be resting," I paused again, "at our house."

"Our house?" He threw me a grin.

I flushed and leaned back in my seat. I didn't even know I had sat forward. "Mandy is delicate right now. She just left rehab. She should be around people who support her sobriety and understand it. This get-together is not a good idea. There's going to be alcohol there. I'm sure there's going to be triggers for her, whatever her triggers are." Why didn't I know? That was what was bothering me the most. I didn't know.

Tray's voice gentled. "You took your sister to rehab and found out a day later that your ex-boyfriend died. It's okay that you didn't go see her."

"They had family sessions."

"And you didn't go because you found out your adoption was a lie. You felt like they didn't want you after all."

"Kevin was forced to take me and he tricked Shelly into wanting me." Tray was right. All of it. I shook my head. "I don't feel like I was there for her."

"Taryn." His tone firmed. His eyes darkened. "You were both going through some massive things. Stop feeling guilty. Believe it or not, you can't save the world. Stop taking on the duties of Wonder Woman when you're not Wonder Woman."

I cracked a grin. "It'd be awesome to have those powers." I frowned. "What powers did she have?"

He chuckled, patting my leg as the car slowed and he turned onto paved driveway. "Does it really matter? Get the lesson here. You're human. Stop acting like you're not."

"Okay, okay."

The driveway went up a hill and curved to the left. There was dense forest on both sides of us and when we saw the house, I saw the amount of cars and my eyes got big. "For real? There's like thirty cars down there." I didn't waste time. As soon as Tray parked, I was out of the car and into the house. The living room was crowded. I couldn't get through to the kitchen, but then I growled and the crowd parted. People saw me coming and moved aside. Sweeping through the kitchen, I went to the patio and there she was. Mandy was at a table, sitting on Dylan's lap.

Jennica and Amber were laughing, but the sound shriveled up as I headed for them.

Mandy saw me and sat upright. "Taryn?"

Her surprise punched me in the chest. "You didn't know?"

Dylan squirmed underneath her. His hand was on her thigh. She was wearing a dress. The hemline rested above his hand and he cupped her skin for a moment before letting out a soft sigh. She turned to him. "Dylan?"

"I invited Evans. Her and him are a deal now, you know."

"You don't want me here?"

She looked back to me. Her indecision was clear, then she shook her head. "It's not that, Taryn. It's…" She bit her lip and scanned the table. Her friends had varying expressions. Amber seemed expectant of something whereas Jennica couldn't look away from the doorway behind me. Then Mandy stood up. "Can we talk?"

I nodded, my neck stiff. Following Mandy as she weaved through the crowd, I wasn't surprised when people shouted their hellos and welcome backs to her. A few saluted her with their cups. When she headed for the stairs, Tray was coming from the kitchen. He paused and his eyes narrowed. An unspoken question passed from him to me, asking what was going on. I lifted a shoulder. I was about to find out.

"Hi, Tray." Mandy gave him a small wave.

He nodded to her. Then as she started up, his hand stopped me. "You okay?"

People were watching us with confusion and skepticism. When they kept looking at Tray, I had a second realization. They had missed their leader. I'd been monopolizing him. Feeling a pang, I said back, "I will be."

"Text if you want to go. I'll meet you at the car."

Reaching for his hand with mine, I squeezed his in response, then squared my shoulders and headed up the stairs. Mandy was waiting for me in the hallway. Her arms were crossed over her chest, and she was leaning against a wall. She gestured to a room. "We can go in there. Dylan uses it when he stays here."

The room had a king-sized bed with a set of couches beside the bed. A side room opened off to the right and I could see a door on the other side that led to a bathroom.

"Where are his parents? And what's his deal again?"

She laughed softly, sitting down on the bed. Her head lowered and her hands played with her dress. "Um...Dylan goes to school in another state, but he comes back when he can. I told you this before."

"Are you together?"

"God, Taryn." Her head lifted and her cheeks were red. "You just dive right in, don't you?"

I shrugged, leaning against a wall. "I have other questions I want to ask. Believe it or not, this is me trying to hold back."

"Oh." She looked back down to her lap. "Yeah. I think so. I don't know. I dumped Devon."

"Yeah." I rolled my eyes, but she couldn't see it. "I thought you dumped Amber and Jennica too?"

"I did, but they came over last night to welcome me back, see how I was doing," she looked up again, "and to apologize."

"I don't really care about your friends or your boyfriend. I just want you to be surrounded by good people. That's all."

"I know and I'm trying that. Devon's emailed and called my phone every day. I haven't taken him back."

"Good."

At hearing that, a small grin appeared. Then she ducked her head back down, stuffing her hands underneath her legs so she was sitting on them. Her feet started kicking at the floor. "As for Amber and Jennica, I love my friends. I mean, I've done some bad stuff too. Who am I to not give second chances?"

"You weren't hurting anyone."

"I was hurting myself."

"Yeah and from how I see it, those two have only hurt you."

Her feet stopped. She looked back. Tears were swimming in her eyelids. They were right there, ready to fall. One did and she brushed at it with the back of her hand. "I have to try, Taryn. I'm not as strong as you."

"What do you mean?"

"You don't need people. I do. I need family and friends. I need to be able to forgive and hope that people will be there for me in the end." She shook her head. "I'm not like you."

"I need people too."

"No, you don't. You never talked to me about Brian. If you needed someone, I would've thought a sister would be that person." A second tear slid down. "You never said a word. I had to find out everything from Austin. You didn't tell me about my parents and your adoption, either.

No one did. Austin just told me that shit was messed up. I hoped you would come to the family sessions too, but nothing."

The truth had been kept from her, and I was one of the people who did that. "I'm sorry, Mandy. I didn't keep it from you on purpose, I just...I don't know what I was thinking. I haven't been myself lately." I wanted to ask, but I wasn't sure if it was the right time. Did I even have the right to ask now? "Why didn't you come to see me last night?"

"I was going to, but Mom said not to. She saw you at the school and it didn't go well. Then I decided to come anyway, but Amber and Jennica showed up. It was late when they left and," she hesitated, pausing briefly, "I didn't know if you wanted me to come or not. Austin told me to go. He said I was being a pussy, but," she rolled her eyes as a small grin escaped, "he's not scared of you like I am."

"Scared?"

"I feel like I disappointed you." She stopped, closed her eyes. "Man, I've been holding that in for a long time. I think, since you confronted me and drove me to rehab, that I disappointed you." A small and bitter-sounding laugh came from her. "Why didn't I feel like that with my own parents, but I did with you?"

"I don't know." My chest had been tight since we left the patio. At hearing her last confession, some of the tightness loosened. I had five massive knots tangled up inside of me and I had four more to loosen. "Let's not analyze that. I can't handle feeling any more right now."

She grinned, tucking a strand of her hair behind her ear. "Too much with Brian's death?"

275

I nodded. I really didn't want to talk about him. Or Jace. I shook my head. "I'm not keeping things from you. It's just that it's so damn painful to even think about it, much less talk about it."

Her eyebrows furrowed together and her lips pressed together. "You've been staying with Tray this whole time?"

"Since I took you to rehab. It didn't feel right staying at the house. I felt like I was going against what your parents wanted."

"You were right. They wouldn't have taken me to a rehab, or at least not to that one. I would've gone to some nice plush one where they wouldn't have pressed me that hard. My dad would've told them to treat me like I was a soft princess. The one you took me to—"

"Is good." I finished for her. "I took Brian there. He needed a place that's like that. They don't bullshit around."

"No." She laughed. "They don't, but that's what I needed. And I think I was tired of lying to everyone. Thank you, Taryn."

I was struck speechless.

There were tears in her eyes, but as she smiled at me, I didn't think they were the bad kind. She said again, "Thank you."

I nodded. "Yeah." My voice was hoarse and that was all I could get out.

"Did you go to the funeral?"

I shook my head. My throat stung. "No. From what I was told, the funeral was kept private. I wasn't invited."

"That's cold."

"Yeah, well, what do you expect? His brother might as well killed him himself. Of course he wouldn't let me go. I'd have questions and demands." I'd have a knife or a gun.

"What do you mean?"

"What?"

"You blame his brother?" She wrapped her hands in her dress and tilted her head to the side, studying me with a frown. "I thought he was robbed at gun point. That's what everyone is saying. Why would that be his brother's fault, unless it was his brother that robbed him, but I doubt that happened. You know, since he had the funeral for him without you and everything..." Her voice trailed off and her head lifted. Her frown deepened, and she sat upright. "Taryn? What's wrong? What'd I say?"

A robbery. Gun point. That's how they spun it? A hard laugh ripped from me. I couldn't believe what I just heard.

"Taryn?" She stood. Mandy started for me, but stopped a few feet away. "What's wrong? What'd I say? Please." A hysterical note etched into her tone. It was soft, hanging there on the end, before it bloomed.

I shook my head. Forcing myself to sound calm, I asked, "Who told you that?"

"Amber and Jennica."

"Where'd they hear it from?"

She lifted a shoulder, but let it drop suddenly. "I don't know. I'm not helping you. I've made it worse. I'm sorry, Taryn. What can I do? Tell me what to do to make this better."

There wasn't anything she could do. "I need to talk to Amber and Jennica."

"Okay." She went for the door. "I'll get them." She opened it, but paused before she said, "I want to help you like you helped me, Taryn. I'm sorry for making this worse."

My insides were burning up. I felt raw, like someone had dragged a rake through my organs and left me bleeding out. "You did. Trust me, you did."

She left and I closed my eyes. *Stay calm. Hear them out*, I tried to tell myself, trying to calm the tornado inside me, but it wasn't working. I used my last resort and counted down from one hundred. When I got to sixty-nine, a knock sounded at the door and Tray stepped inside.

"What's going on?" He closed the door and leaned against it. Voices sounded from the hallway and the doorknob turned. He said through it, "Give me a minute in here."

There was silence and then Mandy said, "One minute, Evans. She's still my sister."

Ignoring her, he focused on me. He was trying to read me again. "What's going on?"

I took a moment and drank the sight of him in. He was gorgeous. Sometimes I didn't see it. I felt his beauty. He was kind. He was patient. He stood up to me and for me. He took care of me, and he fought side by side with me. Those were his qualities, but he wasn't just mine. I saw it downstairs and a part of me was jealous. I didn't want to share him, but I knew I would have to. Now, seeing him at this party, it was like I was being reminded of the other side of Tray. Hazel eyes, sandy blonde hair, rakish grin, chiseled cheekbones, broad shoulders, trim waist, and my mouth watered as I remembered feeling his weight above me.

That alien emotion was back. It bubbled to the surface and spread all over. I shook my head. Shit. That was a whole other level of emotions I didn't want to deal with either.

"Taryn?"

My voice was hoarse again when I spoke. "I'm seeing this through, Tray."

"Okay." His eyes narrowed, growing thoughtful. "Why are you telling me this now?"

"Because you have friends here. These people think of you like family. You're not mine." I hesitated. "Only mine. You're theirs too. And what I'm about to do, it's dangerous. I don't know if you should help me."

A corner of his mouth lifted in a smirk. "Who do you think I am? Someone weak? Someone soft? You're going to come at me, preach to me about the dangerous road you're going down? You think I don't know?" He stood from the door, locked it, and advanced on me. He spoke with each step he took. "I wake up next to you every morning. I hold you every night. I'm there. I'm beside you. This is me. I'm all fucking in, Taryn. Stop trying to scare me away and stop trying to treat me with kid gloves. I taught you how to fight, remember? Do I need to remind you of my life? I found my mom dead. That was me. I found her in bed. I found the empty bottle of pills and booze. I found the note. Me. I was there when my dad decided to leave with Galverson. Jace showed up. He gave my dad an ultimatum: Leave now, go with them and keep his mouth shut for the rest of his life to save mine, or go with my brother and get a bullet in the head later. That was his choice. He left me behind. I was there. I heard the whole thing and Jace saw me. I was standing upstairs. I wasn't hiding, but my dad didn't even look at me. He grabbed his wallet, took out his bank card, put it with a wad of cash on the counter, and left. That's the last thing I remember about my dad."

I swallowed and felt as if he'd struck me across the face. He'd had it hard. So did I. He shook his head. "Stop." He was in front of me now. His hands lifted. He was going to touch the sides of my face, but he hesitated. I saw the agony in him, and he closed his eyes. He closed himself off from me and drew in a breath.

I frowned. He was drawing strength and he was doing it without me. My hands lifted to his before I realized what I was doing. I didn't want him to do that. I wanted him to draw strength from me and as his eyes opened, I was gutted. "Stop."

He did. I saw it.

I added, "I don't want to ruin your life."

"You won't."

I shook my head. I already had.

"Stop, Taryn." His hands cupped my face. His thumbs rubbed over my cheeks, softly and tenderly. "It goes both ways. I'm all-in. I've never been this guy. I've never cared about a girlfriend before, but it's different with you. Everything's different with you. It's too late to go back. I'm in, Taryn. Do you hear that? I'm in. Accept it. I'm here. I'm not leaving. I'm your best friend. I'm going to be your lover. I'm going to fight with you. I'm going to hold you. I'm going to support you. I will not betray you, and I will not abandon you."

Each word calmed me. The storm was there, but it wasn't raging any more, and I cracked a grin. "I don't have a say in the matter?"

He leaned forward. His lips were going to my forehead, but he held back. I felt him struggling with his emotions before he murmured, "No, you don't. You have to deal with it." He touched his lips there and his chest jerked up. The emotion was strong in him. We were the same in that moment. My hands clung to the back of his as he cradled my face, but I tugged him down.

His eyes opened and he looked into mine. For the first time, I didn't hesitate. I didn't look away. I let him stare into me. I let him see everything, and then I reached for his lips. As they touched mine, I claimed him this time.

I was letting him know he was mine.

CHAPTER TWENTY-FIVE

When we headed to Rickets' House, my only goal was to find the girl that I saw with Brian the night he died. When Amber and Jennica came into the room, they said that girl had been asking questions about Brian's death. As we drove up the long, windy gravel road to the house, Tray asked, "So, let's run this over again. What did Amber and Jennica say again?"

"The cops said it was a robbery, but they said some girl was asking people about that night at a party. Amber told her to shut up and to stop asking questions. This girl didn't back down and started saying things like it didn't happen that way and it was all a set-up. Then Jennica told her that they knew his ex-girlfriend and she should respect the dead." I paused. "That's what they told me anyway."

Tray drove past the house, which was lit up and had people spread out onto the front yard. He turned the car down the first row of parked cars, looking for a slot. "You were quiet at Dylan's house. What were you thinking?"

"I have no idea why, but I can't stop thinking about this one night. Jace joined the Panthers when he was young. He quit school and a few years later, he started working for Galverson. He changed and it was almost overnight." The memories flared in my head and I swallowed against the bitterness that came with them. "He was more confident. No, he was arrogant. Their dad started to fear him. Then he started paying for things, throwing his money around like everyone owed him. I wasn't always there. The Panthers aren't a bad gang. They drive around and mostly protected people around the area, but they didn't like that Jace was working for Galverson. I knew there was a divide between him and the rest of the gang. Then, I don't know." I shrugged and turned to the window. I wasn't seeing the scenery. I was lost in my head, in my past. "Then it was like it didn't matter. Jace came to the house one night. It was in the middle of the night and he just sat there. Brian was sleeping and their dad was having health problems by then so he always sleeping, so when I went to get food, he was in the kitchen."

My voice grew faint as the memory reenacted in my head. "I was hungry and I didn't turn the light on, but when I opened the fridge I saw him at the table. There was blood on him, all over him. And he had a gun." I closed my eyes. "I didn't notice it at first, but I saw the jacket. It was his Panther's leather jacket. It was on the table and when I moved closer to him, he covered the gun with his jacket. I didn't say anything. I didn't know what to say. Jace was always…he didn't talk much. I mean, we joked. He used to wrestle with Brian, but all that had stopped for a long time. I was scared of him. He had become Brian's jackass brother, but that night it was like the old Jace was back." I faltered, remembering the haunted look in his eyes. "I never asked him what was wrong. We didn't talk at all, but I sat there and," a grin left me, "I ate a bowl of ice cream. It was the oddest and most surreal night of my life." Everything went back to normal after that night, but I didn't know how to explain it. It didn't make sense to me.

I turned to Tray and found him watching me. I felt the kindness. I felt the understanding and knew Brian would never have reacted this way. That threw me. Brian would've been jealous. He was *always* so jealous, especially of his brother. I shook my head and continued, "Jace changed after that night. I don't know what happened and I always wanted to ask, but now..." It was too late. "I don't care about him anymore."

"Taryn."

I didn't want to hear what he was going to say. It was going to be beautiful and it would probably make me want to cry. I shook my head. "I'm here to kick some ass. Let's save the poetry talk for later, like never."

He grinned, then reached over and cupped the side of my face. I leaned into his touch before I could lecture myself against it. He was there. Strong. Caring. As I thought of what a great guy he was, my heart sunk. I was spoiled for anyone else. He was it.

Shit.

"What?"

"We have to go to the same college."

"Why?"

"Because I'm ruined for guys. No one else will ever measure up to you." He opened his mouth, but I shot a hand up. "I don't want to talk about it, but you're stuck with me. Got it?" I didn't wait for his reply. "Good. Let's go." And I shoved out of the car. As I rounded the back end—when the hell did we park?—I pointed at him. "You and I have to get it on. It's sad that we've not fornicated yet." I grimaced. "I'm not some damn virgin. What am I thinking?"

I started up the hill, but he caught my hand and pulled me back.

I groaned. I knew where this was going. He pushed me against the back of his SUV and lifted me. As I wound my arms around his neck, I said, "I know you're perfect, but that doesn't mean you have to prove it to me here." My legs lifted and wound around his waist and I tugged him so he was pressed against my chest. "Although, public sex does have its own rush, and I have no doubt you'll ace that as well."

"Shut up."

He was serious. All the jokes fled as he leaned down.

"Stop, Taryn. Stop fighting. I thought that we established this at Dylan's house."

I nodded. My forehead rubbed against his.

"Stop fighting yourself from feeling."

"I have to." I felt too much. "I just want to fight." I didn't want to cry.

"Let yourself feel. You need to." He stepped back, shaking his head. "Use your emotions, Taryn. They'll make you stronger in the end."

A wave of sadness rushed through me. His words opened the door and I lowered my head. I felt the tears, but fuck it. I'd feel later. Jumping off the car, I started up the hill. "Let's go. I'll use my emotions. I'll use them to kick this girl's ass if she doesn't tell us everything."

When we got to the house, people stopped talking. The music still blared. People were yelling and laughing from inside the house, but conversations trickled to a stop outside as people turned and saw us. No. I scanned around. They were looking at me. They weren't focused on Tray. All their hatred was coming at me. I lifted my hands. "What? Is there a poster with my head on it somewhere?"

A girl stepped away from the crowd. She was holding a red plastic cup with her purse hanging off her arm. Her hair was braided to the side and it rested over her shoulder. She wore a skimpy black shirt that showed her midriff and baggy jeans. Her eyes were cold. Her lip lifted in a slight sneer. "We know who you are. We don't want you around here."

I frowned. "I'm here for answers. Where's the girl that said Brian's death was a set-up?"

She laughed, rolling her eyes. "You mean every girl? We all know it was a set-up. No one believes Brian Lanser was robbed and killed. We're not dumb."

Tray tugged at my belt loop. He pulled me backwards. "This doesn't make sense. They wouldn't rally for Brian."

I shot him a look. He didn't have to explain that to me.

He tucked me behind him and asked the girl, "What else happened that we don't know?"

"Ask her. The rumor is that she was there, that she was at the Seven8 with Jace Lanser that night."

A shiver went down my back. Someone had seen me, someone that wasn't Jace.

Tray said, "She was there for a different reason. That's when she was told about Brian's death too. She's been in mourning since. This is the first we're hearing about a set-up."

The girl scoffed. "Yeah, right. She saw Brian that night. He died hours later. Gray told me he was going to see her. Now he's missing too. Like I said, we're not stupid."

My blood ran cold, and I surged forward, around Tray. "What did you say?"

"Gray. He's missing." Her eyes were locked on mine and her hatred went up a notch. As she said that, the crowd moved forward. A few people called out, "Yeah, where is he, bitch?"

I looked around. This was it. They were rallying because of Gray, but I shook my head. I didn't want to believe this. "You're kidding me, right? Gray's fine. Gray put you up to this." I raised my voice, "GRAY! Where are you?"

"He's missing."

A guy stepped next to her. "He went missing last night. He wasn't in school today and Dee told us that he went to see you."

"What?" No, no, no. I couldn't go through this again. There was no way. "Who's Dee?"

The girl jerked forward. Her fingers tightened on her cup, and it broke in her hands. She kept glaring at me. She didn't notice her cup or the liquid that was running down her arms and legs from it. "Stop insulting us. I hate you. Do you understand that? Gray is missing because of you."

The guy touched her arm and said to me, "Dee was with Brian last."

"That girl he was hooking up with?"

Just then, the crowd parted and two guys brought a girl forward. She was struggling against their hold. She didn't see me at first and when they shoved her forward, she rounded and punched one of them. Then she turned to the girl. "What the hell, Ro? You guys just grab me?"

Ro pointed to me, her arm dripping with beer. She made no move to clean herself up.

Dee rounded and saw me. Her eyes got big, and she paled. Then she bolted.

"Hey!"

I started after her, but Tray grabbed my arm. "Stay. I'll get her."

"But..." I stopped. He was already gone. The guys who had brought Dee to us took off after her, but Tray lapped them in seconds. One of them stopped and came back, while the other continued after Dee and Tray. He gestured to the parking lot. "I forgot Dee ran track last year."

Ro's lips were pressed tight. She said through them, "Jake will bring her back."

The guy grunted and looked at me. "Evans will bring her back. Jake's there to help in case she knees him in the balls." He nodded to me. "I played against Evans last year. I forgot how quick he is too."

"Shut up, Frank."

He shrugged. "You got your panties in a twist, but she's here. She's not going anywhere." He was still staring at me and I realized he was talking about me. "I don't think she had anything to do with Gray."

The other guy who had first spoken for Ro shook his head. "You're not helping, Frank." He glanced down at Ro. "But I agree with him. We know Matthews. She's not down like that."

"I don't care. Gray's missing. He always took up for her and now he's gone. She's the common factor." Her eyes sliced to mine, cutting through the air. "If you had anything to do with Gray or if he shows up dead like your ex-loser, you're the one I will blame."

I shook my head. I wasn't accepting what they were saying. Gray was fine. He was always fine. "Why don't I remember you?"

"Because I'm not like you. I don't hang out with druggies and criminals."

"You're one of the popular crowd?" She wasn't acting like it, but scanning the guys I recognized them as being a part of the athletes from Pedlam. Gray was popular. She could've been there and I wouldn't have known her. I didn't care enough to know people at that school. Gray and Brian. That was it.

"They're coming back." Frank laughed shortly. "Evans has her."

He swung back to me. I sensed unspoken questions from him and bit out, "What?"

"Nothing. Just never would've pegged you as a girl that would get with Tray Evans from Rawley. He's high-class."

I bristled. I got the insult. "If Gray is missing, you're going to want my help. Pissing me off is not the way to go."

He lifted his chin. "How do you figure?"

"I know Jace Lanser and I can get places others can't."

"She's right." The third guy pulled Frank back. "We all know her reputation. Let's just chill for a moment."

Dee was being dragged by Tray, who had a firm grasp on her arm. As they neared us, he let her go and shoved her in front of me. She glanced around, but the guys formed a circle around her in seconds. She blinked, taken aback by how fast they moved. Then she swung her head to me, snarled, and glanced at Ro. The snarl dropped.

Ro asked first, "Why'd you run?"

"Because of this whore." She nodded at me. "Brian's dead because of her. Gray's missing because of her too."

Ro turned to me, but didn't say anything.

A dark gleam appeared in Dee's eyes as she added, "She probably works for Jace Lanser."

I laughed. "This is a joke, right? I want to *kill* Jace Lanser."

Ro said, "I'm starting not to believe you, Dee. You were with Brian last. You were with Gray last night too. You blamed Matthews today, but she's here. She's acting like she's in the dark. That tells me one of you is lying."

"You were with Gray last night?"

Dee became quiet, and she looked over her shoulder. The guys pressed forward, tightening their circle around her.

"Why'd you run when you saw me?"

"Because you killed Brian. You did something to Gray. You're going to do something to me too." She was pale and began trembling.

I repeated my question. "You were with Gray last night? Why? What happened?"

She started laughing. The sound started out like a genuine laugh, but as she kept going, it turned panicked. Bitterness and a maniacal sound mingled with it. Bending over, she whispered, "Gray didn't believe it. He said Brian wasn't killed in a robbery. I believed him. Maybe I shouldn't have."

I glanced at the other girl, Ro, and asked, "Did Gray say this to you too?"

For the first time, the loathing from her shifted and a look of pain glimmered back at me. My gut clenched. I heard the sadness in her voice when she said, "No. I wish he had, though." It was really starting to sink in. Something happened to Gray.

My own panic was rising. No, no, no. Not again.

Tray had been watching me. He stepped close, his chest brushed against my arm, and said, "Why did Gray only tell his theory to you?"

My eyes closed and I knew what he was doing. He was reminding me he was there for me and giving me his strength. Touching him, hearing his voice so close to me, I clung to it. Gray was gone. Jace killed Brian and he was going to take Gray away too. A darkness was swirling inside of me, lashing against the pain and fear. Rage was taking over, filling every pore in my body, until it blossomed full force.

My control snapped and I lunged for Dee. Grabbing her around the throat, I lifted her until her body slammed against one of the guys. They fell back, surprised by the force from me, but then they grabbed around Dee's waist, lifting her so I wasn't strangling her.

Her eyes threatened to pop out of her head. She couldn't talk. Choked gasps spilled out of her and she tried to kick at me.

My hand tightened.

"Shit, let her talk," someone said.

My hands kept tightening.

Jace. Her. Gray. Brian. Shelly. Kevin. All of them flashed in my mind. Betrayal. Loss. Pain. Lies. Manipulation. All of it. Everything that had happened to me was coming back at me. It felt like I was being seared on the inside, like someone had plunged a hot poker through me. I wanted to hurt someone else. I was sick of being the one to get hurt. In that moment, Jace's face merged with hers, and he was all I could see.

Then I was pulled backwards. I kicked out, trying to get back at him. He needed to pay.

"Taryn!" Tray was yelling in my ear. But I wasn't listening. His voice sounded like a small whisper against the rage that had taken over me.

291

Then Ro was in front of me, between me and *him*. She tried to help with holding me back.

Tray grunted and readjusted his hold on me as I strained against him. I smacked Ro's hands off me and then three other guys stepped between us.

I yelled over them, climbing up, "You killed him. You killed Brian. You were with him last. And now Gray. That's on you!" Tray grasped me around the waist and tugged me back down.

He twisted around, his back to the rest of the group, and wrapped his arms around me. There were other guys there, all holding onto a part of me, trying to help him. He tucked his head down so his lips were on my ear and yelled, "TARYN! Calm down."

I struggled. She was Jace. He was her. He was in front of me. I could get at him.

"You're not making any sense. STOP!" He kept rocking back and forth. "Stop, Taryn. Listen to me. Taryn, listen to me." His head lifted and he said to someone else, "Let me through. I'll calm her down and bring her back."

"You sure, man? She's like a wildcat."

"I'll be fine." The crowd parted and Tray moved me forward. I was in front of him. His arms were holding me in a big bear hug from behind, and he kept urging me forward until we were near the cars. He kept whispering in my ear, "It's me, Taryn. It's me. Calm down. Come on. Come back to me."

When I felt the cool metal of a car, I bent forward and rested my forehead to it. I gasped for air, and my heart raced. Slowly, the panic and hysteria started to ease from me. I felt a tightness in my chest and tears on my cheeks.

Tray was bent over me, still whispering in my ear, "Come back to me, Taryn." His hold gentled and he lifted a hand to my cheek. His finger caressed me, moving back and forth. It was a tender touch and I brought my hand over his. I turned to look him in the eye.

"Tray."

He pulled back, moving so he was beside me. He cupped my face. "It's me."

"I wanted to hurt her."

A soft laugh came from him. "You wanted to kill her, Taryn. You were calling her Jace."

"I was?"

He nodded. "I think they believe you now. If we hadn't been there, you would've done major damage to her."

I closed my eyes. Oh my god. I shook my head. "I can't think about that." Gray. "They did something to Gray. She has to know something. I have to find out."

I pulled away, but he caught my hand. "Hey, hey."

"Tray." I didn't have time to argue. I looked at them, saw they were watching us, and my eyes went straight to Dee's. She was bleeding. Her lip was swelling up and she was holding a hand to her eye, but she shrunk down at my gaze.

I started forward again. Tray didn't stop me this time. He was right beside me. Three guys formed a wall between me and Dee, but Tray motioned them aside. "She won't attack her again."

They nodded and moved aside, but stayed close. I knew they would jump in if I attacked her again. I shoved them out of my mind. They weren't important. "Tell me everything."

CHAPTER TWENTY-SIX

"I don't know what you want me to tell you." Dee was huddled in a corner, sitting on the bed. We had moved inside with Ro and a guy I didn't know. The rest stayed outside and kept the crowd away. Dee crossed her arms and lowered her head, and I wondered if she thought she could hide from us. I snorted to myself at that thought. *Fat chance, honey.*

"What?" Ro was leaning against the wall by the door, her boy toy beside her. She asked again, "What's so funny with what she said?"

I narrowed my eyes. "Why do you care so much about Gray?"

She shot back, "Why do you?"

"He's my friend."

She lifted a hand and pretended to shoot herself. "You think you're the only one that's friends with him?"

I opened my mouth, a retort at the tip of my tongue, when Tray cleared his throat. He straightened from the wall. "Let's stick to the topic at hand."

I turned my attention back to Dee. She was biting her lip, glancing between all of us. I could practically read her mind. "You're not getting out of this. Spill what you know and I'll let you leave with only Ro on your ass."

"And if I don't?"

Really? Flashing a grin, I kicked one of her legs to the side. Her elbows fell down and she almost tumbled to the floor. When a heated glare came at me, I moved my finger from side to side in front of her face. "I would've done real damage outside. Do you want to piss me off again?"

Ro sighed from behind me. "Dee, just tell her. My god, we're not going to kill you. Stop acting like this. We all want the same thing."

Dee's loathing doubled and she pointed at me as she spoke to Ro, "Speak for yourself. She saw Brian last. He was doing something for her and he's dead. Now Gray's gone. All I know is that he didn't want to talk to her for the longest time and the moment he decided to go see Taryn, he goes missing. Those two things aren't a coincidence to me." She swallowed, her throat jerking up and down. She crossed her arms over her chest again. "If I talk, I die. I'm not talking."

I started for her.

She screamed and scrambled back on the bed.

No name guy jerked forward, saw that I didn't do anything, and frowned to himself. He leaned back against the wall. Ro and Tray never moved.

"You're sick, do you know that?" Dee pressed a hand to her chest.

I rolled my eyes. "Do you want to know what I said to Brian? I'll talk, but you talk after I'm done. That's the only way I'm doing this."

She frowned.

Ro cursed. "Say yes, Dee. My god. This is taking forever. She was out for your blood. She's not working with the bad guys. She wants Gray back as much as we do."

"What if it's a trap and she has us all killed?"

"If I wanted to kill you, I would've done it outside. These people stopped me." I gestured around the room and to the door. "They held me back. I do my own dirty work. If I was who you're claiming I am, I would've left, made a call, and had someone kill you off." My eyes flashed. "I'm getting sick of your insults."

Ro shot Tray a look. "She's going dark again. Do something."

He shot her a look back, but said to me, "Taryn?"

"What?"

"Make a call for her too, while you're at it," he said, staring right back at Ro. Everyone got his meaning.

She flushed, rolling her eyes. "I know Dee and she doesn't buckle under pressure like that. You're just intimidating her."

I threw my hands in the air. "Asking her nicely didn't work. Maybe treating her like an idiot will?"

"Whatever." Ro glared at Dee. "Just talk. I'm getting sick of this."

"Your patience has been noted." My hands went to my hips and I turned so I was facing her squarely. "She's not saying anything to you either."

Ro glared at me.

"Hey," Dee murmured, straightening on the bed. "Guys…"

"What?" We turned at once, barking the same word.

She gulped, cowered a moment, and then shook her head. "Fine. Okay. I'll tell you." She stopped and glanced between us.

I made a circling motion with my hand. "Go on. We're all ears here."

"Okay. Okay." She nodded. Her arms unfolded and she patted her legs before moving to sit on the edge again. "Brian left me after he saw you that night at Rickets' House. He wouldn't tell me what he was doing or where he was going, just that you said something and he had to check it out." She faltered, and her head moved down. "He was dead the next day. I didn't know he was dead. I heard about it in the hallways with everyone else, and while I was devastated, I didn't question anything. People were saying he was killed during a robbery. It made sense. He had a lot of money on him. He'd been dealing at Rickets' all night."

"He was Jace Lanser's brother. No one would've robbed him."

Her eyes turned to me. There was no fear. There was no caution or paranoia. I saw hurt and pain. She cared about him too. In that moment, she saw the same in me. I felt it and then she nodded. She murmured, "I know. Gray said the same thing." She glanced at Ro, biting her lip. "He came to me two weeks later and he was asking a lot of questions. He didn't think it was a robbery." She nodded to me. "What you said. No one would rob Jace Lanser's brother. They'd wind up dead themselves. Everyone knows that."

"Tell me about Gray. I know about Brian and that night."

Ro and her friend looked at me, but I ignored their silent conversation. I needed to know as much about Gray as possible.

"He thought there was a different story. He wanted to know what I knew and what Brian said to me. So I told him, but he didn't want to tell you. He said you had enough to deal with. I didn't know what he meant, but he was adamant about not bothering you with this. I believed him. I trusted him." She lifted a shoulder in a shrug. "I didn't know what he was thinking, but I cared about Brian." She looked back to me as she said, "I've since learned about your history with him. I didn't know at that time who you were, but it stung. And hearing that Gray was protecting you, that stung too. Who were you? Did you shit gold or something? That's how they talked about you. Seeing you tonight, I don't know, I was angry and maybe jealous."

I started laughing. I was fed up. "Are you kidding me?"

She flinched.

I added, "My ex-boyfriend, someone who I loved, was killed. Someone else who I care about is missing, and you're jealous? Get. Over. Yourself." My chest was tight and I took two steps towards her. My hands were balled in fists again, pressing against my leg. "We're not playing around here. Brian is dead. I'm hoping Gray isn't. Your emotions don't matter. Ever."

She sucked in her breath, tears welled up in her eyes, and I saw her start to crumble again. I turned to Tray. I couldn't hold back anymore. He saw my impatience and nodded. Gesturing for me to step back, he stepped forward and took my place. "What did you and Gray do?" he asked, his tone gentle.

I crossed the room and took up where he'd been standing, keeping watch outside the window, but I could see from the window's reflection that she'd glanced at me.

"Dee."

She turned to him. "We…" She looked at me again.

"Dee," Tray said calmly, "what did you and Gray do?"

"We teamed up, okay? He didn't want to tell anyone about this, but when he didn't show up for school today, it's like it's happening all over again." She shook her head. "He thought Brian was dead because of Jace. I didn't know what to think of that. I mean, they're brothers, right? But I know that Brian hated Jace and there hasn't been a relationship between them for a while. Gray wanted to ask his brother some questions."

"What did Jace say?"

"Nothing. We never found him. Jace Lanser is missing or," her lip trembled, "he's gone or dead, you know?"

Reaching for the window frame, my fingers curled around it. I didn't dare breathe, the hope was so strong in me.

Looking at Ro now, she added, "Gray didn't want to tell you anything. He said he didn't want you to worry either."

I shook my head and turned around. "Why do you think Jace is missing? He's never been available for just anyone to find him."

"I know, but we staked out everywhere and waited for him. There was nothing. His clubs, his businesses, even the Panther's headquarters. His house. Brian's old house. Nothing. Gray said he had one last place to look and then he was going to tell you what was going on."

"Do you know where that was?"

"I assumed it was your house. Brian always talked about how close you and Jace used to be. He thought his brother was obsessed with you. I just assumed that's what Gray meant."

Nowhere. That's where this interrogation had gotten us. No-fucking-where. I turned to Tray. "Let's go. We have to find Gray."

No one stopped us. We swept through the house and out to the parking lot. Once we were out of earshot, I stopped, bent over, and let out a scream. It had been sitting on the bottom of my throat, waiting for me to let it loose, and I didn't hold back. My hands grasped my hair and pulled on it.

Once I was done, I glanced at Tray. He lifted an eyebrow. "You want to scream again or do you want to hear my suggestion?"

"No." I had one more lead. "I know someone else who might know something about Jace."

"Who?"

"Kevin. The guy he forced to adopt me."

I knew no one was home, but I parked my car around the block and walked anyway. I was dressed from head to toe in black with a red bandana around my neck. There were better items to wear, a black bandana would've been better, but I wanted red. It stood for Brian's death. I was being dramatic, but I didn't care. I didn't know what would happen or what lengths I would go to that night. I wanted information. Kevin was going to tell me everything and if I needed to look like a homicidal maniac to get it, so be it.

Letting myself into the house, I pocketed my key and kept the lights off. Mandy was with Shelly. The two left town for Austin's tournament and Tray texted me that Kevin had driven past him further down the road. He was on his way home. So I sat and waited.

A few minutes later, the car's headlights flashed through the house as it turned into the driveway. The garage door opened and he parked inside. The engine turned off. He was coming. Closing my eyes, I took out my knife. That, also, was intended to strike fear in my adoptive father. When he opened the door, the light switched on and I heard his gasp. Then he belted out an abrupt laugh. "Taryn, you scared the hell out of me."

I was still in the shadows. The kitchen light didn't extend all the way to the end of the table where I was sitting. When he closed the door and stepped closer, he saw what I was wearing. The laughter faded and his eyes dropped to the knife. "What's that for?"

I picked it up and put the end on the table. Then I let it spin. As I held it in place with the palm of my hand, I watched him. He watched it spin. He wasn't laughing anymore, and he moved back a step.

"Taryn?"

I continued to stare at him until I saw his hand slide inside of his pocket. He was reaching for his phone. I asked, "Who are you going to call?"

His hand fell out of his jacket pocket. "I suppose I can't call the cops." He looked down. His tie was twisted, but he let it be. "I had a business meeting. What are you doing in my house?"

I glanced to the hallway. There was a pile of boxes lined up by the front door. "Are you moving?"

"Taryn." He grimaced. "Just tell me what you want to know and I'll tell you. I won't hold anything back. I'm tired of all the lies. I want it over." He closed his eyes. Resting his elbow on the counter, his fingers rubbed at his temple. "What do you want to know, Taryn?"

I laid the knife down. "Everything. Start with what you did for Jace."

He nodded. "Okay." His shoulders lifted and fell. "I did anything Jace wanted. Mostly, I wrote prescriptions for whatever name they gave me. He sent people to me to treat. I was their physician on hand, their medical bitch."

"What did you get out of it?"

"Money. I got a lot of money. Both Mandy and Austin have their futures set. They can go to any college they want, and I put enough in their trust funds so they should never hurt in life. Shelly wanted to adopt a child a long time ago and we started another trust fund for that person." Regret and pain flared in his eyes for a moment. "We had someone picked out. She even stayed with us, but there was a problem with the paperwork and she went back to her real family." He turned away. His hand dropped from his temple and his shoulders drooped. "She died three months later. Her father beat her to death."

"You had another foster kid that you wanted to adopt?"

He nodded. "Yeah."

"Why didn't Mandy or Austin say anything?"

"We never told them. They didn't know who the girl was. We told them she was a daughter of a friend." There was anguish in his voice. He dropped to a whisper. "Shelly cried every night for months, but the kids never knew. We didn't want to get their hopes up."

I frowned. "Let's get back to your work with Galverson and Jace. How did everything start?"

A soft chuckle left him. He nodded. "Yeah, okay." His hand went back to pinching the top of his nose. "Uh, Jace recruited me. He said he wanted a physician on hand to treat their people and to give them pills when they needed. It went on for years. Then things changed a few years ago—"

"How long ago?"

"Maybe five years? I think. I was stupid, Taryn. Jace recruited me when he was young. I took him as a real patient. He built a relationship with me. He came in with broken ribs, bruises all over him. It was obvious that he was getting beaten at home. I'm supposed to report that, but he asked me not to. He told me it wasn't what I thought and that he was getting out. I think I was worried that if I reported anything, something would happen like—"

I nodded. The pieces were beginning to connect and I said for him, "Like the girl who went back home and was killed. You thought Jace would get hurt like that."

"Jace was just a kid to me."

"Yeah." I picked up my knife and stood it upright. The tip rested on the table, grinding into it. "He manipulated you."

"Yeah." His head bobbed slowly. "I can see that now. I think they picked me because of what happened with the foster girl." He looked at me again. A shine of tears in his eyes. They were sitting there, but they never spilled. "He talked to me about Brian, his brother, and about you. He talked about their dad. How their mom left them. I was emotionally involved before I realized it. I cared for Jace like he was my own son. I started talking to him about Mandy and Austin. I told him about the other girl. Her name was Cara. God," he laughed bitterly, "I can't believe I even told him her name, but he knew. Thinking back, he never reacted. He knew all of it. He probably knew everything about my children."

I gritted my teeth.

He kept going, "A lawsuit was brought against me. I messed up in a surgery, and the case against me didn't look good. I was going to lose my practice. Jace picked up that something was wrong, and I told him about it." He paused for a moment. Then another moment. I sat and waited. When he spoke again, his voice was hoarse. "He took care of it. Just like that. The case against me was gone. I didn't know what he did. I didn't want to know, but it was gone and I still had my future."

"That's when you started working for him?"

He nodded. "It started with one prescription, for his brother. Then his cousin. Then his friend. Then there was a list of five every day. I panicked. I didn't want to keep working for him."

He stopped, and I waited.

"Then the money started coming in. He paid me in the beginning, but it was nothing compared to what he paid me after I tried to stop. They dumped money in my bank account. If I had gone to the police, I would've looked guilty. I already looked guilty with the lawsuit. I still don't know what Jace did to get the case dropped against me. I don't know if I could handle that on my conscious."

"This kept going?"

He nodded. "Years. I got in so deep. I was too far in and there was no way out and then I got a call one day. Someone died and the overdose came from a prescription I wrote. I didn't know the person, but I had to pretend I did."

I frowned. "Who called you?"

"It was a family member. They didn't know who I was. They were trying to figure out how their sister got a bottle of pills when their family doctor had referred her to a treatment facility." He stopped again. His breathing was becoming labored and his hand went to the counter. It was balled in a fist, but he forced his fingers to flatten. "I panicked. I hung up the phone and called Jace. He—"

He cut himself off.

"Let me guess." My tone was wry. "He took care of it again."

He nodded. "The protocol was that I was supposed to be eliminated. One of the patients they sent to me dropped a notebook, and there were rules written inside. He came back the next hour in a panic looking for it, but I lied. I told him he hadn't left anything or if he did, the garbage had been taken out so he shouldn't worry. He still did. I could see the fear in his eyes. The next time I saw him was in the morgue. He had my card in his pocket so I was asked to identify his body."

My stomach clenched, but it was faint. As he kept going, a layer of dirt was laid on top of another, then another, then another. There were so many layers, I was growing numb.

"Keep going."

"Yeah." He let out a sigh. His shoulders were slumped so far down that his forehead was almost resting on the counter now. He looked like half the man he had been when he first sat down. "Jace took care of it. I don't know what he did, what he could've done, but he did something. There were no emails in the morning. No more patients sent to me. It was like I had been let go. I didn't work for them anymore." He shook his head. "I didn't ask Jace because I didn't want to know. I'm ashamed of myself. I can barely look at my own children when I'm home. I can barely handle being in the same room as my wife."

"Then Jace came to you about me?"

He nodded. "I was golfing with a few of my friends when he showed up. I almost pissed my pants when I saw him driving towards me in a golf cart. He didn't give me a choice. He handed me your file, said I needed to adopt you, and we were supposed to move. There was even a back story of what I could tell Shelly if she needed convincing."

"That Brian was violent." I remembered Austin's words.

306

"Once I said that, Shelly was all-in. You were her mission. She wanted to save your life, whether you wanted to come along or not."

I glanced at the boxes now. "You were supposed to move?"

"That was the other deal. As soon as we got the adoption papers signed, we were supposed to move. Jace was furious when we didn't go, but I couldn't convince Shelly to go. We didn't want to argue where Mandy and Austin could overhear, so we left. We'd go to a hotel and check in and just fight about it."

"Those were some of your trips?"

"Some of them. I'd get another reminder from Jace that we had to move, so I would call her to meet me. She didn't want to move. That was the one thing she put her foot down about. She didn't want to upset Mandy or Austin's social lives. She said their well-being was too shaky and she wouldn't do any more emotional harm to our children." A hollow laugh came out of him, sounding like it was being dragged from the bottom of his throat. "I told her the truth. Once the adoption set-up came out, I told her most of it."

"What sealed the deal for her to agree to move?"

"Jace threatened to kill Mandy."

I felt as if a knife had been plunged into my gut. It was invisible, but it was there. I could imagine Jace being in the room, smiling as he twisted the knife to the side. Hearing the same threat he gave me from Kevin had me breaking out in a cold sweat. I had to ask the next question. "When?"

"They're already gone."

My eyes leapt to his. "What?"

His eyes grew guarded. "Shelly took Mandy to Austin's tournament, but they aren't coming back. Movers are coming tomorrow, and I'm bringing everything with us. I wanted to take you with us. Shelly was supposed to convince you to come, but I can't make you go. I'm sorry, Taryn."

They were gone. It was already done. The knife was yanked out and shoved back into me, but a part of me no longer felt the pain.

"I haven't heard from Jace for a while, not since his brother was killed." He paused. "I'm assuming that's who that was? Your ex-boyfriend? Unless that was a lie as well."

"No," I whispered. "Brian died."

"I'm sorry about that too. I am, but we can't stay. I believe Jace. I know what he's capable of. After I leave, none of us are ever coming back."

I'd never see them again. Then I asked one last question, "Was the adoption real? Am I really your adopted daughter?"

"No." He didn't look away. There was no hesitation. There was no doubt. "It was faked for Shelly's sake. None of the documents are real. There was no real background check. Shelly just thinks it went fast, but it was all a lie."

I nodded.

I was the lie.

CHAPTER TWENTY-SEVEN

Knock, knock

Tray and I turned to each other. We shared a look.

Knock, knock

"Tray! You in there?"

He ignored him and asked me, "Are you ready?"

I nodded. We had gone to a hotel after I left Kevin. There'd been only one move we could do and Tray pulled out his phone. I watched as he pressed the numbers, and then heard him say, "Chance?"

He had called the DEA. It wasn't a long conversation with his brother. Chance told us to go to a hotel as a precaution and Tray looked at me. I already knew where I wanted to stay. "We'll go to the hotel on Sixth Street in Pedlam."

Tray frowned, but relayed the information. He added, "I'll text the room number." Then he was silent for a moment before he murmured, "Got it. Okay."

As he hung up, I asked, "What was that last part?"

"He told me a code to use in case someone intercepts the text."

"Does he think that's a real possibility?"

"I don't know." He put the phone down and turned the car towards Pedlam. "He said not to go back home, just to be safe. I think they're operating under the 'better safe than sorry' theory."

Knock, knock

I was pulled back from my thoughts as Tray's brother tapped on the door again. Tray went to let his brother into the room, and I stayed by the window.

Chance Evans was an older version of Tray. They had the same hazel eyes, dirty blonde hair, and chiseled cheekbones, but Chance looked more weathered. He was slightly bigger in build as well. His shoulders were a tiny bit broader, but Tray was more defined. After they embraced, Chance gazed at me for a moment. It was direct, as if seeing right through me, with a hint of caution and suspicion at the same time. I felt like I was being interrogated without any questions asked, and I straightened to my fullest height because of it. My eyes narrowed and my chin lowered in a challenge. This was my life. Gray was my friend and I wasn't going to let a stranger cast blame on me.

After a full minute of studying me, his hand clapped Tray's shoulder and he gently shook him. "Are you two nuts?"

Tray frowned. "What are you talking about?"

"This is a Panther hotel." Chance swung his suspicious eyes my way again. The caution was gone. He did blame me. "I know my little brother had no idea, but you did. He said you picked it."

I turned and leaned my back against the wall. My arms crossed over my chest and one of my eyebrows arched. "Yeah?"

"Taryn?"

I ignored the soft undertone of betrayal from Tray's voice. "Jace Lanser is missing. He's the one I want."

Chance narrowed his eyes, turning back to his brother. "You said a friend was kidnapped. You never said it was connected to Jace Lanser."

"Is there a difference?"

"Jace Lanser is a big fucking deal. He's in a different league. Do you know what you've gotten yourself into?" He swung around to me. "What was your agenda coming here?"

"It's a cheap hotel. No one will look here for us." But that wasn't the full truth. I didn't want to look at Tray. When he asked, it had been a split second decision, but I knew I needed to follow it through. I could feel the hurt from him.

"Bullshit."

I shrugged and turned back to the window. "It's the closest hotel to Pedlam's school." *Liar!* My conscience knew I was still holding back.

He shook his head. "You two are going to explain everything, and I mean everything. I want to know when you wipe your ass to the real reason this hotel was picked." He sent the last statement to me.

A good person would've flushed with guilt. I did nothing. There was a good goddamn reason I picked it. Tray gestured to me. "Do you want to start?"

I did. I told him everything. He got all the details, even the events with my fake family and even the conversation from Dee and Kevin. I didn't hold back any of the exchanges I had with Brian or with Jace. By the time I was finished, Chance Evans had a different look to his stare. There was still suspicion, but he looked wary now. He said, "How do I know this whole thing wasn't a set-up and you're not working with Lanser to flush me out?"

"What do you mean?"

He pointed to Tray. "Is this whole thing an elaborate plot to flush us out? If it is, Tray doesn't know anything. I do. If you're a plant and you're working for Jace, you take that message back to him. You got it?"

"You think I'm a narc?" Acid dripped from my tone and I stood upright, moving away from the wall where I was leaning. My arms unfolded and went to my side. I didn't like being called a traitor.

He moved forward, his arm muscles flexing at the same time. "No. I called you a plant. This whole thing could be a set-up. So you tell me. You brought my little brother to a hotel that the Panthers own. You don't think I know what that means? If Lanser's alive and kicking, they've already told him you're here. Now they know where my little brother and I are too." He glanced at Tray, whose eyebrows were bunched forward. Chance turned back to me. "I don't buy your bullshit that it's the closest hotel to the Pedlam School."

Ice was forming in my blood. The more he spoke, the more accusations he sent my way, only made me more firm in my belief. He wasn't there to help. He was there to interrogate, blame, and I had a sneaking suspicion he was going to take his brother with him when he left. Casting Tray a swift look, I wondered if this room would be the last I'd share with him. I had no idea what was going to happen after this conversation, but I knew my destination. Whether he helped or not, I was going to that school. I was going to break in and I was going to find my friend.

I had no idea how I was going to get out, but I had to try.

"Taryn?" Tray asked softly as he moved to stand beside his brother. Suspicion had formed in the depths of his eyes too.

I shook my head and bit out a laugh. "He's right."

Chance's eyes got big.

Tray jerked backwards like I had hit him.

I added, "I picked this hotel for a reason. I want Jace to know I'm here. I want him to come to me. I have to try."

"Try?"

I didn't dare look away from Tray. I moved closer to him and softened my voice, "Tray, you heard Dee. They looked everywhere for Jace. If he was around, they would've seen him. Jace knows Gray. He would've gone out to see what he wanted. The only place they didn't search was the school."

"What's with this school?" Chance asked.

I turned to him. I felt rushed. I needed to keep appealing to Tray to repair the small damage done by his brother, but this was a DEA agent in the same room as me. I needed to appeal for his help too. "They did renovations over the summer. They changed things and now there are cameras everywhere. They have guards too, guards with guns."

Tray told him, "We were in the building. We pranked it one night." He lifted a hand towards me. "She helped us get in, so if Lanser is using the building for something, it's got to be in the basement. We didn't see anything on the main floors and I think we would've."

"Stun guns? Pepper spray?" Chance asked me.

"Guns. Handguns and a couple of them had rifles."

"How do you know this?"

"Because I scoped it out one night. What school has guards like that? You have guards like that if there's something inside you want to protect. What's around here that's so precious?" I shook my head. "Drugs. We're in the center of the country. I'm not stupid. Something's changing. It's why Jace wanted me gone. He didn't want me to get involved or he didn't want me to find something, and he knows me. He knows I'll get in wherever he doesn't want me."

"Why?" Chance narrowed his eyes and tilted his head, reassessing me. "What's so special about you?"

"I'm a thief." I flinched at my words. "I *was* a thief. I can get in wherever I want."

"Yeah?" He lifted his chin. "I've known a lot of criminals and a lot of people who grew up hard like you. They didn't have any special criminal skills like that. Where'd you learn yours?"

My stomach clenched, and I avoided Tray's gaze as I answered, "Because Jace Lanser is the one who taught me."

No one said anything after that. The ball of anxiety that was in my chest dropped to my stomach. The longer I waited for Tray to say something, the lower that ball moved in me. It was almost to the floor when he said, "You never told me that."

Regret seared through me. "I didn't tell anyone."

"It would've changed things."

"It shouldn't have."

"You said Jace was like family, but I didn't believe how much." He shook his head and turned away. "It's why you're so mad. It's why you want to hurt him so bad, it's because you still care about him." He jabbed a finger at the door. "What if he walks through there? What if he comes in here to talk to you? What then? You've been saying how much you want to hurt him, but what if it's not to hurt him? I think you want to see him one last time. You want to see if the guy you loved like family is still inside him. Don't you? This is all about reconnecting with him, isn't it?"

NO! My head screamed, but I couldn't talk. I couldn't move. My feet were glued in place and my body wouldn't move. I was paralyzed, but I wanted to shake my head. No, no, no. A scream was building inside me. My body was betraying me. Tray was looking at me, waiting for my denial. I needed to reassure him, but it wouldn't come out. The longer I couldn't talk, the more I felt him pulling away from me. He didn't move, but the distance was growing.

"Oh my god."

"NO!" Finally. It burst out of me.

Tray moved back another step, shaking his head. "Oh my god. That's it, isn't it? Do you love him?" I could see the wheels turning in his head, but my words weren't forming. I couldn't get them out fast enough. Turning his back to me, he murmured, "Dee said that Brian thought Jace was obsessed with you, but that wasn't it. Brian was jealous for a reason. There was a connection between you, wasn't there?" He turned back to me. The hurt was so apparent in his eyes. He added, his voice so damn soft, "You didn't even know yourself, did you? Did you know that you love him?"

It was like a waking nightmare. I couldn't stop it from happening and I had no idea why. I was frozen in place.

"Taryn," his voice dropped to a whisper, "I have to go. I have to get out of here."

"Tray—" I gasped out and lunged for him, but it was too late. The door closed on me and I was staring into the wood. I heard him walk

315

away. Reaching for the door handle, Chance said from behind me, "I wouldn't."

I turned around. "Why?"

"You hesitated."

I flinched.

He laughed. "The real answer is the silence. Any smart guy knows that. You didn't say yes, but the truth was that you never said no."

"I froze. I was surprised."

Still chuckling, he shook his head and took off his jacket. As he did, two shoulder holsters lifted in the air and he reached back to take the guns out. One was left on the table by the door. He placed the other one on the bedside table. He draped his jacket over the back of a chair. "Now." He pulled the chair out more and sat down. "Since my brother is gone, why don't you walk me through where you think your friend is being held."

I didn't want to talk to him; I needed to go after Tray, but I said, "I don't know where."

"You said the school?"

"Yes." I clipped my head in a nod, but I couldn't look away from the door. I wanted him to come back through it. He needed to come back to me.

"Yoo hoo." He snapped his fingers, tearing my gaze away. He had sat at the table and gestured to the opposite chair. "Tray needs to think. When he gets hurt, he won't listen. He closes up and then he'll weigh everything in his mind. When he's ready for some answers, he'll seek you out. It's pointless. Trust me." He lifted his lip up in a mocking grin. "I'm just like him."

He waited until I crossed the room and sat down, then asked, "So Tray said something about the basement?"

My eyes never left that door. "No. I've been down there."

"Then what was renovated?"

"I don't know—"

"Hey!" He clapped his hands to get my attention this time. A fierce scowl formed on his lips. "Pay attention. I don't give a shit what lovey-dovey thing you have going on with my brother. Your friend is missing. No matter what mixed-up emotions you have for Jace Lanser, you can't deny that he's dangerous. Sal Galverson is dangerous. If your friend is with him, his life is either over or going to be over."

I checked back in. He was right. Gray came first now. "The building was the same, but there was added security so they must've built something underneath the building."

"All right." He stood and retrieved a laptop. "Listen to me."

I was.

"I need you to leave this room."

I opened my mouth, about to question him, but he held a hand up. I closed my mouth.

He added, "Do not go after Tray. I mean it. Give him space. The sooner he thinks over everything, the sooner he'll come back for answers. Now, having said that," he pulled out his phone and gestured to the computer, "I have to call this in. I didn't come with my team. I thought my brother was exaggerating, but since this is dealing with Jace Lanser and Sal Galverson, I have to run the entire op through my supervisor first."

I nodded. "That's fine." My chest was growing tight again.

He pointed the phone at me, studying me intently. "You need to listen to me when I say this next part." He paused a beat to make sure I was listening. And then he said, "I have to get permission to get a team down here."

He needed permission? "What does that mean?"

"There's no prior investigation. There's no evidence except your testimony. If I get a team down here, you're asking us to go in blind. We haven't compiled any recent information. We know nothing. Now," he held his hand up, "I have history down here. My supervisor knows this. Based off that alone, I might be able to get a small team to come."

"How long?"

"Six hours."

"You took half of that."

"Tray texted me earlier that something was wrong. I was coming anyway."

"Oh." I frowned.

"Just give me some privacy and I'll work my magic." He gave me a forced grin. "Okay?"

I jerked my head in a shaky nod and stood. "Okay." Going to the door, I paused and glanced around. "I'm going to get some food." Then I slipped out.

"Wait."

I poked my head back in. "Yeah?"

He stood and pulled out his wallet. Handing me a fifty dollar bill, he said, "Get us all some food."

"Okay." I took the money and slipped back out. When the door shut, I didn't move. I stayed right there and flattened my ear against the door. I didn't have to wait long. His voice was muffled, but I made out enough.

"What are you doing?"

A guy was standing across from me. He was tall, wearing only a leather jacket with the sleeves ripped off. His jeans were cuffed and ripped and he wasn't wearing a shirt. A panther was stitched onto the front corner of his jacket and I knew there was a bigger panther with two skulls on either side of it on the back. This guy, with scars running down his face and over his bare chest, was a member of Jace's gang. This guy had the same jaded look in his eyes that Jace had.

I jerked back. A startled gasp came out, but I clamped my hand over my mouth to stifle it. I shook my head. "Nothing." This was what I wanted. I could say the word and Jace might come to me.

He frowned.

"My dad's an asshole," I said instead. "He caught me drinking and he's calling my mom right now."

"Oh."

I didn't want him to come. As I stood there with the Panther frowning at me, I realized what I really needed to do. I had to get Gray out and never see Jace again. Tray was right. I still cared about Jace. That was why I hesitated. I wasn't even sure if I still wanted to kill him anymore.

"It was a mistake coming here." I said those words before I realized I was thinking them.

The guy grunted. "You don't seem drunk." He moved past me and pointed to the door. "Just tell your dad you're sorry, smile, and quote bible verses. Don't that work for all rich little girls?"

"Rich?"

"Yeah." He looked me up and down. "I don't know you, but I know you don't belong around these parts. Go home. Go back to pretending the world ain't some scary place." The corner of his mouth lifted in a smirk. "Ain't that what your types do? Daydream and turn real life shit into some fucked-up fantasy?"

An abrupt, genuine laugh came out of me. "I look like one of those types?"

He frowned, but didn't answer. He kept going down the hallway. A door opened and he stopped in front of it, still giving me a puzzled look. Then, as he scratched his head, he went inside. The door slammed shut.

I looked this time and made sure I was alone, but it didn't matter. When my stomach growled, I decided to actually go and get food, but instead of heading to a store I went to the lobby and used the phone there to order pizza. After I stopped at the vending machine to grab some sodas and a few bottles of water, I started back to the room. As I turned down our hallway, the door opened. I heard Chance say, "Tray, wait."

"What?"

I stopped. The anger in his tone sent chills down my back.

"Stop. Come back in here before you go and tell her."

"This is real, Chance. Her friend will die. I was there. I saw that girl. Her fear was real." He moved further inside, but the door was left open. "You have to go in. You have to get her friend."

"They won't green-light this mission. I'm sorry, Tray. I am."

I closed my eyes for a second and stood there. Holding three cans of soda and two bottles of water pressed against my chest, I couldn't even feel the cold from them.

They weren't coming. Chance had warned me, but hearing Tray now, I knew it was true. They weren't going to get Gray.

It was up to me.

I knew what I was going to do. And as soon as I made the decision, it was like a piece of the puzzle clicked into place for me. I think I had always known what I was going to do and now, creeping forward, I hugged the wall so they wouldn't see my approach. I didn't know where they were in the room. As I drew closer, I knelt down so my shadow was minimized and then placed the soda and water on the floor.

"Chance, we have to try." Tray's voice drifted from inside the room.

I peeked inside, saw they were in the far corner, and moved back away. Chance said, "I'll figure something out. I promise. Let's wait for Taryn to come back. I have orders to take you both in. They want to question you in depth."

I stood from my kneeling position, but kept myself flat against the wall. My arm moved to the doorframe and I reached inside. Closing my eyes, I used my memory of the room to know the exact location of the table. I used one finger to touch the edge of the table, then paused. I didn't touch anymore. I lifted my hand a millisecond, reached forward another inch and then lowered it. The gun should be there. When my hand touched the cold metal, I let out my breath.

I held still, not making a move, not making another sound. Then I tucked it against my palm, keeping it steady so it wouldn't move and jar the table. When it was in the air, I pulled my arm back around the table.

They had no idea I had been there.

Then I left.

I was going for Gray on my own.

CHAPTER TWENTY-EIGHT

Gray had given me blueprints for the school, but he told me that there hadn't been a lot of changes. When I snuck inside to help Tray with his prank, I knew that was true. The main change had been the security room. That hadn't been there before, but my gut was telling me Jace was beneath it. I didn't know why. I didn't know what for, but they were there. That was my best chance at finding Gray. I didn't have time to search all the other buildings. Gray and Dee already staked out the others. This was my pick, but every instinct inside me was telling me that I was right.

I just had to get in there.

When I got to the school, I walked the perimeter. I couldn't find a weakness. I couldn't get in where I had before. Jace would have the top level covered with hidden cameras. I had no doubt that every entrance to the level beneath the school was monitored and there could've even been a second wave of guards for those doors. I had to find a weakness.

Backtracking down one of the main roads that led to the school, I found a side road and began walking down it. It led past a clump of houses and then curved around a field. The farther I went, the more isolated it seemed. Trees on one side and the field on the other. A flash of headlights warned me of an approaching car and I melted into the trees. It sailed past me and I caught the glint of a rifle from its passenger.

The further out I went, the closer I was getting. I knew it.

As the field ended, the road curved once again, and I was in the forest now, but I knew this forest. There were dense trees that were on either side of the river, which meant that the river wasn't far from where I was. Now things were making sense. The river ran the length of the entire country from north to south. My guess was that Jace used it to smuggle drugs and he stored the drugs in the school, which meant there had to be a tunnel.

I could feel it. I knew I was guessing right.

Hearing shouts ahead of me, I veered towards them and saw an empty truck parked in front of a hill. I looked left and right to check if there were cameras. When I didn't see any, I sprinted for the hill, bending low to the ground as much as possible. I hugged the side of the truck in case anyone could see from a higher vantage point, but no alarm sounded and no one shouted. Rifles were inside the truck, which told me the men were coming back.

"Let's go, Rufus!"

The voice came from inside the hill. I glanced around, looking for a hiding spot. There was none unless I ran back into the woods, but I wouldn't have enough time.

Their footsteps were getting louder. They were coming.

I had only seconds.

I darted forward, and as I hit the hill, a door swung open, blocking me from their vision. As one man left, the door started to swing shut. I bit down on my lip, but held my knife in my hand. I was ready to leap and stab whoever came at me, but I heard a curse and the door was pushed open again. Relief flooded me. That guy went through the door and then a third followed him out.

"Let's get some booze before we have to head back. The next shift change is in four hours," the first one said. He jumped into the truck.

As the other two men filed towards the truck, I slipped around the door. It swung shut just as the truck's headlights flashed on, and a moment later it was reversing. They didn't wait for it to stop, he yanked the front of the truck around and gunned the engine.

As they headed off, another wave of relief came over me. I was inside, but turning around, I had no idea where I was. It was completely black. Running my hand over the wall and ceiling, I could feel it was a big enough hole for a person to walk through. They had covered the walls with cement, but I could hear the river through the walls. My nose twitched from the dirt in the air. Musk, feces, and mold filled the air as well.

As I moved further down the tunnel, the sounds of the river faded and sounds of traffic grew. I was getting close to the school again. I heard a honk, followed by someone yelling, "Pedlam RULES! Eat it, suckers!"

Then it hit me, and I wanted to smack myself in the head. It was Sunday Night Rally. I'd forgotten about their tradition.

When I got to the end of the tunnel, I hit a wall. Feeling around, I could tell the wall covered the entire tunnel so I started feeling for a door handle. Bass music, cheering, and laughter trickled down from above. I knew for sure I was underneath the school, specifically, I was beneath the parking lot. Then my hand hit a door handle and I paused. I started to turn it.

When the door opened, I slipped into another dark tunnel. This one wasn't as compact and I could feel that it wasn't as long. A door slammed shut not far ahead of me and I held still, but my hand quickly felt in front of me, searching for a possible hiding spot. No one came towards me, no light turned on, and I hung my head. The tension had my insides in a giant pretzel.

I scooted forward until I came to another door. Bending down, I felt under the door. A slight draft was there and it was cool. Then I heard footsteps and another door open and close. More footsteps, then a muffled conversation. I pressed my ear to the door, trying to hear their words, but couldn't make them out.

This was it. I knew whatever was on the other side could be it for me. I knelt down, resting my back against the wall. "Never take your time. Get in. Get what you need. Get out. Less than two minutes. That's your goal every time."

I was going against Jace's guidelines, but this was different. It wasn't a mark. What I wanted to steal was a person, but I had to find him first. I had gone in blind, and I knew there was a high risk of exposure once I went through this door.

I reached into my pocket and turned my phone on. In case there was a camera, I pulled my sweatshirt up so it was engulfed inside it, then pulled my hands inside with the phone. I didn't want the light to attract attention, but I had to send this text. Text after text came to the screen. They were all from Tray. Ignoring all of them, I brought up the last from him. It read: **Stop! Don't do what you're doing. Come back. I'll make them help. Please.**

My hands trembled, but I typed back: **I'm in. Back road. Field. Trees. River. Hidden door in a hill. Two tunnels.** I sent that one and immediately started another one: **I'm sorry. I really am. I still care about Jace, but I hate him. I didn't know until the hotel.** That one was sent as well. Then a third, but this one would be shorter and to the point. **I'm going in. I love you, Tray. I love only you.**

Then I silenced the phone and tucked it back into my pocket.

"I'm so dumb," I muttered to myself. Pulling my head back through the sweatshirt, I leaned back against the wall, eyes closed. I waited, one more moment alone, one more moment alive. My phone was buzzing in my pocket, but I wasn't going to read the messages yet.

This was my plan. Get in. Find Gray, and hope they sent an army after me.

It was time to go. I nodded to myself, wiped my sweaty hands on my pants, and stood. I grabbed the door handle and turned it.

Light blinded me for a moment, but I went into the next room and shut the door. Throwing an arm over my eyes so I could let them adjust, I darted forward. It was go-time. The cameras would see me. I needed to move as quickly as possible.

I scanned the room. It was a large basement hallway. A ladder was lowered down like in a submarine and there were four doors, two on each side of the hallway. There were no windows to see in so I started feeling the handles. All of them were locked. I was tempted to climb the stairs and see what was up there, but I heard a door from above open, then the scuffling sounds of feet over the floor.

"Downstairs. An alarm went off. Check it."

Shit. I had seconds to hide.

There was no place to hide in the hallway. I didn't think. I went straight to the door handle that had been the loosest. Kneeling down, I used my pins to crack the lock. I was breathing in and out steadily to keep my heart rate low. Then the door gave way just as the hatch over the stairs lifted up. A pair of boots appeared and then I was pulled inside a room. I was held against the wall. The door started to slam shut, but I twisted. I shot my arm out and the door landed on it. It couldn't slam shut. They couldn't hear that sound. They'd know someone was there. The person softly cursed and held the door from my arm. I pulled my arm back and the door shut. It clicked softly at the same time a guard jumped to the floor outside.

As more guards dropped from the stairs to the floor, I turned. Two inches separated us. I was face to face with Gray. His eyes were wide and shocked. Then his door was knocked on. He cursed and shoved me towards his bed.

"You in there?" a guard called through the door. A key was being inserted into the lock, but it stopped. The guard pulled the key back out. "What the fuck? The lock is all messed up."

Another guard was next to him. Pushing on the door, he said, "What are we going to do? That's our only set. Boss has the other set."

"Check the other rooms. Nothing was on the camera, but they said to still check." He pounded harder on the door. "Answer me, kid, or we'll have to bust down your door."

Gray was holding me behind him. His hands were jerking and his knees were shaking. "I'm here." His voice was hoarse. He cleared it, then called out louder, "I'm here. Here."

The guard laughed. "Don't suppose you'd tell us if anyone got in here?"

The second guard joined in, bellowing loudly. "Right. That tunnel is almost a mile long."

I closed my eyes shut. Good joke, fellas. Good joke.

"Post, you clear?" The guard turned away. The doors were being unlocked and then shut again. We heard, "Clear."

"Clear."

"Last room clear."

"All right. You heard the others. Set that alarm again, make sure it's working right." He paused for a moment. "Let's head to the next level and keep clearing."

They started back up the stairs. As they left, before the hatch was closed over the stairs again, we heard, "We have to clear out the rest of the shipment—" It shut and we couldn't hear anymore.

I started to speak, but Gray slammed a hand over my mouth. He shook his head, then pointed to the hallway and leaned close. He whispered into my ear, "We can't trust the others. I've heard them telling information for food."

I nodded. He lifted his hand and I whispered, "Are you okay?"

His eyes clasped shut and he pressed his hands to his forehead, rubbing his temples. I skimmed him up and down then. He was thin, but Gray had always been scrawny. His shirt was sweaty, bloody, and there were dark smudges I didn't want to inspect. Kneeling down, I tapped his foot so I could inspect the bottom of his shoes. They were still in good condition. That meant he could run in them.

Looking around his cell, I saw that there was one mattress on the floor alongside two silver pans. My stomach rolled over on itself as I saw one had water and the other had crumbs. They were feeding him like a dog. A third pan was in the corner. That was his bathroom.

I took his hand. "We have to go."

He shook his head. "We can't. The door is locked again."

"No." I took my pins out again. "I got my way in. I can get our way out. I think we can make it. There's a tunnel."

His eyebrows arched high. "The mile tunnel they were talking about?"

We were still whispering, but his last whisper lifted in volume. I shushed him quietly and he nodded, lowering his voice again, standing close to me. My nose twitched. The stench from him was foul so I began breathing through my mouth instead.

As I knelt and began working at the lock from the inside, I murmured, "I think the guards use it to change shifts. The other guards said it'd be four hours. We can make it."

"If we don't?" He shook his head. "No, Taryn. They'll find us and kill us. I was looking for Brian. I didn't believe he was dead," he said, his voice growing hoarse.

"I know." My hand dropped to his on the floor, and I squeezed it.

"I'm sorry. I should've told you right away that I was looking for him."

I frowned. "Dee said you were looking for Jace."

"I was, but I didn't tell her that I thought Brian was still alive. He's not."

He sounded so sure and my heart skipped a beat. "What do you mean?"

"I saw his body."

"You saw it?"

He nodded. His forehead fell to rest on my shoulder. He mumbled, "Jace showed me the video. It was Brian in the morgue. I think Jace took the video."

A shiver went down my spine. I didn't want to think about that. "You talked to Jace?"

"I was in another room and he had me moved here. He said it's more secure." A bitter laugh escaped him. "Not that it matters. My friend is gone. We're probably going to die too."

I frowned. He was defeated, but I wasn't. I kept working on the lock. The guard was right. I had messed it up, but gritting my teeth, I felt the second opening with my pin and turned my wrist, pulling it back to the slot.

Then I heard a click and the door opened.

Gray's forehead was still on my shoulder, and I nudged him with my elbow. "Gray."

He started shaking his head. "I can't, Taryn."

"We have to go."

"I can't. I won't be able to walk that far."

I stood up. I hadn't come this far for it to end in failure. Grabbing his arm, I hauled him up with me and then leaned close to his ear. "You will walk or I will carry your ass."

His eyes were still closed. "I'm too weak."

"Then find something inside of you because we're going." I swung the door wider.

I jerked him behind me, and looked at the other doors. They couldn't see us. I twisted around and looked up at the corners. They should've had a camera and there, in the top right corner, I saw one.

It was turned towards the ceiling.

Gray saw where I was looking and whispered in my ear, "They moved it when they shot someone. They didn't want evidence."

I went cold at that. "We are going. Now." I pulled his door shut, then we headed back where I had come from. The alarm was going to go off. I didn't have enough time to figure out how to disarm it. That meant one of two things would happen. They would figure it was a mistake and not bother to check the rooms again or they would break down Gray's door and find him gone. Either way, I made sure I had a cement hold on his arm as I pushed him forward. As we went through the door, I began lightly jogging. I dragged Gray behind me. I wasn't leaving him behind.

We hadn't gone far when I heard the first door open roughly. Then a voice bellowed through it, "WE HAVE A RUNNER!"

The lights in our tunnel flipped on and I looked up. Right there, pointed right at us, was a camera.

They had spotted us.

"RUN!" I yelled at Gray and took off in a sprint.

CHAPTER TWENTY-NINE

We got through the second door and the tunnel was dark again, but we took off. If something was in the way, we were going through it. I glanced back to make sure Gray was behind me. He was. A fierce expression was on his face, and I knew he wasn't going to die. Neither of us were. As we soared down the tunnel, I began to think ahead. They would have men coming behind us, who would be weighed down by guns, vests, and anything else they had to wear for a uniform. We had a slight advantage, but they would radio ahead. Men would probably be waiting at the opening where I came in. They would try to cut us off.

We had to get there first.

A new burst of adrenalin came over me and I ran faster. Glancing back over my shoulder, I saw Gray falling behind. Our eyes met and a shared look passed between us. We had to keep going or we'd die. It was that simple. His jaw hardened and he bent lower, pumping his arms faster. He was back on my heels again.

Their truck had to leave the school parking lot. They would have to go back into town, then through two stoplights before it could turn around. It would have to circle behind the field. We could do this. We could beat them. Maybe.

Then I heard a gasp, followed by a thud, and braked, turning at the same time. Gray had fallen down. He was on the floor. His ankle was

TIJAN

turned sideways, and he was bent over, grabbing it with a hand. The other was holding him up. He looked up, his eyes wide with panic. We both knew what this meant. I couldn't carry him. We were losing our small window.

The blood drained from his face and beads of sweat formed over the top of his lip. He grimaced, bared his teeth, and then waved at me. It was a weak gesture and his hand dropped back to his ankle. He choked out, "Go. You can still get away."

"No." I shook my head.

"Taryn!"

I looked around, tuning him out. I had come for him. I wasn't leaving without him.

"Go, Taryn. What are you doing?"

"I'm looking for something. Maybe I can use a stick to brace your ankle and you could still run then?" I was searching, scanning everywhere. The panic was burrowing deeper inside of me, poisoning every cell of my body. My chest was tight and I knew I was panting from running, but I shoved all of that out of my mind.

The goal was to save Gray. I just needed help. My eyes kept searching for something... Then we heard footsteps in the tunnel. My heart sunk. Gray glanced to where we had come from, but they weren't coming from there. They were coming from where I had first entered the tunnel. We were too late. They had already cut us off and there was no escape. We were trapped.

A wrangled cry ripped up from the bottom of my throat and I dropped to my knees beside Gray. I was frantic. There had to be something—the footsteps were louder, they were almost on us.

"God," a whimper left me. I couldn't find anything. Then I began patting myself down. Did I have something on me that I could use? My knife—Gray wrapped his hand around mine and said, so damn softly, "Taryn. You have to go."

I shook my head. I wouldn't leave him.

His hand squeezed mine. "It might not be too late for you. It's too late for me. You know this. Go, Taryn. Thank you for trying."

Oh my god. A sob tore from me, but I wasn't crying. I wouldn't. There had to be something. "No, Gray. No."

"Taryn—"

I shoved his hand off and glared at him. "I said no." Then I yanked my knife out, tore off the bottom of my shirt, put the knife next to his ankle, and tied my shirt around it. I yanked on the knot, making it tighter, and then I grabbed Gray's chin and forced him to stare into my eyes. "Get. The. Fuck. Up."

He gave me a half grin, but I could see the strain. Pain flashed over his face and he grimaced. "You're such a bitch."

"Yes." I stood, grabbed him by both arms, and yanked him up. "I'm also selfish, and on that note, we're leaving. I don't give a shit how long it takes us." I pulled out the gun and held it in front of me.

"Hold with both hands. Keep the thumbs separate. Firm grip. Support it and it will support you."

Jace's instructions came back to me and I closed my eyes for a moment. We couldn't run any further, but there weren't a lot of footsteps. There was still hope. I could shoot them and we could keep going. Taking a breath, I let it out. Inhale. Exhale. Gray stood behind me and I waited, my heartbeat sounding in my eardrums. The person was close.

"If you shoot, aim for the chest, it's the biggest target. The shoulder will wing. The leg will stop them. The gun is an extension of your arm. It's a part of you. The firmer the grip, the better your aim will be." Jace had been standing close to me when he said those words. We were at a gun range. It was years ago, but it was now too. I felt Jace there. He was still teaching me, as I was getting ready to shoot his men.

Gray knew what I was doing. He placed a hand on my shoulder, giving me support and I raised my gun.

Two seconds.

I wasn't going to shoot the shoulder or the leg. I was going to shoot the chest. Whoever was coming, it was him or us. It was going to be him.

One second.

My throat was suddenly dry. My finger went to the trigger. I was ready.

"Taryn!"

My finger started to squeeze, but I saw who it was and a guttural scream ripped from me. I dropped the gun, and bent over as I dry heaved. My heart was pounding. Oh god. I lifted my eyes back up, horrified. It was Tray. I choked out, "I almost shot you."

His eyes were wide, so wide that the whites of his eyes blinded me. He raked a hand through his hair, but dropped it and shook his head. "We have to go."

A thousand questions flashed through my head. What was he doing there? What did it mean? A look passed between us and we both knew there wasn't time. I jerked my head in a nod, then went to retrieve the gun. Tray went to Gray, studying his ankle. "Can you run?"

"Yes," I said. He would have to.

"No," Gray said, casting me a wary look. "She braced it with her knife, but I can't run."

Tray clipped his head in a nod, then moved so he was in front of Gray. "Get on my back. I'll carry you."

Relief crashed through me, causing a riptide of hope among the panic and terror. We weren't done. We could still get out of this.

Gray glanced at me. He bit down on his lip.

I stepped towards him. The relief faded and the panic surged once more. My voice trembled, "Get on him."

"Taryn," he started, but Tray kneeled in front of him.

Gray frowned, and then Tray threw him over his shoulder. He grinned at me. "Let's go."

I nodded and started forward again, putting the safety back on, but I kept it in my hand.

Tray was right behind me.

Gray groaned. "My head is in your crotch."

"Yeah. Don't get too excited."

There was laughter in Tray's voice. Still going, I closed my eyes as the relief came back in. We could do this. As we kept running, I felt Tray behind me. He was urging me faster so I kicked it up a notch. We needed to get out before they headed us off. Another quarter mile passed. Tray's breathing was steady. I glanced back. He had a firm grip on Gray, who had wrapped his arms around Tray's torso to keep from bouncing around.

Could we go faster? The unspoken question passed between us and Tray nodded. He moved around me and began to lead. I couldn't smile. I couldn't enjoy this, but the sight of him pulling ahead of me almost brought tears to my eyes.

I pushed forward with a new burst of speed, and we were sprinting, going faster than Gray and I had been going.

We would make it. I felt it in my gut.

Seeing light in the distance, I shouted at Tray, "Did you leave the door open?"

"Yes." He didn't look back. He kept going forward.

"Is your brother coming?" I was shouting.

Tray didn't answer.

"Tray?"

He still didn't answer.

My heart dropped. We had no support. I had known, but I had hoped they would come for me. "TRAY!"

A scowl formed on his face and he glanced at me. "They weren't coming." He held my gaze for a second. "Even for you. Chance said they would have to canvas the school first, but the pep rally put everything off."

They weren't coming, echoed in my head. They weren't coming, but he had.

"Thank you."

He looked over at me again. I had so much more to say. I was sorry for the hotel. I was sorry that I didn't know how conflicted I was about Jace. I was sorry for bringing him into all this. But I didn't say any of it. We were almost to the door. There wasn't enough time.

"I'm here, Taryn."

My heart pounded, not from the adrenalin.

He added, "I came."

"I meant what I texted you."

"I know."

When we made it to the door, we paused, slowing down to go outside, but I braked as I saw that the tunnel kept going. I hadn't noticed it when I entered. Tray was outside, but he stopped and turned. I heard his feet on the gravel. Then he asked, "What is it?"

"This tunnel. I bet it goes to the river." That made sense. It was how they shipped their product out. My heart started pounding again. Jace probably had a secret entrance down there.

"Taryn, we have to go—" As he said that, we heard shouts from the road.

I shook my head. Three of us couldn't hide. They would find us. Hearing the engine of their truck and more shouting, I said, "They're at the front of the field."

Tray frowned at me.

I looked around. "Did you drive?"

"No. I walked in."

We had Gray. What could we do?

"Taryn, they'll search the woods for us." They would find us. That was what he didn't say.

A different plan began to form. "Okay." I shoved down the fear and looked around. "There." Pointing at a clump of trees, I said, "Put Gray there."

"What?" He lifted his head from Tray's side.

Holding onto him so he wouldn't fall and reinjure himself, Tray helped him down so Gray was standing on his own again. Then he started for the clump of trees, and called out from behind him, "What are you thinking?"

"Gray, you stay there and hide. We'll draw them into the tunnel. They'll follow us and won't look for you."

Tray helped him sit down, but Gray cried out, "What are you thinking? Stop doing this, Taryn. Whatever you're doing, just stop it. We can all hide."

Tray hesitated. I waved him back over. "Text your brother, to tell him where Gray is."

"What are you two going to do?" Gray was shouting at me. "You can't jump into the river, Taryn. There's a goddamn cliff. It's higher than what Olympic divers do. You can't do that. No way."

Tray had pulled his phone out. He was already texting.

"I know." A knot worked its way up from my stomach, resting at the top of my throat. "I bet it's how they're smuggling whatever they keep in here. They use the tunnel so that means there's an entrance down there. We can try for it."

The truck was right there. A few more seconds and they would see us.

"We have to go. Gray, get down."

Tray reached for me. His hand wrapped around my arm and he pulled me close. A tender look was in his eyes and for an earth-shattering moment, time suspended. Was he going to say it too? Then he murmured, releasing me at the same time, "We have to make sure they see us."

340

Oh. It felt like an anchor dropped to my feet. I forced myself to nod. "Yeah. Good plan."

"We can close the door." Spotting a piece of metal laying on the ground, he picked it up. "We can use this to wedge it closed. They'll still get it opened, but it'll slow them down."

It would give us another head start.

The truck was closer. I started the countdown in my head. Three seconds. I moved back into the tunnel. I glanced at where we had come from, but there was no sound coming from that way.

Two seconds.

Tray was standing in front of me. He gripped the beam tighter.

I looked for Gray, but he was gone.

One second.

Now.

The truck veered around the last bend. Four guards were standing in the back of the truck. Each had a rifle in their hands and as they saw us, they jumped out of the truck before it stopped. They were sprinting for us. Tray heaved the door shut, then wedged the beam at the bottom of the door. They could still open it, but the beam would hold the door shut for a little longer.

Then he turned, his hand touched my back, and we moved as one. We sprang forward.

We soared down the tunnel. Tray was moving at such a fast pace, I couldn't keep up. My lungs were straining. My legs stretched to the farthest stride they could go, and I pumped my arms, propelling forward. We had to get there. We had to find Jace's exit.

341

As we kept going, they were pounding on the door behind us. Gunshots sounded out, then silence for a second, and a deep thud after that.

"Don't pay attention to them." Tray grabbed my wrist. He was pulling me behind him now. "The more you pay attention, the more it'll slow you down. Keep sprinting, Taryn."

I felt his strength. I felt his calm. His hand gentled, slid to fit into mine, and he squeezed my hand. We ran side by side and then I stopped hearing the men behind us. We were getting closer to the river. The current was slamming against rocks below, but we could hear it echoing through the tunnel. It was becoming deafening and we wouldn't have heard the guards anymore anyway.

The tunnel was becoming lighter. We were almost to the end and then the tunnel suddenly straightened and we were there.

The edge was right in front of us. Tray twisted, throwing his body to the side. A scream ripped from me. I was going over. I couldn't stop myself, but Tray yanked me back. I fell into his body and he wrapped his arms around me, shielding my fall with his body. His shoulder slammed hard against the wall and he grunted from the impact, but we had stopped. We hadn't hurled off the edge.

"Shit." His voice was right next to my ear. He tightened his arms around me, holding me for a moment. "That was close."

The drop to the river was high. The tunnel was cut off. There was no platform. It was a complete drop to the river. Even the embankment was dangerous. Boulders and rock riddled the path to the river. If we jumped, we could hit the rocks. Dead. If we jumped and avoided the rocks, we'd be pulled under from the current. Dead again.

Tray was inspecting it with me. "We're screwed." He put it perfectly.

CHAPTER THIRTY

"No, there has to be a door somewhere." I began pushing on the wall. Maybe it was hidden. Maybe there was a rope they used to lower things down? I scanned the floor, but found nothing. "There has to be."

"Taryn."

I was shoving at the cement walls now, but there was nothing. It was a huge slab of cement. That was it. A choked sob was sitting in me, doubling in size. I started pounding harder on the wall. This couldn't be the end.

"Taryn."

He was calm. How the fuck was he calm?

"Taryn." Tray was right behind me. His hand touched mine, coming to rest on top of it. He stood there, right behind me, with that one hand stopping me. His lips grazed my skin and he whispered, "There's no door."

No... He was probably right. A whimper left me now. I couldn't hold it back in. "I'm so sorry, Tray."

His other hand wrapped around me, and he folded his body over mine, hugging me from behind. I bit down on my lip to keep more sobs from escaping.

No, no, no. It couldn't end like this.

He turned me around, then looked down at me. His eyes were full of love, patience, kindness, and strength. I absorbed all of them, feeling them mingling with the storm of rage, fear, and gloom inside me. I choked out, "I'm sorry about Jace, about the hotel."

He shook his head. "Shut up. You didn't even know yourself. I get it." He hesitated then. "Did you mean it?"

My text. I nodded. There was no hesitation on my part. "Yes."

"That's enough for me." Bending down, his lips rested on top of mine. He didn't apply pressure, he just let our lips touch each other, feeling the slight promise of more. He said, "I love you too. It's why I came."

I had gotten him killed. I knew without a doubt that's what was going to happen. I looked up into his eyes. "I'm so sorry."

"Shut up." Then he cupped the back of my head and kissed me. I clutched at him, losing myself in the taste of him. He had come for me. He had done it because he loved me. Euphoria began to fill me. It built, climbing on top of a fevered rush. We were probably going to die, but we were together. It was the best way to go out.

Then a loud bang thundered over our heads. Tray pressed me back, using his body to protect me again. At the same second we moved, a slab of cement dropped where we had been standing. He saved my life again. Shit. We looked up to see a gun pointed right at us.

Jace.

My heart dropped.

Tray moved me back, closer to the edge of the tunnel and Jace dropped down through the hole. A rough voice called down, "Is that them? Open the other hatch."

Still holding his gun steady, Jace knelt, felt under a rock, and pulled it up. The side of the wall moved back and an older man wearing a black button down shirt and tailored black pants stepped through the clearing. His skin was tan and weathered from too much sun. His eyes were beady and they were fixed on me. They narrowed as he asked, "Is this that girl?"

This must've been Galverson.

Jace didn't answer him. He was staring at me. There were bags underneath his eyes and a slight curl in his top lip, so I knew he was furious. His grey eyes pierced through me. A black shirt hugged every inch of his chest, falling over black cargo pants. He was sweaty with dirt all over him. A scrape of mud was on his cheek, as if his hand rubbed his face and left it behind. My eyes fell to some tears in his shirt. Blood seeped through them and the stench of dried blood wafted to me.

"Lanser."

Tray's arm curled around me, pushing me behind him, but I had the gun. My hand was squashed between us. They didn't know I had it, Tray felt the barrel pressed against his back. I knew he was doing this on purpose. We needed any advantage we could get.

Galverson scoffed and turned to Tray. His eyes narrowed. His head tilted to the side, and he pursed his lips forward. "You're that Evans boy?" He hit Jace in the shoulder, whose only reaction was to slide his eyes sideways. Dark hatred stirred in the depths of Jace's eyes, but his boss was clueless. He pointed at Tray. "I thought you were supposed to have taken care of him years ago?"

Jace was barely moving. He stood as still as a statue, but he moved to the side two steps. He moved with such grace it was like watching an animal getting ready to attack.

My free hand tightened on Tray's arm. He felt me shaking, and his finger started to rub over mine, trying to soothe me.

Galverson cast his employee a dark look, and then swung back to us. He jerked his chin up as he said, "You, girl, since this wacko seems mute now, tell me who you are."

"I'm Taryn." I stopped. They heard the trembling in my voice. Brian's face flashed in my mind. The shaking stopped. His memory steadied me, and I remembered the loathing I had for Jace again. He was the reason for all of this. I raised my chin and my eyes narrowed. "You took something of mine. I took it back."

There was a moment of silence. Tray stiffened in front of me.

Galverson started laughing. It sounded genuine, like I was a comedian for his personal pleasure. He pointed his finger at me. "You're funny." He glanced to the side. "You didn't tell me she was a joker."

Jace still didn't say a word. His entire face was a mask now. I was trying to read him, to see if there was any of the old Jace still there, but a cold stranger stared back at me.

"You're like a robot." The words slipped out of me before I could catch myself.

Galverson swung back to me. A speculative gleam formed in his eyes, and his finger moved to stroke his chin. He pointed to Jace, but said to me, "You care for him."

My hand moved from Tray's arm, and I flattened it against his back. I said, "No. I don't." I waited a brief moment. "But I used to, before I realized how much of a monster he is." My eyes held Jace's. His were void of expression. He was so empty. I told him, "You're standing next to the man that killed your brother. What happened to you?"

A flicker of emotion appeared in his eyes, but it was gone in an instant. I wasn't sure if I had seen it. It happened so fast. Galverson was watching him too. He asked, "Is that true?" Then he started laughing again. "You've always been a monster to me. That's a good one." He was shaking his head, but his phone beeped and he took it from where it was clipped to his pants. Reading the screen, he grunted and pointed at us. "The boat's coming. Go on. Kill them. It's time to go."

Jace raised his gun.

"Wait!" I cried out, my heart racing. I was grasping for straws. "There's DEA here. If you kill us, they'll know. There's proof we're here."

Galverson whipped his head to Jace.

The two shared a look, but Jace motioned to the edge of the tunnel with his gun. "Come on. Line up."

Oh god.

We didn't move so Jace started for us. "I'm not kidding. Move, Taryn. Your boyfriend too."

Tray let go of me, but he didn't move. He started to tap the side of my hip, then moved his shoulders a tiny bit, jostling the gun in my hand. As he did, he tapped again quicker. He was giving me a message. Then his shoulder moved forward, as if motioning at Jace. He went back to jostling the gun with his shirt and tapped even harder this time.

He wanted me to shoot Jace. I patted him on the back, confirming I understood and then he stopped. Jace moved closer. Then we heard

Galverson behind him, saying, "Yeah. We're in the tunnel. Complete evacuation. Have the trucks cover us." He paused, then hissed out, "DEA is here. Send all the guards."

They weren't going down without a fight. I was watching Jace, still trying to search if the guy who brought me soda and ice cream was still in there. His eyes narrowed, like he knew what I was doing and if possible, he became even harder. "Move, Taryn. Now!"

I jerked at the hatred in his tone.

"Come on, man," Tray started. He held his hand up.

I calculated the distance. He couldn't lunge for him. Jace would shoot him. It was up to me.

Then Galverson cried out, "Let's go. Kill them. We're on a time table."

"Get the fuck over there." Jace snarled, gesturing to the tunnel's edge again.

Slowly, we began backing up. We needed as much time as we could get. As Tray shuffled me backwards, his hand moved back to my hip so he was still holding me. I started to look for the best angle to shoot from. I wanted Jace and Galverson lined up. I wasn't wasting time. I was aiming for the chest. I could do it.

Jace's voice came back to me as I remembered, *"Don't think. Pull the trigger."*

I had asked, *"And afterwards?"*

"It's you or them. When they fall, watch their chest. Don't look in their eyes. Once they stop breathing, turn around and go. You're the one walking away. That's what you have to tell yourself."

I was going to walk away. When we got to the edge, I tapped Tray on the arm. I was ready. It was time to do this.

Time slowed.

Galverson bellowed out again, "Kill him. Christ, what's the hold-up? You didn't hesitate to kill his dad. Find your balls again, Lanser."

Tray drew in a sharp breath. "My dad?"

I bit down on my lip.

Jace didn't react. He didn't show any remorse. He only raised his hands again and took aim. Hearing shouts from back in the tunnel, he wavered and glanced back. Galverson was on his phone, but he flung his hand in the air and snarled. Then Tray lunged for Jace at that moment.

It happened so quickly.

I was left, stunned, as Tray was in the air. His hands went out to tackle Jace, and Galverson's eyes went wide. Jace twisted back around. He dodged Tray, brought his elbow up and clocked him in the nose. Tray fell to the side, but he tucked his shoulder to help absorb the impact and kicked his leg. Jace blocked his leg, grabbed his shoulder, and turned the gun so he was holding the end. He was going to hit him with it.

I yelled out, "STOP!"

He didn't. He rained it down, hitting Tray above the nose. My stomach rolled over at the sound of it. Tray tried to move aside, but Jace had him trapped. He couldn't move. I raised the gun. "Jace, I mean it." I turned the safety off. "Stop. NOW!"

He glanced up, then did a double take. His hand let go in an instant

Tray scrambled out from his hold, then stood to the side. I looked for a brief second, to make sure he was okay. When I looked back, Jace had his gun pointed at me. It was him and me now. I stared at him, feeling all the old layers of laughter, times he was my teacher, times he was my friend, times when he comforted me, and when he took me to my new home. One by one, those memories peeled away. He had been family. That was gone as well. There was nothing left.

"You're a killer."

Jace didn't respond. He moved forward.

I moved back, just one step. The tunnel's edge was right behind me now. "Stop, Jace."

"What are you going to do, Taryn?" Finally. The stranger fell away, and the guy who had loved his brother stood in front of me now. He began to move so his back was to the wall.

I frowned. What was he doing?

Then Galverson stepped forward. He had a gun pulled as well, but it was held at his side. He was silent, watching us.

Jace continued, "If you fall, you die. If you don't, you still die." His hand loosened on the gun and he softened his tone, "What are you going to do, Taryn?"

I didn't understand what he was doing. "Are you trying to bait me?"

He stared at me, long and hard.

"Taryn." Tray was glaring at Jace, but he pointed to the river. I glanced down and saw three boats below, moving to place a net in the water. My heart couldn't sink anymore, it really was over. If we jumped, they would catch us. There was no hope.

"You and Brian were like my family."

Jace didn't waver. "We were your family."

I flinched. "Then why? Why all this?"

"Because you were supposed to stay away," he ground out. His eyes flashed a heated warning and he moved forward a step.

"Stop," Tray held his hands out. "Stop." His hand whipped up, I glimpsed a knife, but before let it loose, Jace swung his gun to him instead. Tray faltered and the knife fell to the ground.

"No! God, no." I hurried to Tray's side, but he held me away.

Jace shouted at the same time, "Move back, Taryn."

More shouts were coming from the tunnel. There were men all around us, and Galverson let out a growl. "For fuck's sake. This is enough." He brought his gun up. It was pointed at Tray. He was going to shoot him; I saw it in his eyes. I moved without thinking. Tray couldn't die. I threw myself in front of him, yelling, "NO!"

"No!" Jace jerked forward.

Tray fell back, but he grabbed me, trying to cushion my fall. It was too late. We were going backwards. As we tipped through the air and fell from the tunnel, I looked back. Galverson hurried to the edge. He was going to shoot at us, but Jace, never looking away from me, raised his hand to the side, and shot him instead.

I opened my mouth, shocked.

Galverson fell to the side. I couldn't tear my eyes away. Jace shot him in the side of his head. Galverson was dead. We were going to die and Jace was alive.

It was too late. Nothing mattered anymore.

There was no more fight in me so I turned it all off. I savored the feel of the air and the last moments of freedom. Another memory came to me, and I could hear Brian's voice whisper to me, *"Remember when we used to pretend we were flying?" I had laughed, saying, "You're high, Brian."*

He shrugged with a small pout. "But it's the most amazing feeling, Taryn. Try it. Pretend you're flying."

I didn't have to pretend. I closed my eyes and I soared.

CHAPTER THIRTY-ONE

Everything happened in a blur after that. When we hit the water, we were grabbed and pulled aboard a boat. I went in one and Tray went in the other. Then they took off. I wasn't paying attention—I didn't want to see who would be torturing us—but when I was guided to a comfortable seat in the back and two large towels were placed on my lap, I looked up. My mouth fell open.

There were no guards with rifles strapped to their backs. The men wore black coats that had the words DEA on them. I was in a boat full of DEA agents. I rubbed at my eyes and saw the same thing again. One of the men caught my reaction and grinned. He leaned closer to me. "You weren't expecting us?"

"How…" I had no idea what to ask. "A man just killed another man up there. What are you doing? Aren't you going after him?"

He pressed something warm into my hand and patted my shoulder. "One thing at a time, kid. Everything is being handled and all your questions will be answered." He nodded to me. A thread of respect was in his voice. "We got your friend. The one you went in for. He's okay. He's being treated by our doctors already."

Thank god. I looked down, and a small laugh bubbled up.

He started to turn back, but gave me a quizzical look.

I held the thermos up to him. "You gave me hot chocolate." He called me kid too.

He frowned.

Before I knew it, I felt a stupid smile stretch over my face. I couldn't contain it or even dim it. I must've looked ridiculous. I didn't care. For once, I didn't feel any responsibility. Gray was alive. I was alive. Tray was alive. I didn't have to save anyone or protect anyone, the cards would fall how they would fall. I turned to look for Tray and that relieved feeling plummeted.

He was in the other boat, sitting in the same seat I was, except the towels weren't wrapped around him. He held them on his lap as if he didn't realize they were there, and there was no hot chocolate given to him. As I watched now, an officer tried to hand him a thermos, but Tray didn't acknowledge him.

He lost his father.

My responsibility was now Tray.

I watched him the entire time. He glanced at me once. The corners of his mouth lifted up in a brief smile and then he turned away again. As soon as the boats docked and we were allowed to leave, I broke through the crowd to get to him. People grabbed for me, but I evaded their hands. "Miss," one called after me, "we need to question you."

"Let her go." I recognized that voice. Chance, Tray's older brother, was there and he said further, "We'll get their statements in a few hours. They've been through enough."

I ducked around another officer and then was at Tray's side. My hand slipped into his before I realized I was there and after a slight hesitation, he squeezed my hand and pulled me into his side. His arm wrapped around me, resting on my hip.

We were led to a black SUV and I sat next to Tray, scooting so close that my leg was pressed right next to his. Comforting someone wasn't my thing. I didn't like to be comforted and I felt awkward when I tried to comfort others. It was hard to search for words that would ease someone else's pain and in this case, there were none. I only hoped my presence would help. When Tray rested his hand on my leg, rubbing it back and forth in an absent-minded motion, I knew he wasn't going to push me away. I stuck to him like glue until the SUV came to a stop. As we got out, I paused.

Tray got out behind me, his hand came to rest on my hip again, and he turned to the side. "Your headquarters is my house?"

Chance flashed him a grin. His hand raised to the radio attached to his shoulder, and he pressed the side of it, saying, "We've arrived at home base." He released the button and said to Tray, "Literally."

Tray shook his head. "You're still annoying."

It was meant as a tease, but the hollow sound from him caught his brother's attention. Chance frowned, studying his brother for a moment. Tray acted like he didn't notice. A glazed look was in his eyes, and I knew he was remembering Galverson's words from the tunnel. Then Chance caught my eye and raised an eyebrow in question. I looked away. It wasn't my place to say anything.

"Well, okay then," Chance mused. He pointed inside. "I had the guys stay out of Mom and Dad's old room. I saw you two have been using it. Go ahead, shower, sleep, and eat. Do whatever you need to rest up."

Tray nodded and started forward.

"Taryn," Chance called me back.

Tray stopped and waited. I knew what his brother was going to ask so I waved him forward. "Go ahead. I'll be right in."

He nodded, but it was a half nod. As he left, his shoulders were still strong and straight, but there was a slight droop to them. No one noticed. His brother only caught it just now, but Tray was in pain, like the deep aching pain that buried deep inside a person and took root, never to leave. I understood because I felt it too. Mine was named Brian.

"What gives?" Chance interrupted my thoughts. He was frowning in the direction Tray had gone. "We have a lot of stuff to go over, but what happened up there?"

"The guy on the boat said you found Gray. He's okay?" I was stalling. I wasn't ashamed of that.

His frown deepened and he scratched his head. "You're not going to tell me, are you?"

I hesitated and then said, "I would like an update on Gray."

"Okay. Fine. Your friend was taken to a government medical facility. He was mainly dehydrated. He'll stay there to recuperate. When he's cleared by the doctors, he's free to go."

As those words left him, a sense of finality filled me. It really was over now. "Thank you." I started to go again.

"Taryn."

I didn't look at him, but I paused.

"You two will have to undergo an intense debriefing with myself and other officers. You *will* tell me what happened up there."

357

I half-turned to him. My heart was upstairs, wherever Tray was. "You will get all the information, but what you're asking about is personal, and it isn't for me to tell you." With that said, I left.

Different members of the DEA were in every room. Laptops, printers, fax machines, and other machines were placed on the kitchen table. I knew people were sitting there and working. Others were in the living room. A few were coming down the hallway. All of them paused as they saw me, but I ignored every single one of them. I only had one place and one person I needed to be with. When I got to the master bedroom, the shower was on. I didn't pause. After locking the door, I went to the bathroom. Tray was inside, a hand braced against the wall, and his head was bent forward. The water was streaming down on him.

He turned, saw me there, and leaned against the far wall of the shower. He was still in his pants and shirt. The water pelted down on him, making his clothes cling to him.

He was beautiful. And I couldn't move for a moment. God, I loved him.

"What?"

I was damned lucky. Stepping inside, I barely felt the water. He was in my life. Reaching out, I took hold of his shirt and moved closer. Glancing down, my forehead rested against his chest. His hands went to my hips and he pulled me against him. I felt him drop a tender kiss to my neck. My hands fisted around his shirt and I struggled to choke out, "Thank you."

He swept my hair to the side, cupped the back of my neck, and tilted my chin so I looked up. Our gazes met. He asked, "For what?"

"You never left."

A corner of his lip lifted in a slight smile. A fierce expression was in his eyes. I couldn't look away. As his thumb rubbed over my cheek, he said, "I never will."

"See." I tapped his chin, grinning. "Lines like that. How did I get you?"

The other side of his mouth lifted into a full grin. His free hand moved down and cupped my bottom. "With this." He jiggled it, but it didn't move. "A fine ass is all a guy looks for." He moved so he could look at it, then he pulled back with that same wolfish grin. "Although yours is too toned. You should stop working out so much."

Laughing, I pressed a fist to his chest. "It's all your fault. All those training sessions and nights with the punching bag. I never did throw a knife at someone, you know."

His eyebrows lifted. "And you're asking to rectify that? I love you, Taryn, but you're not throwing one at me."

I chuckled, but I caught the pain flare up over him again. Lifting a hand up, I cupped the side of his face. His eyes closed. He moved into my palm and a soft sigh left him.

"Sometimes I don't know what to say." My hand cupped the other side of his face. I turned his face and his eyes opened again. An inch separated us. "I never knew my parents, but I know loss. I know what it feels like to love someone, become attached to them, and have them ripped from you in a day. It happened to me all the time when I left foster homes. I stopped getting close early on, but there was never any words that helped me. The only thing that helped was someone's presence." My finger began moving back and forth again. I wanted him to feel my love. "I don't know what it's like to have parents, but I know what it's like to not have them." I felt tears on my cheek, but my god, I ignored them. The haunted look in Tray's eyes pushed all my demons away. Everything was about him now. "The only thing I can think of to say is that I'm sorry. I am. I am so goddamn sorry." He started to step back, but I held him firm. "I will never leave. I won't. I promise."

He glanced down, while I held his face and then his lips touched the top of my head. His arms moved so he was holding me tight. He bent over me and his lips grazed the top of my shoulder. He murmured against my skin, "I'm trying to tell myself that I shouldn't care. I knew I was never going to see him again, but man, hearing it spoken like that. It's final. He's dead and I'm supposed to be too. I hate Jace, but I'm grateful to him at the same time. I hate feeling both of those things. Not about that guy, not with everything he's done."

My hand lifted to cradle the back of his head and I rested mine against his. "You can feel however you want to feel. Being grateful that you're alive is never wrong to feel."

"I hate him too."

"That's fine too."

He lifted his head, staring down at me for a moment, then another, and another. "I love you."

I opened my mouth, but I couldn't talk. Giving him a shaky smile, I managed to get out, "I love you too." Another nod. "I do."

His eyes darkened. Then he bent, lifted me under my legs, and braced me against the shower wall. As he did, I leaned back, now gazing down on him. My legs automatically wrapped around his waist. His hand moved to my shirt, slipped underneath and began pushing it up.

His thumb rested on my stomach, pausing for my permission. My legs tightened around him in response and then I leaned down. My lips were caught by his, but it was mutual. A fevered frenzy took over me and I wanted him. I needed him. My hands grappled with his jeans, undoing them, and then I shoved them down as he peeled my shirt off. My bra was taken off and he cupped my breast, his thumb rubbing over my nipple. Falling back against the wall, I arched up for him. He held me, caressed me, trailed kisses down my throat until he was bent over me, and his mouth hovered over my breast, I let go. I wasn't innocent, but he was making me feel new sensations again. It would be my first time with him. Knowing that I loved him, and he loved me, made everything right.

It was perfect.

His eyes were lidded and thick with desire. I cradled the side of his face and as I did, he turned to press a small kiss to my palm. Then he tightened his hold on my legs and stood from the wall. As he took me into the bedroom and lowered me down, I pulled him so he was on top of me the whole time.

I didn't want to part from him. And later, as he slid inside me, our hands were clasped together, I had a feeling I wouldn't have to worry about that again. I had found my soul mate.

A discreet knock woke us. Tray's hand tightened on mine and I lifted my head from his chest. The clock said it was three in the morning. We shared a confused look, but the knock sounded again and we both rolled out of bed. As he went to answer it, I grabbed some shorts and then pulled on a loose shirt. He waited. I gave him a nod, and as he opened it,

I ran my fingers through my hair. I must've looked like a mess. Hearing his brother's voice, I forgot about my hair. Going to Tray's side, I hugged myself. "I thought you said we could have our time to rest."

Tray shifted back so I could join the conversation.

Chance's lips were pressed in a flat line. He waited a beat to answer and as he did, his hand lifted to rub at one of his temples. "Uh, Taryn."

"What?"

Tray leaned forward to peer over his brother's shoulder. As he did, his eyes got big and he stiffened.

Chance saw his reaction and shot up a hand. "Stop, Tray. There are reasons he's here."

He jerked forward, but Chance blocked him. Tray brought up his arm and shoved his brother out of the way. He stalked forward. I still didn't see who it was. When Chance saw I was going to follow, he held a hand up. "Wait." He turned. "TRAY. Wait! This is truth time."

He did and pivoted around him. A fierce scowl was on his face. "You better start spilling. Now."

"I will." Chance gentled his tone, and his hands lowered, slowly. "Give me time, and I will explain everything."

"Waiting. Go now."

He swallowed and his Adam's apple bobbed up and down. "Okay, but just you and me. We'll go in Dad's library downstairs."

At the mention of their father, Tray's eyes went to slits and his hands fisted again. Danger emanated from him. He was close to becoming violent. When I started to move again, to see the reason for his anger, Chance shifted at the same time. His hand lifted once more and it held there, his finger extended in my direction. "Taryn," he started.

Then, whoever it was, made a decision. He stood. I could see the top of his head. My eyes followed his dark blonde hair until he stood, clear as day, and five yards from me.

Jace.

He was dressed in a black shirt and black pants. I couldn't comprehend it. My eyes dropped to his side where a gun was holstered. Glancing at Tray, he was waiting for my reaction, but I had none. Why didn't I?

I pressed my fingers to my forehead. "This doesn't make sense."

"Taryn," Jace spoke.

My fingers whisked out, silencing him. "Shut up."

"I have been undercover. I've been working to take down Sal Galverson's entire drug ring."

I shook my head. I didn't want to hear it. Turning my hand, I gave him the middle finger. "I said shut the fuck up." I moved towards Tray. "What do I do?"

Some of the danger had faded from him. His shoulders were still tense, but his hands had loosened. "You do what you want to do."

A million questions flew through my mind, but they all faded, as one was the only one important to me then. "Is Brian really dead?"

Regret and a darkness flashed in his eyes. "Yes."

I stepped back. It was like finding it out all over again.

Jace said softly, "I'd like to tell you everything."

I was still looking at Tray. He would do what I wanted, but I shook my head. "Not alone. I want Tray with me. That's the only way I'll be in the same room as you again."

"Fair enough."

Chance spoke, "The library is downstairs, in the basement."

One by one, we trailed down there. As we got to the main floor, I saw there were still DEA agents everywhere. When I walked past them earlier, their conversations had quieted, but they still continued talking. But now, everything stopped. Fingers froze on their keyboards. No one said a word and all their heads turned our way.

I frowned, noticing they weren't watching me or Tray. Their eyes were trained on Jace. As he walked past them, for those who were sitting, one by one stood. It was a sign of respect. When we went down the other flight of stairs and entered the library, my hand reached for Tray's. Inside, Jace turned to us, and Chance closed the door behind him. For some reason I wasn't scared. I wasn't hurt. I wasn't angry. I was calm. We were going to hear a new story, but mine was done.

My hand tightened over Tray's.

CHAPTER THIRTY-TWO

As we stood in the library, we were told a lot of different facts. We were told that Jace had been recruited by Chance to work for the DEA when Chance returned home and discovered his father was working for the drug ring. Jace was already working for Sal Galverson, but he decided to turn on his boss when he found out the mother of his child died from a drug overdose. Jace said to me, "It was that night when I was in the kitchen and you came out. You sat at the table with me for hours." He hesitated. "I was an ass before then. I'm sorry, Taryn. I know things were bad at the house and I know I'm partly to blame for things over the years. I was messed up for a lot of those years."

I nodded. "I remember." He never talked about his daughter. He mentioned her once; she was being cared for by another family. No one asked any questions because that's how Jace was with us. That had been the dark, scary Jace. That night was when things changed; he had turned into the Jace that I loved as a brother. I saw traces of him again, but it didn't matter. Too much had happened.

"Jace was stalling. He was giving us time to get there and set up the nets."

Tray frowned. "What about Dad?"

Chance cast him a frown.

Jace said, "He's not dead. Sal ordered to get rid of him so we made it look like he was."

Chance spoke up, "He's in witness protection."

Tray asked, "So I'll never see him again?"

"Not unless you want to join him." Chance glanced at me. "Once you go in, you can't come out. Something's telling me you won't go for that deal."

"Do you see him?"

Chance hesitated, then shook his head. "No, but I'd like to. I love him too."

Tray continued to frown, but he didn't respond. He gave a small nod and then looked to me, as if giving me permission to get my answers.

There was a heavy silence in the room. Then Jace asked, "You don't have anything else to say, Taryn?"

I didn't. I really didn't. I should. I knew there was a lot I didn't understand or know, but after jumping from that tunnel and thinking I was going to die, a switch had been flipped. I really had let go of my past. My future was what mattered now. Brian. Jace. I let go of everyone and everything. "I'm eighteen now. I'm an adult. I'm going to finish high school, and I'm going to try and get a scholarship in swimming so I can go to college. I'm going to find Mandy and Austin because I love them. They're my new family and," I lifted my hand that was holding Tray's, "I'm going to be wherever he is," I turned so I was talking only to Tray, "as long as you'll have me."

A tender expression flashed over his face and he pulled me to his side. Dropping a soft kiss on my forehead, he whispered, "That shit goes both ways."

Another stupid smile came to my face and like the time on the boat, I didn't try to hide it.

"Okay then." Jace started for the door. He paused with his hand on the doorknob. "I'm still a member of the Panthers. If you need anything, you can go to them. They'll take care of you."

I frowned. "Why? Where are you going?"

He shared a look with Chance.

I twisted around. Tray's older brother grimaced as he said, "Sal Galverson's drug ring is gone, but he was one member in a bigger network. A few of the guards got away. We were able to capture most of them and the others were killed, but his name will get back to the rest of the network."

"What does that mean?"

"They know who I am so I have to disappear." A wall slid away and Jace wasn't the stranger anymore. I saw the caring in his eyes again and I was warmed by that. Blinking back tears, he was still there in my heart.

I tried to grin, but knew it was shaky. "You really meant it when you wanted me to go away, didn't you?"

He sighed. His hand fell from the doorknob. "If something went wrong, I didn't want Galverson to use you against me. People knew I cared about you."

"And Brian?"

He gave me a crooked grin. "You think Brian would've gone anywhere I told him?"

"Oh." I laughed, but it was weak. "No. He would've done the opposite." Jace reached for the door again. "Wait," I stopped him. His hand went back to his side, and I asked, "Where's he buried? Is he by your dad?"

"I'm having his body moved. I don't want anyone to do anything to it, and these people, they'd do just about anything to get to me." He frowned. "I'll let you know where I have him moved." He glanced at Chance. "Or someone will."

He paused again, staring at me as I stared at him. This was it. This was really the end. "I'll never see you again?"

"Unless something bad happens." His grey eyes seemed haunted and he tried to give me a half-grin. "Let's hope you never see me again." He said to Tray, "Take care of her."

"I plan to."

Then he started to turn again. "Wait." I flew at him. Slamming into his chest, I buried my head there, and he wrapped his arms around me at the same time. This was my last goodbye. With tears streaming down my cheeks, I knew I'd probably always care about him. He and Brian had been family when no one else had been. When I pulled back, he tucked a strand of hair behind my ear and gently flicked me on the cheek. He murmured, "We had some good times."

My heart was heavy. "Goodbye, Jace."

He nodded. He didn't say it back, but that was okay. He dropped a kiss to my forehead and whispered back, "Love you, kid, even when you thought I hated you."

Then he pulled away and left. I didn't turn for Tray. I didn't need to be comforted. I knew what was happening. That old chapter in my life just walked out the door. It was done. There were nothing left to be resolved.

"You okay?" Tray asked me, standing beside me.

I nodded. "Yeah." I reached for his hand. I was okay. I *would* be okay. Hell, I would be more than okay. I was strong. I was a survivor. I felt ready to take on the world. Feeling that rush of adrenalin, I squeezed Tray's hand.

He was my home now.

EPILOGUE

"Matthews, you're diving in five minutes." My coach patted my shoulder as he walked past me.

My teammate laughed next to me. "Way to give us a pep talk." She swung her fist in the air, giving me the thumbs up sign. "That's our coach for you."

I laughed, but I couldn't ignore the knots in me. My stomach was twisted up like a pretzel. We were in the semifinals at Columbia. My dive could seal a win for our team or finalize our loss. No pressure at all.

We were standing against the wall as a diver soared into the water. It was a near perfect execution. My teammate swore beside me. "Goddamn."

Her legs were off, but only a slight inch. I could beat her. I knew it.

Then the assistant coach waved me over. She patted my shoulder and murmured, "Did you see that?"

I nodded. I couldn't talk.

She patted me again. "You can do this, Matthews. You've helped bring us this far."

She was right. I told myself that as I started up the ladder. I was going all the way to the top. The crowd began to become smaller around me and I could see over everyone. This is when I paused, half way up, and scanned the crowd. People asked me why I did this, but I never told my secret. This was my thing to do. Every time, no matter what competition, I always looked through the crowd. It had been a year since Jace disappeared. I wanted to see if I could see him, and there was another slight hope that if I did, I would imagine Brian with him in spirit. It was dumb, but it was a small wish I had. I knew I could imagine Brian's presence with me and at times, I felt him, but pretending he would be alongside Jace—that was a gift I wanted to see just once.

Like all the other competitions, I didn't see him. Pushing forward, I got to the top and rolled my head around. I lifted my arms in a circling motion, loosening my shoulders. Stepping forward onto the platform, I started my other tradition, the one that was the most important. I would look through the crowd again, but I wasn't looking for Jace. The pool was rippling beneath me, beckoning for me to join her, but I ignored her and searched for Tray. My time on top of the platform was only for him.

He was leaning forward, his hazel eyes focused only on me. A few girls were beside him, sneaking peeks at him. The one next to him was staring right at him with a flirtatious grin tugging at her lips. They were trying to get his attention, but like so many other times, his eyes were solely trained on me. We shared a look, his eyes darkened, and a small grin teased over his face. A rush of excitement moved my nerves aside. My body reacted. It wouldn't be long until I would feel his body against mine. His hands would be in mine and he would move inside of me. We would be home again, with each other. Tray was my new home.

Mandy was next to him. I didn't look at her or Austin. They had both come to support me. Shelly asked to come, but I still wasn't ready to open that door. She remained with Kevin and I could never forgive him.

I heard the signal. They were waiting for my dive so I went to the edge of the platform.

I didn't see the pool below. I imagined my hardest dive, and I was brought back to the day in the tunnel. In my mind, I dove from there hundreds of times by now and every time I conquered the fall. I closed my eyes, then flexed my legs, and kicked off. As I completed my dive, my body was perfect. I soared into the pool and when I kicked out, bringing my body right back to the surface, I didn't need to hear the roar of the crowd.

I knew I had won.

ACKNOWLEDGEMENTS

I need to thank two people particularly that helped me get this book out into publication, my editor Ami Johnson and Jay McLean. Ami is the one who emailed and offered to edit this monster (and it was one because it over 150,000 words before I took it to task) for free just so she could own it on her Kindle one day. I laughed, thought she was ridiculous, but sent her the manuscript anyway. That was over an entire year, maybe even a year and a half ago. She did it. It took her a long time (I wasn't rushing, I couldn't believe she was actually doing it) and then she sent me an email eight months later and told me it was in my inbox. I hate to admit it, but that book sat in my inbox for a long time before I finally pulled it back up. I just wasn't ready to tackle it because I knew it would need so much work, but (I'm pretty sure) after a night of chatting with Jay McLean, I learned that she used to love this book when it was posted on Fictionpress for free reading. My mind was blown. She had read it? Then she went on to tell me how much she loved the book and it got me going. I was bound and determined to tackle these edits and get it published. I projected two weeks. I was so stupid. It took me three months. I'm still shaking my head at my insanity, but it's done and those two helped bring it into fruition.

As to everyone else, I have to thank all the Fallen Crest readers because I put finishing AWNC before getting Fallen Fourth Down out for them. Thank you for not reading me the riot act and for being patient with me. I promise, FFD is the next book coming out, but until then I do hope that you enjoyed this one as well.

I feel that all the readers who have followed me from when I first started posting on Fictionpress, then followed me to Livejournal, and are still with me—THANK YOU SO MUCH! I get so nostalgic when I think of the dedication some of my readers have that they keep following me, keep supporting me, and always comment on my posts. Just thank you! And thank you to all those readers who have continued to email me and ask if I was ever going to publish A Whole New Crowd. I'm still getting them, but here it is! I hope I did the original version proud, even though I know it's been changed quite a bit. The original AWNC dealt more with Taryn in high school and all the different groups of people in her school. I cut a lot of those characters out, but I feel that I made the ending better with this version. If you want to read the original, it will also be published, but it won't be edited or polished. You'll be getting the original first edited version that Ami sent back to me.

Other people I want to thank: my author friends (the secret six) and my admins, along with my beta readers. Kerri, Eileen, Heather, Cami, Celeste, Kelly, Lisa. I love you ladies!

Last paragraph, as always, it's dedicated to my significant other and now our dog, Bailey. I'm going to start writing something embarrassing about him, just because he never reads and when he does, he'll laugh so much. One likes to fart and the other likes to go on walks. You can choose which is which. ;) And with this, I'm done. Thank you everyone!!! I hope hope hope hope you liked the story!